Mr. Hooligan

Also by Ian Vasquez

Lonesome Point
In the Heat

MR. HOOLIGAN

IAN VASQUEZ

Minotaur Books
New York

MR. HOOLIGAN. Copyright © 2010 by Ian Vasquez. All rights reserved. Printed in the United States of America. For information, address St. Martin's Press, 175 Fifth Avenue, New York, N.Y. 10010.

www.minotaurbooks.com

ISBN 978-0-312-37811-0

First Edition: December 2010

10 9 8 7 6 5 4 3 2 1

For Nadia and Duncan,
when they're older

Mr. Hooligan

CHAPTER ONE

"Once upon a time," Patricia said, "Charles Lindbergh landed the *Spirit of St. Louis* in a seaside polo field in Belize, or I should say in British Honduras. Which is what they called it back in the late 1920s. That field, you of course know, is where the Princess Hotel and Casino is, and that park, the one out there with concrete animals, swing sets, benches, all those things. Well, just across from the park, on Princess Margaret Drive, there's a bar called Lindy's, named after his truly. It's a nice place, Lindy's, it has a thatch-covered patio, pimento and hardwood walls, a bank of wooden jalousie louvers that're always open to the breeze. One of those places where lots of tourists hang out, a weekend nightspot where the locals enjoy a few before going to a club. But what's really interesting about the place, to me, are the photos along the walls near the bar. Old black-and-whites of Lindbergh in the field, in these jodhpur-like khakis, a white man standing tall in a sea of black faces, lots of children in rough-looking clothes, and all the men in suits and women in long dresses and all of them wearing hats, holding their hats down against the breeze."

"One second," Roger Hunter said with a smile, sitting up in

the hospital bed. "Is this how you're going to begin this story? 'Once upon a time'?"

"All the best stories begin that way, but not all of them end 'happily ever after.' Maybe not even this one."

"Okay, fair enough. This tale, is this the one you've been wanting so long to tell me? Is this about the boy you used to counsel?"

"The boy who's now a man," Patricia said. "Who owns that bar, Lindy's. Who landed himself into some trouble years ago, long before he bought that bar. What, don't you want to hear my story?"

"On the contrary, I do. I just find myself wishing that it'll be worth the wait. You've been hinting at this story for years. Giving me little bits and pieces. Now, I'm about to hear the whole thing. Why now?"

"Because it's time. I really believe his life is about to change. And because finally telling someone about what happened, what he told me—it'll ease the burden on my conscience."

"So, conveniently, you're telling a man who's dying."

Patricia didn't care for that.

"Listen," Roger said, "I didn't mean to sound offended."

"You don't need to keep reminding me that you're dying."

"Pancreatic cancer is a perfectly logical end to life. You who left the convent because of your dedication to truth, it's curious how you can't accept the truth. I'm dying, woman."

Patricia sighed. "Well, you yourself used to say that every counselor needs a counselor."

"So what was this thing that our hero did years ago?"

"He shot a man," Patricia said. "Shot him several times."

Roger whistled, reached a bony hand for the cup of water on the bedside table. He drank and wiped his lips. "I would think," he said, "that qualifies as a story I need to hear."

"Let me tell you what happened, then. Because, actually, in

a few minutes he's coming by the hospital to give me something and I'll have to go downstairs."

"What did you say his name was?"

"I didn't. When he was young, on the streets they used to call him Li'l Hooligan, but now everybody knows his real name."

CHAPTER TWO

"Riley James, get your ass out here, we got to go, man."

Riley lifted two bottles of Lighthouse Lager out of the cooler behind the bar and popped the caps. He turned his face to the window and shouted, "Hold on, lemme get something," and walked through the kitchen, holding the bottles by the necks in one hand, into his small office. He rummaged through a drawer full of a loose pile of invoices, paper clips, rubber bands, slammed the drawer shut, opened another and rifled through some file folders, shut that drawer, pulled open the one near the computer monitor and peered into it. He said, "Shit," and banged it in with the side of his fist.

Stormed outside to check behind the bar. "I'm coming, Harvey, I swear I'm coming," moving bottles of Mount Gay and Bacardi and One Barrel to the side, peeking at the back of the shelf, shifting the tray of clean glasses around for a better view, getting more annoyed.

"Looking for this?"

Gert was holding up his Ziploc of herb, half an ounce of aromatic resin-sticky Belize Breeze.

"Yeah . . . yeah, there it is."

"It was on the floor over there," she said. "Sure it's yours?

I'll just throw it out if it isn't. Drugs, you know, being illegal and all."

"Gert . . ." He walked around from behind the bar, and she handed it over with cool disdain.

"Patrons were in here with a little boy some minutes ago. What if they'd found it?"

Riley stuffed the bag into the pocket of his jeans and ambled past her out onto the deck and down the short stairs into the sunshine where Harvey sat waiting in the old pickup.

"Your wife busted me," he told Harvey, and Harvey laughed and started the engine and aimed north on Princess Margaret Drive.

Five o'clock Friday afternoon. Just a light breeze wafting off the Caribbean, but the promise of the weekend was enough to cool irritations, like that moment with Gert. The exciting hustle of Friday and Saturday nights at the bar to look forward to, the jump in sales, and then Sunday, long and peaceful, the only day Lindy's was closed.

This was what Riley enjoyed—sitting back sipping a brew and cruising through town, the late afternoon light, he and Harvey, just like when they were younger.

"Let's see what you brought here," he said, shuffling through the stack of Harvey's CDs piled on the seat. "Rusted what?" He held up a CD.

"Root. Rusted Root. Good music, sweet percussion. Drop that on."

"*Legend,* Bob Marley. You still rocking *Legend*? Man, that's the equivalent of *Frampton Comes Alive* every American used to own back in the seventies."

"And your point is . . . ?" Harvey's short arm rested on the steering wheel as they made the curve past the old fisheries building and he helped flip through the CDs. "How about Burt Bacharach?"

"Better shut the hell up and watch where you're going."

They settled on playing the radio, the surprises it offered. Riley hung an arm out the window and took a swallow of beer. They were going across town to pick up speakers for the three-man band that was performing on the outside deck at Lindy's tonight; heading on a "mission" like so many others he and Harvey had made since they bought the bar three years ago. Riley had known Harvey since they were about seven years old, the red-faced boy with one short arm who sat next to him one day at the start of third grade and said, "My arm looks like this 'cause when I was a baby I had polio but don't let it fool you 'cause I can still fight." Laying down a challenge that Riley had never felt remotely inclined to take up. From that day, he and Harvey had been tight.

They passed joggers and a woman pushing a stroller along the promenade fronting the sea. In the distance toward the mangrove isles, a skiff tore through the water, a white swath behind, bearing for the cayes. Instead of continuing the scenic route on Princess Margaret, Harvey had turned left on A Street. "Why you going this way?"

"Well, there's a certain person that I got to see if she's home."

Riley groaned. "Now? Really, man?"

"Yes indeed. If she's back in town, I may be paying a little visit tonight."

Riley looked out the window at the fine two-story homes they were passing, kids playing soccer in a big yard. "Careful. One of these days you're gonna get caught."

Harvey looked at Riley. "Gert knows I love her. This thing here, it's nothing to do with love. It's pure beastly, hot, animalistic, athletic, nasty freakiness, yeaaah baby. See, I admitted it." He slapped the horn and gunned the engine, probably feeling the beer already, having never been much of a drinker.

"On that note," Riley said, leaning to one side and reaching into a pocket, "I have a little something I plan to give Candice tonight." He opened the tiny box and showed the diamond ring tucked into the fold of padded velvet.

Harvey grinned, looking down his shoulder at it. He punched Riley's arm. "Look out! R.J. is getting hitched."

Riley drew up his top lip for a buck-teeth effect. "Aw shucks."

"So why now, Riley? Because of the Monsantos?"

Riley nodded, drank some beer. "One last run Monday and I'm through. Debts paid, respect given, and that's it, me and the Monsantos will be square. One more run, make the pickup out by Turneffe reef, drop it off next day and that's all she wrote. Me and old man Israel already had the talk, so I figured the time was right to ask Candice. You know?"

Harvey nodded, looking a little distracted, another question on his mind. On Baymen Avenue he occasionally had to steer to the side for approaching trucks to barrel by, the street narrow and walkers showing no respect for traffic. The usual Friday evening madness.

"Doesn't mean I'm leaving," Riley said.

"Your woman is an American, don't forget. She won't want to live in Belize. Three months after the I do's, you're gone, up to Foreign, you watch."

Riley sipped beer and stared out the window. Harvey was right, of course. Leaving Belize was a possibility Riley had imagined for some time. If it happened he would not be the saddest man in the world. Just because you didn't pursue something didn't mean you wouldn't accept it, and right there lay his ambivalence about his lifestyle, the work he had made a name with, a good living, but which had also produced its share of regrets. Smuggling had been a job he couldn't let go, he told Candice not too long ago. But he'd said it like it was in the past.

She never interrogated him, and he loved it when she said, Well, now you've let that go you've got to just hold on to me. The woman was golden.

"Harvey, if that happens, I leave, like I used to threaten when I got drunk? Listen to this: The bar is yours."

"I can't afford to buy you out."

"No, you'll run it. Send me a small cut."

"So you say now."

"I'm serious. That's Mr. Long Time over there?"

A tall skinny-legged man was coming out of a shop swinging a pack of bread. Riley leaned out the window and hollered, "Yo, get off your hands, Long Time."

Long Time flashed him the finger as they rolled by.

That tickled Harvey.

Riley said, "Pull over, pull over."

They parked on the side and Riley poked his head out the window. Long Time had stopped. Riley said, "Man, get your ass over here, man."

Long Time loped up, self-consciously. "Yo, Riley, I don't got no cash right now. I'll catch you later this week maybe."

"Two hundred and ten dollars, Long Time. Three weeks. What the fuck, brother? Look, don't come to the bar tonight if you don't have my money. Skip tonight. But you better scrape up some change soon, I'm done tired a this waiting."

Long Time nodded, looking away. "I know, I know . . ."

"Let's go," Riley said to Harvey, and they peeled back onto the street.

Coming up to a house on the corner of Calle Al Mar, Harvey slowed down. "Okay, Mr. Picky, tell me what you think."

A cocoa brown young woman in shorts that revealed the corners of ample cheeks was walking up the stairs. Harvey tooted the horn and she turned around. Harvey twiddled his fingers and the girl grinned and sauntered into the house. Harvey said, "God*damn.*"

"All right, I must admit, you're beginning to show some taste. She was very nice."

They rolled past the house, Harvey still peering up, a couple of cars cutting around and zipping by.

"No, that's not her. My one lives across the street there, but her car's not in the yard," and he floored it. "But I think I want to get to know her neighbor. Oh, my gentle Jesus."

They hit Cinderella Plaza, Riley explaining to him how they'd still manage the bar together if he left, and that was a major "if" since, first of all, Candice had to say yes. Harvey had his doubts, saying would Riley hand over the keys to the place he'd dreamt of owning for years, just like that? Could Riley really trust that he and Gert would run the bar to his satisfaction, especially Gert? Harvey said, " 'Cause you know how you and Gertrude butt heads all the time."

Riley said, "It could happen. We'll keep talking, but listen," tapping his watch, "we're late, I've got to meet Sister Pat at Caribbean Hospital, too, so let's move it."

That's all Harvey needed to hear, speed freak that he could be, banking a hard right onto Freetown Road and zooming past bicyclists and parked cars clogging the narrow street.

"All right, you don't need to get crazy."

Harvey slowed down a little. "The old Ford's still got it." He pushed the clutch and tried to downshift but it resisted, gears grinding.

"Yeah, but the driver's got no skills."

Harvey cursed, located the gears and picked up speed. "Natty Dread rides again!"

They were coming up on a crowded intersection, a little girl dashing across the road, cars waiting at stop signs on both corners. A bunch of people milling outside the donut shop. Harvey eased off the gas, downshifted.

A woman and a young boy were riding bikes, the woman on the outside. A few yards ahead on the other side, a man walking a dog was chatting with a woman. Kids outside the donut shop were horsing around, pushing each other, one of them running onto the street, scampering back, and Riley, about to take a sip, lowered his beer, to wait until Harvey navigated this cluster fuck, the streets seeming extra narrow and Harvey going twenty miles per hour too fast.

A car at a stop sign nosed out and Harvey steered left to avoid it, then after that everything happened in a second. A basketball from the technical college court flew over the fence, bounced high off the sidewalk and onto the street, startling the boy on the bike, who toppled, knocking the lady off balance. She fell, Harvey swerved left, heading straight for parked cars, someone shouted, people scurried out of the way, Harvey cranking the wheel right, mashing the brake and *thump,* the truck slammed into something. Riley flew into the windshield, beer bottle leaping into the air. He heard and felt his head hit the glass and sensed that he was blacking out, hearing voices and a woman screaming. . . .

When he came to—how long he'd been out he didn't know—he heard shouting. Saw the spiderweb crack in the windshield, felt wet all over. He swiped his face, no blood. He looked down, shirt soaked with beer. Where was Harvey? CDs were scattered across the floor. He opened the door, stumbled out, steadied himself till his head stopped swimming.

"Oh shit," a man said.

A woman shouted, "They killed Miss Solomon, oh Lawd, they killed Miss Solomon."

Kids came running from the donut shop, shirtless guys from the basketball court, drivers leaving their cars.

The pickup was stopped at an angle in the middle of the street, blocking traffic. Riley noticed Harvey's door was wide open. Holding on, he walked to the front of the truck and saw people crouching, a woman standing amid them, hand over mouth, crying. Beyond them, Harvey was hunched over, hands on knees, saying, "Oh but fuck, oh but fuck . . ."

Riley stumbled again, and the woman kept saying, "They killed Miss Solomon. They killed her!"

More people joined the crowd on the street. Bicyclists stopped and looked on. Car horns blared.

Standing at the front of the truck, Riley saw blood on the asphalt, near the left front wheel, but he couldn't be sure and didn't want to venture farther, wasn't prepared for more evidence just yet. A man in a tie and a woman were crouched over administering to someone on the ground, and that damn annoying woman in the middle of the crowd kept squawking, "Poor Miss Solomon, she never had a chance. Never had a chance."

Traffic was backed up in both directions, and a driver behind the truck caught Riley's eyes and hollered, "Move that shit out the way, man."

But Riley didn't snap to until he spied the police Land Rover up the road inching forward, parting the crowd. He slipped around to his door, reached in and got the two beer bottles off the floor, swept the beer puddles out with a hand. As sneaky as he could, he walked holding the bottles close and low in front, dropped them in the high grass by the open drain, knowing somebody was probably seeing this but he couldn't give a shit right now.

A policeman had gotten out of the Land Rover in the middle of the street and was walking toward the scene.

The weed. Oh, man. He dug the Ziploc out of his pocket and balled it tight in a fist. Looked around, acting real cool, saw no one's eyes on him, and underhanded the thing into the grass. He stepped away, thinking about how to explain his beer-smelling shirt if the cops questioned him.

Because they were already talking to Harvey. The crowd was melting away, then the man crouching in the street rose holding the limp body of a blue-gray dog and carried it to the side.

Riley moved to the front of the truck and saw nothing on the street but the bloodstains, people leaving, cars squeezing by, and Harvey coming over saying, "Cops said I better pull to the edge of the road."

Riley said, "But . . ." and moved out of Harvey's way. He watched Harvey park streetside and traffic began flowing again. Harvey rejoined him, wearing a cheesy grin. "I was sweating bullets for a couple minutes, I can't lie."

Riley stuffed his hands in his pockets and watched the man in the tie lay the dog gently in a car trunk and shut it. His muscles slackened with relief. "Miss Solomon," he said.

"Miss Solomon," Harvey said, nodding.

They exchanged a glance and fell apart laughing, pure relief, Riley holding a hand to his head, Harvey saying, "All right, stop, stop, I have to talk to the police now," and trying in vain to stop. He drew a deep breath and set his face serious, but as soon as Riley looked his way, he collapsed into snorting laughter. Riley said, "Oh, Lawd, they killed Miss Solomon, they killed her," shaking his head at how scared he'd been a minute ago. Not that he didn't like dogs, but he'd take this any day.

Harvey said, "Lemme go, hear? You'll get me in more trouble," and crossed the street to where the policeman stood talking to the dog owner.

Walking to the truck, Riley crunched something underfoot

and looked down—the Bob Marley *Legend* CD cover. How the hell did that fall out? He picked it up. The CD was cracked down the middle. Farther along, he came across an Elvis Costello that was salvageable. He gathered the CDs from the truck floor and stacked them into the disarray on the seat that Harvey favored, the man genetically incapable of understanding the concept of organization.

Riley sat in the truck and watched the policeman talking to Harvey and the dog owner, a stoutish, middle-aged business type—dress slacks, long sleeves, dress shoes. Not like he and Harvey, T-shirt and jeans. The policeman left, and Harvey and the businessman kept talking, the man not seeming too upset. They exchanged pieces of paper, and Riley remembered the bag of Breeze.

The bottles were there in the grass where he'd dropped them. He scanned the area farther out, close to the drain. Nothing. He saw Harvey waiting for a break in the traffic so as to cross the street and saw the businessman get into his car, and that's when he noticed the license plate, a government plate. So the man worked for the government.

Harvey sidled up. "What you looking for, last of your senses?"

"The kali, man. I coulda sworn I pitched it over there."

"You threw the weed out? Is it because they killed Miss Solomon?"

Riley said, "Maaan," and went back to searching.

"It was a pretty dog though. I feel bad."

"Tell me about it." Riley hopped over the drain onto the sidewalk for a different vantage, checking between tufts of grass, toeing scraps of paper and cans aside. "Healthy dog, too. You could see it was well taken care of. Which kinda has me wondering how come the owner didn't look too pissed. Was he pissed?"

Harvey shrugged. "Couldn't tell. Dude kept it all quiet and official. That's not it?" pointing at the ground, to Riley's left.

"That's grass, Harvey."

"Isn't it grass you looking for?" and he slapped his thigh. "Man, I kill me."

"And Miss Solomon, too."

Harvey shook his head. "You're a cold son of a bitch, Riley." He went to the truck. "Forget that shit and let's get . . . Wait, check this out."

Riley turned to see what he was looking at. Two teenagers on a bike, one standing on the rear-wheel step nuts with hands on the other's shoulders, were casting backward glances, riding away on the sidewalk.

Harvey said, "You think . . . ?"

"I *know.*" Riley cupped his hands around his mouth. "Yo! Yo, come back here and pay for that."

The boy on the back grinned and said something to the pilot, who pumped the pedals faster.

Riley waved them off. "Screw it," and leaped over the drain onto the street and headed for the truck. They got in and Riley buckled up, prompting a questioning look from Harvey.

"With you behind the wheel, I should get a helmet too. Let's hit it, we're late." He groaned. "Man, what an expensive day."

Harvey started up and the truck roared onto the street.

Riley said, "See what I'm talking about? You just cut somebody off."

"They were going too slow. Not my fault they can't keep up with traffic."

"What an expensive day."

"You keep saying that."

"Know how much that kali cost me?"

"Boys went down a street up here. Want to go after them?"

"Forget it, they're long gone. Oh, by the way, the *Legend* is dead."

"What?"

Riley lifted the crushed Bob Marley cover in one hand and a half of the CD in the other.

Harvey hit the steering wheel. "Aw man, how the hell . . . ?"

Riley tossed the stuff on the seat and looked out the window, feeling the wind on his face, smelling the beer rising off his shirt. "Expensive day."

"I *loved* that CD, man."

Riley smiled at him. "Oh, Lawd, they killed the legend. They killed him!"

Harvey was honestly irritated, scrunching his brow, face reddening. "Man, that's not even funny."

Which made Riley laugh even more.

CHAPTER THREE

Sitting by Roger's bed at Caribbean Hospital, Patricia continued with the story of Riley James.

"He used to live in an old clapboard house by the river," she said, "a house with peeling paint, rusting zinc roof, not much different from other houses in that area. His mother was a terrible drunk. She was a secretary at St. Catherine Academy when I was there. So imagine this little brown boy sitting by the window overlooking the river, waiting for her to come home from the bar down the street. Waiting for her or his father, who rarely came home. The man was a hustler, you see, a bushman, he smuggled Mayan artifacts, contraband, anything of value that can be taken from the land. A hunter, a carouser, a womanizer. The rumor used to be that he had families all over the country. So, anyway, soon Riley was fifteen, and the streets and his alcoholic mother had done the job of raising him, and let me tell you, the results were mixed. At St. John's—yes, he went to your school, Roger—he's known as a bad egg. His expulsion was so entirely predictable, the only surprise was that he lasted till his senior year."

"You know if I ever taught him? I can't say I remember the name."

"You may have, but the question is, did you reach him. Chances are you didn't. I say that because in no time he fell in with a dangerous crew. You know the Monsanto brothers?"

"The Monsantos . . . who own that store on Albert Street? Oooh boy."

"My sentiments exactly. Try as I might I could not get through to Riley. He was following hard in his father's footsteps. The old man, by this time, was somewhere in his late seventies, feeble, but he'd garnered a reputation that many people with an underworld persuasion quite respected. His mother was ill—cirrhosis. Riley was, in effect, his own man. Age seventeen, bringing home more money than most adults in his neighborhood, for god's sake. See, he'd become a messenger, he knew the rural roads, the rainforest, the coastal waters, he learned all that in those few summers he managed to spend with his father. So Riley, now a tall, dark young man, he ran packages and money and guided traffickers through the channels in the reef, or up the rivers inland to their drops. He was valuable, no one in the Monsanto crew knew the land like he did. Then one night he gets stopped by a policeman on a motorcycle. And this is how he got in trouble, this is what started him off on a long, bad trip with the Monsantos that may be finally coming to an end."

Roger said, "How long ago did this happen?"

"About twenty years ago. Sometimes it feels like last week."

"Patricia, I know I'm jumping ahead, but just tell me. This person that he shot. Did this person die?"

Patricia took a deep breath.

"Patricia?"

She nodded.

Roger leaned back on his pillows propped high against the headboard. "Can I get a little more ice, please?"

Patricia filled the cup with cubes from the plastic ice bucket, poured water and sat down again, watching him drink. She looked around the room, the large white tiles, blue cement walls, the closed aluminum jalousie windows. In the upper corner of this new building, a cobweb. Some things never changed in Belize. Caribbean Hospital, by the seawall on Marine Parade, had been built in the style of the old Belize City Hospital, which was at one time the only hospital in the city and the premier one in the country. But neglect, shabby medical care, and lack of funds had closed the colonial-style tin-roofed buildings of heavy shutters and echoing breezeways. Not too long afterward, the buildings were torn down.

When Roger had heard that a group of doctors had opened a new place—only the third hospital in the city—cement-walled but with fortified steel roof and colonial charm, he returned from self-imposed exile in Mexico and chose it as the spot he wanted to die.

Outside the open door, a nurse passed by in the hallway which had screens that faced the sea. There was only one other patient in the five-bed ward, the old man sleeping in his bed near the window.

Roger gave her a tired smile and folded his hands on the sheet. "Go on. I'm listening."

Patricia closed her eyes, imagining again the events that Riley had told her so many years ago.

"So, the policeman stops him," she said. "It was a simple traffic violation. But Riley made a big mistake. He knew the Monsantos had sweetened many officials' pockets over the years, and so he thought he was protected, and so what does he do? He mouths off to the policeman. The policeman promptly lets him eat his backchat. Now, this officer just happened to be notorious in Belize City, not only for his rouge style, but also because of his distinctive features. Light-skinned black man with freckles and red hair. Everyone called him Red Boy, and in some quarters, where he gambled and boozed, they called him Red Dread. So Riley goes home that night having been soundly roughed up by Red Boy—in his words, bitch-slapped, the ultimate humiliation on the streets. And the slaps, well, they come with a message for the Monsantos: You use my streets, you've got to pay a fee for me to look the other way."

"Uh-oh," Roger said. "Knowing what I know about the Monsantos, that sounds like retaliation."

"And that's what Riley thought, too. But the Monsantos are shrewd businessmen, above all else. They know Red Boy's reputation and they know you don't antagonize the police. They give Riley a fat envelope to deliver to Red Boy. Riley is *furious*. Shouldn't the Monsantos be protecting *him*? Just look at the bruise on his face, this Red Boy embarrassed him. But no, take the envelope, the Monsantos tell him, take it. One day you'll understand. And so, Riley obeys, and from then on, the last Friday of every month, he drives to an alley off North Front Street by the Holy Redeemer School playground, and he drops an envelope into a mailbox at a house gate and rings a bell. And then an old woman, Red Boy's mother, comes down the stairs to get the envelope. Month after month, that's how it happens."

Roger said, "But then . . . ?"

Patricia nodded. "But then one day, Riley drives to the agricultural show in Belmopan to pick up an envelope for the Monsantos. He meets a man behind a stall, pockets the envelope, and finds he has a couple of hours to kill before he drives back to the city."

Patricia paused, guilty that she was betraying Riley's trust but relieved that she was finally sharing the story with someone. "Roger, I know this story by heart, he told it to me so many times. But every time I think . . . I wish when I come to this part I could change it, say something else, change the ending." She shook her head briskly. "Anyway, anyway . . . Riley starts walking the show grounds, checking out the sights. He stops at the rodeo grounds and peers through the fence at the calf roping. He meets a young woman he knows from his neighborhood, they start chatting, flirting a little. He leaves to get her a Coke or something. When he comes back, Red Boy is there, talking to the girl, he and another man, a Lebanese known only as Tarik, a small-time drug dealer who had done some business in the past with the Monsantos. They're rather openly coming on to the girl, especially Red Boy. Even being rude and aggressive about it, trying to hold her hand, making suggestive comments about how tight her shirt is, things like that. He's drunk, Red Boy, and he keeps it up even after Riley hands her the Coke. Red Boy ignores Riley, like he's not even there, a nonentity. So Riley takes the girl's hand and leads her away, leaves Red Boy and Tarik standing there just *glaring*."

"How long before they come after him?" '

"On his drive home. Not even two hours later. He was driving alone, an envelope filled with money stuffed in a pocket. It was around five o'clock, the sun was beginning to set, he was behind the wheel of an old Volkswagen he paid for himself, in full, so he had every reason to feel good. He's just cruising, the radio on. Soon he notices a truck in the rearview, a hulking thing with massive tires and tinted windows and fog lamps and roll bars—not that I would know what those are but that's how he describes it. Anyway, the truck begins to tailgate, edging close to his bumper then easing back. Taunting him almost. He can't make out who the men are in the truck but he knows it's two of them and he can see their teeth when they laugh. He speeds up, the truck speeds up; slows down, the truck slows down. He's nervous, he has all this money. He waves the truck ahead. The truck stays behind. This dance continues for miles and miles till finally the truck darts out and rolls beside him, the window slides down and it's Red Boy telling him to pull onto the Manatee Road when he gets there and drive a little ways, he wants to have a word."

Roger adjusted the pillow behind his head. "That doesn't sound promising."

"Manatee Road back then, this is almost twenty years ago remember, it used to be a washboard dirt road, very dusty in the dry season. There was hardly anything on that road then."

"Isn't it still that way?"

"I think so, but back then, all you saw was brush and the occasional fence or the gate of some farm hidden in all that dusty vegetation. One or two rusting car wrecks hauled to the side, certainly no foot traffic. Just desolate enough to be unsafe. Which is what Riley was thinking when he turned onto the road. He was getting anxious, thinking he was in for a beating, two against one. What chance did he have? I'll tell you. There was a gun in the glove box, an old .45 Carlo Monsanto had given him and taught him to use. It was perfectly illegal, just like the source of the cash in his pocket, so he takes the cash envelope and shoves it under his seat. Except for five hundreds. So now, he has parked on Manatee Road. It's growing dark. He gets out and waits for them, leans against the car, arms folded."

"Trying to strike a posture of cool," Roger said. "Saw that so many times with those boys when I taught."

"He admitted that's what he was doing. He was young, somewhat insecure. Figured he needed to show these two older, bigger guys he wasn't scared. The way he told me, he even greeted them first. 'Hey, what's up,' sorta like that, trying to be casual. But Red Boy wasn't having it. He grabbed him by the front of his shirt and banged him hard against the car. He feinted a backhand slap and Riley flinched, I mean, it's reflexive, but it elicited howls of laughter from Red Boy and Tarik. Then Red Boy says to him, he says, 'Don't piss yourself. I ain't gonna slap you this time.' He says, 'But I want you to know, don't ever fuck with me again when I'm doing police work.' Riley says, 'Police work? I don't know what you're talking about.' So Red Boy looks over at the Lebanese and says, 'Tarik, tell this boy I was questioning that beautiful young lady at the fair as part of an ongoing coochie investigation.' Tarik laughs and says, 'Oh look his face, he is wanting his momma and going to cry.' "

Roger was smiling. "You do a good accent, Patricia."

"Well, it's like I was there myself, I've imagined that evening so completely. So listen, the second Red Boy releases his shirt, Riley opens his fist and lets the hundred-dollar bills fall to the ground. He says, 'I think you dropped something just now.' Well. It was an ill-advised and clumsy bribery attempt. You see, what he didn't know because he'd never dared fool with any of the envelopes he delivered for the Monsantos, he didn't know how much money they were giving Red Boy. Five hundred dollars? Chicken feed. Red Boy starts acting ever so insulted. He picked up the money and said something like 'That's it? You waste my time making me follow you out here for this?' Starts cussing. Things like, 'Bitch, you must could do better than this.' That's when they start to search him. Red Boy throws him up against the hood, legs spread, and Tarik pats him down and Red Boy keeps asking him, 'Where the money? Where the money?' He tells Riley, 'I know you're making collections. Tell me where you got the money and I won't throw your ass in jail.' Riley refuses to talk. Finally, Red Boy slugs him in the stomach, doubles him over and says, 'Look, give me my money now and tell Israel how you needed to dip in to avoid a little trouble.' Then Tarik lifts his head up by his hair so they can look into his eyes. Riley, poor Riley—he caves. He blubbers, 'Under the seat, it's under the seat.' Red Boy finds the envelope and helps himself to a couple thousand dollars, tosses the envelope on the seat and he and Tarik walk back to the truck."

Patricia smoothed the front of her skirt, taking a moment. Down the hall a child was crying. The fan on Roger's table click-click-clicked as it oscillated, throwing warm air in her direction. "While they walk, Riley begins to agonize. Later on, he'd say that their walk back to the truck seemed to take a whole day because so many thoughts tumbled through him, so many fears. Not to mention the shame. He said to me he noticed a button on his shirt had popped off and that set him off thinking how weak and sorry he'd look if he went back to the Monsantos with this story. He would lose their confidence, hell, if what people said about them was true, he could lose his *life*. And the humiliation, too, even then it was burning inside. He checks the envelope, feels how light it is now, and remembers what was in the glove box. He doesn't want to open the glove box so he starts repeating, 'It's okay, it's okay, just drive off, just drive off,' like a mantra, you see, but he can't lose the feeling, it's stuck inside him, and so even as he's saying, 'Don't do it, don't do it,' he's opening the glove box and taking out the .45. He checks the magazine, he flips the safety, and meanwhile, behind him, they haven't even gotten inside the truck; they're at the doors, talking low, casting glances at the Volkswagen, like they're considering—to Riley's mind anyway—taking the rest of the money. By this time, Riley has *his* mind made up. He's thinking no dice, no fucking way—pardon my language, but that's what he says he was thinking, he was in a dark, dark state of mind. He jumps out of the car and marches up to them, points the gun at Red Boy and says, 'Gimme the money. Now.'"

Patricia shakes her head. "You know what this fellow, Red Boy, does? He laughs. He says, 'Really?' and opens his door, reaches in, comes out with a shotgun, this scary sawed-off thing,

Riley said, and Red Boy says something on the order of, 'I'll fix your little ass,' and before he can raise it, Riley runs up pointing the .45, but he's shouting, 'No, no, put it down, no,' pleading with Red Boy. The thing was, he'd realized right then that the situation had gotten out of hand, and he wants to stop, he wishes somehow they could just hop into their vehicles, drive away and try to forget this ever happened. But of course, it's too late and Red Boy's shotgun is coming up and Riley has a finger on his trigger and he has to go through with it, he has to or he'll be killed."

Patricia breathed out, shoulders drooping.

Roger waited.

"So Riley shoots Red Boy. At first, he thinks he missed, but he sees the sudden expression on Red Boy's face, like somebody threw boiling water on him. But he's still holding the shotgun, so Riley shoots again and Red Boy grabs at his face with both hands and tries to run but he falls in the middle of the road. Meantime, Tarik, who must've scampered for cover behind the truck, Tarik runs around and looks to pick up the shotgun. Riley is no longer thinking, he's reacting now. He fires shots until Tarik falls. He said that even though he saw Tarik heaped motionless there against the front tire, he was so panicked that he would've shot him some more if the gun hadn't jammed.

"So he's standing at the side of the road holding the gun with two hands, and shaking. Just shaking. Two men bleeding on the ground and he's thinking that's it, his life is over, what did he just do? Red Boy is twitching and groaning so he's still alive but Tarik—Riley could tell he was dead. Stone dead, sitting against the big tire with his eyes wide open and not blinking. Riley decides he's got to flee the scene, but first, his money. He finds the cash folded in Red Boy's front pocket. Thing is, some of the bills have blood on them. He'd shot him right above the hip. He wipes off the blood on Red Boy's shirt and that's when he noticed that he'd also shot him in the eye. He starts feeling sick to his stomach and runs back to the car, and that's how he sees the little boy."

"Little boy? What—"

"Yes. Standing at a gate. He's half concealed behind a cluster of trees. It's off to the left, a few dozen yards up the road and it's easy to miss, just a chicken-wire fence set back at an angle, a dirt path, probably leading to some shack way in the back. The little boy just stands there staring through the wire, sucking a pacifier. Riley walks up, gets close to the gate and looks down at the little boy. The boy is expressionless, staring up, sucking that pacifier. Not frightened, not curious, just a blank look. Riley raises a finger to his lips, goes 'Shhh.' He nods at the little boy, gets into his car and drives away.

"He heads back to the Western Highway. He passes no other car in either direction on that dirt road and he's thinking he just might get away with this. The child at the gate? Riley says he didn't fear him. He looked no older than three, and there was something in his face that . . . well, suggested retardation. At the intersection with the Western Highway, there's a restaurant, a two-story concrete building, unpainted, you probably know it. A couple yapping on the verandah hardly pay him any mind when he drives by. He's thinking, good, he just might get away."

Roger said, "But I take it, he's wrong."

"He keeps driving—"

"Wait, one moment there, Patricia. You said that he killed someone. But it sounds like he killed *two* men."

"He killed one man. And one devil."

"Oh, come on, now, you don't even believe in a deity anymore. Listen to you with this metaphysical talk. Devil?"

Patricia rose and went to the window. She cranked open the

aluminum louvers. Only a few cars in the parking lot, one with a cab driver behind the wheel reading a magazine. She watched a paper bag skitter across the dusty pavement. "What time is it, Roger?"

"Around five thirty or so. Why?"

"I'm supposed to meet him outside about now, and he's usually pretty punctual."

"Another counseling session?"

Patricia returned to her seat. She said, "No, he's through with counseling. Not that he'd even call it that. More like 'talks.' Soon he might be through with the talks, he might be getting married. No, today he's just meeting me to drop off something."

Roger inhaled deeply. "Feel that lovely breeze, so nice. That lovely Belize Breeze," smiling at her.

"You're so very clever. My, I can't get anything past that steel-trap intellect of yours, can I?"

"Only concerned that you're not driving."

"So I can't drink anymore, but some nights I could use just a little help to take the edge off."

Roger raised a hand. "No excuses necessary."

"None given."

Roger cocked his head. "When Riley drove off, past the restaurant and nobody noticed, is that the end of the story? Did he get away with it?"

"Well, that's what he hoped. But no one really gets away, you know that. No, Roger, Riley's problems were just beginning. The news about Red Boy and the Lebanese came over the radio the next day—remember we didn't have TV news back then. They said that Corporal Lucius Myvette and Lebanese national Tarik El-Bani were found dead on Manatee Road, victims of multiple gunshot wounds, police were investigating and so far there were no suspects and so on and so forth. Riley said that started one of the worst weeks of his life. It was the waiting, the fear, the paranoia that any day, any minute the cops would come knocking at his door, rouse him from bed. He said he even had nightmares they busted into his bathroom while he was on the toilet. I mean, he was a physical and mental mess. Still, still—he hadn't told anyone. He didn't tell me until much later. And by the end of that week he thought he was home free. The radio, the papers were saying there were still no suspects and very few clues. But he'd overlooked something.

"Remember the cash Red Boy had taken and he'd taken back from Red Boy? Well, some of the bills, he hadn't completely wiped off all the blood. Israel Monsanto had noticed the stains, and when he heard that Red Boy had been shot on the same day Riley had gone to make his collection and in the same general area? He remembered how Riley had appeared really nervous that evening, how he wouldn't stay for a beer or have any of the chips and guacamole Mirta Monsanto had prepared. So he started making inquires. People like the Monsantos have connections everywhere, you understand.

"Riley's fears came true, but it wasn't the cops who showed up; instead it was Israel and Carlo Monsanto who knocked at his door early one morning. 'Come,' Israel said, 'let's go somewhere private we could have a little talk. And I want you to wear the same shoes you had on the other day you went to the agri fair.' And Carlo, the younger one, said, 'Also, the .45 we lent you. We'll be needing it back.'

"Imagine the fear. Riley just about collapsed. But he held his composure, for a good while, he surprised himself. The Monsantos drove him up the Western and turned onto Manatee Road and parked on the roadside after about a half mile, and Israel said, 'It's right around here the police found those boys. Know who I'm talking about?' And he stared directly into Riley's face, waiting for a reaction. Then Israel just laid it out for him. He said that when you decide you're going to shoot someone you must be smart enough to conceal the evidence, and that means you must pick up after yourself. Then Carlo, he's always had a temper, broke in with, 'Three things that cops know already, okay? Those boys were shot with a .45, footprints matching a size eleven Adidas were found at the scene on this dusty road, and a small yellow Volkswagen was seen racing with the Lebanese's truck on the Western Highway that evening.' He told Riley, he said something like, 'You have a .45 in your possession, *my* .45. You are wearing Adidas tennis shoes, size eleven, and you drive a yellow Volkswagen. You dumb shit.' Israel had to settle his brother down. Israel told Riley, 'Tell us what happened, and don't lie or we turn you in this morning.'

"So that was that. He told the Monsantos everything. Except he wasn't racing, he said. Red Boy had been following him and he was trying to get away. Israel didn't care about that, he'd heard enough and he was all about what do we do now. First, they got rid of the tennis shoes, flung them deep into the bushes off the Western. Next, they disassembled the gun and that night they dumped some parts into the West Collet canal and some in the Belize River. The car? Israel said there was nothing to be done about the car. Two friendly policemen were coming to question Riley next morning. He advised Riley to just relax, stick to his story and everything would be fine.

"The police did come. They talked to him for five or ten minutes. They explained to him how people saw him racing with the truck, making threatening gestures at Myvette and the Lebanese, how people had seen them arguing at the agricultural fair—they tried different angles, they mixed truth and fabrication, to see if they could trip him up, catch him in a lie. When the police left, Israel Monsanto paid a visit and said, 'You're goddamn lucky.' That was the closest the police ever got to Riley. They never came around again, and the investigation fizzled out. Life went on as before, Riley doing collections and guiding drops—a little wiser, though, and the Monsantos profiting from it. Carlo was never shy about reminding him that if they hadn't helped, if not for their pulling strings, and if the police were more capable? He would surely be living the rest of his life behind bars—as Carlo would say, as someone else's bitch.

"Which brings us to the present concern. It's been almost twenty years and Riley—he's not so young anymore, he's middle-aged, he's an upstanding citizen, a business owner, taxpayer, a father, though his marriage didn't work out, but he's a good father—"

Roger Hunter said, "Wait wait wait. What are you saying, Patricia? This man isn't an upstanding, law-abiding citizen, he's part of the criminal element. Or am I living on some other planet? Did the standards of responsible civil behavior change and no one informed me?"

"But that's not my point. He *has* changed. In the eyes of the law, he is law abiding. And over the years, if you must know, he's pulled away from the Monsantos, little by little. As a re-payment for them saving his skin, he started taking a reduced payment from them. It has become an unspoken agreement. Then after his son was born, he cut back on the number of jobs he did for them, started saving, bought that bar, he and a friend, remodeled it. Now he seldom makes runs for the Monsantos. They resented it at first but they've come around, slowly, accepted that they'd go separate ways one day. Last month he told them that his next run would be his last. Didn't go over too well with Carlo, but Israel, the boss, gave it his blessing. As Riley says, 'I can't keep paying them back for the rest of my life.'"

Roger said, "So what's the concern?"

"Will they be true to their word? That's the concern. Not

pressure him into taking on another job? He wants no more of that life, he says, and he plans to marry again, start afresh."

"Ahh, this idea—the New Beginning. Such a common delusion."

"You're a cynic. One must always try, or else slit your wrists now, why don't you?"

"True, we've got to practice hopefulness. Question I have, and I assume you know Riley better than most, has he really changed? Does he have the discipline to live by the strength of his convictions, live a normal, one might say, boring existence compared to the one he's led before?"

"I believe he does."

A nurse entered the room with blankets slung over a forearm. "Mr. Hunter, you're getting another roommate. Fellow came in here this morning for an emergency appendectomy." She went over to a bed on the far side of the room, laid the blankets on it and peeled back the sheet.

Roger said, "That's fine. I need some company. Not that yours isn't exceptional, Patricia. You know, you're quite comely with makeup. When we were an item you hated makeup."

Patricia glanced at the nurse, who was adjusting the bed height, wheeling a side table out of the way. "Are you trying to flirt with me?"

Roger smiled, downright pleased with himself. "Know what else? That story was really something. Since when did you become such a raconteur?"

"For goodness' sake, Roger, don't pretend we don't know nearly everything about each other." Glancing at the nurse again, she said, "Private matters for instance. Like that very dark asymmetrical mole on the left tip of your penis."

Roger's eyes bulged and he fell into a fit of coughing. Patricia jumped up, wearing a little smile, and filled his cup with water and handed it to him. The nurse finished up hastily and hustled out.

Roger drank noisily while Patricia patted his back. He lowered the cup and said, "Woman, you're rude."

She laughed and retook her seat. They passed a few minutes in silence, enjoying the light breeze that had started flowing through the room, hearing the voices outside and the waves lapping against the seawall.

He said, "So you truly think he can change? Think he can become a new man?"

"I do, Roger. I do. I worry about him, he's like a son to me, but Riley has matured. Sometimes he's—dare I say—introspective. He's become a surprisingly thoughtful and cautious man. I want him to change, but to change he might need to leave here to get away from his old influences, and I don't want to lose him. He's ready to change, but some people might resent that, and it could be dangerous for him."

The fan clicked-clicked and blew a warm breeze over her face.

"I don't want to lose any more of my friends," she said.

Roger smiled sadly, stretched a skinny arm over the bed rail, and she reached over and clasped his hand.

CHAPTER FOUR

Riley dropped the truck into third gear and took the curve hard, then building speed, pressed the clutch and slipped into fourth and bulleted into the straightaway, ripping past A Street and the fork in the road and on toward home. Man, sometimes when he'd been cooped up or stressed out all day, he lusted after that piece of asphalt perfection.

He slowed down when he passed St. Thomas Street, having dosed himself with just enough adrenaline to last till suppertime. Night had fallen and he had long hours ahead. After he and Harvey had picked up the speakers, he'd helped Gert behind the bar, served some beers, shot the breeze with the Friday evening regulars. Then it was time for home and a warm shower, maybe a power nap if he was fast enough, before he had to head back.

Riley lived on Lizarraga Avenue, behind the Belize Telemedia building and the antennae tower visible for miles around. It was a street of nondescript homes and lower-middle-class incomes, children always running about, cars parked on the verges, some yards overgrown, but pretty quiet most of the time, generally safe, with friendly neighbors who liked him.

His house was a concrete tin-roofed bungalow, two bedrooms, a porch out back and a covered one in front, where he always kept a light burning for safety, and the comfort of never having to come home to darkness. He strived to make his life as routine as possible—difficult considering he made much of his money in ways that were anything but routine.

His custom was to park the pickup out front. Unlatch the rickety wooden gate and stroll up the seashell path, maybe stopping at the carport to check the van with DUNCAN'S TOURS painted on the side, see if the windows were rolled up, doors locked. But the part of it he was tired of—coming home to an empty house. Sometimes, just seeing his son's name on the van gave him a lift; other times it was only painted lettering. For the past year, however, he'd had an American neighbor next door whose attractiveness was worth every second of all the time he spent admiring her.

He stood in the center of his yard and stared up at her house. Lights were on in two rooms, windows open. He edged toward the fence. Smelled cooking. Onions sautéing, meat. Heard her voice. High-pitched singing. Through the tall living room window he could see the ceiling fan whirring, a high shelf of photographs, the walls. Couldn't see her, though, and he was in need of a glimpse.

When she moved in last year, he'd introduced himself, helped carry boxes up, and from that day, he'd been checking her out. His neighbor across the street had been as well—Bill Rivero had seen him helping and later that week said, "Boy, you don't play. You're Mr. Swift," and winked.

She was a tight, muscular woman, thirty-six, pale skin, red hair, features untypical in Belize. She liked snug jeans and they never disappointed her, baseball caps sometimes. She ran four mornings a week, seven-thirtyish, and looked surprisingly softer, leaner, and girlish in running shorts.

Clearly, Riley had a thing for her.

He saw her glide past the window. Long T-shirt, bare legs. Was her hair damp? It looked damp. He listened to frogs bleating in the empty lot behind his house, crickets cheeping. A light came on in another room and he followed her, staying close to the fence, going into his backyard.

There—another glimpse. She was folding clothes, stacking a high shelf in a bedroom closet . . . man, those legs. He had the perfect angle, perfect view with the lights on . . . and yeah, her hair was wet. Like she'd just stepped out of the shower. She turned around and he ducked, holding his breath, feeling stupid. No way she could've seen him, she in a lighted room and him down here in the dark.

He felt self-conscious, and naughty. His other neighbor's windows were closed, Bill Rivero was too far across the street to see him, and the house behind hers, well, if someone there looked out, they might see him, but it was dinnertime, plus who'd think anything wrong about a man standing in his own backyard?

Riley was massively turned on right now, and he did mean massively as in uncomfortably tight jeans. He thought about it, then he put a hand on the post of the chain-link fence and launched himself over, dropping low into the grass on her side.

He remained still. Heard her singing. Sounded like . . . something by Prince?

". . . don't have to be rich to be my girl . . ."

Riley passed a palm over his face and thought, Okay, let me reconsider this, and didn't, stepping over to her back stairs, where he rested a hand on the railing, one foot on the bottom step, looking up. Light slanted onto her back porch through a screen door.

He sat on a step, listening to her voice going off-key. *"Women, not girls, rule my world, I said they rule my world,"* the clank of a spoon against a pot. He imagined her, back and forth between the fridge and the stove, what she was wearing under that T-shirt, or not wearing. Jesus, he had to take a look.

He stood up, counted one, two, three and bounded up the stairs, two at a time, and braked right beside the screen door, flattened his back against the wall. He looked over at his house, the weedy lot behind it, at the square of light from the other neighbor's window. He was satisfied there was no one watching this. Inch by inch, he pushed his head around and peeked in.

She was in the kitchen, shaking a bottle of spices into a small pot bubbling on the stove. Bopping her head, earbuds plugged in, wire leading to an iPod clipped to the hem of the T-shirt. She screwed the lid on, turned to put the bottle on the counter, and Riley pulled his head back.

His heart was thudding. Wow—she was so damned good-looking. No makeup, wet stringy hair, baggy T-shirt, but this was what was so cool—the plainness made her prominent jaw and blue eyes and milky white skin more striking. He poked his head around for another moment of appreciation.

She was dancing now, twirling in the middle of the tiled kitchen, pivoting on the ball of one foot, eyes closed, head thrown back. Clapping now, swinging her hips in that loose T-shirt that reached to the middle of tight runner's legs.

God*damn,* Riley was breathing hard. He felt like Harvey, like some slack-jawed ogler.

She did a move where she struck a pose, hands on chest, then flung her hair and tossed her arms out into a series of serpentine gestures, hips rocking, toes pointed, and calves taut. Riley put a hand to his heart and thought, Oh, my, god.

He drew back. Without a second's doubt, he removed his shirt and dropped it there on the porch. His left hand roamed his chest, traveled down to his navel, unsnapped his jeans, unzipped. Reached in and . . . man, oh, man. . . .

What the hell was he doing? Touching himself, thinking,

I could get arrested for this. Thinking, I don't give a shit, no one can see me. . . . He was rock hard, breaths coming shallow.

Clapping—she was clapping again. When he pushed his head around, she was facing him, dancing into the kitchen, eyes directly on the door, and he froze.

But it was like she couldn't see him even though she had looked straight at him. He stepped back, knowing he'd just been caught and that she did not care, the woman was teasing him, pretending to be oblivious, as she enticed him further. Tantalized him.

He pulled his Levi's down and it sounded *thock* when it hit the floor, and he remembered the engagement ring in his pocket. But it was in a box, well protected. It would survive.

He tugged off his briefs and flipped it onto the pile and stood there naked and stiff and pulsing. He felt wicked daring and crazy and jungle virile. The air licked at his backside, and he really liked that.

She was singing a different song, or more like speaking, about rain on the barn roof and the horses wondering who you are and about thunder and lightning and how you feel like a movie star. He stood still as she launched into the chorus. *"Raspberry beret . . ."*

Her voice moving away. The air thick with delicious cooking, his head reeling, he made up his mind to do it. He reached over and finger-hooked the door handle gently. The door opened with a creak of the springs.

He stepped into the kitchen, the tile cool under his feet. She danced into the living room, her back to him, swaying those hips. There was a leather sofa on one side, a love seat on the other, and he wondered on which one he'd do it—or maybe right there on the rug she was dancing on.

If you're going to act crazy, might as well act crazy all the way.

He wanted her to turn around, see him naked and solid under the kitchen light, before he made his move.

Throwing her arms out, she twirled and stopped. A hand flew up to her mouth and she let out a scream. "Oh my god!"

He charged, she put out her hands but he ducked under and tackled her around the waist and lifted her easy, slinging her over a shoulder, her body so soft and light. She squirmed and shrieked with laughter and started spanking his butt. "You're crazy, Riley, you're so"—spank, spank—"totally crazy,"—spank, spank, spank—kicking her legs and laughing hysterically.

He said, "You like that? Didn't expect that, did you?" He thought better of the sofa and moved toward her bedroom. She was pinching his butt and he couldn't stop laughing, rushing and tottering with her to the room. He stumbled. "Oooh, my back, I think I hurt my back."

She said, "Don't you *dare* drop me," and whaled away at his ass, giggling.

He heaved her onto the bed and pounded his chest like a gorilla and roared as she rolled around laughing uncontrollably, tears in her eyes. He raised his arms and executed a short dive onto the bed, landing on elbows and knees, straddling her. "You're trapped now, baby, nowhere to go but to the land of extreme pleasure," and he leaned in for a deep, long kiss full of giggling.

He lay on the damp sheets and languidly took in the room in the light leaking through the half-open bathroom door. Wood-framed photos decorated the walls—a kayaker bobbing on the blue-green near the barrier reef; the ruins of the Maya temple at Xunantunich at sunset; Riley and his five-year-old son standing on rocks, grinning in the mist of the Thousand Foot Falls at

Mountain Pine Ridge—all of them photos Candice had taken. And one snapshot on the dresser of her fiancé, Albert, who had died in a car crash years ago. To honor him, she said. Riley respected that.

She said from the tub, over the noise of the faucet, "Baby, can you put the mince on simmer for me?"

Passing the bathroom door, he said, "Girly-girl, you wore me out proper, I can hardly walk." In the kitchen, he turned the stove to simmer and sniffed the pot. Ground meat, onions, peppers, and carrots swimming in a curried stew. In a pan cooling off, thin-sliced potatoes, crisped in a light coating of olive oil and a sprinkle of kosher salt. The sight made him happy and ready for the big question. He retrieved his clothes from the porch and padded back into the bedroom with a quickening heart.

She was toweling off in the bathroom, smiling at him occasionally in the mirror. He stepped out of view and pincered the little box out of his jeans, removed the ring and searched for the best place to put it.

She came out and dropped the towel, a message that she just might be in the mood for more.

He said, "Heavens, you're too sexy for your own good."

"Oh yeah?" She teased him with a pose, hip jutting to the left.

Her skin was flawless in that light. Down there, he was rising again. He said, huskily, "Walk across the room."

"Like this?" and she sashayed, snapped her chin in line with a shoulder, with attitude. Pivoted and swaggered back.

He said, "I think you dropped something, over there. No . . . by the closet," and admired her shapely apple cheeks, which she pointed his way.

Legs together she bent forward from the waist perfectly and said, "Oh where but where could it be? I don't see anything here," in a girly voice. Playing with him. She straightened, dropped her arms on the dresser, stuck her rear out and said, "I believe I shall just have to look again," and Riley laughed, leaping onto the bed.

On his knees, he said, "Looking at you makes me want to growl."

She spun around, shoved her hips to the left—bam—took a couple of steps, shoved to the right—bam—and bent over again, offering a side view, the flat of her thighs, breasts, long damp red hair tousled over a shoulder. "Is it here, you think?"

He was quiet, waiting.

She straightened, a hand over her mouth. She stared at the ring she was holding. "Riley . . . ?" She looked at him. "Riley?"

For days he had planned what to say and now the moment had arrived, he was mute. So he grinned. "Uhmmm . . . well, yeah . . ."

She came to him, and they hugged, then she stepped back and examined the diamond. She slipped it on her ring finger, daintily.

He felt awkward and nervous and just couldn't wait any longer, so he said, "I'm ready for loving," but that wasn't what he wanted to say, and when she smiled he played it up, posing with fists on hips, Superman now. "Riley James, the indefatigable lover."

She frowned. "No, say it with style. Say lov*ah*."

"The indefatigable lov*ah*."

"Yeah, like that."

"Come to me, my fairy sweet."

She did, sneaking a peek at the ring. They embraced hard, and he wrestled her to the sheets, tasting her mouth, tartish wine, her nipples, salty with dried perspiration, her neck. Her legs parted for him, and he covered her with his body, their abdomens barely touching, until he moved in, hoping for the right answer.

CHAPTER FIVE

Riley awoke in his own bedroom with the sun in his eyes, nightstand lamp burning. His reading glasses were perched crookedly on his nose, his worn paperback of the *Tao Te Ching* open on his chest. He yawned, stretched, and reseated the glasses. Watched the haze of dust in the sunrays, trying to remember what time he'd left Candice's house to go to the bar, then what time he'd left the bar. After a while, he took up the book and read half a page with half his attention and put the book down.

He got out of bed, rolled his neck and bent backward, joints cracking and popping nicely. He sat on his kneeling meditation bench, and when he was ready, relaxed, he watched his breath rise and fall. After a few minutes, his attention slackened and he started scratching his arm, and he gave up on the sitting.

Driving to Lindy's, he called Patricia on his cell. Her machine picked up and he said, "Sister Pat, listen, sorry about yesterday evening. I had a . . . little situation, an accident, and I couldn't meet up with you. I apologize, but this evening maybe I can get something, if you're home? Call me, please."

Then he called his ex-wife's house to chat with his son, but the phone rang and rang and no one answered.

Arturo was already at the bar, picking up cups and bottles from the outside tables and off the deck, his old bicycle chained to the fence. The boy nodded at Riley. "Mistah James."

Riley nodded back. "Turo." He took out his keys and opened the padlock to the corrugated shutter, slid it up. Turo followed him into the bar area. While Riley opened the wooden jalousies and fixed a pot of strong coffee, Turo got the deck broom and garbage bags from the storage closet in the back. They drank coffee, looking out at the road.

Riley watched Turo pour more cream, spoon in two hills of sugar. Riley went into the kitchen and returned with a container of chicken fried rice and plastic utensils, put them on the bar. "If you get hungry, help yourself, hear?"

Turo was embarrassed, so Riley said, "Look, I bought too much last night and I'm not gonna eat this. You don't want it, no problem, just toss it," and he moved away, opening the cooler and taking inventory, giving the boy room.

Riley inventoried the soft drinks, the liquor, bottled beer and kegs, jotting numbers on a slip of paper. Turo sat eating at the bar. Riley told him he was leaving to pick up a few crates of Cokes, some rum, a couple kegs, they were running short 'cause of the holiday crowd. He should be back in an hour, the phone rings, just take a message, and please go ahead and clean the lines so they could switch out the low keg.

Turo said, "Mistah Riley?"

Riley paused at the stairs.

"Think you could help me write a letter? My landlord wants to, like, you know, kick me out. Saying how I stole his wheelbarrow and sold it."

"Wheelbarrow?"

"Yeah. And plus pilfered a few baubles."

Riley fought back a smile. "Pilfered a few baubles?"

"Yeah, that's what he said."

Riley said sure, he could do that, and didn't chuckle to himself until he was in the truck.

The first stop, Ramirez Brothers on New Road, should have prepared him for the problematic morning. But he was expecting nothing other than an ordinary transaction, and when the girl at the front, Sarita, told him they were out of Blue Parrot rum, and sorry but Cane River, too, he still didn't think there was anything strange. It wasn't until he walked to the far end of the counter and glimpsed the stack of Blue Parrot cases in the back room that he figured something was off. "What's that there?"

"Sold."

"Everything? That's . . . five, six . . . seven. Seven cases."

"Sorry. Sold."

"So you're telling me Ramirez Brothers, manufacturer of four kinds of rum, has no rum to sell customers?"

Sarita wouldn't look at him.

"Did I square my account with you last month?"

Sarita stapled a sheaf of pink and yellow invoices together and reached for another stack. A man walked in, exchanged nods with Riley.

Riley said, "Sarita?"

She straightened her glasses and sat forward, folding her hands on the desk. "I'm sorry, Mr. James. I'm just . . . That's what Mr. Ramirez told me this morning, everything we have here today is sold."

The other man came down the counter. "You got Blue Parrot, miss? I'll need like a case."

Riley looked at Sarita.

She turned to the man. "Uhmm . . ."

"They're sold out," Riley said.

The man said, "What's that?"

Sarita raised a finger and said, "One moment," and rose and

clip-clopped in her heels down a narrow corridor to an office in the back.

Riley asked the man, "I take it you haven't paid for yours in advance?" The man said no, and Riley asked, "And you don't have an account?"

The man watched Riley. "Since when you need one?"

Sarita returned. "Mr. Avila? Mr. Ramirez would like to see you in his office. Come around the counter over here, please."

Riley walked out of the store and stood by the front door. What the hell was that all about? He mulled it over, then strode back inside. "I want to talk to Mr. Ramirez."

Sarita sat back, blinking. The other man, Avila, was leaving the back storeroom lugging a case of Blue Parrot. He came around the counter and shrugged at Riley, saying, "Hooked one. Good luck."

Riley stared at Sarita. She raised that finger again, said, "One moment," and clip-clopped back down the corridor. A minute later she returned. She folded her hands down in front of her and said, "Mr. Ramirez is in a meeting at the present time but you can call him later if you'd like."

"What time?"

"Well . . ." She raised her eyebrows. "Why not give him an hour."

"Today is Saturday, you close at noon on Saturdays. In forty-five minutes, you'll be closed and you're telling me call in an hour?"

She glanced away.

Riley took a deep breath, fighting to control his tongue. He wanted to stare at her long enough to provoke some response that might sound like a reasonable explanation for the game being played, but the phone rang and she reached for it. So he walked out, annoyed.

He drove to Bowen and Bowen on King Street for soft drinks

and beer. Fuming. He was perspiring, felt it under his arms, face flushed, but it wasn't from the heat. All these years and it didn't take much for his youthful temper to rear up again, needle him. Truthfully? He wanted to punch something. Telling himself no worries, you'll talk to Ramirez soon.

At Bowen and Bowen, he bought four crates of Coke cash and loaded them in the back of the truck. He thought, All right, at least I got one job done this morning. He trotted up the stairs to the office to buy his two kegs of Belikin, settle his account fast so he could surprise Ramirez with a visit and get to the bottom of—

His cell chirped. He dug it out of his pocket, thinking this must be Ramirez now—yeah, right. He read the number on the screen: the bar's. "Yes, Turo."

"Mistah James. Like sorry to bug you, but the health inspector didn't want to talk but he asked me a whole pile a questions, you know, and by the time I catch a break to phone you? The man already left, and he dropped off some papers in your office so I—"

"Whoa, hold on, Turo, slow." Riley entered the small office and found a corner free of bodies. It was pleasantly frosty in there, a relief from the heat and his frustrations. "Health inspector?"

"Yes, mahn. Two of them. The main one, I tell him you're not there, he didn't care, just walked into the kitchen like he own the joint, you know? And the other one, he went through—"

"On a Saturday? You sure they were from the health department, Turo?"

"Yes, mahn. I saw his papers. And the truck said it, too, on the side."

Riley said he'd be there real soon and hung up. Didn't bad news come in threes? Let's see what would happen next. He approached the counter, working on his positive mood, his charming smile. "Terri," he said to the heavy woman at the desk. "When are you going to take that trip to San Pedro with me, Terri? Everybody needs a little romance in their lives, Terri."

"Listen to you, sugar mouth. Your white woman's got you under heavy manners so you better fly right."

They laughed. He said, "All I need this morning is two kegs, and let me go ahead and pay off the balance on my account," pulling out his wallet. "Didn't think I was gonna be here so soon, but that crowd hit us hard last night. I'm not complaining though."

Terri heaved her considerable bosom, gripped the side of the desk, and hauled herself to her feet. "Wait one second, Riley. I think Raymond needs to talk to you." She lumbered over to a small window and slid it back and called for Raymond.

The office manager came out of one of the doors and shook Riley's hand. "Yes, Riley J., how's things," one hand on Riley's shoulder. "See you inside my office a minute?"

Walking in with him, Riley said, "Gertrude didn't pay the bill last month or something, Ray?"

"No, it's not that," Ray said, closing the door behind them. It was a cramped office, AC vent rattling. Ray dropped into a creaky chair behind his desk. "It's just . . . you know, if it's up to me it would be business as usual, I'd sell you the kegs."

"Yeah, but . . . ?"

"I got a call this morning from my supervisor. I don't understand it, but he's telling me to cancel your account."

"Cancel my account? The hell you talking about?"

"No more purchases. The man, I don't know why, the man said he doesn't want to sell Lindy's draft beer anymore." Ray cleared his throat. "Matter of fact, Tuesday morning I'm supposed to send a truck to your place to pick up the draft machine, kegs, and whatnot. But I could hold off on that for a couple weeks." Ray shrugged, put up his hands. "I'm sorry, man."

Riley sat down. "What the fuck, Ray?"

"Riley, me and you go way back, but you understand it's not like I have a choice. I mean, if it was up to me . . ."

"I know Ray, I know," Riley said, getting up suddenly. He opened the door, not wanting to hear anything else.

Ray stood up. "So this won't affect things with us?"

Riley walked out of the office and through the main one, Ray following. Riley opened the door and stood half in the sunlight, half in the air-conditioning. "You know I don't do business that way, to retaliate. The five sixty you owe got nothing to do with this. Pony up and you're back at the poker table immediately, Ray. The VIP room is always open to friends."

"Five *sixty*? More like four eighty, I think."

Riley said, "Ray."

"You're right, you're right. I might be miscalculating." Ray extended a hand. "Sorry again, partner."

Riley was getting into the truck when the phone rang again. He took it out, checked the number on the screen. "What now, Turo?"

"It's me," Harvey said.

"What? Impossible. Harvey Longsworth would never be out of bed at this ungodly hour of midafternoon. You, sir, are a flimsy imposter."

"Yeah, well, I wish I was in the mood to fuck around but we got ourselves a little complication here ain't no joke."

Riley sat back. "Hey, don't mess with me, it's been a curious kinda morning. Like nobody-wants-to-sell-me-anything kinda morning that makes no sense."

"Exactly what I'm telling you. Some people here to see us, you and me. To discuss 'any obstacles Lindy's might be encountering.' I'm looking at them right now out there on the deck. How soon can you get here, Riley?"

CHAPTER SIX

Harvey's Honda was parked in a space by the fence. Beside it, near the gate, was a white Range Rover with government plates, angle-parked, occupying two spaces—the work of a driver who didn't want anyone near his ride, and who was also just plain inconsiderate. A small Belizean flag hung from a pole on the hood. Riley pulled up near the gate, and Turo helped him carry the crates of Cokes inside.

A man and a woman were sitting out on the covered section of the deck. They had drinks full of ice in front of them, and with a cooling breeze off the Caribbean, the woman looking relaxed, Riley could have mistaken them for contented patrons, but he knew from Harvey and Gert's expressions when he passed by to wash his hands that the pair outside weren't here for pleasure.

Riley came out toweling his hands. Gertrude was behind the bar, elbows on the counter, staring at them.

He said, "Any coffee back there?"

"No."

Riley pitched the hand towel on the bar.

Gert was glaring. "That's Eva Burrows. Minister of finance and development. The man is her driver."

"Where's Harvey?"

Gert's eyes were flat. "In the kitchen. Slicing a lime. 'Cause the minister requested a slice of lime to garnish her drink, don't you know."

Riley said, "So what's this all about?"

Harvey came bustling out of the kitchen with a saucer of lime wedges. "Ready?"

"Ready for what?"

"Talk to these people, see what the hell they want."

Riley said, "After you," and followed Harvey onto the deck, Harvey stiff-backed like a waiter, smiling at the man and woman, saying, "Here you go. Sorry that took so long. Wanted to get the pick of the lot for you, Mrs. Burrows." Acting unusually nice, and getting Riley concerned.

It wasn't until introductions were made and Riley shook the man's hand that he recognized Victor Lopez as the man whose dog Harvey had killed yesterday.

They all sat down. There was a manila folder on the table next to their drinks.

"I'm so sorry about what happened yesterday, Mr. Lopez," Harvey said. "Again, I'll pay for any expenses. Your family wants a new dog, anything like that. I mean it."

"I'm not the one," Lopez said in a slow rumble, "that you should apologize to. Miss Solomon was Minister Burrows's dog," and he stretched out a palm, giving her the floor.

Minister Burrows released a dramatic sigh. She touched the base of her throat and started to speak but nothing came out. She was a slim biracial woman, midfifties, hazel eyes, proud bearing. Waiting for her emotions to settle, or putting on an act—that's how it struck Riley.

"I loved that dog so," she said, shakily, barely more than a whisper. "Had her for five years. My Miss Solomon. Smart as a whip. She was the prettiest pup in the litter. I went up to Tampa,

Florida, to get her. The sweetest little Weimaraner pup, just gorgeous. Did you notice her coloring?" The minister's face turned briefly to Harvey, who shifted in his chair. "Sable, an unusual color in dogs. I almost named her that—Sable. But from she was a pup she had this way about her, strong maternal instinct." The minister seemed to choke up then, and paused. "She was pregnant, did you know?"

Harvey shook his head. "Aw, hell, didn't know that." Pursed his lips. "I don't know what to say."

"It's sad. A litter of six pups. She was due in a few weeks."

"I mean what I said, Mrs. Burrows. I'll buy a dog to replace her. I know in your heart she can't be replaced but if you allow me to make that gesture, I'd like to do that."

"You can call me Minister Burrows. I'm not a Mrs."

The woman was stern, eyes cold, gazing over Riley's shoulder at the park, the clouds, or who the hell knows, but Riley was beginning to have suspicions.

When she refocused, she said to Harvey, "Miss Solomon was AKC registered, from a long line of registered Weimaraners. She can never be replaced." Then she clasped her hands in her lap, lowered her gaze and seemed to withdraw into herself.

Riley piped up, "So what can we do to, you know, make this unfortunate incident more bearable, Minister Burrows?"

The woman didn't even look at him. "Tell him, Victor."

Victor Lopez sat forward. "We came here today to discuss fair compensation." He put a palm on top of the manila folder. "What we have here is the means by which we can consider some arrangement."

Riley looked at the beefy hand on the folder, the expensive gold watch in the coarse arm hairs, and thought: This guy is a straight-up gangster. Running with the Monsantos for twenty years had well attuned him to the type.

"First matter to discuss," Lopez said. "Miss Solomon. You

know how much a dog like Miss Solomon costs? She was the offspring of a show dog. The minister paid one thousand dollars U.S. for her. Those six pups, God rest their little souls, were also the offspring of a show dog from Naples, Florida, called Big Un, a champion in his class. The minister had to pay for that mating. And those six pups?" He shook his head. "It was tragic seeing that. You could understand, the necropsy. The vet lifting those small pink bodies out of Miss Solomon." He mimed it, hands together, picking the puppies up and setting them on the table. "One, two, three . . . My heart was breaking, man. Couldn't save any of them."

Minister Burrows's chair scraped the floor and she shot to her feet. "I can't listen to this, I can't." She was near tears. "Where's your facilities, please?"

Harvey stood up. "It's toward the bar and hang a left. I'll show you."

"Sit. I'll find it." She said to Lopez, "Let's hasten matters, okay?" and she hurried away.

"So sad," Lopez said, watching her leave. "You know, each one of those pups was worth a thousand. That was gonna be the asking price. Six thousand dollars. Dead. Not a lot of money, but still, you know. It's money."

He turned to the folder. "Let's see here now," flicking it open. "Mr. James, you bought this—" He looked up. "That's a curious name, uh? James, Riley James, like two last names or could be two first names, whatever pleases. You wouldn't happen to be related to Otto James?"

Riley nodded slightly.

A smile crept across Lopez's face. "Ahh, thought as much. You must be his son. Yes? Sure, who doesn't know about Otto James. Your father, boy," wagging a fat finger, "he was a character, I'm telling you. Salty exploits, run-ins with the law. Somebody ought to write a book."

Riley jerked his chin at the folder. "You were saying?"

"Ah, yes." Lopez scissored a page out with his fat fingers and shook it, produced small black-framed reading glasses and slipped them on. "Now, Mr. James, you bought this bar three years ago from one Mr. Paul Gillette. Says here . . . for one eighty grand—that's a good price, prime seafront property like this, walking distance from the Princess Hotel down the street there. . . . So what else?" He squinted at the page, slapped it down, found another. "You made renovations to the place, expanded. Business picked up." He peered over the top of his glasses at Riley. "Your subsequent divorce from Mr. Gillette's daughter didn't appear to damage the deal any." He leaned in. "Or was that part of the deal?"

Grinning, thinking he was funny.

Riley said, "Go ahead."

"Well, yes, let's see here." Lopez frowned, all business again. "You built a back room, it appears. Remodeled the kitchen, what else, added a deck." He lowered the paper. "This one right here?"

Riley nodded.

"Handsome deck. Fine work in the back. Before you came I took a little tour of the place. I knew you wouldn't mind. The place is much improved. Mean to say, judging from what I used to hear about it, how run-down it was getting and so." Lopez adjusted his glasses and made a face, inspecting the paper. "The only problem I see here . . ." Tilting his head back, making big eyes. "No permit. For that work, thousands of dollars' worth of work I got to assume, and not one permit pulled with the city? Not good. No permits and therefore no inspectors for all that electrical work among other things you had done in the kitchen." He sucked in air, raised his eyebrows. "Not good," and slapped the page on the table. "Dangerous, Mr. James."

"Mr. Lopez," Harvey said, scooting forward, "it was minor, minor stuff in that kitchen, we simply—"

Riley put up a hand and said, "Wait, let's hear what the man has to say." Throwing Harvey a look. *Be quiet, please.*

Lopez had another paper in hand. "There was a health inspection this morning. The results here, not good at all. Says here, 'Roaches found in mop room and under utility sink area.' 'Garbage bin outside back door left uncovered.' 'Cutting utensils improperly cleaned.'" He waved the paper, glancing from Riley to Harvey. "Long list. I could go on if you want."

"No," Riley said. "I think I'm understanding your point." Meaning he had picked up the unmistakable scent of a shakedown.

"Already, your establishment is facing a hefty fine."

Harvey said to Riley, "The paperwork's in the office. Haven't had a chance to tell you."

Riley shrugged, said to Lopez, "So you finished, now?"

"In addition," and Lopez raised a finger, "last but not least, as they say. That back room. A legal question. I have it from good sources that if I was to enter there, say, on a Friday or Saturday night looking for, oh, maybe some poker action, I hear tell I just might find it. I hear that Lindy's has a VIP room. Don't know how true but being a gambling man I'd like to find out." Lopez sat forward, smiling. "In other words, Mr. James, I would like in on the game. If you know what I'm saying."

Riley let a moment pass—a car rolled by, Harvey was rubbing his forehead—before Riley forced a smile, becoming serene. "So like I asked your boss. What can we do to make this incident more bearable? Why don't you go ahead and name your price?"

Lopez shook his head emphatically. "It's not just a matter of price. This is about *principle.*"

Riley said, "Name your price, please," and fixed the man with a stare.

Lopez sat back. Folded his arms across his chest. "Sixty percent ownership."

Riley squinted at him. "Ownership? Of what?"

Lopez pointed at the floor. "This place right here."

And Harvey said, *"What?"* gesturing and knocking over the minister's drink, glass tumbling onto the deck, water spreading across the table.

Lopez picked up the folder and shook off the water that had touched the corners. Harvey jumped to his feet and said, "Shit. Turo, Gert, somebody get me a towel." He flapped the legs of his shorts, the front wet. "You must be out of your fucking mind," he said to Lopez and stalked away.

Arms folded, Lopez sat there, looking amused. Watching Harvey leave, he said to Riley, "No need to get emotional about this."

Riley turned in his chair so that he was facing the road. In the park across the way, palm tree fronds were fluttering in the breeze. Soft sunlight on the water out there under low-lying clouds. "You have no idea—"

"Who I'm messing with?"

"Not what I was going to say, but anyway . . . ."

"Believe me, I know who you are. Police records might not show any convictions but your name is known. Everybody knows you're involved with Israel and Carlo Monsanto, and everybody knows how they acquired their money and it ain't from no dusty downstairs dry goods store. Many years ago, two men were assaulted out on Manatee Road, middle of the day. Your name came up. Don't think I know that? I'm very aware of who you are. Now let me tell you what you're up against. Besides the health department, the building codes department," he said, raising the folder. "Consider where you buy your goods and services. Think about what happened this morning and imagine how much worse it could get. Electricity bills high? Who knows, soon they might become exorbitant, unaffordable, the faulty meters, you know? You might have a faulty meter back there, something like that. City water. Sure you paid your bills on time? Wouldn't want to get your services cut off, would you? Mr. James, you consider how easy things like this could happen and you'll come to understand you're up against the whole *government*. Which is why I'm telling you, this is not just about a dog."

Riley repositioned himself in the chair, leaned elbows on knees, invading Lopez's space. "Now you know I ain't just gonna hand over half my business to you or anyone else, so we want to keep on talking, give me a *figure*, man."

For a moment, Lopez hesitated. He sort of sighed, nodded, and pulled a paper from the folder. Set the paper on the dry side of the table, slid it to Riley.

Harvey returned with a rag, started blotting up the water. Riley held the paper against his chest, waiting for Harvey to finish. Harvey looked at the paper and said, "What's that?"

Riley held the paper out at a distance and read. It was a column of figures, a tally of health and permit fines, the cost of Miss Solomon and her six pups, the estimated legal fees "should a lawsuit be deemed necessary" and the bottom line, the sum required for all these problems to vanish. Using spectacular effort to maintain composure, Riley put the bullshit piece of paper on the table, spun it around for Harvey to scrutinize.

Harvey leaned forward, narrowed his eyes at Lopez. "You are fucking insane. For a *dog*?"

"For a business, my friend."

"I'm not your fucking friend."

Riley lifted a hand. "Easy now, let's settle down." He canted his head, smiled tightly at Lopez. "I'm sure we can come to an agreement, the terms of which will be satisfactory to both parties."

Lopez, smirking, nodded. "I do like the sound of that."

Harvey stood there shaking his head, looked at Riley then at Lopez.

Minister Burrows reappeared on the deck, chin high in queenly fashion. "Are we finished, Victor?"

"For now, I believe we are." Holding Riley's gaze. "I get the feeling we are well on our way to an understanding."

"There are some lovely old Lindbergh photographs and engravings on the walls in there," the minister said, examining her fingernails. "How did you come by those?"

Riley realized he was being addressed. Returning the favor of casual indifference, he kept his eyes on Lopez. "Came with the place. Have a good day, Minister Burrows. Mr. Lopez."

Lopez stood up with the folder. "I expect by tomorrow morning you'll have an answer for me? Or we could make that noontime, being the reasonable people that we are."

"Noon it is," Riley said, keeping his smile, but now a pressure inside his rib cage was building.

The minister led the way off the deck and down the steps. Lopez opened the passenger's door for her, shut it carefully and quick-stepped around to the front. Riley stayed in his seat and watched them drive away.

Harvey came to stand beside him, rag hanging over a shoulder. Neither of them spoke while they watched the Range Rover disappear around the bend. Then Riley said, "Let me hear it."

"No, I'm just thinking, that's all. . . . Don't mind me."

"What you thinking?"

"Hey, just wondering, silly old me, just trying to think out of whose ass we're gonna pluck two hundred grand. Two hundred grand, Riley. C'mon, man," and he threw the rag at the railing.

Riley rose and walked away, suddenly dizzy, like he'd been holding his breath. The pressure under his rib cage had surged to the back of his neck, muscles clenching. Behind the bar, half floating and heavy-headed at the same time, he snagged a plastic cup, pulled the beer handle for a swallow of Belikin draft, just a quick one, but nothing poured.

Gert said, "It's out, remember?"

He said, "Yeah, yeah," swinging around to the cooler, getting a bottle out, fumbling with it as he popped the cap, the blasted thing slipping from his grasp and hitting the floor. He groaned, beer chugging out onto the wood planks over his Nikes.

Eventually, he got half a bottle of beer into his system and held on to the side of the cooler, looking out the window at the street, the park, the sea, while his heart thudded into his ribs. After all these years, two words could still do this to him. Manatee Road.

Behind him, Harvey said, "You all right there, Riley?"

"Yeah," he said, squeezing his eyes shut. "Just a little . . . just a little dizziness. Gimme a couple minutes and I'll be my old self."

Riley had been saying that for years.

CHAPTER SEVEN

Riley, Harvey, and Gertrude were sitting at a table on the deck, cups of coffee at their elbows, table piled high with invoices, order forms, Quicken spreadsheets, calculator. All business here. Turo had been sent home to return at opening time. The three of them had been plugging away for the last two hours with no headway.

Harvey rubbed an eye with the heel of his palm, and Gert, shaking her head, tossed a pen on the papers. "We can't do it. Unless we come into an infusion of cash but otherwise . . ."

Riley was the only one trying to stay positive. "Okay, look, what if—"

"Good god, you're not listening?"

"I'm listening, Gert."

"Look here." Gert pushing a spreadsheet forward for him to read, Riley following her finger down to a column of figures. "That's funds available. After regular expenses, that's all we have to work with."

"Twenty-eight thousand five is a start."

"Are you serious? They want *two hundred thousand*."

"I told you, I can start collecting on the back room, what the poker players owe me."

"Whoop-dee-doo. Add eight thousand more."

Harvey said, "We're fucked, Riley. We need to get the money from elsewhere, a loan, something."

Riley saw the hint, ignored it. "What if we forego salaries for a couple, three months?"

Gert's tight lips crimped tighter. "We can't do that. We have bills to pay."

"And I don't? Like I don't have a child?"

Gert said, coolly, "You the one that had that back room built. I didn't realize you didn't get a permit."

"Your husband was in charge of that."

Harvey said, "You're blaming me now? I used the guy you recommended, I didn't know he didn't pull a permit."

"Okay, good, I'll forego *my* pay then, damn."

Gert shook her head. "Still far, far from the goal." Picking up the spreadsheet, reading. "What we can do, however, is finally collect all outstanding tabs." She lowered the paper and smirked. "Like the sixteen thousand Carlo Monsanto and his crowd owe, for starters."

Riley knew it was another dig, but let it go. "No problem. I'll tell Carlo again. But his tab isn't the only tab."

She leaned forward to scan another page. "Some others here . . . piddly compared to that, few hundred at most."

Riley finished his coffee and sat back, fingers laced across stomach. He sensed them waiting.

Gert examined the spreadsheet again, scratching her scalp with a pen. "We'll need to take out a loan. Can't see any other way. And we'll need time to collect on those tabs."

Riley nodded. "I have some savings. I'll contribute that. See what else I can scrape up."

Harvey and Gert, as if on cue, reached for their coffees and sipped. It was the offer they'd been waiting for all along. "That would be a big help," Gert said. A finger rimming the cup. "About how much altogether?"

"About eighty thousand."

Harvey cleared his throat. Looked away, looked at the papers on the table. "I may have hit the dog, but the health department thing, you the one insisted on keeping Turo, that boy so dense and incompetent he can't do the easiest thing like clean this place properly. I've been telling you, but, no, you still want to keep him."

Riley furrowed his brow. "What's wrong with you, Harvey? I'm here devising a financial solution out of this shit, shit that *you* caused, and you're over there still wasting time playing the blame game?"

Gert hooded her eyes with a hand and said, "Look here, stop this. Just . . . stop. So"—raising her head and exhaling—"eighty thousand, Riley. Plus about twenty from our funds, and let's say," scanning the spreadsheet, "we collect, realistically, about twenty thousand in outstanding tabs. That's only one twenty."

"But like I said, I might be able to scrape up some more."

"*Scrape up*? Eighty grand more?"

Riley thought it over. Had to accept it; the answer was no. "And what about time? We need some time."

He stood up, gathered some papers. "Finished with that?" he said, motioning at their cups. He took the cups away.

Gert said, "Where you going?"

He kept walking. "I'll take care of this."

"What you mean?"

Riley went around the bar, dropped the cups in sudsy water in the sink. "I mean I'll take care of it, don't worry about it. Lopez will get his money, we won't have to spend ours and everything'll be cool." He snapped off the coffeemaker, dried his hands on a towel.

"You're gonna get another eighty grand, in addition to your eighty grand."

"That's right."

"And it won't cost the bar anything?"

"That's correct."

Harvey and Gert exchanged a look.

Riley folded the towel on the bar and waited for questions he knew were brewing. None arrived. They'd rather not ask where the money would come from. They were going to spend it, thank him, treat it like a business expense to be repaid over several years maybe, and carry on with their guiltless lives, and he couldn't fault them. If he were in their position, he'd probably do the same. Except he wasn't so sure about the guiltless part. Their practiced silence about the source of his money and how it benefited them was a hypocrisy that aggravated him. Made them, in his eyes, less honest than if they'd simply acknowledged that it was "dirty" dollars, and that they were no more righteous than he.

Riley got his keys from the office, checked e-mail, traipsed into the kitchen and pulled two roaster chickens from the freezer for tonight. Since Lindy's had started a menu of *panades, salbutes,* and chicken enchiladas, he was the only one who consistently remembered to prep food, encourage the cook to maintain the quality. Forget that it brought in good money on weekends—or no, Gert wouldn't forget that, money being her primary concern. The work? Someone else could do that.

He was in no smiling mood, so better to split. But Harvey stopped him on the way out. "Yo, just remembered. Last night, how'd it go?" The friendly bantering Harvey now. "She say yes? Tell me."

Riley put his hands in his pockets, shook the keys. "She said she loves me."

"Uh-oh."

"No, no, it's just that she wants to get married but didn't plan on it being so soon. She says she wants to be sure about her answer."

"Think she's scared?"

"Maybe. We're having dinner tonight at her place. Says she'll give me an answer tonight."

Harvey said nothing.

Riley appreciated that Harvey did not make of this an opportunity for humor. When it came to emotions, they weren't often open with each other, probably like most men who are friends. But when a man speaks plainly and directly about an affair of his heart, listening silently and nodding like Harvey was doing was the most considerate response.

"Good luck, buddy. I'm crossing my fingers."

Riley's irritation dissolved. He left, thankful for Harvey's grace.

CHAPTER EIGHT

The Monsantos lived in a broad three-story wood-frame on Albert Street, with a red zinc roof and a steep stairway with a second-floor landing. Old man Israel and his wife occupied the second floor; a divorced Monsanto sister, her two boys, and Carlo lived on top. The ground floor was half a storeroom in the rear and half Monsanto's Dry Goods. It was an untidy shop with an arched doorway, a perpetually dusty store window, and bare concrete floor.

Riley picked his way past the tables of cheap men's shoes and Chinese-made flip-flops and around a messy rack of grandmotherly dresses. There were a couple of customers in there, a woman at one counter being tended by Carlo, and an old lady and a little boy admiring soccer balls and rubber basketballs on shelves behind a glass counter that displayed pocket knives. Riley could've sworn he saw some of those very knives when he was about this boy's size.

Riley caught Carlo's eyes and Carlo nodded. Riley stepped off to the side, scrolling through missed calls on his cell phone, thinking of calling Sister Pat to say he'd drop by.

Carlo had taken down a bolt of brown cloth and put it on the counter. He unfurled it some, and the woman rubbed the cloth between thumb and forefinger. "Color is right, but, I don't know, it's too stiff."

Carlo, with his slicked-back hair and loose, flowery shirt, smiled. "You mean you don't like it stiff?"

The woman pulled her hand away and stepped back, chin tucked in. Carlo rolled up the cloth. "We have something else you might like, same brown, in polyester."

The woman said, "No, that's fine," tugging her purse higher on her shoulder. "Thank you very much," and she made her escape.

"What's troubling Mr. James this fine morning?" Carlo said, climbing the stepladder with the bolt of cloth, sliding it up on a shelf.

"Man, I must be getting wrinkled like you if you're thinking I look worried."

Carlo came down from the ladder and shook Riley's hand across the counter. "Must be worried 'cause I can't tell you the last time you set foot in here." Gripping Riley's hand, he said low, "Ready for Monday night?"

"As always."

"No change of heart?"

"Not even palpitations."

"So what I'm hearing you say, you're gonna keep on working with us? Continue making good money for your son and your retirement?" Carlo still holding Riley's hand. "How's that boy, Riley?"

"Getting tall. And sorry, but this is the last job for me."

Carlo narrowed his eyes, nodded, sizing up the truth of that. Riley knew him long enough to know that's exactly what he was doing. Of the two brothers, Carlo was the more shifty one, more volatile, would just as soon hug and offer you a drink as threaten you, which was one reason why some people in the street called him the Serpent. Another reason was that he resembled one, oiled hair, stoop-shouldered and smooth-cheeked, an overbite. Look at this, unbelievable, still gripping Riley's hand and thinking he was being intimidating.

"You sure, Riley?"

Years ago, that might've worked, but not anymore. Riley was too experienced to be mistaken for a pushover. Now, Carlo's act was merely tedious, the clip of his pocket knife showing as always. Abruptly, he released Riley, his face not as congenial as before. "So what then? To what fabulous surprise do we owe this visit?" Lolling his head, adopting sarcasm.

"Just popped in to see Israel. He available?"

Carlo went down the counter, picked up the phone on the pillar. He spoke into it, saying if your uncle's up there, tell him Riley's down here to see him. He listened, said all right, hung up with a loud clack and turned around. "Go ahead on up."

Riley headed through the store, past a mound of garden hoses and a row of wheelbarrows, toward the door in the shadows at the back. He stopped, turned around. "Hey, Carlo?"

Carlo lifted his chin.

"Think you could hook me up with a little something when I get back down? Half ounce, say?"

Carlo strolled away, pausing to rearrange bolts of cloth on low shelves, drop a pair of scissors into a drawer. "Don't know, Riley, that depends."

Riley shifted from one foot to the other, working on patience. "On what?"

"On a C-note."

"For a half ounce?"

"Half ounce of White Widow. That's what's in stock. Furthermore, another half ounce? Just two days ago at the bar I dropped off—" He nodded. "Okay, okay, I see it now, Mr. Riley is diversifying. Got his hands in a little side *dealing*. I see how it is."

"It's not like that. Seriously."

Carlo tilted his head back, appraising Riley. "So you say, so you say. Awright, half ounce. But let's get this straight, you re-selling my stuff you need to step up to a bigger cache, quit play-ing small change and wasting my time. I might could offer you better pricing even."

Riley thought, Yeah, whatever, and headed out the back door and into the cool concrete backyard, in the full shade of the building, and up the steep stairway. Whenever he climbed these stairs, he wondered how old Israel negotiated them and why he just didn't get another house, it's not like he couldn't afford it.

Before Riley could knock, the door opened and a little boy with a pageboy haircut greeted him. "My uncle says to tell you, could you please have a seat out in the parlor 'cause he's on the toilet."

"Boy!" Israel hollered from another room. "What's the mat-ter with you?"

The boy scampered away, feet resounding on the wood floor, down a corridor. Riley took his place on the settee—that's what the Monsantos called it, not *couch*—covered in heavy, transparent plastic. It was next to the speakers of an old hi-fi—not *stereo*. Nothing about this room seemed to have changed in twenty years. Same bouquet of artificial flowers with stems stuck in green Styrofoam in the same wooden bowl on the same dark mahogany coffee table atop the same ultracolorful—though more faded—Mexican rug. Same statue of the Virgin laced with rosaries in a corner, and the same old photos on the wall, a memorial to the Monsanto ancestors from Yucatán.

The Monsantos all looked alike, even the wives—straight black hair, bushy eyebrows, concave mouth, and rounded fa-cial structure. It gave rise to rumors of inbreeding somewhere in the line. Riley didn't put too much value in the slander, but he had to admit even on his most charitable days, this wasn't a family he'd ever accuse of being attractive.

Riley heard the *dunk, dunk, dunk* of Israel coming down the hall before he saw him turn the corner, skinny and stooped, bald skeletal head, limping with his cane. "Good morning, my dear man."

If Carlo was the tough, Israel was the gentleman, but only in relative terms. They embraced, and Israel fell into his crusty leather recliner across from Riley and studied him through huge black-framed glasses. He leaned both hands on his cane between his knees. "I heard you're getting married."

Jesus. "Where'd you hear that from?"

"Never mind. Is it true?"

Riley shook his head. "Maybe, maybe not. Not sure. Who told you this, Israel?"

"Maybe, maybe not? What kind of answer is that?" Israel's lips curled up in a smile. "My sister spoke to your friend at your place last night, what's his name. The one with the wife from Guyana, the fellow with clock hands."

"Harvey?" Riley thought, Harvey's got a big mouth.

"So what can I do for you? Better make it fast, son. I just drank a glass of that nasty stuff, that Metamucil stuff. Prune juice chaser too. Might have to excuse myself quite soon."

"Yes, well," and Riley sat forward, cleared his throat. "Israel, I have a favor to ask. I got this, aah . . . financial emergency that came up, and I might require a loan to get out from under. I'm thinking I'll be able to pay you back within a few months, if the terms I have in mind are acceptable to you, and if they're not, then I'm flexible, I understand if—"

Israel said, "Shhh," fanning away the preamble. "Tell me how much you need."

Riley said, "Hundred and twenty thousand."

Israel whistled. "Kind of trouble you in, boy? How soon you need this money?"

"Soon as possible."

Israel squeezed and released the cane handle, squeezed and released, looking at Riley and sorting out the odds. "Terms. What terms you proposing?"

"Well," and Riley scooted to the edge of the settee, forearms on knees. "This run Monday night. We've never discussed compensation and I know you and Carlo may assume that my past cuts may apply in this case, but I don't see it that way, Israel. No disrespect. This is gonna be one of the biggest shipments for us in the last couple years, and considering that you're coming to me and not using anyone else, like that Robinson boy, it's because you have a certain level of trust and confidence I'll see things through."

"No one will dispute Julius Robinson's still got to prove himself, whereas you don't, but what's your point?"

"My cut. I'm saying that for this run, forty thousand. Not twenty or twenty-five, like all those previous times. Forty grand—to be deducted from this one twenty loan."

Israel adjusted his glasses. "If it was anybody else coming into my parlor saying this to me I'd tell them to get the fuck out, right before I whip this stick in their mouth, you know that, son?"

Riley sniffed, nodded.

"But because it's you," and Israel canted his head. "Tell you what, I promise to give it due consideration."

"The loan or the forty?"

"Same thing, isn't it?"

"No. If you can't see your way to offering me the loan, fine. I'll go elsewhere. But the forty large is what my price is for this run. My final one with you gentlemen. Forty, or I'm not doing it, Israel. You can use somebody else."

Israel sat up, one hand squeezing and releasing the cane. "Don't get too sure of yourself, okay?" He studied Riley for a few seconds. "So, one hundred twenty?"

"There's the issue of a sixteen-thousand-dollar tab that your brother has run up at the bar. Which can be deducted from the loan. So when that tab gets paid, that sixteen plus my cut of forty cancels out fifty-six grand, making the true loan amount sixty-four thousand."

"Where that bar tab is concerned, you're talking to the wrong person. You'll need to speak with my brother."

Riley shook his head. "It's Carlo and his crew responsible. Julius Robinson, Boat, Barrel, Jinx, all of them that work for you. That surprise party they threw for you that time? Part of the tab. Your sister, Mirta, when she and her friends pass through, they put drinks on that tab."

"So you're saying within a few months' time you'll return sixty-four of the one twenty—*plus* my twenty percent interest."

"Twenty percent?" Riley did a quick calculation. "Jesus, twelve thousand eight?"

"Exactly. You sure you want to put yourself under that pressure, Riley? I *will* be expecting my money in full. No excuses. In full. Things are tough right now, price of blow almost in the cellar, you know that."

"The bar is doing pretty good. Who knows, I might be able to pay you back in five months, four maybe."

"Not doing so good that you could take care of your emergency yourself though, see my concern? This problem you have—something I can assist you with in any other way? Talk to someone, use my powers of persuasion?"

Knowing what that could mean, Riley passed. "I can take care of it quietly, with money."

"And you want this soon and in cash, I presume."

Before Riley could answer, Israel touched his stomach and

said, "Gracious me, good gracious, here we go." Bracing against the cane, he struggled to his feet. "You could wait here if you want, but I warn you, I might be busy a good long time. Or you could go downstairs, I'll tell Carlo to take care of you."

Riley considered it. "I prefer—"

"Prefer not to deal with Carlo on this."

"Don't want to say it blunt like that, but yeah."

Dunk, dunk, dunk—Israel limped down the corridor to the bathroom, saying, "That's why I like you, son, always the diplomat. I shall return. Don't fall asleep."

CHAPTER NINE

Riley was sitting in one rocking chair, Sister Pat in the other, her living room windows open to the verandah and the light breeze. A plate of Danish biscuits and two cups of tea on saucers sat on a card table between them. It was late afternoon and Riley knew he should be going but he wanted to stay a little longer, as always.

"I had another one of those attacks," he said. "Couldn't breathe, felt like my chest was being squeezed, my lungs, too."

"Out of nowhere?"

"No, I was talking, at the bar. Somebody mentioned the Manatee Road, and that triggered some rapid thoughts and then, boom, I was in it. Dizziness, the whole works."

"What did you do?"

"Breathed. Focused on my breathing, slow and relaxed."

"And?"

"The feeling passed."

"Of course. Breath is the essence of life. In turmoil, return to the breath. Simple." She motioned to the plate. "Have another."

Riley munched a biscuit, raisin-filled and buttery. They sat facing the white curtains swaying in the window. Passing voices rose up from the street below.

"You know, Riley, you still might want to consider Lexapro."

He shook his head.

"Still not going there, huh?"

"I'll be fine."

"Are you relieved about Monday night? You're out of it now, liberation day is finally here."

"Very relieved." He picked crumbs off his shirt, dusted his fingers off over the plate. "But I had to borrow some money from the old man. So I'm not really out of it yet. I ran into some problems with the bar, needed the cash. Soon as I repay him, then I'll be out."

"Sorry to hear. These problems, they aren't major, though?"

"Minor business complications."

"Okay. If you say so."

Her cup rattled on the saucer when she picked them up, sipped her tea. He did the same. Ate another biscuit, chewing meditatively. Sister Pat asked had he read any good books lately. He said he was in the middle of one now but it was ponderous, a book on genetics, why we are the way we are. Hey, did she ever get around to watching that DVD he lent her, *The Lives of Others,* beautiful flick? Tonight, she said.

The rest of their conversation followed an established pattern. Flitting about from one topic to the next, like the butterflies at her front yard hedge, never settling on one petal too long; conversation that was just as beautiful to Riley for its effortless dance, and as nuanced as the colors of a Blue Morpho's wings. Once or twice a month, he visited Sister Pat, no longer of the order of the Sisters of Mercy, but he couldn't stop calling her Sister, it just didn't feel right. And they'd talk about books and belief and everything he could never speak of with most people. She'd serve tea, and they'd sit. Today it was Darjeeling with sugar and milk for him, green with a dollop of honey for her.

"About this elephant in the room," she said. "How'd it go with Candice?"

"You calling my girlfriend an elephant?" he said, all mock horror.

"Silly boy."

He stretched his legs out, ankles crossed, laced his fingers over his stomach. "Well, tonight I'll find out how it went. She's thinking it over."

Sister Pat's gaze rested on his face, searching. "You're certainly handling it well."

"I have no other choice. If I show my anxiousness, she may flee." He smiled at that, not believing it completely but liking the compliment that he was being cool. He looked out the window at the pale sky, hearing passersby. Sister Pat's street dead-ended at a lagoon. On the other side of the lagoon was Bird's Isle, a tiny island connected to the city by a narrow road that was the venue for sports events, dances, concerts. He said, "Last time I went to Bird's Isle . . . man, let's see. My friend Miles Young was making his comeback." He shook his head. "God, time ain't nothing but one bit of nostalgia after the next."

"I wish you all the happiness, Riley." Her eyes had never left his face.

He admitted something to himself. "I'm nervous."

"That's understandable."

He finished his tea and stood up. "I better get going."

She nodded at the dining room table behind them, the rolled-up Ziploc of marijuana on a place mat. "Thanks. It'll last me a while."

He crossed over and hugged her, Sister Pat giving his arm a squeeze as they said good-bye. At the door, he asked, "How should I do this, you think? If she seems doubtful, should I be polite, accept it? Or should I try to make my case? I don't know, Sister Pat. I love her. But I'm not gonna beg."

"Just be yourself. And relax."

"Hmmm." He saw himself standing tall in front of Candice, her red hair and blue eyes, a smile curving her lips and him saying, "I want you to be happy . . ."

He said to Sister Pat, "I know what I'll say. I'll say this: 'I want you to be happy, and if you think marrying me . . .'"

"If you think marrying me won't help to make you happy, then I'll respect that and do my best to accept it, and let's still be friends. . . ."

He stood tall. He was wearing a crisply ironed white long-sleeve, thought it glowed against his dark skin. He was freshly shaved, sweet with cologne but not overly so. He waited. Felt a frown and relaxed it, all easy now.

His reflection stared back at him from the mirror.

Nah, that didn't go right, the tone too high, the timing off, and his expression would need to be self-assured from the start. He shook out the tension from his shoulders and arms, clapped once, looked down then slowly raised his head. "Candice, I'm tired of living alone. I want to live with you. Want to marry you. But if you think marrying me won't help make you happy . . . if you think . . ." Wait. "I want you to be hap—"

Know what? To hell with this. He shouldn't be trying so hard. He patted down his hair, straightened his collar, and headed out the door. The words that would come at the moment he asked would be the best ones.

Riley sauntered through his yard in his white shirt and clean chinos and shined Rockport oxfords. At his gate, confidence ebbed. But as he closed the gate and turned to the street, a little boy on a bike hailing him, confidence surged. He halted at her gate when he noticed her car wasn't in the yard.

Car problems maybe? She might be upstairs, waiting, while

her Honda was in the shop. She *had* complained weeks back about the engine sometimes not kicking over. He trucked on. Up the driveway and up the front stairs, onto the tiled front porch. He shaded his eyes, peering through the slightly parted louvers into her quiet house.

It was obvious no one was home. He corrected himself: that *she* was not home. Sitting on the top step to wait, he thought, Not like anyone else but Candice could be there. Wasn't like she was messing around.

It was nearly sunset but the day still carried heat and humidity that had begun to soak the back of his shirt. Was there another someone in the picture, someone she was visiting, the reason she was having difficulty giving him an answer? A simple yes or no, that's what he needed. He was a big boy, he would deal, but don't prolong this thing is all he asked.

He undid three buttons, regretting not wearing an undershirt. He got up to wait on the porch, it was cooler there. He put both hands on the balustrade and looked down at her yard that needed mowing, the street. Where are you, Candice? When he saw his neighbor Bill Rivero's black Taurus coming up the street, he returned to the top step. Minutes passed, his patience slipping away. Riley was not a gloomy guy, and Candice was not an evasive, complicated person that his fears were making her out to be, so why couldn't he shake the thought that maybe he'd misread her all this time. That somewhere, maybe some private restaurant corner, a dark hotel room, something was going wrong?

CHAPTER TEN

They were holding hands high atop the main temple at Lamanai, the Maya ruin on the New River Lagoon in Orange Walk. On the floor at their feet were photographs weighted down with pieces of Mayan pottery and stone knives.

Malone said, "That's what these are? No kidding? They look like ordinary old stones to me."

"They were excavated at Lubaantun. That's way south of here, the Toledo district." Candice looked at him. "You've been there, Toledo?"

"Toledo, Ohio, sure."

"You're really in need of an education, you've got to get out of the office more."

She couldn't tell if Malone was sweating because of the climb or his fear of heights. "Can I let go of your hand now?"

"I'd rather you didn't." But he was wearing a dirty old man's smile.

She removed her hand. "Now this one," crouching and pointing to a dark, pointy stone, "was found at Cahal Pech, out in Cayo. Medium-sized ruin."

"What does that mean, any idea? Cahal Pech."

"Place of the Ticks."

"Niiiice. And what does this place mean?"

"Lamanai? Submerged Crocodile."

He panned the view around him, hands on hips. Treetops in the rainforest, the wide lagoon that stretched south.

She said, "This used to be one of the largest ceremonial centers. People lived here thousands of years."

"Sure doesn't look like much. And, I know, I know, it's a *ruin,* but . . ." He was looking down at the smaller, rougher pyramids, a guide leading a group of tourists across the grassy plaza.

"They say people lived here from before Christ till up to the nineteenth century."

Malone, looking around, said, "That long, huh? I did not know that. But these guys," and he walked closer to the photos on the ground. "Now these guys I know. I know all about these scumbags."

Five photos. Carlo Monsanto in a loose Hawaiian shirt, smoking a cigarette on the sidewalk outside his store. Israel Monsanto on a bench in Memorial Park, big sunglasses on, cane between his legs. Two photos of a red and white speedboat with chunky twin outboards, *Ravish* painted on the hull, roped to a pier. Riley James, smiling, good-looking in his understated way, chatting with a woman outside the entrance to Monsanto's Dry Goods.

"Tell me about this boat," Malone crouching next to her, tapping a photo.

"This is the one I think they're going to use. They've been back and forth checking it, Carlo Monsanto or Riley James. It's docked at the boatyard on the Belize River getting repairs. Note the stripes on the side, and this picture here shows the writing on the back."

"Any idea what time Monday night?"

"I extended that invitation for an early dinner that night like you suggested, and expectedly, he declined. Business engagement, he says."

"You asked him what kind of business?"

" 'Course. He says it's the bar."

"You tried pushing for details?"

"Sure, but Riley's a very private man. Doesn't offer up a whole lot, and kind of clamps down when you ask too many questions. Far as anyone's supposed to know, sure, these are things he *used* to do. Way back when. He can't run from the rumors, but I think if he gets the sense I'm being nosy, he'll just shut down. He's sharp, so I try to be delicate."

Malone had been watching her sideways. He stood up and folded his arms across his chest, looking over the trees to the east. A small wind blew and she put a hand on a photo to keep it down.

Malone said, "So you like this guy?"

She rearranged the stones unnecessarily. "He's a good neighbor." That's as much as Malone was going to get.

"You have special clearance and I know we've emphasized you should do what you need to do to get information, but you ever find you're getting too close, you need to step back."

"I'm fine."

"Good, good. No hope for me and you I take it?"

"Henry Malone, quit." She straightened, stretched. "How's your wife doing, by the way? She acclimated yet?"

"You don't care, do you?"

"I'm asking."

"Don't use her to put me in my place. Hell, I can't help it if I find you incredibly striking."

What to do with this man? Let him have his obligatory flirting. But back to the subject: "What have you found out?"

"They're doing it this way because they've been having difficulties with their wet drops. Considering we've intercepted three of the last five, nothing major, six hundred kilos alto-gether, I understand the reason they're doing it by ship. Not along the Mosquito Coast either, the Coast Guard planes out of Puerto Rico are putting way too much heat on them that route. This time, it's from Colombia to Venezuela to a con-tainer ship of Honduran registry."

"So the speedboat will upload somewhere on the water, but where?"

"Calmer waters. We don't know where yet. As of this morn-ing, the ship is bearing northwest, toward the Turneffe Islands. Monday's a national holiday here, which means more people out on the water so one more boat going out probably won't draw notice. Coming back in will pose the challenge, and we're pretty sure that it's gonna be at night. We need to keep tabs on Mr. James all day Monday."

"And what about help?"

"We've already cleared it with the locals. I informed the hon-chos, police commissioner all the way up to the deputy prime minister. We got the typical delays before the approval went through. Some of them here might not like the DEA but they understand, you better believe they understand, they want to keep Uncle Sam's loan spigot flowing, cooperation is in their best interest."

Candice only listened.

"What's wrong?"

She said, "I don't want to be at the office Monday night."

"You don't need to be. We have a sizable local contingent behind us. Coast Guard, members of the defense force."

"I'd rather not be there . . ." her voice trailing off as she turned away and gathered up the photographs. She slid them into a manila envelope, stuffed her collection of Mayan pieces into a pocket of her backpack. More than ready to leave. She handed over the envelope. "Here you go, I'll also send copies electronically." She hefted the backpack, shouldered it, watching him slip the envelope into a smooth black leather satchel best suited for the office. He hung the satchel over one shoulder and across his body.

"You're looking kinda pale," she said. Wanting to insult him for being part of this operation, hell, for being DEA like her. But she was more upset with herself for painting herself in a corner from which she could foresee no clean escape. Didn't matter if this was her job—the sense of betrayal was caustic.

"Last time we met, you said you were shocked by how skinny my legs were. Now I'm pale. What's next, my nose'll be too big?"

She went ahead of him, turning around and grasping the rope and placing feet carefully on the steep steps. She started down. Realizing, she stopped about halfway and looked up. Malone was standing at the top, scared. She climbed back up, leaning into it, and reached out to him. "Come. Like this. Keep your chest close to the wall . . . and take your time."

Near the bottom, he apologized, saying he didn't know where this phobia came from, he'd never liked heights but it was never a phobia for god's sake. He wiped his face when his feet touched grass. Gave a nervous laugh, but he was clearly embarrassed and walked ahead across the plaza toward the boat waiting for him at the dock. After a minute, he slowed down and said, "So where did you learn all this Mayan history? Been doing some reading?"

"And some traveling. You need to get to know this country, Malone. Been here almost two years and never been to a Mayan ruin?"

"These faces," he said, tapping his satchel, "are all I need to know about this place for the time being. Maybe when my assignment is up, hey, I might take some road trips, island jaunts."

"Don't sound so enthusiastic. Anyway," she said, gesturing

toward the lagoon. "Your boat's about to leave. We should say good-bye here."

"Remember. He makes any move, you tell us."

She said of course and walked away toward the small building that housed the restrooms, pretty sure he was watching her ass.

"Hey," he called.

She turned.

"May I ask how you came by those little bits of artifacts in your backpack?"

"A friend," she said, tiredly. "An American archaeologist friend gave them to me. You gonna turn me in?"

"Well, let me think about that. I could blackmail you. Why don't you and I go on a field trip, give me an education. What's the name of that other place you told me about? You've got to cross by ferry to get there? San . . . something or the other?"

"San Jose Succotz. That's the village. You're talking about Xunantunich. And if I say no?" Smiling. She adjusted the backpack straps, turned and walked to the restrooms.

"C'mon," he said, "what about it?"

"I'll have to think about that," she said, without breaking her stride, and already she was remembering the ferry slipping across the glass-green Mopan River. She and Riley sitting together on the bench, legs touching, while the ferryman turned the crank, pulling them along on a cable strung across the banks, and Riley's truck engine ticking in the heat, then the rocky road into Xunantunich. She and Riley sharing a canteen of cold water on the climb to the pyramid. Still one of the tallest structures in the country, he told her. Then she and Riley kneeling by a replica of a stone tablet in a display under a thatch shed in the plaza, their fingers tracing the hieroglyphs, and she remembered the smell of Riley's skin that afternoon.

She imagined her fingers in the grooves of his abdomen, her

white hand on his chocolate skin, his abdomen rising and falling in the evening light on her damp blue bedsheets.

Riley unbuttoned his shirt and hung it over the bed rail. He
removed his pants, folding them deliberately over a hanger,
hung it in the closet, hung the belt on a hook behind the door.
Going about this unrushed, fluidly, letting the rhythm placate
him, not wanting to make a big deal of his hurt feelings.

So he guessed that was her answer. An absence louder
than words. His disappointment was strong, but in due time, he
thought, washing his face, sliding on a comfortable T-shirt, cargo
shorts, it would lessen, you just watch. Such is the flow of life.
What did the *Tao Te Ching* say? *Sometimes one is up and sometimes down.*

And yet one wouldn't argue against a stiff drink. He walked
into his kitchen and took down the half bottle of Knob Creek
from a cabinet and poured two fingers into a coffee cup. From
the freezer he plunked in three ice cubes and swirled the drink,
thirsting for the melt.

He looked out the window, over the fence and into her yard,
but he refused to let his eyes wander up to her windows. He'd
try to avoid looking at that house for a while.

His cell phone chirped and he searched the kitchen counter,
found the phone behind the coffeemaker. "Yes?"

"Riley?"

"Yes?"

"Yes."

"What? This is Riley. Who's this?"

"Yes."

"Candice?"

"Yes, Riley. You asked me, and I'm answering you. It's yes.
Yes, yes, yes."

Oh, man. It stunned him. He couldn't help it—his face split into a grin. He laughed. "Wow, really and truly, huh?"

"That's right. Ask me now."

"Wait." He took a gulp of bourbon, held some on his tongue to savor it. So nice, everything suddenly so nice. "Candice, will you marry me, love and honor and especially *obey* me for the rest of your life?"

She cackled. She told him come on, be serious, and he was so giddy it required considerable effort. Then he asked it straight and she gave him the yes once more in a level voice. She apologized for not showing up. No, it wasn't cold feet, it was a difficult client who kept her back, and she'd forgotten her cell phone at home. He said sitting on those steps waiting and sweating, he'd made up his mind to divorce her two times for revenge, but first, first maybe he wanted to undress her slowly in his room, middle of the afternoon after a shower, lie down under the ceiling fan. He said, "How about a little celebration? A party?"

"Like what, an engagement party? I don't know . . ."

"Something small, at the bar."

"Very small."

"A few friends. Tomorrow night?"

"As long as it's small, sure. Why not?"

"Tomorrow night then." He drank his bourbon, grinning like a happy idiot.

CHAPTER ELEVEN

Next morning, business before pleasure: Before giving Harvey and Sister Pat and his buddy Miles Young the news, he made one important phone call and showered, dressed, and drove to Lindy's.

Harvey and Gertrude were already there, drinking coffee at the bar, and Turo was hosing down the deck and sweeping water off with a deck broom. Riley fixed himself a cup, creamed and sugared. "You guys didn't have to be here."

"This is half our place," Gert said, "and you're paying off somebody to ensure our survival and we don't have to be here?"

"You got a point." He sipped his coffee, looking at Turo coming, unfolding a sheet of paper from a pocket of his baggy pants. The sun was out, but rain clouds hung on the horizon, a bluish shadow far out on the water, a Sunday morning breeze.

"Mistah James, remember that deal about my landlord?" Turo stopped a ways off, meaning he wanted Riley to go there, wanted a private word.

Riley came around and Turo gave him the paper. "I wrote this letter that you could please proofread for me?"

The paper was folded into about sixteen squares. In the middle of the page, a block of neat letters:

Dear Parter,

There has been a rumor said by a certain loqwacious arsist on Pickstock Street that I am defrauding you of your prize tools. Two persons, certain pessimistick nonentittys are suspected of such ficticious acusations. I am gathering clues for the discovery of such infidels and to assist no one.

Yours gradigually,
Arturo Godoy

Riley said, "Quite a letter you got here. Maybe a few misspellings."

"Keep that copy for your corrections. I got another one home."

"Good thinking." Riley folded and slipped the letter into a pants pocket. "How soon you need this back?"

Turo reflected on that. "Next Wednesday before five P.M. That's when my landlord comes back from Cancún."

"His name's Parter?"

"No. That's, like, German. For father. His name is Joseph Jones."

"Okay, I'll get right on this."

"Appreciate it. It's very important," and Turo picked up the broom and got back to work.

Riley exchanged a look with Harvey and shrugged.

The Range Rover pulled in at 10:30 sharp, and Harvey and Gert swung around on their stools to watch Lopez scurry around to open the minister's door. Riley was standing at the railing and set his coffee down while they came through the gate. He heard grumbling behind him and Harvey telling Gert, Be nice.

Lopez was dressed in a spiffy bowling shirt and Minister Burrows had on a white strapless dress with low heels, both of them looking post–Sunday brunch. Riley wondered about them. What was their real connection? Were they sleeping together?

Everyone traded greetings, and Lopez, Riley, and Harvey went to sit at one of the high tables with bolted-down stools on the inside deck. Riley looked over his shoulder and beckoned Gert to join but she wouldn't. Stood right there shooting the minister daggers.

Minister Burrows clacked around examining the Lindbergh photos on the walls, the drawings of the *Spirit of St. Louis* etched into the bar counter.

Riley said, "Well," and was about to begin, but Lopez pointed his chin at Turo rolling up the hose. They waited until Turo wheeled the hose cart away, broom in the other hand.

Riley said, "I think you'll be pleased. Took some doing but I was able to come up with a hundred and fifty grand."

Lopez made a face, turned his head slowly, and looked along his shoulder at the minister.

Leaning forward to inspect an etching on the bar, she shook her head slightly.

"No," Lopez said.

"No, what?"

"No deal. I precisely remembered us sitting here and agreeing on the amount needed and that has not changed, Mr. James."

"Agreeing on the amount. Was more like you dictating to us the amount. Furthermore, what's to stop you from coming back asking for more? We need a guarantee that won't happen."

Harvey said, "That's right," arms folded across his chest.

Lopez put a hand on his forehead and massaged his temples. "Look, you two. I leave here today unsatisfied, it's because when I return," sweeping his hand across the table, "you won't be here. Not one trace that you ever owned the place. And the keys to the house will be in *my* pocket." He looked at Riley, putting on the befuddlement. "You must think I'm playing a little game with you. I will shut this fucking place down," he said, finger stabbing the table. "By noon today, you and you," pointing at them now, "will be the former owners of the establishment once known as Lindy's."

At the bar, the minister cleared her throat loudly, stepping over to the bank of windows, very casual, fiddling with the knobs.

"Okay, then," Lopez said. "Okay, you want to go smaller than two hundred grand today, here's an offer. In addition to the payment today, give me a five percent cut of your monthly gross, five percent or a thousand a month, whichever is greater. You do that and you won't see me here again. But one fifty today? No, that won't do it. Understood?"

Riley looked at Harvey.

Harvey turned down his lips. "Five percent or a thousand? I don't think so. Let's go with one fifty-five today and three hundred a month."

"That sounds reasonable," Riley said to Lopez. "If not that, you'll get nothing because giving you a grand a month will put us out of business."

Lopez scratched his weekend stubble, smiling.

Riley said, "One sixty. Three hundred monthly and one sixty today, but you're absolutely killing me, you're killing me."

"You don't believe a word I just said. I'm beginning to think I might need to go ahead, prove myself to you."

Riley plucked the cashier's check from his shirt pocket and slapped it on the table. "It's what I got."

Lopez rubbed his palms together and looked down his nose at the check. Sat staring at it.

On his periphery, Riley saw Minister Burrows swipe the windowsill with a finger, give the finger a disapproving look and flick away the dust. Harvey's right knee was pumping, and Riley reached under the table and held it down.

Riley and Lopez studied each other. Lopez shook his head.

Riley said, "Damn," slumping his shoulders. He scooped up the check, tucked it in his pocket. "Well," he said and threw up his hands, slapped his thigh. "I tried, I really tried."

Harvey turned to him. "Wait, hold it now . . . that's it?"

"What you want me to do, Harvey? Blood outta stone?"

"This is how you're going to take care of it? This how you say you got things covered?"

Riley turned his head away. Rested elbows on the table and admired the sunlight on the palm trees out in the park.

"One sixty," Lopez said. "That's the best you got?"

Delivering the opening line Riley was waiting for. "I suppose . . ." He nodded, scratching an ear. "My personal savings, you know . . . I suppose . . ." He detected the change in Lopez's body language, a small forward tilt, raised eyebrows. "One moment," Riley said and got up and walked away, past Gert and the minister, their eyes following him, into his office.

When he came back, Burrows was saying to Lopez, "I think if we knocked this wall down and added more feet to the deck, it would be just as nice, or keep the general airy feel of the big windows, only put them farther out."

Oooh, Gert's eyes were afire.

Riley stepped to the table and set the check down, in front of Lopez. Next to the check, he plopped a paper sack.

Lopez cracked his knuckles before he picked it up, tested the weight, the sack chunky with cash. "Added some sweetener?" He unfolded the top, peered in, and set the sack back on the table. "How much?"

"Ten grand cash. Plus the check. One seventy, absolutely all I got. And don't forget, the five hundred guarantee."

Lopez took a deep breath and stood up. He glanced over at

the minister. If something passed between them, Riley missed it. He watched Lopez eye the sack . . . one second, two seconds, hand hanging loose at his side, twiddling his fingers. Then he snatched up the check and the sack, held the sack to his chest. He gave a little laugh, an embarrassed boy caught stealing.

Harvey lifted his eyes to the ceiling and pumped a fist. "So we're good?" He looked around at everyone. "We cool?"

Lopez said, "Well, there is another little matter," with a sly grin.

"What now?"

"We're cool if you could fix me a good Bloody Mary. How I like it is with not too much black pepper, put a stalk of celery in there, fresh celery. The minister may care for a little refreshment, too."

"A ginger ale would be fine," she said.

"We're all out," Gert announced from behind the bar.

Harvey said, "Maybe I can find some in the back?"

"No bother. A Sprite will do."

Harvey sprang up to get behind the bar.

"Tell you what I *must* insist upon, though," the minister said, "is this photo here."

Riley turned to see her pointing at a photo on the wall: Lindbergh crouched by the propeller, repairing the plane in the field, amid a group of onlookers.

"Gives me the feeling of those old days. Just look at their clothes," the minister said, easing up to the photo. Her hands moved up to it. "Do you mind? A little gift for me?"

Riley met Gert's eyes, and Riley said, "Sure. Not a problem." Gert was fuming.

The minister took the frame off the nails in the wall and held it out, admired it.

Harvey just about ran up bearing a tray with the drinks,

although later he'd say that wasn't the case, Riley was exaggerating and he didn't say, "No, masah, yes, masah," either, but he did admit it was probably the best Bloody Mary he'd ever prepared and the tallest, prettiest glass of soft drink over crushed ice he'd ever poured.

CHAPTER TWELVE

Monday afternoon, Riley awoke to the sun glaring on his bed—no, not his bed, this was Candice's—a jagged glass splinter in his brain. His mouth tasted like stale beer and cigars. Candice lay twisted in the sheets beside him, snoring.

He stumbled out of bed, shifted back into last night's smoky clothes. Just about everyone he considered a close friend had attended the get-together at Lindy's. Sister Pat came offering kisses and congrats, but left around eleven, way past her bedtime. Miles Young, whom he hadn't seen in weeks, came with his little girl, Lani, and sipped a couple of beers with Riley in a corner. "I got a feeling this time, marriage will settle you down," Miles said. "Just the medication you need." They tapped bottles and drank in full agreement, then Riley excused himself to speak with the other guests. His neighbor, Bill Rivero, showed up, too, and drunkenly informed everyone within spitting distance that he'd known all along Riley and Candice were gonna march up that aisle. Candice rolled her eyes. Given the fact, Bill said, Riley was always ogling her from his front porch when she took her morning runs and *she* knew it, too, 'cause those shorts got a little shorter as time went by, got a little tighter. Candice walked away when Bill kept going on and on.

This person was there, that person—friends who brought friends. Candice seemed uncomfortable but relaxed after a second glass of wine in the smoke, loud music, and raucous laughter. Riley remembered one or two shots of chilled Don Julio with lime and snuggling with Candice and people shouting at them to get a room. He remembered Miles waving when he left, carrying his sleeping daughter.

Harvey had invited a woman, Jawanda, who said she was from Chicago, but Riley had doubts, and whenever Gert's head was turned, Harvey would rub Jawanda's shoulder or hold her hand, in full view of everybody, guy had no shame when he drank. When one of the kegs ran dry at the same time the vodka finished, Riley trekked to the back with Turo to fetch more and they heard a *clink clink* coming from the back porch. Quietly, Riley cracked the door and looked outside.

Harvey was standing out there in the semidarkness, his back to them, pants around his ankles, bare-assed. Jawanda's legs wrapped around his back as she sat on a stack of beer crates, the empty bottles inside going *clink clink clink*. Turo said, "Disgusting," but didn't move, edging forward to peek some more. Miles shut the door and said, "At least he's doing it *gradigually*." Together they left to make sure Gert was in the front or wasn't on the way to the back for some reason, but it made Riley want to take a shower.

It was a noisy, blurry night, all right, but four in the morning, Riley toppled into bed happy, and now despite the pain racking his cranium he was most assuredly happier, knowing that after tonight, no more runs, no more anxiety over schemes; he was hours away from being a free man.

He nibbled Candice's right ear, and she stirred, then swatted at him. She said, blearily, "You're leaving? What time is it?"

"About two o'clock."

"My God. I have such a headache."

"Got to run a few errands, meet somebody for business out at St. George's Caye." A kind of truth. "I'll be back soon as I can."

"Sounds like breakfast tomorrow then?"

"I know. I'm sorry. Pancakes?"

"Yeah," she said, groggy, and closed her eyes again.

Two hours later Riley was in a nameless Panga-style skiff, a thirty-three-footer with twin Yamaha 200s, roomy cockpit, and V-berth, cruising down the Belize River with an icy Lighthouse Lager for a hair of the dog. He was pasted in sunblock and sported a Tilley hat, scratched-up shades, feeling fair to middling in the warm breeze as he passed under the swing bridge. Then he glided by the sailboats and tugboats in the quiet harbor, a man with a black Labrador on the deck of a Catalina waving. At the mouth of the harbor, near the Baron Bliss Lighthouse, he stood up and pushed up the throttle and the bow lifted with a deep growl of the engines. Wind in his face, he tucked his hat strap under his chin. The boat bounced over the light chop as the water changed from brown to green and he ripped out into the Caribbean Sea.

In fifteen minutes, he came within sight of the mangrove islands and aimed the boat for the cut. He eased back on the throttle, skimmed through the calm water, past a fisherman's shambling house on stilts at the edge of the island. Back in the rolling waves he picked up speed and banked east toward St. George's Caye. When he neared the kraals and boats lined up at the piers, he slowed and came off plane, the bow dropping and knifing through the clear waters toward the island of coconut trees and two-story houses along the white-sand path.

There were a few more holiday boaters out than usual but nothing historic. He tied the boat at the Monsantos' pier and walked barefoot down the pier to the Sandy Reef, a restaurant and bar at the north end. He sipped a bottled water on the upstairs verandah, feet up on the railing, watching kids playing by lobster pots in the front yard, and farther out teen girls sunning on towels around a kraal. Beyond the line of piers a windsurfer struggled to stay upright, losing the fight repeatedly. In the distance, surf rolled in a white line on the reef. Riley tipped his hat over his eyes and dozed. When it got too warm, he retreated down the beach to the Monsantos' house.

In keeping with their low-key style, it was an old stilt woodframe in need of paint, behind a stand of cocoplum trees. The house was shuttered, and the only key Riley had was to a room off the back porch. He entered. Inside it was musty, glass buoys hanging off one wall, a hard bench by the window, and a table with a marine VHF radio on top. He opened the shutters to air the place but closed the door. He checked his watch and turned the radio on. He spun the dial to 65, a rarely used channel. He checked his watch again, waiting for six o'clock.

He remembered the first time he stood in this room, when he asked Carlo if he wasn't afraid police would see his tall antenna on the roof and put two and two together, come after him. Carlo took him out on the porch and pointed out the roofs of houses down the row that had antennas, about five others. "Everybody knows," he said, "that VHF works through flat waves so you want to reach over the horizon, you need an elevated antenna, dig? Nothing wrong with that."

Fifteen years ago, just about, but it felt like last weekend.

At 6:05 he clicked on the mike and put it to his lips. "*Dover, Dover,* calling motor vessel, *Dover,* whiskey tango five eight one five. Calling motor vessel *Dover,* whiskey tango five eight one five. Do you read me? This is Hooligan, over."

The radio crackled, clicked. Then, "This is *Dover,* whiskey tango five eight one five responding. Come in, Hooligan."

"Good evening. Please give me an ETA."

A static-filled delay. Then, "ETA is . . . nine thirty, over."

Static again, which could mean bad weather. "Copy that. What are the skies like? Over."

"A little rain. No bother, over."

"Good to hear, over and out."

And until he was on the salt again, that would be the last communication with the *Dover*—which wasn't really named the *Dover* and which didn't have the call sign WT5815 either—all of this to avoid detection. Standard operating phoniness for this type of trade.

Riley locked up and went down to the pier in the twilight. Most of the holiday crowd had left; only a few boats were docked at the other piers. Someone was having a barbecue in a yard to the south. He could smell the meat roasting and hear laughter and voices, and that stayed on his mind when he pushed out in the cool air, heading for Robinson Caye.

He reached it in ten minutes, the sliver of white beach amid mangroves, a long wooden pier with an engine house, and farther back, a glimpse of red tin roof among tall coconut palms.

The Robinsons' dogs trotted onto the pier barking when he glided in, three salty mutts. He called their names and spoke to them while he tied up, got their tails wagging, the little yellow one whimpering. They circled around then ran ahead, yapping, leading him down the pier and across the hard shore of crushed shells and down the sandy path that snaked through trees to the back of the island.

About halfway to the red-roofed house, he passed a short picket fence squared around a white cross in the ground, under a stately coconut tree. Old brown coconuts and palm fronds dotted the sand all the way to the front steps.

Miss Rose was at the stove as usual, stirring a steaming pot, banging the spoon against the rim, seemingly unaware he was behind her.

"Miss Rooooose. I'm starving. A hungry man is an angry man."

"Come see what I have for you, Riley," and she made room for him at her stove and lifted the lid of another pot on a front burner. Like they had been in the middle of a conversation.

Riley threw an arm around her shoulders, leaned over and sniffed the pots. Fluffy yellow rice in the small one, an aromatic boil-up of onions, potato, carrots, cabbage, and fish bubbling in the other. "Heavenly," Riley said, making the face of a man in unbearable ecstasy. "I'd kill for a bowl of this stuff, Miss Rose. What else in there, okra? What kind of fish?"

"Snapper and kingfish. Okra, no, but some malanga," and she reeled off all the spices, Riley nodding, knowing she liked discussing her food almost as much as he liked eating it.

She spooned up a bowl of rice and ladled the stew on top, chunks of fish in there, potatoes, the bowl so hot Riley used a dish towel to carry it into the next room. Miss Rose sat across from him and watched him eat. "It's nice?" Amusement shining in her eyes.

"With all this deliciousness in my mouth," he said, mouth full, "how can anyone find words to express," chewing, closing his eyes to show delight, "how divine this experience is, Miss Rose?"

She laughed. "Oh, lass, you funny, boy," and she pushed up and limped back into the kitchen, Riley noticing her elephantiasis looking more swollen than ever.

Oh, lass. That was one of her expressions Riley figured must come from old-country Creole, Miss Rose with the front of her frock perpetually wet from cooking and washing dishes. Not a dress, a *frock,* as she would say. Living out here almost twenty-five years with her husband, rest his soul, and now maintaining the island and her house at her age, you had to admire that. The house was a simple setup: two bedrooms off the porch, a kitchen, a bathroom, and a vast main room that served as dining and living area, with a long wooden table and wicker-bottom chairs. Huge screenless windows propped open with sticks in every room, and in some corners, the remnants of mosquito coils clothespinned to the top of Coke bottles.

Through the doorway Riley saw Miss Rose shuffle past in her slippers out to the porch. She returned after a while and sat with him again.

"I went and woke that boy up. Not like he didn't know what time you coming. Ay, lass," she said and put a hand to her cheek. "Don't know what I'm gonna do with that one."

Riley slurped the last of the stew, wiped his lips with the dish towel. He nodded, didn't want to say the wrong thing.

"Drink rum and smoke that dope all night, you see him there, don't want to get a steady job. My god, I named him like his father but not one ambitious bone in his body."

"He's not helping 'round the place?"

"You see how the yard looks? How I'm gonna clean all that up with my feet acting up like this?"

Riley looked down, playing with the spoon. "I mean, not to get in your business, but he's contributing financially at least, correct?"

"Last piece of money I ever get from him was seventy-five dollars. Last month." She rested her chin in a hand and studied Riley. "You always said one day you're getting out of the trade. Me and Tito used to talk about us doing it one day, you know, just tell Israel Monsanto we can't store his gas for him anymore. Tito used to say everybody always say they're getting out soon, this or that, but once that easy money grab hold a you, it's hard to let go. Look at me, Israel's rent money is good business for me."

"Here's the thing. The money's not easy for me anymore. Mentally."

She nodded at his bowl. "Want more?"

He touched his stomach. "Better not. Got to keep on my toes, stay light."

"For your last trip ever."

"You don't believe it?"

She smiled in a way that reminded him of Sister Pat. How her eyes gently fell on you as her mind gave your words due consideration. "I'm rooting for you. I'm proud of you, with your bar business and everything. Don't let these people swallow you up, these are some bad people. Tito used to say if it wasn't that they paid him good he wouldn't even want to say hello to them."

"I'm getting out, trust me."

"One person I know, only one left the Monsanto fold, years back. Remember?"

"Brisbane Burns? Only because they had a personal falling out. Nothing to do with business."

"Hear what happened to him? Know he lives by Buttonwood Bay, by your friend there, the Romeo, what's his name, Harvey? Well, they broke into Brisbane's house some days back. I hear this from my son that they docked at his private pier, broke in, stole a safe full of guns."

"Brisbane still loves his guns, I see. If he's still the same way, somebody better watch their back."

Heavy footsteps sounded outside on the porch and Riley looked up as a lanky guy in dreadlocks sloped past the main room door. "What's up, Julius?"

"What up, yo," Julius said, heading to the bathroom.

"We might get a little rain out there," Riley called.

"Uh-huh." The bathroom door creaking open, slamming shut.

Miss Rose said, "Hear that? *Uh-huh*. Not even have the courtesy to give people time of day, please and thank you. You give him something. *Yo*. Not thanks, *yo*! Tell him thank you, hear what he says? *Uh-huh.* I didn't raise him like that. And all this ghetto street talk or whatever the hell they call it. When he talks to his friends it's always big talk and things like, 'Know what I'm sayin'?' No, I don't know what you're saying, I tell him, 'cause that's all you keep saying. 'Blah blah blah, know what I'm sayin'?'" She shook her head. "He thinks he's a Rasta. Riley, I wish you could maybe talk to him so he could think of getting out the business, too. Offer him a job maybe?"

"Don't think he wants one, Miss Rose. I've brought it up before, about something at the bar we could work out. Didn't seem interested. Miss Rose, honestly? I don't think Julius likes me too much. Generational thing, could be, I don't know."

She sucked her teeth. "He don't even like himself, that one. Don't mind him." She got up and took Riley's bowl. "But suggest it again for me, please?"

Riley said he could certainly do that.

Julius walked ahead when they left, Riley taking his time, checking out the island he might never see again. The dogs skipped and played around him. He liked Miss Rose but he had no real reason to come back except to say an occasional hello and he could easily do that on her market days in the city. He'd always told himself, when you end it, end it, clean and complete.

He tarried at Tito Robinson's grave behind the picket fence. The sand there had been raked smooth and there was a bottle of white rum lying by the cross. Julius passed by rolling a fifty-gallon drum of gas. Riley hopped to, rolled out another fifty-gallon drum from the concrete shed and onto the pier. Julius was laying out the fuel storage bladder on the floor of the boat. Riley hooked up the hand pump to a drum and Julius connected the hose to the bladder. They pumped a drum each, swelling the bladder. Riley rechecked everything—radio working fine, flashlights had batteries, flares in the glove box intact, two cold Belikins in the cooler for much later.

He sat back in the chair and watched Julius untie the lines. It was full night now, seas mild. Julius was wearing a long white tee, oversized denim shorts, and as usual no shoes, which was why he had island-man's feet—calloused, toes curled like claws. The guy's only concession to good grooming: dreadlocks bundled neatly in the back with a ribbon. A pink ribbon.

Riley said to himself, shit, he shouldn't judge this boy. He said, "Hey, Julius, what's the significance of the rum by your old man's cross?"

Julius threw the ropes in the boat and hopped in. "Holiday today. The old man liked his rum on a holiday."

"That's right," Riley said, nodding, thinking of what else to say. "Tito did like his taste, all right. Your dad was a good guy."

"Uh-huh."

Julius pushed off from the pier and Riley started the engines, thinking he'd better raise the subject, get it out of the way. "Listen, one time we were talking and I said I could use somebody dependable three nights a week at the bar?" He looked at Julius's expressionless face. "Been thinking about it?"

Julius, sitting on the gunwale, turned his shoulder away slightly, put his attention on the water. "After tonight, this is it for you in this business, right?"

Riley said, "Yeah," knowing where Julius was going. "But I'm talking steady job, steady pay. Nothing underworld. Know what I'm sayin'?"

Julius nodded, gazing away. "I hear you."

Riley waited.

That's it? What more could he say? When a man shows disregard by not wanting to converse, you don't talk. So Riley thought, To hell with it.

CHAPTER THIRTEEN

They headed for the reef. The waves had picked up some but not enough to slow them, the boat skimming unperturbed toward the break. Through St. George's cut and then into the vast blue, the boat rode the swells and the movement became a rhythm to the drone of the engines. Every now and again sea spray lashed them. Night had chilled the air. Riley broke out the rain slickers for comfort's sake and offered Julius one. The macho man refused.

When you're on the sea, the mind drifts. You let matters surface that you've held at depths. Riley was thinking how Duncan would love a boat ride, so long since they'd been on the water together. He was thinking of the boy's big round eyes, his mother's, and bushy eyebrows and that raspy voice. Riley was beginning to forget how that voice sounded.

Now the night was ink, the sea a rolling momentum. In the distance the Mauger Caye lighthouse winked at them as they moved north along the Turneffe Atoll. Riley picked up the radio mike. "*Dover, Dover,* come in, *Dover.* This is Hooligan. Calling motor vessel *Dover.*"

The bow pitched and cold spray splashed Riley's face.

"*Dover* responding. Come in, Hooligan, over."

"How far away, over."

The radio crackled. "Fifteen minutes, over."

"I read you. Over and out." Couldn't have been more perfect.

Not ten minutes later, Julius hollered into the wind, pointing out the lights of a ship . . . while Riley was thinking of Candice. That it felt right with her because she was a woman, as opposed to his ex-wife when she said I do at age twenty-one and was really still a girl.

He cut his running lights when he saw the long shadow of the container ship holding steady in the current, on the leeward side of Bushman's Caye, bow to the waves. Lights were off all down the ship. Riley pulled back the throttle and idled around the wide stern to its port side, the dark wall of steel towering above.

Riley radioed up. He told Julius get ready. Two figures appeared at the ship's railing, then the bulk of a net started down slowly, slowly, six white, ten-gallon buckets inside, knocking the hull as the net was lowered. Riley pulled up under it.

The cargo thudded into the boat, and Julius worked fast, loosening the net, freeing the buckets. One fell on his feet and he cursed. Riley thought, That's why you should be wearing shoes, fool.

Julius signaled up, the empty net rose, swinging against the hull. Julius slid the buckets into the V-berth to make room for more. They repeated the process. Before the net went up for a third and final time, eighteen buckets in all, Riley motioned to Julius to take the helm. He tottered over to the buckets, holding the gunwale for balance. He took out his Spyderco and cut away the plastic-wrap seal on one of the buckets, pried the cover off. Got a flashlight and shined it on the contents. Seven tightly taped bricks. He hefted one, about five kilos—he could tell from experience. He sliced open the tape and cellophane, exposed the hard white underneath, and chipped off a tiny piece with the blade. Tasted it. High grade, yes sir.

He dumped the brick back in, covered the bucket, quickly uncovered another. Results the same, he waved to the figures peering down.

See you later, nice doing business with you and so long. Eighteen buckets of thirty-five kilos each equal six hundred thirty kilos, and at the Monsanto price of seven thousand per to deliver—yeah, Riley knew the price, he'd checked around—you're talking four point four million effectively in his boat tonight. And he was asking for a mere forty thousand? The Monsantos were getting away with an insult of a bargain.

They returned the same path they came except this time Riley threw the throttle wide open and cut the running lights. They passed through St. George's cut back into the calmer Caribbean and sliced south toward Belize City, making good time. Unload this cargo at the Monsantos' dock in Buttonwood Bay and Riley would be in bed before midnight.

He eased back the throttle, idling through the channel between mangrove islands, city lights on the horizon. Feeling good, a little tired, but that sea air in his lungs kept him steady. His thoughts slipped into the wake of an earlier reverie, of why he was drawn to Candice, her physical presence. He mused on the image of her sun-weathered shoulders and the lines at the corners of her eyes that said she was experienced at living.

Then the Coast Guard boat whipped around the corner with hardly a sound and headed toward him.

Even in the darkness, Riley knew from the shape, the number of heads on board, it was Coast Guard. In the nanosecond that he decided to throttle it, get the hell away, he heard Julius say, "Fuck, behind you," and Riley whirled around to see another one, coming up fast.

Searchlights blazed on, front and back, blinding him.

He thought he could still make it, shoot the gap to the west, so he spun the steering wheel, turning the bow fast, saw the shape of rifles pointing, a man yelling at him cut the engines now, fucking *now*. Julius standing straight, hands in the air.

The boats advanced, so much light Riley couldn't see. He turned off the engines, kept his eyes down, the lights hurting.

The voice said, "Driver, get your hands up! Get them up."

Riley's hands went up.

"Two of you, walk to the center of the boat with your hands up, do it now."

Riley took two exaggerated steps so there'd be no mistaking that he was complying. He could feel the heat from the lights.

"Now, two of you, lie down on your belly with your arms out, do it now."

Riley lowered himself in stages, no fast moves, first one knee, then both and folded forward, face-first like he was doing yoga, sun salutation to these blinding lights. Julius was already down there. The floor was wet, salt-crusty. Either Julius knew the drill, or he was just as scared as Riley.

Both of them lay prone, jammed up against the buckets. A Coast Guard boat bumped them from behind, then from the front. Their boat rocked when the policemen boarded it, and instinctively Riley raised his head to see. A black boot landed in front of his face and a rifle muzzle poked him in the ear.

"Face down," a man said, "eyes to the ground."

But Riley had seen. Their faces were black. They were wearing black ski masks. Blue coveralls, boots, like ordinary police, but black ski masks?

Movement all around, the boat swaying, buckets being picked

up and carried off, low murmurs. Someone planted a knee in the middle of his back, twisted his arms behind him and snapped zip ties around his wrists, tight. He heard them doing the same to Julius. Heard the bucket handles clanking.

The boat rocked and tilted to one side, the masked men leaving. He heard a deeper rumble of engines and one boat pulling away, and the searchlights went out, and in the darkness he heard the other boat leaving as well, engines fading. After that it was only the night and the smell of gasoline in the breeze and he and Julius lying there on the hard floor, the boat rocking in the wake.

Riley rolled onto a shoulder and struggled to his feet. Julius staggered up, grunting. They stood, arms tied behind their backs, staring into the dark. Nothing but mangroves and empty waters and far off, too far, the glow of Belize City.

Black ski masks?

Riley said, "Who the fuck just jacked us?"

Julius looked him. "Coast Guard, man. What, you didn't see that?"

Eighteen buckets of high-grade cocaine gone. Riley saw that they'd taken the ignition key. No arrests, no fuss, and the two of them left drifting in the dark. He let out a shout over the water and sat down hard on the edge of the gunwale. "Coast Guard my ass."

CHAPTER FOURTEEN

"Somebody beat us to it, we don't know who. What we do know, our man didn't take that water taxi, the *Ravish*. By the time we realized and deployed, he was probably halfway to his pickup."

"No leads on who may be responsible for the ambush?"

"None yet, but we have some ideas," Malone said. "Is this bench okay?"

Candice stopped to consider the surroundings, the sunlight. They were in Battlefield Park, downtown Belize City, traffic noisy on the streets on the other side of the wrought-iron fence, homeless men sleeping on cardboards in the grass and slumping on the benches in the noon heat. "Why don't we try this one instead," pointing to another bench in the shade of a Royal Poinciana. That spot was perfect, the old courthouse in the background.

Malone wanted photos of himself amid the local scenery to send to his folks back home in the Midwest; well, he was about to get authentic ones, bums included.

He sat stiffly on the bench, pleated khaki shorts and purple polo shirt, canvas shoes, no socks. A few threads too preppy, especially with his shirt buttoned up like that. She told him to loosen the button, hey, loosen up in general, act like you're enjoying this.

"But I'm troubled," he said. "Two months we've been expecting this drop. Do they have a contact on the local force, that's what we need to know. Someone who leaked that we were on to them? Or it could've been a handoff. Staged as an ambush." He undid the buttons and flicked a cold eye on a barefoot bum shambling past, scrutinizing Candice setting up her light stand.

She said, tightening her Canon strobe onto the hot shoe, "You might want to wait until I start shooting before we continue this conversation."

She switched out her zoom for the 50mm prime lens, her good glass, stuffed the zoom into her camera bag that sat close at her feet. The city was abundant in purse snatchers and gold-chain grabbers who could easily lose a tourist in the maze of narrow streets.

She positioned the strobe stand at a forty-five-degree angle between her and Malone. Raised the camera, found his face in the viewfinder in suitable shade, no shadows. "You *could* smile," she said, snapping test shots and examining the LCD screen.

"Do I have a nice smile?" Malone flirting.

"You have a lovely smile." Bullshit, but mildly so, and effective encouragement for getting good pictures. She adjusted the strobe power, thumbing the wheel and saying, "Was there no one following him?" But she knew the answer to this already.

"They were staking out the boatyard. We figured that once he got there, he'd be on his way, so that was the most logical spot."

Candice took a couple more test shots, checked the effect on the screen, adjusted the strobe accordingly. "Okay, smile from the bottom of your heart now." She raised the camera, he smiled and she fired off three shots, came in close and crouched, snapped another. "Nice . . . nice, I'm getting the courthouse, that old church in the back . . . great."

Strands of hair falling into her eyes were bothering her, and she blew them away, tried to refocus. But that wasn't the thing bothering her, really. When she spoke again, her palms were perspiring. "What happened to him? Did they hurt him?"

"Which one? There were two of them."

"Our man."

"No one was hurt. We heard from this pilot the Monsantos hired that they were handcuffed and left in the boat. The Monsantos had the pilot fly all over before he found them lodged in the mangrove out there, about four miles off the coast. They'd been drifting for some time."

Candice wanted to say it must have been several hours, she'd seen Riley entering his gate that morning looking sun-blackened and exhausted.

Malone said, "You okay?"

"What?"

"What are you thinking about?"

She said, "Let's try another spot. Over there looks good. Brodie's in the background. Did you know that for decades that used to be the country's only department store?" She slung her camera bag over a shoulder, picked up the strobe stand, asking herself, Whose side are you on? You're going to have to make up your mind whose side you're on. She said, "Come, look alive."

Malone rose and walked through the grass toward the other bench. "You mean chirpy like you?"

"Chirpy? God, don't say that, I don't do chirpy." Couldn't even fake it now that her stomach was in knots. She wiped her palms off on her shorts, inhaled deep. This double life was more nerve-racking than she'd expected. Malone said he was troubled. *He* was troubled? He didn't know the meaning of the word.

Because, Candice, she told herself as she positioned Malone on the bench, set the strobe stand at the proper angle, acting normal in this scene in her own drama—because, Candice, in your other world, you're in love with a criminal. But the DEA didn't know the *man,* and she did. The qualities that made Riley a successful drug runner—loyalty, patience, determination— were the qualities she would admire in anyone. Put him in any line of work, she always told herself, and he'd succeed. Before they met, he was only a name and a photo, and she'd wanted the man she was about to deceive to be mean and all-around dislikeable, but the day she moved in, his kindness threw her. Riley lugged her boxes up those stairs all afternoon, showed her a photo of his son, and in the weeks afterward when she saw more of his laid-back sweetness, his goofball humor, saw that smile on his face whenever he talked about his son, she lost her balance. She understood only one thing the night they first shared a bottle of wine on his porch, after they kissed and she tasted Chianti on his tongue—she could never hate this man. And the next morning, when she awoke and saw him propped up in bed, reading, glasses low on his nose, she got the sense that it was too late for her to return to her old self. Her priorities had been rearranged, seemingly without her volition, and Riley James now lived in that space that her fiancé's death had left.

"Smile," she said, talking to Malone there on the bench, talking to herself as well.

Behind him, a homeless man was sitting against the fence Indian-style in the grass, eating a ripe mango. He was into it, yellow juice running down his hands, forearms, dripping on the grass. The *scene* looked delicious; she snapped it. She edged closer, aimed the lens at the gnarled black hands clutching the moist peeled-back mango skin just above the grass, against the backdrop of the black iron fence.

Click, a perfect photo. Except her pleasure was short because when she lifted her eyes from the camera, she noticed a
familiar face observing her from the sidewalk across the street.
Sister Pat, Riley's friend, was holding a Brodie's plastic bag,
shading her eyes. She waved, hesitantly.

Candice waved back, offered a tentative smile.

Sister Pat's hand went down, she smiled, stood primly watching her and Malone and the homeless man. Waved again and
left, down the sidewalk, into the crowd.

Candice scrolled through the last shots, walking over to
Malone. She said, "Not that anyone here knows your job, but
next time, let's make this business-pleasure meeting somewhere
less public, shall we?"

CHAPTER FIFTEEN

Carlo Monsanto passed the bowl of grapes to his brother, sitting there with two hands on the hook of the cane between his legs. Israel screwed up his face at the grapes and shook his head like the grapes had insulted him. All he had to do was say no fucking thank you, none of this snootiness, like Carlo's Chilean seedless weren't sweet or juicy enough.

Israel said to Julius, who was sitting next to Riley on a metal chair in the center of the bare storage room, "The main question is in fact the only question we need to answer, is who ratted us out. We find this rat, kill it, we could resume operations. Until then, hell, I wouldn't even consider to plan to try to ponder to give any thought to want to attempt one single shipment more. Not one." He banged his cane on the concrete floor three times, saying, "Until we kill that rat!"

Carlo flipped a grape into the air, tipped his head back and caught it in his mouth. He chomped, Riley and Julius looking at him intently, the sideshow to Israel's seriousness. Carlo had made a point of kindly offering them some grapes, to hide how pissed off he was. Get them relaxed, let them believe he was kicking back, not agonizing over the bad news. Let them feel comfortable and not realize he was checking out their body language. Make them comfortable and wait for a slip of the tongue.

"Think, tell me the truth," Israel was saying, "you didn't talk to nobody at any time about this? Think hard."

Julius was quick to answer no, shrugging and shaking his head vehemently, dreadlocks moving. Riley now, he was relaxed, not happy but not scared. A tougher one to read.

Israel said, "Riley?"

Riley cocked his head. "How many years I been doing this? Why would I talk to anybody about my business?"

"That's a good question," Carlo said, "why would you?"

Riley looked at him, but Carlo wasn't ready to engage him yet. He was only tapping, poking for weakness. He kicked out his legs, crossed them at the ankles, and tossed up another grape, leaned his head back to catch it, but it bounced off his front teeth and onto the floor. When he bent to pick it up, he saw a trace of a smile on Julius. The fuck was wannabe Rasta smiling at? Carlo simmered. When he was a kid, people always teased him about having horse teeth, so call him sensitive. But, anyway, what happened just now, he wasn't in the proper position, legs too far out. Okay, he'd let Julius have that smile.

"Call Barrel in here," Israel said.

Carlo unlocked the door and walked across the pavement to the store's back door. His sister's two boys scampered past, screeching and shouting, shooting each other with plastic guns. He said, "Whoa whoa, slow down there," entering the shop.

Barrel was at the counter, chatting up his sister. Mirta laughed at something he said, playing with her hair. Watch, she was going to flip it in a second. There was a customer in the store, a man she was paying no attention to. Barrel leaned in and said something. Mirta laughed and . . . there, the flip, look at that. Soaking up the attention.

Carlo said, "Hey, Barrel. You're needed."

Barrel turned away from the counter and waddled to the back, leading with his belly. Carlo had no inkling what Mirta saw in this fat dude. Carlo said, "Mirta, those boys eat lunch yet?"

"What?"

"Your boys," he said, jerking his thumb over his shoulder, "the reason I ask—"

"Of course they ate," she said with a scowl.

"Don't look at me like that. Yesterday you shoulda seen them, digging out chocolates and cookies all afternoon, and when Ma stopped them, they said because you didn't give them any lunch, what's up with that?"

Mirta strode down the counter and came at him. "Look, don't tell me," her voice steely, "about my kids. Like I don't take care of them properly. You have no idea—"

"All I'm saying—"

"I don't want to hear what you're saying 'cause you don't know what you're talking about."

Carlo said, "Barrel, go on back." Fat man had stopped to listen. He rolled on out the door, and Carlo said to Mirta, "You're here wasting time talking to him and like usual you're not aware what your boys doing. Running through the shop causing chaos, that's what."

She slapped the counter. "I know damn well where my boys are. Don't you even—"

"Wasting your time with somebody like Barrel. Ink on your divorce papers hardly dried yet and you're in the market already."

She rolled her neck, saying, "Unlike somebody I know, at least somebody finds me attractive."

"What's that supposed to mean?"

"Look at you."

He wagged a finger at her. "Better watch yourself, Mirta, that mouth. Next time you need my money, probably tomorrow, just wait, we'll see how smart your mouth is when I tell you keep walking." He said, pointing with his chin, "Look, you got a customer."

She shot him one last glare and swiveled around.

He said, "Hey, by the way."

"*What.*"

"Pedro's been calling for you. Left two messages yesterday. I'm just saying."

"I don't want to talk to Pedro."

"What's wrong with Pedro? Give the guy a shot, he's got a good job, a house. Stays out of trouble. All the things you like to insult me with—right after you take my money. What's wrong with Pedro?"

She narrowed her eyes. "What's wrong? He's our *cousin.*"

"So?"

"I'm not having this conversation." Throwing up a palm and turning away, smiling at the man waiting at the counter.

"Second cousin, that's all. You can't be choosy like that, you know." She ignored him, talking to the customer. He left, but he paused at the back door for one last word. "You're not young anymore, Mirta."

Shit. He headed back to the storeroom. Yeah, but she was still pretty. Thing was, he'd never kicked the habit of sneaking peeks at her in the bathroom. That hole in the wall across from the shower had been there since the night he gouged it out with a steak knife when he was thirteen, maybe a little wider now, concealed by a picture frame. He'd felt a keen shame that afternoon their eyes met through the hole and he darted off—he was about sixteen when that happened. Over the years, that shame fell away, like the clothes that dropped off her body time after time when she stood there in front of the tub, in full view, casting backward glances at the hole. Knowing he was there.

Stripping secretly for him all through her two marriages whenever she came to visit. The only times she took a hiatus was during her pregnancies, and, okay, Carlo could respect that, she wasn't too appealing then anyhow. He still wanted the best for her, but, man, nobody could tick you off like family.

Like Israel now, let's see how far he'd reached. Carlo reentered the room, locking the door behind him. He took his seat. Barrel was standing in the center of the room, near Riley and Julius, talking to Israel about the conditions of the marijuana trees they had planted in the middle of a friend's cane field in Orange Walk, another subject entirely.

Israel said, "Sounds like that's in good shape, but why I called you in today was, tell your cohorts here what you told me concerning how long you waited last night for the drop-off."

"Like I told them. I got there around ten o'clock. Parked by the pier and smoked a cigar, didn't—"

"Tell them, not me."

"Yeah, yeah," Barrel said, shuffling around to face Riley and Julius. "I was saying, right? I didn't come out the truck till closer to the time I figured you'd get there."

Israel said, "Even though it's a private yard."

"Yes. Didn't want to take any chances, see? Maybe somebody next door might could spot me hanging out. They call police, next thing you know . . . Remember that time—"

"Go ahead with you story. Tell them, not me."

"Yeah, man, so I didn't come out the truck till I looked at my watch and I said what! Almost one o'clock. So I begin to start worry, you know? Start to wonder maybe something went wrong with you two."

"You had legitimate concerns," Israel said.

"Correct."

"So you called me."

Barrel nodded. "That's what I did."

"On your cell phone."

Barrel turned back to Israel, confused as to whom he was supposed to be addressing. "Yes, but—"

"But nothing," Carlo piped in, "you called on your fucking *cell phone.*"

Barrel nodded stupidly.

"Where were you, may I ask," Israel said, "when you called me at one o'clock on your cell phone?"

Barrel hesitated. "Outside, by the truck."

"Not on the pier, or *in* the truck, but outside, in the yard, by the truck. Tell them, don't tell me."

Barrel said, "I was in the yard. Why I called, Riley, I was worried. Figured you guys got touched or something."

Carlo watched Barrel begin his deference to Riley, shifting from one leg to the next in his long white T-shirt and jeans shorts, badly stained and crusty down the front like he'd been cleaning fish. And this filthy dude is the one trying to sweeten up Mirta?

"In the yard," Israel said. "In sight of neighbors on two sides. Who if they walked onto their porches coulda seen you easy. Some strange man down there talking on a cell phone in the middle of the night. Which anybody, any fool knows you do not use a cell under any circumstances in these transactions because why? Cell phones can be tracked." Banging his cane, he said, "On your cell phone. To me, on my home phone, imagine. Anybody listening in would know it's me. Tell me what happened when you called me."

"What you mean?"

"I said hello and what?"

"You asked what's the problem."

"And then?"

Barrel looked lost.

"I asked if this was a cell phone you were using, did I not?"

"Yes."

"And . . . ?"

"You, like, hung up."

"I hung up. I *slammed* the phone down is what." Israel said to Riley and Julius, "How late did I say it had to be before any calls?"

Riley sat up. "Midnight. If we weren't out by the pier by midnight, then a call."

"Midnight. And from where," Israel said, turning to Barrel, "did I say make that call?"

Barrel wiped his forehead. "See now, I remember that part but how I understood that, it was just a suggestion."

"What?"

"Israel, the way you said it, you said you suggest I use the house phone to call."

"A *suggestion*?"

Carlo said, "But still, anyway, what time did you call? A whole hour after the time you shoulda called."

Israel said, "A *suggestion*?"

Carlo stared at Barrel, shaking his head. "Simple things he could not understand, this fool that's part of the plan. Whoa! Somebody write that shit down, that's classic."

Israel braced himself against the cane and stood up. The waist of his pants looked to be above the navel, folded high-water cuffs flapping around black socks and skinny ankles. Carlo, curious to see what his brother was going to do, watched him limp over to Barrel. Like Israel still thought he was young and robust. Old boy had better calm down, getting worked up, look at him. Better watch it or he might stroke out again.

"I *suggest* you have a seat," Israel said to Barrel.

Barrel looked around, got a folding chair from behind the sink and dropped his big butt down.

Israel said, "To me, your biggest asset is not your muscle,

young man, it's your brain. Unfortunately, anybody who does what you did and got the temerity to look at me and say 'it was a suggestion' illustrates that your balls are bigger than your brain. I do not need men with brass balls and no brains in my operation. I need some intelligence." He stood over Barrel and glared at him. "Young man, you are an appallingly dumb shit. Out of whose ass did you pop from?"

Barrel opened his mouth to say something, but then sucked his teeth and looked off to the side with attitude.

Israel swung the cane so fast Carlo didn't realize it until it had already belted Barrel's face and was coming around for a second time. Barrel yelled, "Ow!" and caught it on the elbow, the cane snapping and a piece flying across the room. Barrel jumped up and scurried away from Israel. He stood looking at Israel and rubbing the elbow, a red welt across his jaw. "This ain't right, man, this ain't right."

Israel was muttering—a red flag, a sign he'd lost his temper. He started shuffling over to get Barrel but Carlo stepped in, put a hand on his brother's shoulder. "Easy there, wait. Don't fluster yourself over this. I got this," talking nice and gentle so he wouldn't have to hear any complaints from Israel later about undermining him or making him look weak.

Israel said to Barrel, "Today's your lucky day, boy. Hope you understand that," and he headed for his chair. He sat, breathing hard, and looked at Riley, who was picking up the handle half of the cane off the floor. "We need to talk."

"I know," Riley said, handing Carlo the cane.

Barrel walked past rubbing the elbow and saying, "Fuck, Carlos, that ain't right, dawg."

Carlo spun and smashed the handle into the side of Barrel's head. Barrel wobbled, tried to take another step and lurched face-first into his chair, knocking it over with a clatter and sprawling on his side.

Julius leaped to his feet. "Damn!"

Carlo walked up and stood over Barrel, the man groaning, a raw scrape on his chin. Carlo bent low and screamed into his face, "My name is Carlo! Do not call me *Carlos*. My name is not Carlos, you fat fuck." He clubbed him again and Barrel curled up and took cover behind his arms. Carlo feinted another blow and then just dropped the idea, dismissing this dumb ass. Too much energy spent on him already.

Carlo washed his face at the big sink while Israel and Riley talked. He dried off with an old towel, saying to Julius, "Help him up and drive him home."

Barrel was sitting on the floor, touching his face here and there and checking his fingertips. "I could drive myself."

Julius helped him to his feet. Stood with him until he regained balance then guided him to the door.

Carlo said, "You drive or he drives, I don't give a shit. I just don't want to see you for the rest of the week."

Julius unlocked the door and turned to the room. "I'll be right back, then."

Israel broke off the conversation with Riley and shook his head. "No, that's all right, son. We'll give you a call when we need you again."

"Okay, but Barrel don't live too far. I'll circle back."

"It's all right," Carlo said, "we'll shout when we need you again."

Julius didn't like that, you could see it on his face.

Carlo said, "Hey, Barrel. What's my name?"

Barrel didn't answer.

Carlo smiled, watching them leave, shut the door. He sat beside Israel, who was saying that they were pursuing some quality leads.

"Since we know it's a Coast Guard boat involved, we know where to start looking and what questions to ask. There are only a few people out there with the kind of pull to put to-gether something like last night. So that's the good news. Bad news is we got somebody in Mexico waiting for the stuff. Last time, by plane, we lost that three hundred kilos, those boys went elsewhere. We can't afford to lose another shipment or we lose their business for good. When I find out who has my stuff, I'll promptly assemble a crew to retrieve it, and I need you to be part of that crew."

Riley squinted. "To go out and get it?"

Israel said, "See now, I know what you're going to say and I don't want to hear that. Of course you'll help me get it back."

"I mean I'll gladly complete my end of the deal and trans-port it like every other time, but this other business, you know that's not my expertise."

"But it's your responsibility. This thing happened on your watch. Directly to you it happened."

"And has never happened before. So it's my fault?"

"Riley, there is the issue of a loan that you're forgetting. You're in a bigger debt than you expected. I find it surprising you could even think of resisting this plan, leave unfinished business."

Riley shook his head. "You know I'm not into the rough-neck trade. I don't want to be part of that."

"You hear anybody telling you carry a gun?" Carlo said, easing back in his chair. Riley looked down at the floor, Carlo enjoying watching doubt rattle his head. Sometimes lately, Riley was too confident for Carlo's taste, on the border of arrogant, and Carlo found himself itching to take him down a peg.

Israel said, "We need somebody who knows the waterways, the in-country. We don't know yet how this situation will turn, but we need somebody who'll know how to reach the places we might have to search, reach there fast, you understand?"

Riley nodded, coming around. "Okay, okay . . ."

Israel leaned forward. "Yes?"

Riley, rubbing his eyes, said, "Yeah, yeah, I'm on board."

Carlo smiled. "Riley, what's my name?"

Riley looked up. He took a moment. "They call you the Serpent."

Carlo grinned. Reached a fist across and tapped Riley's face. "My boy, Riley."

Riley, cool as ever. If Carlo found out he had gotten lazy last night on the water, though, wasn't paying attention to his surroundings, let's see if this motherfucker was still cool after Carlo got through testing him.

CHAPTER SIXTEEN

It started raining in the afternoon and continued into the evening. Riley pulled up outside Lindy's and sat in the truck, listening to music and waiting for the rain to abate. Business would probably be slow because of this weather, but he wasn't complaining; he needed the quiet for his mind to come down off the high-wire tension of the last several hours.

He dug out his cell phone and dialed his ex-wife's house for the third time that day. He waited for the machine. "Vicky, where oh where are you guys? I've been trying for days. Are you guys on vacation? You didn't let me know. Duncan, I love you and I'll see you soon. Give me a call, please, Vicky."

When he felt sufficiently placid he got out and walked through the cool drizzle and up the steps. Two tourists, a man and a woman, sat at the bar eating tacos and conch ceviche and swigging Lighthouse Lagers, Gert bartending. He twiddled his fingers at her and passed through to his office.

Before he could settle in with paperwork, he heard her fussing at Turo that he forgot to get the customers the Marie Sharp's habanero sauce, always serve the tacos with a bottle of Marie Sharp's, why's that so hard to remember?

Riley tried to concentrate but every little noise bothered

him. Gert barking orders at Turo, who was moving furniture out of the poker room in the back, rearranging it—they were closing it down temporarily, until they were confident Lopez would leave them alone—Turo muttering, "Tell me where I should put the chairs, then. Don't delay no time."

Riley set down his pen and puzzled over that one. Don't delay no time? He unpeeled Post-its Gert had stuck to his computer monitor and turned his face to the half-open door. "Hey, Turo? Come in here a second?"

Turo walked in blotting his face with a sweat towel. Riley swiveled his chair around and motioned for him to grab the chair over there. Turo squeezed past and sat, their knees inches apart in the cramped office. Riley held up a Post-it. "Duncan's Tours. A group of five. Altun Ha, then Progresso, a day trip. You did good last time we went out together. Think you could handle this one by yourself?"

Turo nodded, smiling. "Yeah, mahn, sure. No doubt, Mistah James."

Riley said, "Awright then. I'm a tourist. I ask you what does Altun Ha mean?"

"Sir, Altun Ha is a Mayan word stands for Water of the Rock."

"And what's so special about this place?"

"Hmmm." Turo looked off into space a moment. "Well, sir, Altun Ha, located thirty-one miles north of Belize City, that's where the Jade Head was found. That being the biggest jade object of its kind in the entire Mayan region. And if you look at any Belizean dollar note, you'll notice the Jade Head in the corner. So that's what's special about Altun Ha."

"Good. Your driver's license in order?"

"No tickets or nothin'. And check this out, too. Altun Ha was a major ceremonial center and trading center way, way back, like twelve thousand years back. The history books say it connected the Caribbean shores with other Mayan centers in this region."

Riley said, "Well, I for one am impressed."

"I got skills, you didn't know?"

"Which reminds me," Riley said, reaching over and plucking a sheet of paper from a pile and handing it to Turo. "Your letter to your landlord. I rewrote it some, not much. Sprinkled in some corrections, now it's good to go. But, I gotta tell you. 'Gradigually'? I checked *Webster's,* checked my *Concise Oxford,* sorry. No such word."

"Serious? I could swear to god I read that somewhere." He read the corrected letter. "Yeah, yeah . . . I likes, I likes."

Riley said, "So Friday morning at eight, outside the Great House guest house. Party of five. Got it covered?"

"Definitely."

Riley told him what time to come by his house for the van, it would have a full tank, and Turo left, excited.

Not a minute later as Riley pored over an electricity bill, Turo returned to the door. "Mistah James. I could ask you a question?"

Riley pushed back his chair and looked up. "You already started."

"How come you the only one 'round here that trusts me?"

Riley frowned. "Turo, you think I should trust you?"

"Of course."

"Then that's why I trust you." Riley tilted his head. "I remember this from a book I always read. It goes, 'I am good to people who are good. I am also good to people who are not good. Because Virtue is goodness. I have faith in people who are faithful. I also have faith in people who are not faithful. Because Virtue is faithfulness.'"

"Preach it."

Riley smiled with him. "But you get my meaning?"

"Definitely. Mistah James? Something else, what's up with Mistah Harvey? He's like, I don't know, extra jumpy. Drinking harder, messing around, like that other night? Just wondering."

Riley said, "Harvey is going through a phase. It'll pass."

"Like a midlife crisis?"

Riley pointed at him. "There you go." Turo turned to leave, but Riley said, "One question. Something from your letter. What's an 'arsist'?"

From down the corridor, Gert called, "Riley, someone here to see you."

Riley said to Turo, "We'll talk later," and went out. There were a few more patrons now, a man at the bar and two young men at the high tables on the sheltered part of the deck, eating tacos. A tall man in a black straw fedora, back turned to Riley, stood near the stairs shaking water off his umbrella. From that view alone—long sleeves, creased dress slacks, leather loafers, and the elegant hat—Riley knew who it was. "Brisbane," he said, smiling despite himself.

"Riley, it's been too long." They shook hands and Brisbane drew him into an embrace, slapping his back. "Too long." Brisbane stood tall and examined him. "How you doing, Riley?"

"Can't and won't complain," Riley said, turning to one of the deck tables, putting a hand on Brisbane's shoulder to lead him there.

Brisbane said, "Somewhere private we can chat?"

As Riley had feared. But what could he do? To come off reluctant or unfriendly in any way would be rude, they hadn't seen each other in a couple of years. Brisbane Burns, a former cohort, a firearms expert, and a man with the unnerving quiet of a guard dog.

When they walked past the two young men on the deck, one of them mumbled something to the other and they both turned to look at Brisbane. If he noticed, he didn't let on.

Behind the closed office door, Riley sat across from him and said, "So what's new with you? Last time we spoke you were planning that house out by Buttonwood Bay. I've seen it, man. It's beautiful."

"I'm enjoying it. We fish out by the dock every weekend. Can't beat it."

Riley nodded, idly twisting a paper clip. "I could only imagine."

"I understand I live right down the road from your business partner."

"Harvey? Yeah, that's right."

"He's the one built that house with that huge turret on the roof?"

Riley cracked a smile. "He's the culprit."

Brisbane chuckled. "What an unsightly . . . a *turret*? It doesn't go . . . You know what? I better stop." And he and Riley laughed some more. "Can't say I see him around much."

"Well, that's 'cause nobody sees *you*. You're in seclusion."

"I don't go out much, that's true. Don't have a reason to. Living the life I always dreamt, Riley. That's why I played around in that old business in the first place."

"I'm happy for you. Just kinda wish you'd parted ways with the Monsantos on better terms."

"Hey, it is what it is, what can I say? I have no regrets. They'll always believe I led that girl on, and you know me, I wouldn't do that."

"Mirta's been married and divorced since, you know that?"

"No, I knew she was separated," Brisbane said, picking lint off his slacks and flicking it away, "I didn't know she got divorced. Wish her all the best." He removed his hat, hung it on his knee.

"How's Roberto?"

"Fine. You look at him, you wouldn't even know he's sick.

That AZT is the best drug combination out there, we can attest to that."

"I wish you two a long, happy life, buddy."

Brisbane touched Riley's knee. "I really appreciate that."

They regarded each other in silence, then Riley said, "I know you didn't come here just to catch up, as nice as that is. How can I help you?"

"Maybe you heard," Brisbane said, "about my guns."

That could be taken two ways—that Riley had heard some of his guns had been stolen, or that Riley had heard who might be responsible. It was the cleverness of men like Brisbane that had unwittingly educated Riley over the years, though Brisbane was only a few years older, late forties at most, so you'd expect that he'd know Riley would not be jooked by trick questions. He ought to know better, but Riley didn't take offense—after all, he'd built a life by lying low and being underestimated. He remembered another line from the *Tao Te Ching,* which he'd just told Turo about. *Why is the sea the king of a hundred streams? Because it lies below them. . . .*

He was honest with Brisbane. "I heard about that," watching Brisbane perk up, "from Miss Rose Robinson. She said they stole one of your gun safes? How much did they get, Brisbane?"

Brisbane shook his head. "We were on a little weekend getaway, went to see *The Bourne Ultimatum* at the multiplex in Chetumal? Lovely weekend, then we came back and discovered the break-in. They came by boat, used my dock, broke into the house through a downstairs window and went straight to the safe. Didn't take anything else. Not a thing. None of my neighbors saw or heard it. It was a group that did it, because that was one monster safe, and it was loaded."

"What did they take?"

"Shit, what *didn't* they take." Brisbane released a sigh. "Five of my assault rifles. You know I have an affinity for the AR. They took my Rock River Arms, my two Armalites, the two old Colts. You know my Garand, the World War Two rifle I refurbished—that's gone. My Mossberg shotgun, gone. Don't even talk to me about the handguns. All the .45s I've been working on, the two Ed Browns, my Kimbers, and a couple of 9mm Sigs. Not to mention thousands of rounds—.23 caliber, .45s, and four brand-new pieces of body armor."

"Damn, very sorry to hear that. Any ideas who could be behind it?"

Brisbane nodded, looking directly into his eyes.

"You're thinking the Monsantos."

Brisbane said, "The reason why I believe it's somebody who knows me, nobody else but some friends and former associates know I stock weapons in that special back room I've got. Reason I know it wasn't the contractor that built it, that gentleman isn't around any longer."

"What you mean?"

"He's not around. Completely different incident. He did something and I had to take care of him." Brisbane made a backhand gesture, crossed his legs, impatient with the turn of conversation. He noticed Riley had canted his head and was staring at him, so he obliged. "He called Roberto a faggot, okay? One day we're haggling over some detail in the construction costs and he decides to get personal, insult Roberto, and I can't have that, Riley."

Riley nodded, feeling a pulsing in his neck. "So that's how come you know it couldn't be that guy," nodding, telling himself this is exactly why he wished Brisbane wasn't here. "And how can I help with this problem today?"

"By keeping your ears to the ground. Should you hear any rumors or happen upon any hearsay concerning my guns, or any guns for that matter, let me know?"

"You bet."

"Putting my feelers out, you see, enlisting the aid of people with connections, people I can trust."

"In other words, ask around, but don't raise the subject with the Monsantos."

"Or any of their crew for that matter."

Riley told him he could surely do that, and offered Brisbane a drink, but he said he had to be going, put his hat on and stood up.

"You caught me at the perfect time," Riley said.

"How's that?"

"I'm traveling the same road you did, and I hope to be out of the business in a few weeks, after I tie up some loose ends."

"Then this makes my visit all the more urgent." He touched his hat brim.

Riley opened the door for him.

"You taking care of that .45?"

The Kimber .45 that Brisbane had given Riley as a gift years ago. "It's well oiled and loaded."

"I hear a 'but' in there somewhere."

Riley smiled, embarrassed. "But I haven't run it in a while."

Brisbane tsk-tsked. "Got to keep your hand in, Riley, got to keep your hand in. When last you been skeet shooting?"

"Probably"—Riley feigned an effort to recall—"probably the last time I went with you."

"Aaah, shameful, just shameful," Brisbane shaking his head as they walked out. At the steps, he snapped open his umbrella and turned to Riley. "Any news, you let me know immediately?"

Riley assured him he would and stood at the rail gladly watching him leave, posture erect, steps quick and neat. Turo sidled up next to Riley and watched Brisbane get into his Lexus, swing onto the road and drive off, Riley exchanging a wave.

Turo said, "You were asking me what's an arsist?" He jutted his chin at the car going down the road. "*That's* an arsist."

"That he is, I guess. And he's also a sociopathic son of a bitch you don't want to cross, son, so never let him hear you say that."

Riley poured himself a glass of beer to take back to his office, finish the paperwork. Gert, a rag over her shoulder, was staring at him. He said, "Yes? What did I do wrong now, Gert?"

"I'm just thinking how nice it is that soon we won't have to see people of that kind anymore popping in for a surprise visit."

Riley sipped beer, pretending to mull that over.

"Because I've never trusted that man for a second. He might dress oh so clean and fancy, act so sniffy, and you don't hear any bad news about him, but he doesn't fool me."

Riley wiped foam off his lips. What did she want, an argument? "You're right, Gert," he said, cruising to his office.

Once in there, he locked the door, put the beer on his desk, plopped down and closed his eyes. He thought, Guns? Like I need anything else on my plate. Sure, Brisbane, I might ask around for your guns. In your dreams. Shit.

He needed to feel, and soon, that he was through with the Life, but the Life was like swimming across the Sibun River on a trip he'd made with Candice. That's what it was beginning to feel like. Sinister. As soon as he had reached within a few feet of the grassy bank, stroking hard, exhausted, a cold, swift current would turn him slantways, far, farther away from Candice waiting for him on the blanket with their picnic basket of cheese and sliced watermelon, the river tugging him back to the deep spot he'd started from.

———

Green tea in rustic clay bowls. A stack of books—*Zen and Japanese Culture, One Hundred Years of Solitude, Hombre*—all different genres, on the kitchen table. A plate of homemade oatmeal raisin cookies, his favorite.

Sister Pat finished knocking ashes out of her glass pipe and washing her hands. She came away from the sink, tucking the pipe into a pocket of her apron then drying her hands. She sat across from Riley and double-palmed her bowl of tea, warming her fingers.

Riley liked being here. Books and candles everywhere, on shelves high and low, in the built-in bookcases out in the parlor, on the side tables in the sparely furnished living room that smelled of polish and wisps of marijuana. She kept her stash in a Russian nesting doll, in the second innermost doll, among the knickknacks on top of a bookcase. She smoked only in the evenings, using her Pyrex pipe, a sturdy double-blown piece beautifully swirled inside with red and green streams. She was proud of her pipe and considered it part of her smoking aesthetic.

She never offered Riley a hit. Not because he wouldn't partake; they simply both understood it was her private ritual, that pipe in her living room while a bowl of green tea awaited.

She asked, "Which one will you read first?" talking about the books on the table.

"Probably the Western. You can't beat Elmore Leonard for a crackling good story. Besides, it's the slimmest and lightest of the three, probably the most funnest."

She groaned. "The most funnest . . ."

Riley munched a cookie. "I'd told her I'm prepared to leave my life here behind, but now that it might really happen, that she's willing to marry and we're ready to start afresh? I don't know . . ."

"Don't tell me you're having doubts. About leaving that business."

"No, not that. The bar is the one. I like running the bar. I like the smell of cigarettes and beer. Seriously. Hearing voices and people laughing, having a good time, glasses clinking, bottles smacking that counter and feeling crumpled dollars and hitting the register? I like all that. Even seeing all my utility bills ready to mail out, checks signed, envelopes with stamps placed just so, and knowing we got through another month? Sister Pat, nothing can't beat that feeling."

Sister Pat sipped her tea. "Maybe because it's your own business, something you're honestly working hard at."

"If honestly means legal, yes, I agree."

"A legal and above-board enterprise, the success of which depends on you. So that's one reason you're having doubts. Any other?"

"Don't you know?"

"Duncan."

Riley said, "It's not like I wouldn't come back to see him, spend some time, maybe summer vacations. But it's when I think about him I still see a Buddha-belly baby, and he isn't, he's six. In a few years, he'll be a teenager that probably won't even want to hang out with his old man, but it's the years in between I don't want to miss. I want to be around. In a way my old man wasn't."

"I completely understand."

"I haven't seen Duncan in almost two weeks. Unprecedented. I keep calling the house but no one's ever home. I'm a little irritated. But I know when I see him again, that's all gonna wash right off, I know it."

"And another reason you're having doubts about leaving, could it have something to do with the fact it's because, well, you're leaving with someone you've known only a year or so? That maybe you don't know her that well? It would be only natural to have doubts."

Riley considered the question carefully. "Actually it's thirteen months," was all he could come up with.

Sister Pat looked down, circling the rim of her bowl with a finger. "How well do you think you know Candice, Riley?"

Riley sipped some tea. "How well do I know anybody?"

"Oh, don't give me that, you know what I mean."

"You're asking me if I could trust her to be the person she appears to be?"

"That's it on the nose. And who does she appear to be? Someone who'll enrich your life, make it fuller. A sound influence, a faithful companion? All those things we've discussed so many times?"

"Yes to all of the above. I'll tell you the truth, she's an artist to me, Sister Pat. She's got a mind that attracts me. Stop me if this is too much information, but it's way more than physical and I enjoy the hell outta that part, but it's—hey, it's *deeper* with her. We can hang out, cook together and we're in this zone where it's peaceful but full of energy at the same time, and we riff about anything, God or if there isn't a god, music, art, and maybe I don't know that much about Edward Hopper but I'm learning. Sometimes she talks about her fiancé who got killed in a crash, how much she missed him, and I could see a part of her is still hurting, so I listen, and I think it makes us closer. I've taken her all over Belize. The cayes, the ruins, camping in Placencia, snorkeling at Half Moon Caye ... I guess I'm saying it feels natural with her, Sister Pat, it feels *effortless*. Real. We argued a couple times, yeah, but basically there're no pretense between us. Either that or I'm fooling myself."

Sister Pat said, "I like what I'm hearing, but more than that, I like what I'm seeing as you're telling me this. Drink your tea, it's getting cold."

They sipped tea together, Riley scanning the spines of the

books on the credenza across the room to see what he might borrow next.

Sister Pat said, "I saw Candice this afternoon as a matter of fact."

"Really? Then you beat me 'cause I haven't seen her all day after that thing that happened to me last night."

"That thing I don't need to know any details about, thank you very much."

"I know. Where'd you see her?"

"Battlefield Park. Taking pictures of a man. Looked like an American."

"Maybe one of her Peace Corps friends."

"I don't think so. This fellow was somewhat too well dressed. Too clean cut."

"Sister Pat. My personal spy. Hey, I'm teasing."

"That's okay. This man, I've seen him before. Driving a U.S. embassy SUV."

"And you can tell it's embassy because . . ."

She set her bowl down and glowered. "Boy, don't insult me. I know what an embassy vehicle looks like. From the tags. Which say U.S. embassy." She let him off with a little smile.

Riley shrugged. "Who knows? Candice's business has taken off recently. She gets all these different clients. She sold two photos to *Condé Nast Traveler* last month, I told you about that?"

"That's wonderful."

"Yeah, she's got an eye. Like I said, she's an artist."

Sister Pat pushed the plate of cookies toward him. He took one, bit into it and said, "So an embassy vehicle, huh? Cheating on me with The Man. That evil woman." He chewed the oatmeal raisin, thinking Okay, who could this guy be? He looked at the cookie and put it down, his appetite gone.

CHAPTER SEVENTEEN

One evening, Riley peering over her shoulder, Candice had ordered a bunch of skimpy panties from the Victoria's Secret Web site. Riley pointed to this and that on the screen, saying oh, yeah, that's perfect. No, scroll down—yeah, look, right here, Brazilian string. But wait, better yet, get the *extreme* string. Rubbing her shoulders and fitting his chin into the crook of her neck.

She was wearing one now, a racy, black sliver of a thing—there's something delicious and naughty about black panties, he told her, and she was inclined to agree—the panty tight with strings high on her hipbones, and a sleeveless form-fitting blouse hugging her midriff, while she sliced sweet red peppers and dropped them into a bowl with onions and potato wedges.

The pan hissed when Riley spooned the red curry paste into the hot oil and stirred. He was sporting silky blue boxers she'd bought him, which he had vowed he'd never wear. Aromatic fig candles were burning on the far kitchen counter and on the dining table, the houselights were low, jazz drifting from the living-room speakers. An open bottle of chardonnay and two glasses of wine stood over there on the counter.

"Where's the chicken?" Riley asked, fanning away the spicy fumes rising from the pan.

"In the fridge," she said, opening a can of bamboo shoots, "where you put it ten minutes ago."

Passing by, he spanked her butt, took out the pan with the chunks of seasoned chicken breast. He stuck his head farther in the fridge.

"What do you need?"

"The fish sauce. I know I saw a bottle of fish sauce in here somewhere."

"It's in the cabinet over there, by the sink."

She didn't keep a close eye on him and when she looked up again he was rummaging around, toppling spice bottles, in the wrong cabinet, so she told him the *other* one, *by the sink,* you don't listen, and he shook his head and said the fish sauce shouldn't have been in there anyway, since anybody knows it belongs in the fridge or it goes bad, refrigerate after opening, right there on the label. She argued otherwise, and he cut her off and said now, dammit, he needed garlic powder, was that in the spice cabinet or maybe, should he like check the freezer?

She went after him with a spoon and they ended the argument laughing through a ferocious kiss. When he lifted her up and sat her on the counter, water from the can of bamboo shoots spilled, and he stood between her legs kissing her, long and deep.

She continued cooking, tipsy from the wine and all that loving, she said. She slid the onions, potatoes, and sweet peppers in with the chicken chunks coated in red and browning juicily. Next came a can of coconut milk, whitening the pot then picking up swirls of red curry as she stirred. Next, the bamboo shoots and a cup of frozen peas that he handed her, then he dipped across and sluiced cold wine from his mouth into hers, pressing his bare chest against her, and the room felt hot and smelled of figs and red Thai curry and his skin, that sharpness he had.

They ate at the table, curry ladled over mounds of basmati rice, refilled wineglasses. Rain was falling outside. They ate messily, they didn't care, commenting on the food. Playing footsie under the table.

She jiggled her eyebrows at him. They had all night for things to progress. Let the anticipation be sweet.

Somewhere between putting the plates in the sink and draining the bottle of Chardonnay into her glass, he lost his boxers, and she cackled and clapped her hands once when she noticed. Before you know it, her clothes were off, too, and she was leading him astray, into the bedroom. The rain had picked up, smothering the music, and rain-breeze washed over the bed. Giggling and kneeling over him, she flung the sheet over their heads, and they set about pleasing each other, while the rain drummed the tin roof.

The sheets were drenched. He was drowsing, pillows scattered on the floor. She kept the bathroom door open and spoke to him as she sat on the toilet peeing. "Are you listening to me?" He mumbled. She saw herself in the big mirror over the sink, hair mussed, face flushed, and she was happy.

He said, "You musn't tell your friends about me. They'll all want a piece. I can't be expected to rock every woman's world, there's only one of me."

She said in a monotone, "Okay, you stud you."

He said he liked some of those pictures she had on the wall, were those ones new? She said a few were. How could he see? Put on a lamp. Look at the ones by the closet, Lamanai, that one with the yellow rope leading up to the temple, the angle and the color contrast. He snapped on the light. He said man, how cool. She'd pumped up the color saturation on the computer to bring out the yellows, and the blues in the sky. She flushed the toilet, washed her hands, smiling giddily at herself for some reason, maybe content mixed with chardonnay.

He said, "Could you take a portrait of Duncan and one of Duncan and me? I'll bring him over one day."

She said, teasing, "Sure, and bring your ex, too," but when she walked out of the bathroom, saw that he was serious. She said, "I'll finally get to spend a little time with him?"

He nodded. "Maybe one day this week, in the evening, I'll bring him over."

"Perfect." She saw no trace of a joke on his face. "I could whip up something. What does he like to eat?"

"That'd be nice, but not necessary. Some of those Oreo cookies and some ice cream would be cool."

"The cookies you've been scarfing and there's only a quarter pack left?" She found a bottle of body spray from the night table drawer and spritzed her neck and her arms.

He heard his cell phone chirping, looked around. "Now where's that thing?" He lifted his jeans off a bench by the wall, patted the pockets.

"It's outside."

"Outside, what would it be doing outside?"

"Hmm, let's see. Because maybe you left it in the coin tray like you always do?"

He snapped his fingers, walked off to get it and spun around fast. "You were checking out my ass, weren't you?"

"You know I was."

She sat Indian-style on the bed and flipped through a textbook on color management, hearing him on the phone, her mind wandering. She slapped the book shut, heaved it on the ground, and covered her face with her hands.

What the hell was she doing?

That man outside, the man who just rose naked from her bed, was he the slippery drug runner of the "ruthless organization" police had been trying for years to nail? That man outside? That silly, sweet gentle man? Riley James? *Her* Riley James?

She sighed, she felt like such a heel. There was a golf ball in her throat, but she was not going to give in to emotion, no way. Not tonight . . . it had been so perfect.

She lay on her side, curled around a pillow. He was not the man she thought she knew when the investigation started. Not a streak of meanness in him that she could see now. Like a father should be. Occasionally, she'd dropped hints, spoken well of him to Malone. "The best neighbor I've ever had. I'm not lying." "What an easygoing guy." "Why do some criminals turn out to be such nice people?"

Malone said, "You sound like every single woman I know. 'Why are all the handsome guys gay?'"

Malone must've picked up on her warming up to Riley, or growing cool toward the operation. Picked up on her doubting her role. He showed her pictures, two men lying bloody on a dirt road near a pickup. He pointed to the one slumped against a tire. "This guy, Tarik El-Bani. This other guy, a local officer in El-Bani's pocket. The agency had been following El-Bani's movements for months back in the eighties, he was getting big. Do you know how these men died?"

"Shot, it appears."

"Multiple times. You know by whom?"

She hesitated. "I think I know."

"So do we. In fact, we're pretty damn *certain* Mr. James was the gunman. Everything we know about the local investigation points to him, which is how he came on our radar. A young member of a loose organization run by a rival drug family takes out our target and makes himself a target. Candice, the bad guys never get away. The shadow they cast, it's too long, they draw too much attention, clever as they think they are, they can't hide forever. It's simply in their nature to be deviant, and

what does law enforcement need to do? Pay attention, be patient. Like going fishing."

She thought, Sure, whatever you say, John Wayne. But then,
in the days that followed, she wondered if what he said next
was true.

"Sooner or later, people like Riley James, they all taste the
hook."

After he got off the phone, he brought a hefty chunk of cheesecake on a plate with two forks. They ate in bed, propped against
the headboard, licking the forks clean and listening to the rain.
"One mile more tomorrow morning," she said, stabbing a piece.
"Mmmm . . . Two more miles," digging in again.

He said, "Yeah, all one hundred and twenty pounds of you."

"One eighteen."

"Excuuuse me."

She teased him about his calloused toes, some of the ugliest
she'd ever laid eyes upon. He wiggled them, cracking them to
annoy her. He scraped off the cheesecake stuck to the plate and
said, "I've got to meet somebody tonight. I shouldn't be too
long, okay?"

That surprised her. "In this weather? Do you have to?"

"It's this man I do business with, he just called. He's being
unreasonable, and I think I better get this meeting over with so
I don't have to hear his complaints anymore. I'm sorry."

Why was she so upset? She wasn't faking, there was something else. . . . She bounded off the bed and hurried into the
bathroom, slamming the door.

Riley called, "You all right?"

She sat on the toilet, lowered her head. "I'll be okay. . . . It's the
cheesecake, I think." Her forehead was cold with sweat—she'd
lost her flipping mind, hadn't she. She felt a knot of indigestion

high in her stomach, her breath was shallow, her arms suddenly clammy.

To expect that she and this man were going to live some normal, stable life was ludicrous, a fantasy, a child's game. For that to happen, she saw it plainly: She'd have to betray the DEA completely.

How the hell did she take this long to admit that?

Riley rapped on the door. "Want me to get you something? Tums?"

"No—I'll be fine." She flushed the toilet. She ran cold water and stared at herself in the mirror. She leaned over, splashed water on her face, laved it over her neck and straightened, cool water sliding down her back. And the night had been so beautiful. . . .

Or maybe that was all too superficial. Behind her giddy grins, the girlish glee, the other woman inside her skin, the adult, was screaming. She thought, You are so messed up, Candice.

When she said yes to Riley, she'd narrowed her life to two choices, and the day was speeding her way like a tunnel train—with Riley dashing off somewhere in the middle of the night, which she knew was because of his shadow life—that moment was hurtling at her, when she'd have to decide: Let's start a family, my love. Or turn coldhearted: So long, Riley, you should've known better.

Riley said at the door, "Sure you don't want anything? You're going to be all right?"

"I hope so, Riley," she said, wiping her eyes dry. "I sure hope so."

CHAPTER EIGHTEEN

Riley didn't like the vagueness. Why did they have to meet now, an odd hour like this, on a rainy night? This matter can't wait, Carlo said, that's why. Could Carlo at least give him a hint what it was about, he was in the middle of something here. "Just come, Riley, we got two men who'll help us I need you to meet. Can't say any more at the moment."

So Riley borrowed Candice's umbrella and returned home in the rain. His yard was soggy and thunder rumbled deep in the pitch blackness to the west. He strapped on tattered Chaco sandals, got his rain slicker off the peg behind the bathroom door, and what else . . . ? Looking around, considering. The vagueness had put him on edge, the suddenness of the call.

In his bedroom, he opened the closet and cleared shoes and boxes out of the way to reach the small safe in the back, bolted to the floor. He dialed in the combination, tugged open the door, surprised at how heavy it was. It had been several months since he'd opened it. Inside was his passport, assorted house and business documents, and right behind an emergency bundle of cash and a twenty-count box of Spear .45 ACP rounds, there it was, looking intimidating, the Kimber 1911 Brisbane had given him.

Riley took it out, and in swift moves dropped out the magazine, cranked the slide, checked the empty chamber, like it was yesterday. He fondled the pistol, held it out straight and looked down the sights and thought, Naah.

He reseated the mag and returned the gun to the safe and shut it, feeling wise about his decision.

He drove his truck through empty streets, no radio on to distract him, just the pleasing swoosh of tires in the rain. He headed up the BelChina Bridge and realized there was a blackout on the other side of the river. It didn't take much of a storm to knock the power out in some areas of the city.

He rolled onward on Youth for the Future Drive. He liked that name, especially considering that a good bunch of the youth on this street were seeing to their future doing odd jobs for the Monsantos. He hung a right on Ebony Street and another right down a pothole-riddled lane with no name sign, headlights beaming for the river. He jounced along in the blackout and hard downpour on an unnamed lane to meet unknown men for some unclear reason. Men who could "help them." Great, sounds fabulous, please, get him out of bed for this, count him in for sure.

Riley punched the high beams on just in time to see where the lane dead-ended at the river. He stomped the brake, telling himself to cool it, check your attitude at the door. He parked behind a wreck of a car on cement blocks and made sure he locked all the doors. In areas like this, you paid for your carelessness.

He flipped up the hood of his slicker and walked through puddles toward the boatyard at the river's edge. He made his way along a trail of planks thrown on the ground, past the shadows of tugboats and skiffs under open sheds and a chained pit bull barking at him.

In the back, behind a stack of lumber and boats on dry dock, was the watchman's shack, where Carlo told him to go, but the plank windows were down and the door closed, the whole place in darkness. Listening to the dog and the rain pelting his slicker, Riley cursed, thought of going back to the truck for his flashlight, when a back door opened and a figure stood in the doorway, silhouetted by a wavering light from the room.

"Hey, Riley? That you, Riley?"

Riley said, "Hey," and advanced, raising a hand.

"The one and only, the mystical one," Carlo said, escorting him into the house.

The room was hot. Riley hauled off his slicker, dropped it by the door. Two men were sitting at a table jammed against a wall of the small room that passed for a kitchen. A kerosene lamp burned in the center of the table, the flame fluttering when Carlo swung the door shut. He pulled out a chair for Riley. Riley nodded at the men, sat down.

Carlo said, "Riley, this is Temio and Chino. They came in from Mexico this evening."

Neither man offered a hand, faces expressionless.

Tinny calypso was playing in the next room with walls that didn't reach the ceiling. In the flickering light, Riley didn't recognize either Mexican, one with a thick mustache and male-pattern baldness, the other lean and dark with straight black hair and Indian features. Riley didn't know, because Carlo didn't make clear, which one was Temio, which one Chino, probably not their real names anyway, but Riley had a feeling he was going to find out, whether he wanted to or not.

Carlo fixed Riley with a stare. "What took you so long?"

Riley figured he was trying to pull rank in front of the Mexicans so he let him have his show, Riley not taking it too seriously. "Like I told you on the phone, I was getting ready to have some cheesecake."

Carlo's brow knotted. "What?"

There was movement at the other side of the room and Riley turned to see Israel coming from behind a curtain in the doorway to the other room, toweling his pate dry. "Nasty weather," he said. He removed his glasses, dabbed at his eyes, pushed the glasses on and took in the room.

Carlo said, "Fucking cheesecake. He's late because of cheesecake."

Israel shrugged. "Must've been some tasty cheesecake."

Carlo seemed to ponder that. He said to Riley, "What kind, one of them fancy ones like *dulce de leche*?"

"Plain. With a little strawberry topping."

"Strawberry syrup running all down the side?"

"Yeah."

"A fat slice, like with a couple beefy strawberries on top?"

"Yeah, you know it."

Carlo nodded deeply. "Very nice."

Israel stepped forward and said, "Riley, you know why we called you here?" looking for a place to put the towel among the pots and pans and stacks of canned goods on the counter. He finally tossed it by the sink, by rotting backboards and a dish rack. He faced the room, holding on to the counter, no cane tonight.

Riley said, "I have a feeling."

"Tell me."

Riley's eyes passed over the two Mexicans. "Something to do with the shipment."

"Excuse me a second," Israel holding up a hand and cocking an ear toward the other room. He raised his voice at the gap between the wall and ceiling. "Turn up the volume, please."

There were footsteps behind the wall, and the calypso music got louder.

"Regarding that last shipment," Israel said. "Our friend El Padrón is giving us some assistance. We located the shipment.

Thanks to a little double-crossing bird named McCoy that flew in and sang a sweet song over the phone. He told us who has it, and now we're getting it back. For a nominal fee to this McCoy."

"When?"

"Tonight."

Riley said, coolly, "Okay," but he was thinking, *Tonight?*

"These two gentlemen are professionals in the retrieval arts. We don't expect any difficulties, but they're also highly skilled in techniques of persuasion. Your job is to take them where they need to go, in the shortest time possible, and return with the cargo intact."

"Tonight?"

"Yes tonight," Carlo said, walking into Riley's line of vision. "You got a problem with that?"

Riley tried to look past him and address Israel, but Carlo wasn't moving. Riley expelled a breath and relaxed. "Where we going?"

"On the water," Carlo said.

"Where on the water?"

Israel said, "Caye Caulker, Riley."

"Twenty-odd miles out on the sea, in this weather?"

"The element of surprise," Carlo said.

It figured he'd come up with B-movie shit like that. Riley stood up and walked around him so he could reason with Israel. "Look, I understand how important it is to get this thing back ASAP, but you think maybe we could wait until tomorrow night? We're talking serious waves out there tonight. If you can avoid it, you avoid it."

"It can't wait," Israel said. "We've set up the meeting for tonight. McCoy says he can't guarantee things will be in the same spot more than twenty-four hours."

One of the Mexicans mumbled something.

Carlo waved a finger and said, *"No, vamos esta noche."* He shook his head at Riley. "Bullshit."

Israel said, "Riley, think of it this way. You do this tonight? Tomorrow you're retired, enjoy all the fancy cheesecakes you want. But let's get this job done. That's only sound business sense. Weather? Weather is beyond our control. We've got to be practical businessmen regardless of the weather and bad roads and bellyaches and other such vagaries. Experienced man like you, you ought to understand this."

Something moved at the doorway curtain, and Riley saw a little face poking out. Carlo said, "Hey," snapped his fingers, and the little girl pulled back.

Riley smiled at that and thought, Let's get this over with then. When he looked at Israel he didn't need to say a word.

Israel shuffled toward the table and spoke to the Mexicans. *"¿Tiene sus cosas?"*

They nodded.

Carlo turned to Riley. "The *Ravish* is out there. You need to gas up out at Robinson Caye. Other than that, the boat is stocked up and ready, flares, flashlights, everything."

The Mexicans reached under the table and pulled out long black canvas duffel bags. They put on raincoats and stood holding their bags. Soldiers waiting for orders.

Israel came close to Riley. "They already know where they need to go. They have McCoy's money. You just take them to Caye Caulker and dock at the back bridge, direct them to Chapoose Street and stand back. Now, you can't wait by the boat because they might need your help to carry the stuff to the boat. If for some reason the shipment isn't where it's supposed to be, then our night will be a little longer, but don't worry, they'll fill you in, and then it's the same routine—you take them to the destination, stand back, wait till they say go. You got that?"

Riley said he understood, and picked his slicker off the floor, checking out the bulk of the Mexicans' bags, their loose T-shirts, perfect for concealing a carry piece or two, and the nervousness he felt at the start of the visit surged back. He shrugged into his slicker.

Carlo stood at the door and looked at them. "Everybody good?"

Hardly. But Riley nodded along with the Mexicans.

Carlo opened the door and a blast of rain swept in.

CHAPTER NINETEEN

One way Candice liked to relax, aside from shooting photographs, was by cleaning her cameras, the whole careful process of it in the spare bedroom. Making sure the fans in the house were off and the windows shut so there was no dust blowing in; laying the cameras and the cleaning accoutrement on the cloth on the carpet; sitting down and setting the camera on the slowest shutter speed, and unscrewing the lens to begin. The steps had a meditative quality that eased her.

She wiped the lens down with a microfiber cloth, triggered the shutter while she squeezed puffs of air from the blower into the sensor. Screwed the lens on. She snapped a couple of test shots and examined them on the screen. Cruelly, one image showed the phone in the corner, the phone she'd been trying to ignore.

She needed to make a call, didn't know if she wanted to make that call. She wiped the camera body down, looking at the backdrop stand set up against the wall and picturing how Riley's son would look standing there, or sitting on a stool, whatever made him comfortable. She couldn't remember how tall he was, wondered if he still looked like the little boy she met once.

She didn't want to make the call, but Riley had left almost twenty minutes ago. She folded the lens cloth on her lap, preferring to think about photographing Riley's son, how much fun that might be.

She hoisted herself from the carpet and picked up the phone. Looked at it. Set it beside her camera bag. Sat on the carpet. Thinking about Riley's son had made her remember the story he told her once when she asked how he got along with his ex's new husband, Miguel, and Riley said he almost didn't.

He explained that during the first year of the new marriage, from time to time Duncan would complain that Miguel was teasing him and Riley—trying to be mature and agreeable about the state of things—didn't make a fuss and distracted Duncan whenever he brought up the issue. Weeks passed, Riley thinking bruised feelings were healing, and Duncan and his stepfather were beginning to bond, until one day he picked up Duncan for the weekend and the boy ran down to the truck in tears.

Said that Miguel had been calling him a musclehead, over and over, and he hated it and he hated Miguel. All Riley said was don't worry, he'd talk to Miguel, and that weekend he worried about how he was going to approach it without being too confrontational, or appearing jealous.

Sunday evening when Riley took Duncan home, he walked upstairs with him, said hi and bye to Vicky and Miguel, kissed Duncan and left. But instead of returning to his truck, he lingered at the bottom of the stairs, listening to the voices in the house, the TV going, Vicky telling Duncan to please take off those filthy socks and go wash his hands, dinner would be ready soon.

Riley said he heard chairs scraping, plates being set and no more TV, and Miguel saying, *Come with me, musclehead, it's time to eat,* and Riley started climbing those stairs. He'd already planned an excuse—"Stupid me, I think I left my keys up here"—now all he needed were the calmest words to address Miguel. At the screen door, he stopped and knew after he peered in that he didn't need to carry it any further. Quietly, hoping no one inside had seen him, he turned and trotted down the stairs and got into his truck. On the drive home, he felt a bittersweet relief that his boy wasn't only his, but was the son of another man now. Miguel, Vicky, and Duncan, the picture of them he kept seeing, the one he glimpsed through the screen door— Miguel lifting Duncan onto his shoulders in a fireman carry, roughhousing with him on the way to the dinner table, Duncan shrieking and Vicky spooning potato salad onto a plate with a look of good-natured exasperation. And Riley said he heard Miguel going, *Come with me, musclehead, it's time to eat. I don't know how in the world you got so big and brawny, must be the food, must be all this food.*

Riley told Candice he saw how Miguel loved the boy, and that soothed his fears.

And this was one reason why she loved Riley.

And that soothed his fears. In *her* mind, nothing was soothed. She felt crazy, she wanted to go for a run. She said, "Candice, Candice, make up your mind," and she picked up the phone. She thumbed out the number and waited.

"Hey, it's me. Calling to check in."

Malone said, "What's the good word?"

Candice didn't know what she was going to say until she said it. "No word. No action here. The game looks like it's been rained out tonight."

"So all is quiet but for the thunder?"

"Yes," Candice said, and as if Malone was there watching, she stood up and crossed over to the window, opened it and gazed through the rain at Riley's house, the porch light shining. "House is all locked up like the owner's fast asleep."

"The perfect thing to do on a night like this. Or maybe the second perfect thing. 'Western wind when wilt thou blow, the small rain down can rain, Christ if my love were in my arms and I in my bed again.' Don't be too lonely, Candice."

"Say hello to your wife for me, Malone."

Malone chuckled. "One of these years, one of these years soon, you may need to take a lover in the spring."

"Good night, Malone."

She leaned her forehead against the screen, stared out into the rain feeling sprinkles on her face and arms. She pressed her torso against the screen, enjoying the cold droplets. She wondered if the screen and the louvers could hold her if she pressed hard with all her weight. She wondered how much they could take before they broke and sent her hurtling over the edge.

CHAPTER TWENTY

Riley heard the clink of metal inside the black bags when the Mexicans slid them into the V-berth. Even in the pounding rain he heard the clink and didn't need to guess that the only techniques of persuasion these two knew were the kinds conveyed in calibers.

He didn't like what was going down, but it was useless to argue that it didn't have to be this way. The possibility of violence had been inherent from the first run he ever made for the Monsantos; he should consider himself lucky a night like this hadn't happened sooner.

They made their way slowly down the river and under the swing bridge in the blinding rain. Coming through the mouth of the harbor, at the lighthouse, he saw the bald Mexican reach into an ice chest by his feet and offer his *compadre* a can of Red Bull. The man didn't hear, huddled under his raincoat, and the bald one said, "Chino," loud enough for Riley to know now who was who.

That was about the last thing Temio, the bald one, said for the rest of the trip, sitting in front of the wheel, head bobbing with the rolling waves. Chino sat on the other side of the cockpit, slump-shouldered, looking down at his tennis shoes getting soaked with the spray lashing in and the boat pitching and yawing. A few minutes later, the rain and waves eased and Riley gave the boat throttle.

Satisfied with the speed and feeling less antsy, he decided to make small talk, asking Chino if he could help himself to a Red Bull. Chino didn't hear so Riley reached across and touched his shoulder and said, with a bad accent, messing around, *"Oye, mi amigo, dame un—Toro Rojo, por favor."*

Chino didn't crack a smile. He wiped his eyes and looked at Riley. "We speak English. Say in English you want, I understand."

He stooped over to get Riley a Toro Rojo, but Temio had a foot on the cooler. Chino tapped Temio's leg and said something in rapid Spanish, and Temio turned lazily in Riley's direction, turned back and kept his foot on the cooler just long enough.

Chino handed Riley the can without looking at him. Riley popped the Red Bull and said, "Cheers."

Chino said nothing. Riley said, shouting into the wind, "You guys been to Belize before?"

Chino nodded.

"Where about have you been?"

Chino raised a finger. *"Mi hermano,* please." He touched the finger to his head. "I need to think. I need to focus." It sounded like *I nid too fuckus.*

Riley said, "No problem," lifting his drink. You go ahead and fuckus, *mi hermano,* just don't fuck me tonight, I want to get this over with and be back home without any blood on my clothes.

The rain had ceased but the air was brisk, colder as they neared the mangrove islands, and a wind picked up. The boat weaved through the mangroves, and then Robinson Caye rose out of the dark, Riley pushing back the throttle and the bow setting down to a slow glide toward the dock.

Chino helped moor the boat, but when Riley climbed out, no one followed. Chino had pulled the black bags out of the V-berth and was stooped over, checking something. Temio was using a flashlight to read what looked like a black day planner. Riley told them he was going to a shed down the trail for a drum of gas, roll it over.

Temio nodded, handed Chino the book, and Chino put it in one of the bags.

"Don't get up," Riley said, "you gentlemen sit tight and let me handle this."

He went down the pier, thinking, Such pleasant chaps.

The dogs greeted him, nipping his fingers, scampering about. At the cement shed, he untaped the key off the top ledge of the door frame, opened up, fumbled around on a shelf in the dark until he found the Coleman lamp and turned it on. In the dull glow, he rapped the side of the metal drums standing on the sand floor. He found a full one in the back, lowered it onto its side and rolled it out the door. Rolled it down the trail, crunching seashells. It was drizzling.

The Mexicans crossed the trail, looking like old-fashioned seamen in their big raincoats, taking a leisurely tour of the island.

"Nice night for a stroll," Riley said, pushing the drum, gas sloshing around inside. He rolled the drum onto the pier and stood it up by the boat. He went back to the shed for the hand pump, sweating lightly and feeling a chill. He didn't see the Mexicans when he returned from the shed this time. He stood in the drizzle searching the darkness, holding the gas pump. He couldn't distinguish anything but the shape of coconut trees, the outline of the Robinsons' roof in the distance, and no sound but the trees stirring in the breeze.

Filling up the boat, cranking the pump lever, he yawned and rubbed his eyes, sleep creeping up on the Red Bull.

A burst of firecrackers woke him up. He spun around, toward the island. *What the hell?*

There they went again—*pak pak pak*—and now he recognized that sound, dropped the pump and started running up the pier. He raced along the trail, veered right, through a stand of coconut trees. He saw the stilt house, nobody outside, a light on in the kitchen with one window propped open.

He slowed down to a fast walk, staring at the house, under the house, straining to hear something. Footsteps thundered on the plank floor inside the house, somebody shouted and Miss Rose came lumbering onto the porch, cradling a stick and rocking from side to side on her elephantiasis legs.

Riley called out, "Miss Rose? Miss Rose, what's going on?" and when she brought up the stick to her shoulder and aimed at him, he realized what it was and dove as the shot exploded. He stayed on his belly, covered his head with his arms.

He looked up, getting ready to run, sand in his mouth. He saw one of the Mexicans run out of Julius's room and level a long gun at Miss Rose and fire two shots as she was turning around. She flew into the railing and her shotgun clattered down the steps.

Riley got up on one knee. Then everything started happening strangely fast in his head but in slow motion outside. He saw the Mexican, Temio, step over Miss Rose and walk down the steps. Under the house, a light beam flashed on and Chino appeared out of the darkness with a flashlight, a carbine slung over his shoulder, and Riley understood now—when they had crossed the trail they'd been carrying carbines under their raincoats.

Chino shined the light on the storeroom under the house. Riley stood up, knees trembling. He moved his feet in the direction of the stairs. He stumbled up and crouched for a moment by Miss Rose. There was no helping her. He headed into the house and slipped on something, almost losing his balance.

Blood slicked the kitchen floor. Julius lay on his stomach, limbs twisted at unnatural angles, and a piece of the back of his head was gone. His hand gripped a small Glock, finger on the trigger. His eyes were open, lips parted.

Riley pried the pistol from his fingers. He checked it: a round in the chamber, a stoked magazine. No small bullet casings on the floor; the boy probably hadn't even gotten a shot off. Riley jammed the pistol in his waistband and left the room, passing Miss Rose without looking at her and going down the stairs. The double-barrel shotgun was lying in the sand. He picked it up, broke it open and plucked out the shells. He tossed the empty one and stuck the unspent one back in. He snapped the barrel shut and strode under the house.

The storeroom door was open and the Mexicans had their backs turned. Temio stood in the doorway and Chino was inside, messing with something. Riley halted about ten paces from Temio's back and, clamping the gun stock under his right arm, he slowly raised the double barrel. He had a clear shot. He pulled out the Glock and held it in his left hand. Soon as Temio fell, Riley would start firing the pistol. He needed to be fast. He didn't doubt himself, but his knees were still trembling. He stepped closer, muzzle aimed at a spot between Temio's shoulders, and he heard Chino say, *"Aquí lo tienes,"* and watched him come to the door holding the handles of white buckets in each hand and Temio stepping aside.

Riley lowered the shotgun. Pushed the pistol back into his waistband.

Temio set his carbine down and went into the room and emerged with two more buckets. Riley propped the shotgun against a house post, and just like that, because Riley James considered himself a practical man, his allegiance to the memory of Miss Rose and her son was gone, and he moved forward to give the Mexicans a hand.

Eight buckets. Five minutes later, eight buckets of high-grade Colombian blow was in the V-berth, and Riley felt disgusted with everything. What the hell was Miss Rose thinking? Couldn't have been Julius behind this, he wasn't that smart. And what kind of people were these two Mexicans here? Riley watched them slip their carbines back into the black bags, zip them up, Chino yawning and Temio looking relaxed like all they'd done was a little target practice at the gun range.

For the better part of the ride to Caye Caulker, Riley pushed the worries away. It took intense concentration. The seas were less choppy, and now and again lightning crackled across the sky to the west.

The engines droned inside his skull. His body was humming. All the way to Caye Caulker the Mexicans didn't say a word. It was cold and drizzly when the boat sliced through the calm waters around the back of the island, lights on in the wooden houses on shore. They idled past sailboats anchored in the deep near the long concrete dock, the Back Bridge. There was nobody there. Raindrops pattered the dock.

Chino climbed out and helped Riley moor the boat to the cleat on the dock. Temio consulted his black book again, hunched over, raising a finger to his mouth to wet it and turning the page daintily.

Pressure swelled in Riley's chest, he felt a need to sigh. He shook off his raincoat. He leaned over the gunwale, cupped water in his hands and splashed his face. When he straightened, Temio was staring at him. Riley wiped his face with the front of his shirt. "Something you need?"

"We are meeting McCoy here. You take us to Chapoose Street. To a bar. Mariners Bar. Wait outside. We finish, we go home. Easy, no?"

Riley nodded, afraid of what he might say if he opened his mouth. His head felt tight, his limbs jangly with adrenaline. He knew he needed to calm himself even more or he could get in trouble with these two.

Chino hopped down into the cockpit and once again rummaged through the black bags. This time Riley waited in the boat while they fiddled with their weapons. Steel clanked and clicked. He watched them screw suppressors onto the muzzles of two pistols, push the pistols into the deep side pockets of their military pants.

Chino stood tall and said, *"Vamos pues."*

Riley watched them, two ordinary-looking middle-aged men who could pass for someone's father or uncle or your old friend from high school but hardly cold killers. So as someone associating with them, what did that make him?

Riley climbed out of the boat and led them down the dock. The empty wet street reflected the streetlights. Riley turned left on Cruzita Lane, thinking about Miss Rose sprawled on the porch, the image stuck in his head. He passed a group of men on the verandah of a house talking and laughing uproariously, and he lowered his gaze, wishing he'd kept his raincoat on. The Mexicans had dropped back, one of them smoking a cigarette in a cupped hand.

Riley took a right on Pasero Street, sorting through what had happened, and the pieces he'd put together looked like this: One or both of the Robinsons had helped set up the ambush last night; people who you'd never accuse of craftiness had thought they could outcraft the Monsantos. Dumb move.

He went left on Atux Street, the Mexicans several steps behind. Spanish music floated out of a small bar on the right and a man in the doorway holding a beer bottle waved. Riley stepped over a puddle and carried on, staring straight ahead into the misting rain, to Chapoose Street. He turned right at the corner and pushed his hands into his pockets. His hair and shirt were soaked, he felt cold.

Mariners Bar occupied the ground floor of a square concrete building. There were wood and zinc-roof houses all around, and next door a shop that was closed. Riley went under the overhang of the shop.

He stood there like he was taking cover from the drizzle and saw the Mexicans glance up and down the street before they walked into the bar. He leaned a shoulder against a post and watched raindrops glittering in the glow of a streetlight.

A young girl came out of a gate across the street holding a newspaper over her head and dashed across into another yard. A covered golf cart with two teenage boys rolled past and left a scent of marijuana. Riley could hear voices in the house directly across, its porch lights on, a swing there, flowerpots hanging from the ceiling.

Life going on as usual all around him. He was shivering violently and it wasn't only because of wet clothes. He had no idea how long the Mexicans would take but he wasn't going to stand here too long.

A man came out of Mariners, then another right behind him. They headed in opposite directions. Two minutes later, two more men stumbled out and passed by in the drizzle.

Riley waited until they had gone down the street a ways before he detached himself from the post and strolled by the bar. The door was open. A jukebox playing reggae pulsed light from a corner in the semidarkness. The place was empty except for beer bottles on the tables, and Chino sitting at the bar in his long raincoat. Riley stood at the window and peered in. The bartender was standing still, not talking, just looking seriously at Chino, and Temio was nowhere to be seen.

Riley returned to the overhang and wiped rain from his eyes. He inhaled, deep and slow to control his shivering. A woman stepped onto the porch of the house across the street, hugging a baby bundled in a white blanket. Thunder rolled across the sky.

In a flash of lightning Riley saw the woman sitting sideways on the swing, legs out as she unwrapped the baby like a fruit, hiked her blouse and put the child to her breast. Riley lowered his eyes. Wished he had a cigarette even though he didn't smoke, something to do with his hands so he didn't look odd standing there. Hell, he wished he wasn't there at all.

The woman, a young face, was gazing in his direction, but he wasn't sure she could see his features. He heard something from the bar and glanced over. Someone had shut the door. Just in case, Riley smiled up at the woman, playing casual, then looked down the street.

Lightning flashed and thunder cracked, and Riley waited until it was dark again before he ambled over to the bar. He could hear shouts from inside. He peeked through the window and saw chairs and broken bottles scattered across the floor, puddles of water or beer.

Temio and Chino were walking around the room, then Riley saw two men lying on their stomachs, hands roped behind their backs. Temio was speaking to them; Riley couldn't hear what he was saying, the music was too loud. Temio squatted by one of the men and said something. The man twisted his body to the side and replied. Riley recognized the bartender. Chino rushed the man and delivered a kick in the ribs. The man curled up tight.

Riley said, "Goddamn," and looked up and down the street. He checked the door: locked. He hurried back to his post. He was hating this, made up his mind: If anybody who faintly resembled police arrived, he was gone, no looking back. He was getting in that boat and speeding off and fuck the Mexicans.

He adjusted the pistol in his waistband, knowing he might

need to drop it in the sea. He kept breathing deeply, not shivering so much anymore. A long flash of lightning lit up the street and the houses all around and he saw the young woman on the porch turn her face, and their eyes met.

She was stunning. Black hair in twin braids over her shoulder and almond-shaped eyes. The sky went dark again and thunder clapped, and he could still see the image of her face and it disturbed him, something about her; it struck him deep.

He knew she must've seen his face as clearly as he'd seen hers, so now he had to move. The rain had intensified, drilling the street and the zinc roofs. He scoped another house farther up the street with a verandah overhang he could use for cover. It would take him away from the bar but he needed to move, and it wasn't only to avoid her identifying him, it was to get away from a kind of innocence he'd recognized when she looked at him. He didn't care for the way it made him feel.

He lowered his head and headed into the rain. The bar door creaked open just then and Temio poked his head out and called, *"Hermano."*

Riley trotted over, the pistol loosening under his shirt. He fixed it in place, walked into the bar, Temio locking the door behind him. The room was a mess.

Temio motioned for him to grab two white buckets by overturned bar stools. Riley hesitated, but in his mind he saw the Mexican shooting Miss Rose, and Riley picked up the buckets.

Chino stormed out of the restroom at the back, near the jukebox. He rattled off something in Spanish to Temio and Temio marched over to him.

Riley put down the buckets and followed him through the pounding funk from the jukebox, and he walked into the flooded men's restroom. The white tile wall was splattered with blood and there was a dead man lying under the urinals.

Chino had opened a utility closet and was taking white

buckets out from behind mops, brooms, and cardboard boxes. He set the buckets on the floor, four of them. Riley saw shoes sticking out from under a bathroom stall, the legs splayed.

He said, real tense, to the Mexicans, "Let's get going," and left the room.

He was seething. Things had gotten way out of hand. These guys were insane. He stood by the two buckets outside and waited. They were taking too long and he said, "Let's go, man," just as they came out of the restroom. Temio shot him a look, but Riley didn't give a shit now. He needed them to understand he wasn't putting himself at any further risk; he was not going to be an accessory to any more killings tonight. Fuck them, fuck the Monsantos, and when he returned to the city, he'd let Israel know it straight up, he wouldn't hold back. You want to sink fast? he'd tell him. Keep working with El Padrón and these two wackjobs.

Riley and the Mexicans carried the buckets, two apiece, through the streets in the hard rain. All around, windows and doors were closed. Wind gusts shook trees in the yards. More than once, Riley looked back and saw that the Mexicans had stopped to rest. Standing in the middle of the street, hands on hips like two cowboys. Idiots, no other word for them.

He reached the boat and rearranged the other buckets in the V-berth to make space. He pushed his two buckets in and put on his slicker, took the helm and started the engines. While the Mexicans slid their buckets in, he undid the lines and swung the bow away from the dock before they could properly take their seats.

He didn't know exactly when he'd stopped shivering, but he was wide awake, testy, in fact. He didn't speak the entire ride back, glad to be occupied with the rough waves. Glad when he saw Chino grip the edge of his seat, looking like he was about to puke.

The rain had slowed and the sea had leveled out to a medium chop when they saw the city lights, the Baron Bliss Lighthouse blinking. Temio stood, tucking away his black book and holding on to the back of his seat for balance. He gestured to Riley, pointing north. "Buttonwood Bay!"

Riley steered the boat north, cutting across the direction of the waves. They hugged the coast for a couple of miles and headed around Moho Caye, a shadowy clump of mangroves and moored sailboats. Riley was counting down the minutes. First thing, after they unloaded at the Monsantos' bay house, he was going to shed these wet clothes, poke around in Carlo's closet for something that looked decent, slip into them. Then maybe warm up with Scotch or bourbon or whatever they kept in their cabinet. Prepare himself for Israel's and Carlo's rants when he told them they were short four of the eighteen buckets. He'd sip his drink and listen, let them lean into him for a bit, then he'd warn them about ever dealing with the Mexicans again. He'd say his farewell to working with the Monsantos and he'd be done with it.

If they wanted to be difficult with him about the four missing buckets—what was that, 140 kilos?—well, maybe he'd offer to work one last shipment for free. . . .

What the hell was he thinking? He'd *never* do that. Losses were part of the trade, and he'd done enough. Get your head right, Riley. Seems that being out on the sea in this weather with two lunatics was corroding his brain.

But hold on—what was Temio saying? He was pointing northwest.

Riley leaned in, against the wheel, cupping an ear.

Temio said, "This way, this way."

They were in the bay, lights dotting the coastline, and out of habit Riley had been steering the boat toward the land, the Monsantos' dock less than a mile away. Now, Riley pulled back on the throttle. "You know where you going?" he said to Temio.

Temio had taken out his black book again, reading with a flashlight. He said, "Go to the canals. You know the canals?"

"Just around the bend? The new development?"

"Go down the second canal, to a house. I show you, okay?"

So that's where the missing buckets must be. The long night wasn't over yet. He idled close to the land so he wouldn't miss the canal but stayed far out enough to avoid the shallows. It seemed to take forever before he spotted the entrance to the first canal, a towering white house on the edge, terraces, private seawall.

Temio pointed to the second canal up ahead, and Chino crouched by the V-berth and started pulling out the duffel bags.

Riley eased back on the throttle and steered the boat to the left, gliding into the canal, and he was shivering again. Temio and Chino were crouched by the bags, getting their weapons ready. The boat rumbled slowly past two-story houses, most of them dark, a dock here and there. Temio told Riley to keep going. Chino slung his carbine over a shoulder, under his raincoat. Temio pushed a loaded magazine into a pants pocket.

Some of the yards were lighted with spotlights from the houses. Cars and SUVs sat in carports. A dog behind a chain-link fence barked at the boat. Temio pointed to his right.

Riley's throat had tightened; he was pretty sure where they were going.

Temio counted off the houses with a finger. One, two, three, and yes—that one, with the light in the upstairs window.

The one with the turret. Riley's world turned darker. He steered the boat toward the dock, his fingers ice cold. The Mexicans stood up, ready. The boat edged closer to the dock, tapping the rubber tires nailed to the posts. Chino climbed out to tie the lines, while Riley looked up at his friend Harvey's house.

Harvey, man, what did you do? What did you get yourself into?

Riley felt like he'd been punched in the heart.

Chino secured the lines and Riley cut the engines. Then all he could hear was the rain pattering his slicker and the lonely barking of the dog. The boat dipped when Temio stepped off and stood on the dock beside Chino.

Riley couldn't be certain if they knew that Harvey was his business partner, his friend. He figured the Monsantos must have filled them in but he couldn't be certain about anything tonight except this: Whatever he thought was of no consequence to the Monsantos and these two killers marching down the dock. Riley looked up at the window light, looked at the Mexicans, near the end of the dock now. He and his buddy Harvey were two zeros, one friend hired to lead two stone killers to the other friend's house so they could slaughter him.

If Riley did nothing, he was worth nothing. He said, "Hey, wait up," and climbed out of the boat.

The Mexicans continued walking.

Riley trotted up the dock and said, "Hey!" and they stopped and turned, almost casually. Riley raised his hand to tell them to wait, like he'd forgotten to mention something.

"I know the guy who lives here." He waited to see if either face registered concern, however slight. Nothing came, and he said, "I know where he might've hidden the stuff," walking past them now, taking the lead. "Two places. A pump room under the house, over there. Or it could be upstairs, like in a rec room closet."

He had reached the end of the dock, but the Mexicans hadn't moved. Deciding what to make of him.

When he spoke again, he couldn't help the tremor in his

voice, the pleading tone, "Look, we rush in there, let me handle things. We could get this stuff clean, no shots fired, no trouble."

Temio approached, shaking his head. "No, no, we need to talk to this man. We need to leave a lesson tonight." He called over his shoulder, "Chino, *vamos*."

Riley hurried to stay well ahead of them, blowing on his hands to warm them. He said, "Look, I'm begging you, let me handle this, let me do it the easy way. Please." But he glanced back and saw they weren't listening anymore. He might as well have been that dog still barking on the other side of the canal.

Riley trudged through Harvey's muddy backyard and thought, Well then. What else you got? The answer was nothing. So his hand ducked under the slicker and folded around the pistol in his waistband. He took two steps, spun around and said, "This can't happen."

They were about five yards back, coming up fast. Temio stopped, seeing him blocking the way. "What you say?"

Riley's hand flew up from under the slicker and he shot Temio twice. Temio stumbled back, and Riley shot again, swiveled from the waist and swung the gun on Chino and fired as flame spurted from Chino's carbine. He was carrying it low, how he'd produced it so fast Riley couldn't say, Chino firing, muzzle jerking. Riley fired back, feeling heat ripping through his abdomen.

He tried to lift himself off the ground. He didn't know how he'd gotten there. He rose on hands and knees, his ears ringing. The shooting had stopped, he didn't know why.

Chino was walking away, holding his throat.

Riley knew he'd been hit, his stomach was on fire. He knew Chino was hurting, too, staggering away, gripping his throat, coughing, a gurgle. Riley groped around in the mud for the pistol, glancing at Chino tottering toward the dock, Riley tossing handfuls of muck. *"Shit, shit, where is it. . . ."*

Chino's carbine fell, clanging on the dock. He reached the boat, hunched over, two hands clamped over his neck like he was trying to hold something in.

Riley found the pistol, wiped it off with one hand and shook water out of the barrel. He pushed himself up, his knees buckled. He took one step, another step, body clenching against the fire in his torso.

Chino was trying to untie the boat lines from the post. It was drizzling again, and the dog was barking crazily. Riley stiffened his back as tall as he could bear it and walked through the pain. Moaning. It hurt so fucking bad.

Chino had untied the boat and jumped into the cockpit, holding the rope. He swayed, lurched toward the helm and crashed into a seat. Riley walked to the boat. Chino used the steering wheel to pull himself up, hands slipping momentarily, but he was up and standing and he looked at Riley. He lifted a palm and said, *"Espera. Por favor. Espera."*

Riley reached the boat with his pistol held straight out, and he let off two quick shots. Chino shouted and dropped back against the gunwale, and Riley shot him two more times. Chino's head slumped forward and he toppled sideways onto the floor.

Riley's ears were ringing hard. Lights had come on in house windows across the canal. Lightning crashed across the sky and he could see Temio lying in the mud in Harvey's yard. Rain was falling harder, and he needed to move, but his legs felt frozen.

Then some primal part of him took over, the old street Riley. He jammed the pistol back under his slicker. Looped the boat lines around a post. His torso clenched and he sucked in a breath before he continued.

He dragged Temio's body by the legs down the dock. Stopped to rest. Dragged it farther and tumbled it into the boat. Went back for Temio's carbine in the mud, picked Chino's carbine off the dock and carried both rifles into the boat. Then he collapsed in the captain's chair.

He moaned, pressing a forearm against his abdomen. He said to himself, "Come on, punk, get your ass up, get moving." But it took forever—to lift himself off the chair and haul the rope in; fumble with the key and turn the ignition; push the throttle—every movement hurt.

Swaying in the chair, he navigated the boat through the canal at an unsafe speed. Emergency speed, because he had no doubt he was bleeding to death. He'd reached a hand under his slicker and under his shirt and touched a warm ooze. His fingers had come away sticky and covered in blood.

Out on the sea, the boat tossed and rolled from the high waves and his clumsy steering. Visibility was poor, but he knew that if he held to a line along the shore and followed the houselights he'd be able to pick out the Monsantos' dock, the only question, would he pass out before he arrived.

He didn't want to look at the wound. He feared how his mind would react when he inspected the damage. Recognizing a pattern of houselights, he guessed the distance he'd traveled from the canal, then aimed the boat at the shore. He batted the throttle down to idle and he closed his eyes, couldn't help it, as the boat dipped and rose toward land.

With a start, he remembered, and pulled the pistol out. He pitched it overboard. He stumbled around while the boat listed. Found the rifles and thought, What am I doing? You don't need to get rid of these. You're not thinking straight.

At the Monsantos' dock he secured the boat as firmly as his trembling fingers would allow, threw the rifles into the V-berth and padlocked it. Pressing both forearms against his abdomen, he walked down the dock, wincing all the way, through the backyard and up the stairs.

On the front porch he dug into the soil of a bamboo tree in a big clay planter, plucked out a matchbox and took out a house key. He opened the door and walked into the foyer and then the kitchen, trekking soil and water and drops of blood on the marble tiles. He grabbed the phone and bumped along the hallway walls and into the bathroom. He flicked the lights on and set the phone down. Self-consciously deliberate, he took off his slicker, his shirt, and looked at the vanity mirror.

His abdomen was smeared with blood. The front of his pants soaked dark red. At first he couldn't find the hole. At one point, he thought he was going to vomit. He found it, just under his navel. Two holes. In and out—the bullet had passed straight through that fatty middle-age pouch.

He said to the mirror, "All right, you son of a bitch, you might live."

He picked up the phone and dialed his friend's house.

"Miles, please. Yes . . . tell him it's Riley." After a few seconds, "Miles? I need your help. You better . . . come quick."

He gave Miles the address and hung up, dropped the phone on the counter. He stripped naked, kneeled in the tub and turned the faucet on. He washed the wound gently with warm water and a bar of soap, letting the tub fill up. After a while he sat far back, water sudsing pink with blood, rising to his waist.

To his chest.

He shut his eyes and waited for Miles, the fast-rising water lapping at his neck.

CHAPTER TWENTY-ONE

The waiter set the platters of stewed snappers and the bowl of yellow rice on the table, and another glass of Sprite for Candice.

Malone rattled his glass of ice at the waiter. "I could do with another Johnnie Walker Black. Less ice this time?" He handed off the glass brusquely.

After the waiter left, he said, "Notice he didn't bother asking me if I wanted a refill." He leaned over the food, examined it. "What's this on top of the fish?"

"Those are onions," Candice said.

"Huh. Why are they red?"

"If you look closely, the entire fish is red. It's a local seasoning. You ever heard of *recado*?"

Malone eyed the fish. "Why do they serve it like this, with the head?"

Candice said, patiently, "Because that's how this dish is prepared. A whole stewed snapper. That's what it's called. It's not a fillet, Henry."

"I don't know about this . . ."

Candice spooned yellow rice onto her plate, Malone watching her. She broke off a section of her snapper with the edge of the spoon and put it on her plate. She ladled some of the broth and onions over the rice.

Cautiously, Malone followed her lead.

She said, "What's wrong with you today?"

"I could ask you the same thing. I've been watching you. Your body's here, but your mind is out to sea."

She lowered her eyes and ate some rice. Yes, she *was* a ball of nerves. She didn't know where Riley was. She'd called his house and the bar several times. No answer. She couldn't stop thinking about him.

Malone tried to shake salt on his food but nothing sprinkled out. He banged the shaker on the table and tried again. "Couldn't they have put a little rice in here? Haven't they heard of humidity before?" Banged the shaker again. A woman at a window table turned to look at him.

They were at the Château Caribbean, windows open to the sea air, and before Malone's little snit-fit everyone had been having a quiet lunch. Candice reached over and calmly pried the shaker away. Malone laid his forearms on the table and exhaled heavily. She unscrewed the cap, turned it over and cleared the holes and the opening of the bottle with a finger, screwed the cap back on and set the shaker down in front of him. "Would you look at that. The magic of patience."

He sprinkled salt over his fish. "Sorry." He picked up his knife and fork, looked out the big windows facing the sea. "Just in a pissy mood today."

After his drink came, they ate in peace. He admitted the fish was much tastier than it appeared, except he might have to pass on the head, those teeth. Like the fish was grinning at him.

Candice said, "But we get the last laugh because we're eating him and he's so yummy," hoping to lighten things up.

Malone wiped his lips with the napkin. "My wife is leaving."

Candice set her fork down.

"She said she's had enough. Enough of this heat, the dust. How there's nothing to do here. She says she misses all the conveniences of the States. She wants to catch a sale at Macy's, she wants to swing by 7-Eleven and grab a Slurpee, I'm not kidding." He tossed the napkin on the table and sat back. "As if I don't have enough to think about."

"I'm sorry to hear."

"Well, what are you gonna do, right? Maybe now I can put more time into smoothing out this new wrinkle. This wrinkle being that we have reason to believe the people who stole the Monsantos' shipment are local police officers."

Candice said, "Why does this not shock me?"

"Furthermore, our sources identified who might be in possession of the shipment, and guess what? One of the men whose names came up was found dead in a bar this morning. Shot in the back of the head, execution style. No witnesses. No suspects so far. No drugs found on the premises."

"Premises being where?"

"A bar on Caye Caulker. The place was ransacked, and if drugs were there, they've been taken. By whom is the question. We may yet answer that if we continue to investigate, but the bigger question is whether this operation will continue or not. We've got to sit down with the police commissioner and the head of the Coast Guard. I've arranged a meeting for tomorrow."

Candice said, "We'd heard from the start that some of the local police were not to be trusted, isn't that the case?"

"What's your point?" Malone getting defensive.

"I'm simply imagining the conversation tomorrow. The commissioner, he'll say the same thing he said last time, you remember? Bang that desk a few times, act huffy, bluster, 'No, never, not on my watch! We've rooted out all the rogue elements from this force.' Might even imply that Mr. Yankee shouldn't come into his office making these unsubstantiated accusations if he expects cooperation."

"He might, but it'll be hard to ignore the facts. The man killed last night in the bar was a police officer. Furthermore, we have reason to believe—and this comes to us from another person involved who didn't like the way the stolen shipment was divvied up and he complained to someone who just happens to be our informer—we have reason to believe that a person with considerable authority spearheaded the robbery."

"Someone on the police force? The defense force?"

Malone spread his hands. "Pick one. But it's someone with muscle. Political clout."

Candice put her knife and fork down and pushed her plate away. "Okay, I see where this is going."

Malone sipped his drink. "If we can't be assured of getting local law enforcement support we're in for a tedious campaign. If we uncover something that some big shot wants uncovered, then . . ." He shrugged. "At this point we don't have a clue how high up the hierarchy this is going. We're tugging one way, someone or some group is tugging the other. We need to find out where we stand in this game or we just might not play anymore, and that's why I'm arranging this meeting. To tell them how it's going to be."

Candice needed to understand something clearly. "And where does this put us as far as tracking the movements of the Monsantos—and my neighbor?"

The waiter appeared at the table. "Uh . . . miss? Excuse me?" He held out a folded slip of paper. "A lady in the lounge," he gestured to the wide-open doors to another room, "she asked me to give you this."

Candice opened the note. It was written in neat cursive: *A moment of your time to talk about Riley? Thank you.*

Malone said, "Something wrong?"

Candice shook her head briskly. The coincidence of the moment was too much; she managed a phony smile. "Can you excuse me a sec? Just a client wants to speak to me." She rose from her chair, dropping the napkin on the floor. "It's about a photo shoot. Let me get rid of her, it'll be quick."

Malone checked his watch. "I need to be somewhere in a half hour."

"This won't take long."

There were only a few people in the lounge, two men at the bar and a young couple at a table by an open window. From the far corner, Sister Pat raised her hand.

They exchanged hellos. Sister Pat motioned for Candice to have a seat. There was a plate of Chinese food on the table, a glass of Coke with ice and a straw. Candice sat down across from her. "What's going on, Patricia?"

"Thanks for calling me that. You know how long I've been asking Riley to call me by my real name? He says he just can't. 'Sister Pat,' it's like a habit." She sighed. "Riley is in the hospital, dear."

Before Candice could make a sound, Sister Pat said, "Now, now, it's not that serious. . . . Well, it could've been, but he's doing fine. As a matter of fact, he could be discharged as early as tomorrow."

"What happened?"

Patricia took a big breath. "He was shot."

"*Shot?* When?"

"It happened last night. I don't know the details, and frankly I haven't asked. But I paid him a quick visit this morning and he looks fine, considering."

"What hospital?"

"Caribbean."

Candice, without realizing it, had put a hand to her chest, and now she could feel her heart pounding. "How did—I don't mean to sound resentful, but why didn't he call me? Do you know?"

"He didn't call me either, his doctor did. A childhood friend of his. Alfred Gonzalez knows I'm about the closest thing he has to family and called me this morning."

"This is a shock." Candice stood up. "I should go. . . ." She looked again at Patricia sitting there with her uneaten plate of Chinese food and full glass of Coke, sitting for a solitary lunch. In a bar. And Candice remembered Riley telling her once months ago, explaining his close relationship to Patricia, that she was a recovering alcoholic. The other nuns at St. Catherine used to be awakened some mornings by liquor bottles clinking in her market bag as she skulked by on her way to a downstairs garbage bin.

Candice said, watching her tone, "Patricia, why didn't you call to tell me this as soon as you found out?"

Patricia put down her drink. She looked hurt. "Dear, I don't have your number. It's unlisted, and when I went to your house this morning, you weren't there."

"I see."

"I was hoping not to upset you too much, but I'm beginning to realize that I did. I'm sorry."

"When you visited Riley, did he ask you not to tell me because he didn't want me to worry?"

Patricia looked at her tenderly. "Yes. He wanted to tell you after he was discharged."

Candice didn't know what to make of that answer. She thanked Patricia and tried to smile. But on the way to the dining room, something struck her as odd, and she turned back.

Patricia looked up, surprised to see her there again.

Candice said, "Can I ask you something? How did you know I was going to be here?"

"I didn't."

"You didn't? It just seems a bit strange, that's all."

Patricia folded her hands in her lap and leaned forward. "Candice? This is one of a handful of places in this little city that makes a decent lunch. I come here every other Wednesday for the buffet, my dear. See over there, near the wall?"

Candice saw the silver chafing dishes and pans on the long buffet table for the first time.

"Sometimes I come on Thursday, though I find the Wednesday selection to be more consistent. Their jerk shrimp salad is divine. I'm assuming you're here for lunch? The buffet runs until two, so if I had to guess I'd say meeting you here is serendipity. That's all it is, okay?"

Candice felt her face getting red. She said, "Then my apologies, and thanks again." As she was leaving, Patricia called after her, "Oh, Candice?" and Candice turned around. Patricia beckoned to her, and Candice came closer, annoyed.

"Riley needs to see you at his bedside, no matter what he thinks. Don't waste another minute being distrustful of me, Candice, go see Riley. It'll be good for him."

Candice kept her mouth shut and headed back to the dining room before she made another mistake.

CHAPTER TWENTY-TWO

Riley sat by the window screen in the hallway enjoying the sea breeze on his chest, eyes closed, shirt open. So pleasant he didn't want to move. Some of the bliss was probably the Demerol Dr. Gonz had given him for the pain, but he wasn't complaining.

This might be his last restful moment for a long time, and he didn't think he was being pessimistic, but realistic: He had fallen into a snake pit last night and now had to do some scrambling to get out.

Gonz had dressed the wound this morning, wrapping the bandage around Riley's midsection and propping bed pillows high for Riley's comfort. "Sure you don't want a private room?" he had asked Riley. Riley declined, said he didn't intend to stay very long.

"Riley, what did you get yourself into this time?" Then Gonz shook his head. "On second thought, none of my business."

Riley had given his friend a smile, a family man whom he hardly saw anymore, a man who, unlike Riley, had always known what he wanted to be and had excelled in high school, breezed through college in the States then med school in Jamaica. Time and lifestyles had separated them, but Riley understood that the friendships you made in childhood were the ones that lasted.

Like his friendship with Harvey? It was too soon to know if Harvey would be the exception. What Harvey had done hurt as much as the gunshot.

How about Miles? Yeah, Miles was a man he could count on.

Riley said, "Gonz, how do you make outgoing calls?"

"Press nine. Listen, I told Sister Pat. Don't be mad at me. I thought she'd like to know."

"I'm not mad at you. Hey, could you bring that phone this way?"

Gonz had rolled the table with the phone over to the bed, said he'd return in a few hours to check on him then take it from there, but honestly?—he'd like to keep Riley in for at least two days for observation, make sure the wound was cleaned properly. "Now, let me give you some privacy." He nodded at the two men sleeping in the other beds in the room. "Privacy, as it were."

After Gonz left, Riley had telephoned Miles.

Miles answered, "Big boss, how's it hanging?"

Riley said, "Thanks for last night. Got a minute? I think I'm going to need your help again."

They had talked briefly, but long enough for Riley to feel confident that he was taking the correct measures to protect himself.

Now, woozy, he lifted himself off the chair by the screen and walked gingerly back to his room. He climbed into bed slowly. The bullet had ripped through the outermost muscle in his lower abdomen, and the pain radiated from his wound to his groin. Recuperation time? According to Gonz, at least three weeks.

Well, then consider doctor's orders defied, because Riley wouldn't have three weeks, and he couldn't half step. He was in the Monsantos' sights—he wasn't going to fool himself about that one. When he had called at noon, Israel listened to his story, asking in a tone of great concern if Riley was sure he was okay and was there anything he needed. Magazines maybe, or a good hot meal that didn't taste like hospital food? Then Israel suggested a transfer to Karl Heusner Memorial, he had friends there. Riley knew that the Monsantos' connections ran deep and they'd be able to keep tabs on him better if he were there, could exert their control if they reckoned it necessary, so he'd brushed off the suggestion.

Israel had accepted his story for the time being, but more questions would come, and Riley was preparing.

He lay in bed listening to the waves outside and thinking about last night, remembering only some spots with clarity. He did recall early this morning, talking to Sister Pat through the haze of Demerol, a strong dose he was grateful for. Though he had wanted to talk, he kept the impulse in check and simply held Sister Pat's hand, telling her he'd be okay, he'd be just fine, don't worry.

He remembered, as she got up to leave, he motioned to her and she brought an ear to his lips and he whispered, "I did it again . . . I did it again, Sister Pat," and the tears came. He covered his eyes. He told her, "Two men again. Just like the last time."

Sister Pat placed a warm hand on his cheek, then over his mouth. "Now isn't the time, dear. We'll talk later." She kissed him on his head and was gone.

Then he slept a long time and woke up to find a lunch tray on the bedside table and Candice walking into the room. A scene similar to Sister Pat's visit replayed. He tried to be honest without being honest all the way, saying, "Candice, there are some things you better know about me. I'm in a little situation here."

"Are the cops looking for you?"

"No—not as far as I know."

"Is anyone else looking for you?"

He said, "No."

"Then shhh," and she put a finger over his lips. "I want you to recover. Don't waste your energy worrying, just rest."

He lay back on the pillow and looked at her, her eyes glistening. "It's going to be all right. The doctor is a friend of mine, I trust him."

"Have I met him?"

"Not through my introductions."

"I'll have to meet him sometime."

He looked up at the ceiling so he wouldn't have to stare at her face and feel so alienated from her. Like a part of him had changed. "I was thinking how much I respect you, you know? You not being from here but how you mixed in well with people. How you probably heard all these stories about me but you never brought those things up. I respect that." He studied her face, then turned his eyes back to the ceiling and said, "But I was thinking, even though I love you, and I do love you, I can't deny it, I might not be the best person for you. It could be I'm trouble, like a lotta people think. Bad news."

"Stop, Riley."

He shifted around to get comfortable and grimaced from a tug of pain.

"You okay?" Her hand reaching out to his shoulder. She left it there.

"It might be," she said, "there's something you don't know about me either."

He agreed. She said, "So there," and they sat in silence for a while as the room cooled with the afternoon breeze. Nurses passed by in the screened hallway. An old white man in a Cardinals baseball cap was parked by the screen in a wheelchair.

Every now and again he'd smile at the nurses and one time he smiled at Candice. Riley asked if it had rained today; she said no, and they held hands, Riley understanding that they'd talk about the important matters in private. There might be time. For now, just be with her.

He fell asleep that night remembering those quiet minutes.

A jolt of pain woke him up and he hurt himself when he sat up fast in the dark. One of his roommates was snoring softly, the other one talking in his sleep. The air-conditioning hummed but the room was stifling. Riley slid out of bed and walked to the half-open door, testing the ground for any Demerol tilt. The breeze in the hallway felt nice, and he found a plastic chair and dragged it closer to the screen and sat down.

He had a notion that his life had altered irrevocably. The man he thought he could be was never going to be. He was a killer and he was going to have to learn to live with that. When you do something, do it fully, be absorbed by it. Where had he read that? Didn't matter. It was true. He would have to burn with the will to survive and do whatever it took without judgment and regrets. It scared him somewhat to think like that, but fear was good if it kept you alive.

He heard someone coming down the hall, turned to see the old man in the Cardinals cap rolling up in his wheelchair. The man paused to rest, smiling at Riley. He eventually parked beside Riley, facing the screen. He blew out a sigh, then coughed, pasty skin between his collarbones sinking in. Wiping his lips and gazing ahead serenely, he said, "Can't sleep either, uh?"

Riley said, "Panic attack." For some reason, he felt it didn't matter if he told anyone. In fact, it felt good to tell someone; he'd suffered them off and on for years.

"I see. Can't say I've ever experienced one. But I know what it is to be terrified." The old man nodded, looked Riley in the eyes. "Full of dread. Weepy with existential horror."

Riley thought, Whoa. Who's this guy?

The man said, "I'm dying. That's how I know."

Riley took a moment. "I'm sorry. What are you sick with?"

"Life. Hoping too much, wanting too much. But they call it cancer. Of the pancreas."

"I'm sorry." Riley not knowing what else to say.

"I'm angry. Well . . . maybe not. I'm beginning to accept it. My mind. My body gave in to it a long time ago. Life is like that, I'm afraid. The human brain, it's always playing catch-up to nature's will."

Riley nodded, staring at the darkness beyond the screen. He could hear crickets chirping downstairs, waves lapping.

"Roger Hunter," the man said, sticking out a hand.

They shook. The man's wrists were bony but his grip wasn't bad. "Riley." He looked at the man closely. "Where do I know you from? I think I know you from somewhere."

"I used to live here, in the city, many years ago."

"Roger Hunter . . ." Riley musing on the name. Then, "Yeah," snapping his fingers and grinning at the old man. "Father Hunter, Jesuit."

"You were a St. John's boy?"

"Yes. But you never taught me. I think you left a couple years before I got kicked out. Father Hunter, man. It's been a long time."

"So, I suppose I left behind some stories?"

"Maybe. You quit the priesthood because of a woman, that's what they say. Among other things."

That brought a smile. "So that's what they say? It's not true. I quit because, well—why did I quit? Because I hated being a priest. I wasn't a very good priest."

Riley smiled. "Heard that, too."

Roger Hunter lifted his chin and shut his eyes, inhaling a deep draft of sea air. "I wish I could say I'm ready to go, but I'm not. Are you afraid of dying, young man?"

Riley said, "I don't think so. I figure when you're ready to go, you go. Like falling asleep. What's there to be afraid of?"

"Then are you ready to die?"

"Now I wouldn't go so far as to say that."

Roger Hunter focused straight ahead. "Because you still have too much living to do. Long walks. Books to read. A glass or two of single malt in the evening. Women to hold." He turned to Riley. "Funny, I find myself craving a woman's company. Which I find perplexing. Assaulted by that sort of desire when my body is withering away like this?"

"Can I ask you a question? Something I heard, way back. They said you fought alongside rebels in El Salvador. Is that true?"

The old man shook his head. "Rebels? Funny how the word gets twisted and appropriated by the people in power. They were *campesinos*. Poor farm workers. Dirt poor. That was Salvador, late seventies. I took up arms, yes, I walked with them, but it was all too brief."

Riley said, "What do you mean 'walked'?"

"Do you know what liberation theology is? No? It's the name books give to the movement I was a part of. Christian socialism, they call it. I prefer to call it justice. Christian justice for the poor and oppressed. Being politically active on behalf of those whose daily existence is an unfair struggle, not merely preaching about it and praying for it, but *demanding* it. It's what I did for several months there. I believed in it." He smiled and patted Riley's forearm. "Didn't mean to preach at you like that."

"You didn't. Believe me, it's better listening to you than to sit here just champing at the bit to go home. So go right ahead, tell me more."

"Not much to tell. After Romero was killed and nothing was done about hunting his killers, no one brought to justice . . . I fought. I fought like hell. But we were outgunned, we weren't as organized, we suffered too many causalities, and I lost faith in some of the other leaders. So I folded. Gave myself a break from the constant fighting."

"You left?"

"I've always wanted to return. But that time has passed. Sometimes, I think that my friends should've picked up guns *before* Romero died." Roger Hunter shook a fist. "*Create* change. Seize the power. You know who Romero is, don't you?"

"I remember a priest if that's who you mean. Assassinated during a mass or something?"

"An archbishop, but yes, it was during a sermon. A single shot to the heart. I was still in the priesthood then. I was in El Salvador for his funeral. It was huge, I tell you. Over two hundred thousand people from all over the world gathered in the Plaza Barrios for the funeral mass. Never seen so many people in one place. It scared the government. They thought they had silenced that one loud voice—Romero—now they were hearing thousands. A chorus."

Roger Hunter sniffed the air, eyes closed. He said, softly, "I was a damn fool. To think that the powers that be wouldn't perceive that as a threat, that they would tolerate it."

There was a long silence. Riley said, "So what happened?"

"Too much," Roger Hunter said. "About twenty minutes before the mass began, a bomb went off somewhere in the square. It felt like someone had thumped me hard in my chest. People started running and screaming, then the shooting started. I didn't know where it was coming from at first. People were pointing here and there at the surrounding buildings, people were scattering, some were falling down, and only when they didn't get up I realized, only then, that it was because they'd been shot. It took me *that* long to accept that it was really happening. I ran, ducked my head and fled to a building to take cover behind some columns. It was mass panic. Women, men, teenagers—everyone was a target. I saw gunfire flashing from rooftops, and everybody was running, absolutely terrified. Good god, it seemed to go on forever.

"When it was over, when the shooting finally stopped, there was this chilling quiet, I'll never forget it. Then the people on the ground started moving. Some of them were trying to crawl away, you know? Moaning and crying. Me? I was transfixed. There's this image I can never shake. Piles of shoes in the square. People who had escaped had practically run out of their shoes, and I couldn't get over that. I couldn't stop staring at the shoes. I was in complete shock."

Roger Hunter shook his head, returning from the far-off place in his mind. "What a day. That day—that was the day I most felt that I was going to die. And yet, that was the day I felt most alive. And what brought me to that point? The fact that I dared, by my presence alone, ask for what I thought was right, something those very rooftop shooters would've asked for themselves if they'd been poor and struggling. A chance for a better life, just a chance. Not charity, not welfare but *opportunity*. And then to be shot at like a hunted duck? No, no . . . that was much more than my psyche could handle. Never again, I told myself, never again. You want something in this life, you cannot plead, you cannot appeal to the better nature of people, you must be firm and do your best to meet them on equal terms, and if that means leveling the field by the necessary tools—you understand what I'm saying?—then that's the way it must be."

Roger Hunter coughed, covered his mouth, and coughed again. He was worked up, his face had reddened. Riley tapped his feet for want of something better to do and said, "I agree with you," wishing he had something meaningful to add, but all he could think of was, Don't worry, I know where you're coming from. Riley felt like explaining that since he was a kid he'd never waited for someone to deign to give him opportunity. He had created it himself, maybe by undercover means, but it had worked for him. Just like it works for certain government ministers with their hands in the public till. Justice? Riley's method had its own justice. He'd dispensed some last night and now he'd have to live with that, his psyche would have to overcome that.

Roger Hunter said, "Listen to me sermonizing like this. I'm filled with this fire and self-righteousness, and all for naught now. I used to fancy myself a man of action. Up until a few months ago, I'd have wild dreams of being in the thick of battles, honestly. I still want to hear gunshots, yells, warnings. *Look out! Watch it!* I never thought it was going to be like this, death coming so quietly and slowly, maybe visit me when I'm unprepared in the middle of the night."

Riley nodded with understanding. The screen trembled in a gust of breeze.

"Uh-oh," Roger Hunter said, "I should get back to my room." He was looking past Riley, down the hall. A short nurse in bright whites tramped toward them, a stern Caribbean Florence Nightingale.

Roger Hunter rolled his wheelchair backward and spun it skillfully up the hall. He looked over his shoulder. "Didn't mean to depress you. I hope that gunshot wound heals fast and you can get out of here, back to your life. All the best, young man."

He wheeled away. At the room two doors down from Riley's, he spun to his left and rolled in. The nurse marched past Riley, muttering.

Riley sat there for a moment before he thought, Wait. I didn't tell him I'd been shot.

He guessed word just got around. He returned to his room on steady legs, feeling like he could sleep now. He lay in bed and covered himself with the thin sheet and heard one of his roommates peeing into a urinal bottle.

Before Riley shut his eyes, he thought how he didn't want to be full of rage when he died. He wanted to be at peace with his life. At the same time, he didn't want death visiting unexpectedly, slipping into his room in the darkness. He wanted to see it coming.

When he awoke, his eyes were blurry in the morning light and he rubbed them hard, and the first thing he saw was Israel and Carlo Monsanto sitting on either side of his bed, Israel displaying his skeletal grin.

CHAPTER TWENTY-THREE

Carlo said to Riley, "Morning, sunshine," but caught a look from Israel and said to himself, All right, let's do it your way, Israel. Always wanting to be the gentleman diplomat, to do the soft shoe like no one knows what you're really all about and the business you're in.

Israel said to Riley, "Don't mean to pounce on you first thing in the morning but we need to talk. You need to freshen up first? Or we can talk now if you want."

Riley pushed up to a sitting position carefully, obviously feeling some pain. "Guys, you should've told me you're coming by. What you want to talk about?"

"Clarify some things. Shouldn't take long. We thought now would be the best time for a visit. We have other goals to accomplish today. Bear in mind, a certain transaction remains incomplete."

Riley got out of bed and padded over to the bathroom in socks and hospital robe. For a second, a split second, Carlo felt the urge to stick a leg out, trip him and send his ass flying. Juvenile maybe, but it would appear that Riley deserved it.

While Riley busied himself in the bathroom, Carlo and Israel sat there quietly. Carlo didn't know why Israel was so surprised about the turn events had taken. He'd always told him his boy Riley was going to fuck them over good one day.

Riley came out of the bathroom looking brighter, patting down his hair, and Carlo stuck a leg out fast, like he was changing position, simply trying to get comfortable. Riley walked around it. If he noticed what Carlo was up to, he didn't pay it any mind.

Carlo nodded at the other two beds, one empty. "One of your roomies was checking out this morning when we were walking in. That other guy, I hear a nurse say he's got Alzheimer's?"

Riley said that's what he heard.

Israel said, "You're looking better this morning. What's the prognosis?"

"I should be out in a day or so. Rest about two weeks and take it easy." Riley sat on the bed, swung his legs up carefully and leaned back on the pillows so that he was sitting up.

"You okay?" Israel watching Riley grimace.

"Soreness, that's all. It's actually worse than the first day."

"My wife had our last two by Cesarean and she couldn't move without something hurting her. You'd be surprised how much you use your abdominal muscles."

Carlo said to Riley, "No big damage there for you though, that's fortunate. Bullet went through and through, huh?"

"Hurt like a bitch, though."

Carlo rubbed his stubbled jaw with the back of his knuckles, listening to the scrape. "So tell me again what happened at Caye Caulker." He dropped his voice, "You're there at the pier fixing to pull out, and somebody just walked up and started firing? That's how it happened?"

"That's about it. Didn't see him coming."

"Damn. You got lucky." Carlo looked around the room, at the Alzheimer's patient sleeping in his bed, partly hidden by the curtains. "Poor Temio and Chino got riddled. Chest, throat, belly, all over, it was bad, and you only got it once. Man, talk about luck."

"That's because they were on the pier. I was farther away. Down in the boat."

"Yeah, that's what you said, I remember," Carlo nodding, scraping the stubble and putting on a frown.

Israel said, "It was a nasty sight, that boat. But we got it cleaned up, and more important—those Mexicans have been interred."

"Listen," Riley said, "I want to thank you for this."

Israel raised a palm. "Thank me after you hear what I'm thinking. Carlo, get that door for me?" After Carlo did and had sat down again, Israel continued, in a grave tone, "Our friend in Mexico. I had to tell him. Explain the circumstances. He understands. He knows sometimes there will be casualties. We took care of this cleanup and whatnot on our end and as a way of compensation for any ill feelings, we're giving their families a little something to help ease their grief. Chino had a little boy, just like you, a young wife. Temio left four children behind, two of them in high school. These were family men, it's very sad. Very sad." He paused to reflect on it. "So we think, me and Carlo, that it would be fitting if you were a part of this gesture to these families in their time of mourning."

Riley's eyebrows lifted. "You're asking me to contribute?"

Israel nodded.

Carlo said, "That a problem?"

Riley looked away, like he was searching for an excuse. "You're asking me, who got shot in the belly and I could've died out there on that water, you're asking me to contribute?"

"Yes," Carlo said.

"Then let me put it like this. A hole in my belly and a couple pints of my blood—that's my contribution."

Silence followed.

Israel said, "Never known you to be such a cold son of a bitch, Riley."

"And I've never known you to hire such malicious mother-fuckers like those two."

"Speaking ill of the dead," Carlo said, "shame on you."

Israel leaned forward on his cane. "I acknowledge the situation got out of hand."

Riley raised his voice, "Out of hand? That's how you're describing it?"

"Calm down, now."

Carlo sat back and folded his arms, beginning to enjoy this.

"We need to clarify something first and foremost before we go any further," Israel said. "I want to understand, I want to believe that you, Riley James, the boy I've known for eons, is with me completely. Look here, we helped clean up a mess for you. Don't want to rub your face in this, son, but we cleaned up after you. A full explanation of what happened out there, you owe us that."

Carlo stood up and walked over to Riley's bed. He stared down at him. "You ask me, that whole deal don't pass the smell test. Top to bottom."

Riley, as he always liked to do, ignored him, saying to Israel, "What do you want to know?"

"I'm having a hard time picturing it. Let's see if I got this straight. You're on the back pier. You, Temio, and Chino. Then this person just appears out of the dark and comes down the pier shooting?"

"I was in the boat, I told you that. Temio and Chino were on the pier. They were just about to load the buckets. A guy comes running down the pier. I'm thinking he must've followed us from the bar. Next thing I know, gunshots. One of them, I think it was Temio, fired back. I felt something hit me and I went down, hid in the boat 'cause I didn't have a weapon. Shooting stops, I look up. Temio and Chino are down and the guy, he probably got plugged 'cause he's getting up holding his arm and he runs off. And that's it. I help them in the boat, and we speed off."

"How did this guy look?"

"Young, kinda slim. Spanish. That's about all I remember."

"What kind of gun did he have?"

"A pistol. Don't ask me what type, or how big. It was raining, and it was dark."

"So you just needed to put Temio and Chino in the boat and then you're off."

"Some buckets were still on the pier."

"So you loaded them in the boat yourself. Shot and bleeding you did that by yourself?"

"Those guys weren't in any shape to help."

Israel said, "Hmm," fingers squeezing and releasing the hook of his cane. "Because when we talked the other night you said the buckets, all of the buckets, were in the boat, and Temio and Chino were untying the lines and you were about to push off when the shooting started."

Riley took a second to adjust a pillow behind him. "Then it must have gone that way. Obviously I'd be fucking confused over the moment-by-moment occurrences on a night that was dark and rainy when I almost got myself killed, all right, Israel?"

"Slow down, chief," Carlo said and touched Riley's shoulder. "Don't get all upset, you might hurt yourself."

Israel said, "So you think Chino hurt this guy when he fired back?"

Riley stared at Israel. "What are you doing?" He looked up at Carlo. "Get your hands off me." Back to Israel, "You know I told you it was Temio who fired back, so what game are we playing?"

In the long silence, Carlo walked away past the sleeping Alzheimer's patient. He stood at the window and parted the blinds with two fingers and looked out at the wet hospital square. "That's the question we want to ask you, buddy."

When he turned around, Riley was standing up, taking off his robe. He had a wide bandage tight around his torso. He fished a shirt out of a plastic bag on the floor by the bed and slipped it on. Buttoning the shirt, he looked squarely at Israel. "You're accusing me of something, lay it out."

Israel scooted forward with the help of his cane. "Yes, the six-million-dollar question. You don't hear me accusing you of working a little deal under my nose with the assistance of a few friends. Like Harvey Longsworth and Miss Rose Robinson. You haven't heard that from my lips yet but you tell me how this sounds: Harvey gets wind that a shipment is coming in—" He stopped, looked at the other bed.

Carlo glanced in that direction. "Sleeping."

Israel said, "A shipment is coming in, he gets wind maybe because you let it slip accidentally on purpose. Or maybe it could've been you and Harvey set things up. Who will help? Easy. Julius Robinson. Where to hide the stuff? Robinson Caye, of course. An ambush is staged, and you and your friend Harvey, the masterminds, then stand to make significant money. What do you think about that?"

Riley was climbing into a pair of jeans. He paused, then tugged them on and zipped up. "You already answered that question."

"How so?"

"When you sent me to go retrieve the stuff. You don't send the man that stole your goods to retrieve your goods."

Israel cocked his head and started to smile.

Riley stepped toward Israel and said, steely, "But you sent me on a trip to take out Harvey Longsworth and Julius and

Miss Rose." He leaned over, pushed his face closer, almost nose to nose with Israel.

Carlo tensed up. The gall, Riley had better watch it—Carlo wouldn't hesitate to intervene, hit him in the stomach quick, watch him drop. Go ahead, Riley, test the size of your balls.

Riley was saying, "You put me out there with two killers to off my friends and expect me to be down with that, and you come here today and look me in the eye and say you want me to help compensate grieving families? You obviously have no respect for me, so I'm thinking now it's perfect we're parting ways."

Israel and Carlo watched Riley walk away and fold his robe, lay it on the bed. "This isn't finished," Israel said. "We have four buckets missing."

"I'll get them."

"We have a transaction to complete. People are waiting. After we get everything, we'll need a courier. Are you in?"

Riley faced him. "First, I'd like you to tell me that after I get your stuff, you do not touch Harvey Longsworth. You leave him to me."

Carlo snorted. "What are you gonna do? Fuck him up? Gimme a break."

"Leave him to me," Riley said, voice rising.

"We'll think about it," Israel said.

"I don't want to hear 'think about it,' I need to hear you'll do it."

"So now you're giving me orders, Riley?"

Riley stepped close again and said through his teeth, "You sent me to assist in knocking off my friends, Israel. Why? What did I ever do to you?"

Carlo had had enough, rushed over and got in Riley's face. "Fuck that. *We* are your friends. We are the ones that pay you. We are the ones got you where you are today, pretending to be respectable, Mr. Big Deal business owner, so do not imply that we owe you a goddamn thing. If not for me and my brother, your ass would be *under* the jail, motherfucker, and you know what I'm talking about." He jabbed the air with a finger and said, "So watch your step and come with more respect when you talk to us."

Riley wiped flecks of saliva off his face and rubbed it on his jeans. He said, "So I take it that's a no." He turned away and slouched over to the window. He said, softly, looking out the blinds, "I'll get your stuff. Don't worry." He looked over a shoulder. "And then that'll be it between us."

Israel breathed hard through his nose and lowered his head, a tired man. He said, "That loan I gave you, that's also financial aid to your business partner. You're asking me, in effect, to help someone who's trying to screw me over. You're asking for plenty, son. You must've mistaken me for a Christian." He shook his head and pointed his cane at Riley. "But you know something? I'm gonna go along with it. Only this one time, and only because it's you, Riley. Because you won't last long without me. You're going to come back to me one day after your business fails and you need some fast cash, you're going to come back and beg for a job. Because this work we do, that's what you do best, so don't fool yourself. And if I hire you again, I want you to know: It'll be on my terms. You'll take whatever I give you and you'll kiss my ass and thank me. I promise you that day will come, it will. So I'm not worried. Have your little freedom, but I want you to do something. Tell that piece of shit, Harvey Longsworth, we know. We *know*. And we will have our eyes on him, and he better not fuck with us again. Now, as for our friend in Mexico, I can't vouch for him, but I'll talk to him."

Riley chewed the inside of his cheek. "It's you who is running things here, Israel."

"It was the Mexican's goods, and he considers this partly his channel. But he takes my counsel, so you may be in luck."

Carlo said, "When can we expect the stuff?"

"As soon as I get discharged."

"That doctor, Gonzalez?" Carlo swirled a finger by his head. "Off with the fairies. I asked him what kind of bullet it was went through you, you know? Hear what he said? 'A big one.'"

"I'm expecting you'll have the stuff in less than forty-eight hours," Riley said.

"Then we're back on," Israel said and pushed himself up to his feet with his cane. "Happy to hear this. Let me leave you now. Call me as soon as you come through. We don't have much time and we need to make arrangements."

Riley said all right, he'd call, and sat on the edge of his bed as they made their way out the door.

Carlo stopped and popped his head back in. "If you don't find the stuff, then it's me who'll be visiting Harvey, and you know what that means, right? Talk to you soon, Riley."

The long hallway was crowded with nurses and plastic bags of linen outside room doors and a couple of patients hobbling along, pushing IV walkers. Carlo had to help Israel navigate the traffic, a hand occasionally on his elbow.

Carlo said, "You know he was lying his ass off."

"I don't know that at all. He might have been, but I don't know it."

They started down the stairs. Carlo said, "I know you see what I'm seeing, only I don't know why you can't admit it."

Israel didn't say anything, clacking down the stairs.

Carlo said, "Jesus Christ, I hate the smell of hospitals. Smells like medicine. Like dead people." He hurried ahead of Israel, through the lobby and out the door. Once outside, he sucked in some fresh air and stuck his hands in his pockets and waited for Israel.

The last time he'd been in a hospital it was because Israel insisted. They'd come to visit a guy Carlo hadn't meant to stab, but his temper had taken over, a guy who'd been skimming bagfuls of marijuana from shipments, back when the weed pulled crazy profits. Carlo had told Israel this morning how much of a coincidence it was, one of their guys in the hospital and them paying a visit under strained circumstances. He asked Israel if he thought this was a similar story, someone skimming shipment—Carlo wanting to hear Israel admit to doubts about Riley, his blue-eyed boy. But no, all Israel said was, "We shall see."

Well, what did they see now?

Israel came out and they walked together to the car, Carlo opening the door for him. Behind the wheel, before he started the car, Carlo said, "Know what? You don't want to say it, I'll say it."

Israel breathed through his nose and stared out the window.

Carlo said, "It was Riley shot those guys. That's the only story, the only one that makes sense. It was fucking Riley."

Carlo waited for his brother's reply. Israel's silence said a lot, but it gave him hardly any satisfaction.

CHAPTER TWENTY-FOUR

Roger Hunter rolled into the room without knocking and stopped to look at Riley lying on the bed, one foot on the floor. He had a hand over his eyes and was breathing evenly. Roger cleared his throat.

Riley didn't move. He knew the man was there but he needed a moment to get over the last visit. Eventually, his hand slid away from his eyes and his head turned on the pillow. "Hey, Roger."

Roger wheeled closer and pulled up next to the bed. "How're you feeling this morning?"

"Not too bad. Eighty percent. And you?"

"So-so. You look good, like you're recovering. Slower than you want, faster than you expect."

"Indeed," Riley said, sitting up carefully. "No sudden moves, nobody gets hurt." Roger was wearing the kind of smile Sister Pat would call beatific, a priest's smile, all patience and kindliness. Riley said, "Let me ask you something. Last night I didn't tell you I was shot. How'd you know?"

Roger shrugged. "Maybe a nurse told me?"

"Did a nurse tell you?"

Roger just smiled. "News gets around."

Riley thought about that, then something became clear to him, something that had been hovering in the background found words. "I have a good friend, an older lady I've known for years. She has a friend she's been visiting in a hospital who's very sick. Sick with cancer. This lady used to be a nun, and years ago there was a rumor that she was having a romance. With a certain Jesuit priest. Only a rumor, far as I know. But here you are—former Jesuit, in a hospital. Hmm, makes me wonder . . ."

Roger removed his Cardinals cap and put it in his lap, smiling. "Yes, I know Patricia Pierce very well. We're longtime friends."

Riley nodded. "It's all coming back to me now. So I guess you know who I am?"

"I certainly do. You're the young man she used to take care of, way, way back. I'm glad I've gotten the chance to finally meet you." Roger appraised Riley, like seeing him for the first time. "You're like a son to her, Riley, one of the anchors of her life, I've always thought."

"And I'm glad to meet *you*. Well. Little did I know the Father Hunter they said used to fight with the rebels is the same priest from those long-ago rumors about Sister Pat."

"Revelations abound."

They grinned at each other. Roger brought the wheelchair closer to the bed. "If you think it's none of my business," he said, his expression turning somber, "just say so and I'll shut up. Those two men who just left here—are they your friends?"

The question surprised Riley.

Roger reached out and clutched Riley's forearm, surprising him even more. "I mean, *real* friends. You know, as in good for you." His grip was clawlike.

"I wouldn't necessarily say that."

"Are you in trouble?"

The old man was so close Riley could smell his stale breath.

Could smell the talcum on him, see the veins in his eyeballs, the deep blue irises, and Riley felt no need to lie. He said, "You could say that."

Roger let go of Riley's arm. "I know those men. Don't know them to talk to, but I know who they are. I know what they do." He reversed the wheelchair, folded his hands in his lap and regarded Riley from a distance. "When I lived here, I used to run a youth summer program on the south side. I learned a lot from those boys in the program. Who they respected, who they feared, who was—the Mac Daddy, is that how they used to say it? I'll tell you something, over the years I heard an awful lot, too much, about the Monsantos. Quite powerful, aren't they?"

Riley wasn't sure where Roger was going.

"I'll just leave you with some information, and you can do with it as you please," Roger said. "I may know someone who knows someone who may be able to arrange a trip for you with accommodation to a Central American destination."

Riley said, "Okay," meaning, go on.

"This place wouldn't be the Hilton but it would serve as a getaway, if you will, a quiet retreat for someone in—in a spot of bother. An isolated village far from any major city. Cold and colder running water, electricity sometimes, yet there are amenities like a dependable propane stove, a kerosene refrigerator. Mosquito nets, blankets. Books on socialism and Catholic theology for your entertainment. It's a place not even our dear Lord would find."

Riley pretended to consider.

Roger said, "Don't let me presume that you've even imagined leaving. But if it's assistance of this kind you need, only say the word."

"I can't go anywhere," Riley said. "Not immediately anyway."

Roger picked up his cap and inspected it, turning it around. "If it's something along the lines of protection you need . . ."

Riley met the old man's eyes. There was no joke in them, not a twinkle.

Then he smiled. "As you can see, I'm still very much a fool for adventure." He sat back and groaned, fanning himself with his cap. "Listen to me . . ." He trailed off, squinting at the light in the window. "But you know something? I lived in a different world once. So maybe I can understand your problems. There's this world we live in every day, then there is another world below it," Roger making chopping motions, "and another below that one. That bottom one, I'm familiar with it. I think you are as well."

Riley felt like he had nothing to hide. "You're probably right."

"I think I can tell you this." Roger leaned in. "When I was in El Salvador, I knew the gun routes. One from Chalcuapa, or the one from Santa Ana, I knew them well. I drove trucks to transport arms for my friends. It was a thrilling time, scary, oh sure, but worthwhile. Guns would flow through Mexico, sometimes they made a stop right here in Belize. Even till today, I sometimes get word from old traders and former associates that M4s or Glocks or bullets are available down south in some village in Punta Gorda. Can you believe that?" He shook his head. "Different world . . . Not healthy, but exciting. I wish I could feel that way again, the exhilaration I used to feel when I was younger."

They sat and listened to the sounds in the hallway. Riley poured two cups of water from the ice bucket and they sipped and talked some more, the conversation turning to St. John's, the other place they had in common. But it had changed, Riley said. The Jesuits had put up new buildings on campus, broad walkways from the high school to the junior college.

In a little while, Roger Hunter's eyelids drooped, and a minute later when his chin sank to his chest, Riley reached over and took the cup before it spilled, and he sat watching the old man, who had reminisced so much about excitement, dozing peacefully in the quiet.

CHAPTER TWENTY-FIVE

Three hours later Riley received his third visitor of the day. Miles Young stood at the door with his handsome smile and said, "You ready?"

Riley took the pen and notepad he'd asked Miles to bring. He scribbled a note to Dr. Gonz, explaining why he couldn't stay (because he had better things to do than stare at hospital walls, and thanks for the special attention and why didn't Gonz come on over to Lindy's one night, to the cigar/poker room, which was officially closed but could be unofficially opened for certain VIPs?)

Riley left the note on his pillow and slipped out the door with Miles.

Two hours later, Riley was sitting behind the wheel of Miles's old Camry, alone, observing a tall concrete stilt house on the other side of an unpaved street. All the windows were down, but he mopped sweat off his face and neck yet again, and yawned, thankful that at least he wasn't on any pain meds stronger than Advil or he'd be taking a siesta here in this heat.

A truck rumbled by, dust billowing. The truck rattled and bumped through potholes and disappeared around a curve. The stilt house with the turret on the roof was three lots south of the curve, and from where he sat, he could see the iron scroll-work gate closed and the carport empty and a glimpse of the canal shimmering behind the backyard.

No cars passed for the longest time, then an SUV drove by and immediately after that came the green Honda Civic he was waiting for, Gert at the wheel. Riley slid lower in his seat.

Gert turned right and stopped at the gate. She got out, opened it. As she was returning to the car, a head popped out from the backseat—Harvey—then went down. Gert drove into the yard. Seconds later, she closed the gate, and Riley saw a swatch of Harvey's shirt disappearing into the downstairs entrance, then everything was still again.

Riley waited five minutes to see if there was anybody tailing Harvey. Satisfied there wasn't, he drove across the street and parked in front of the gate. He opened the gate quietly and went to stand at the downstairs door. He could hear murmuring coming from a window facing the backyard and the canal. He pressed the doorbell; the murmuring stopped. He pressed again and heard the bell loud and distinct, but no other sounds.

He went around to the back window. Gert's big cat, Sir Belly, was on the sill and meowed thickly at him when he peeked in. "Harvey, it's me, Riley. Open the door." The cat pawed at the screen, purring.

Riley returned to the door, it opened and Gert stood there, solemn. She didn't say a word when he walked in, didn't fake a smile or cut her eyes or do anything Gertlike.

"Where's Harvey?"

She pointed her chin at the computer room down the dark corridor. He headed toward the open door. There were two suitcases at the foot of the stairs to the bedrooms and he paused to check them out, knowing Gert was watching him.

Harvey was sitting behind his desk looking scared. He had thick stubble and glasses on, no time for a shave and contact lenses. There was a loose pile of cash on the desk, U.S. currency. He pushed his chair away from the desk and started to get up. "Riley, I guess I owe you an explanation."

Riley said, "Sit down," and walked around the desk to see what was on the computer monitor. A schedule of rates and flights from Orbitz—flights to where? Riley leaned closer. Miami to New York. Riley said, "Hmm," nodding.

Harvey was shrinking back, like a man expecting to be hit.

Riley picked up a handful of the U.S. bills, old and thin— who knows how long Harvey had them—let them fall from his hands like dry leaves. "Who's been minding the bar, Harvey?"

"It's—we closed it temporarily."

"I've been in the hospital almost two days," Riley said, "and I didn't hear a peep from you." He examined the room, casually, boxes on the floor, filing cabinets open, a satchel stuffed to overflowing with papers up on the shelf of a bookcase. Riley said, "How you been keeping, Harvey?"

Harvey had pushed his chair back to the wall and said, "Jesus Christ," and he buried his face in his hands. "I didn't expect any of this to happen." He started to sob.

Riley looked down his shoulder at him. "You heard what happened to me?"

"I heard, I heard it. Gert told me it must be thunder but I knew it sounded different, I knew it was gunshots, but I was scared, Riley . . . I was too scared to go out there and check." Harvey pulled off his glasses and tugged the front of his T-shirt over his face, sniffling into it. "I'm sorry . . . I'm sorry . . ."

Riley wanted to hit him. Seeing a friend in pain had always depressed him, but he believed he could punch Harvey with full force in the temple right this second and feel satisfied. He said, "They shot me, Harvey, but don't you worry, I'll be okay."

"I'm sorry, man, I'm so—"

"Shut up," Riley swinging around and pointing at him. He

waited until he had Harvey's eyes before he said, "I'll be okay, but Julius and Rose Robinson, they can't say the same. In fact, they can't say anything, they're fucking *dead*."

Harvey put his palms to his face and threw back his head, letting out a groan.

Riley wasn't impressed. "Two other men died that night that I could give a shit about. Only thing I care about now, where are the buckets and who the hell is McCoy?"

Harvey dropped his hands to his side and shook his head. He put on his glasses, shaking his head, eyes brimming. "There's . . . there's nobody named McCoy."

"Don't do that. Do not lie to me."

"Riley," Harvey whined, "there's no McCoy."

Riley slapped him, Harvey's glasses bouncing against the wall and onto the floor. Harvey's short arm went up in case Riley swung again. Riley watched Harvey roll the chair back and pick up the glasses, averting his eyes. Riley said, breathing harder, "Who is McCoy?"

Harvey ran a palm down his face and put on his glasses. He swallowed hard. "It's just a name I made up."

"You? Why?"

"I just thought it'd be cool, you know? Tell them to meet—" He exhaled through his mouth, looking down at the floor. "Tell them to meet McCoy if they want their coke back, like the Real McCoy."

"That's real cute. You dumb ass."

"Stupid, stupid, I know, okay? But we didn't want to sit on all that amount of coke we didn't have anywhere to sell so fast, so we thought it sounded good if we arranged to sell some back to them."

"Who's *we*?"

Harvey shook his head. "Riley, believe me, I wouldn't've done this if I didn't have to, he pressured me."

"Who's *we*?"

"It's Lopez, who else?"

"The minister's driver?"

"Yes, yes," Harvey spluttered. "He pressured me, Riley. Was *his* idea, *his* plan."

Riley straightened up, nodding. "And you had nothing to do with it."

"Listen, all right. Lopez came to me after we already paid him off for that dog and he told me he knew everything about you. Said he had a stack of files this high on you and the Monsantos and did I have any info that might help with any investigation or some shit like that."

"And you said, Why, certainly, I'd be happy to help."

"No no no, I told him no way, I didn't know nothing about nothing but he kept pressuring, pressuring. Telling me it's in my best interest, he could see to it that the government seizes my business, things like that. So he offers me a deal, okay? I tell him something I know, he'll funnel some of the dollars my way, and Riley, forgive me, man, please, but I'm thinking you're getting married soon, you'll be leaving the bar, but that's all I got, man, that's *all* I got. If I didn't do this, he'd take it away, somehow. You've seen how he is. He's got a fucking government minister behind him, Riley."

"So you went in with him. You and Julius."

"I *had* to. Once I told Lopez about the shipment, he did the planning. He was the one reached out to Julius and Miss Rose, like he already knew about them. He went out there to see them, made them an offer. They had no choice. He could've tried to work it so the government seized their property. For aiding and abetting drug traffickers, that's what Julius told me."

Riley just about spat out the words. "Don't give me that shit you didn't have a choice. You coulda come to *me,* you coulda warned *me*. We would've worked something out, we've always worked things out."

"I was scared stupid, I know I know—"

"Now you know, yeah. You know you're in over your head and it might cost you your life."

Harvey said, "They're coming after me, right? I *knew* it." Looking like he was about to start crying again, shaking his head.

"Didn't expect they'd find you this fast, did you? Don't you ever doubt they know where you are. Think you're going to fly away somewhere? Good luck with that, son."

Harvey raised folded hands. "Look, put in a good word for me? Tell them I'm cooperating?"

Riley looked at him and walked to the door. "Where are the buckets, upstairs?"

Harvey's hands came down. "Yes, they're—"

"In the rec room?" Riley already walking out the door.

Harvey showed him where the four buckets were upstairs, in the locker by the foosball table. Harvey carried two, unbalanced because of his short arm, and Riley carried two, feeling a strong burn in his abdomen. They set them at the foot of the stairs, Riley in pain, Gert glaring from the kitchen, arms folded.

Riley looked at Harvey, who seemed to have lost weight, T-shirt wrinkled, pants droopy. "I thought I knew you," Riley said, "but I never would've believed you could do this to me." He bent down, grabbed the handles of his buckets. "Let's go."

"I-I can't go outside. I don't want nobody to see me."

"Afraid they might shoot you?"

Riley took the buckets out to his car and put them on the backseat floor. He saw Harvey peeking out through the cracked door. Riley came back for the other two buckets, sweating, pulled the door wide open; Harvey recoiled. Riley smiled and marched on to the buckets.

From the kitchen, Gert said, "Look at you, like you got some right to decide who makes money and who doesn't on something that's illegal and nobody has license on. Who made you the—the arbitrator, Riley James, you're a fraud."

Riley stopped for a second, to see if she had more to say, then lifted the buckets.

Gert started up again. "You don't think everybody knows about you? All these years we've been right by your side, thick and thin, but you can't stand to see anyone making money the way you've been doing your whole life. Pulling the same shenanigans you pull, oh, you can't stand it, so you turn against us friends that had your back and defended you against all those rumors people always spreading about you. 'Oh, no, Riley isn't like that, he'll pay you on time.' 'Oh, no, Riley cares about his customers. Have another beer, on the house!' " Gert launched into a girly voice. " 'Your conch fritters too greasy? Sorry, our deepest apologies. Riley wants you to know you can have anything else on the menu on the house.' *Please.* I see right through you, acting so nicey-nicey, but it burns you up when other people succeed at anything, that's why you had to cheat at it. All those years a cheat. A cheat and a thief."

"Stop it," Harvey said.

"No, I want him to hear me and I want—"

"Shut up, Gert!"

That shocked her. Harvey and Gert stared each other down, Gert's nostrils flaring. Harvey's lips curving downward, trembling. Riley and his buckets caught in between these two.

Harvey turned to Riley, palms upturned. "Riley . . ."

Riley thought of responding to Gert but it would've made

no difference. He wasn't sure of anything nowadays except this: Gert would always be a jealous woman.

As Riley was going out the door, Harvey said, "Please, man, you know these people. If I can't get to the airport safe, where do I go? What's gonna happen to me?"

Riley, walking out the gate, said, "Those are fine questions," not looking back, trying to ignore the burning in his midsection and the disappointment that was weighing down his heart.

Harvey called from his door, "What's gonna happen to me, Riley?"

Riley kept moving, opening the car doors, putting the buckets on the floor. He walked around to the driver's side, hearing Harvey say, "Riley, what should I do now? Come on, talk to me. What's gonna happen to me?" and on and on, his voice high and sharp as a blade in the sunlight as Riley started the car and drove away.

CHAPTER TWENTY-SIX

Carlo sat slouched on the edge of his bed, a pair of slacks across a knee, waiting for his sister to finish her ironing. He was wearing nothing except boxer shorts but still felt hot. The windows were open wide and the ceiling fan was going but perspiration was trickling down his back.

He could hear Mirta in the corridor outside humming at the ironing board. He fought the urge for a moment then went to the door again. She was in bra and panties only, peach ones, and he let his eyes linger. Telling himself to cut it out, go back and wait. But her skin . . .

He knew that she knew he was admiring her, just from the way she canted her head as she slipped the white blouse over the board. Her long hair, by supposed accident, swept to one side so that her neck and jawline were exposed. Now look at this, jutting out a hip, putting her weight on one leg. Her legs were fleshier than before she had kids, understandably, so dropping a few pounds wouldn't hurt, twenty minutes or so every day on that recumbent exercise bike in her room she never used. Tightened, leaner—she'd be back to her old knockout self.

He returned to his seat on the bed. Time hadn't changed the house that much—the walls in his room still brown and white, her room still the same one from childhood, seven paces down and across the corridor, the biggest change being that what used to be Israel's room was now taken over by Mirta's boys. There was still that parlor where they watched TV, with the bank of louver windows looking down on Albert Street, and they still ate meals in the dining room on the second floor, which was where Israel and family lived. And Carlo still felt his groin stir whenever he watched his sister like this.

"Mirta, you almost finished?"

No response. But after a minute she called, "All yours," and he got up and hurried into the corridor with bogus exasperation. He caught her right before she turned to go into her room, a full rear view, and he also caught that second of hesitation, that glance over her shoulder as she half shut her room door. She laid her clothes on the bed, walked to her bathroom. There, a small flip of the hair, another over-the-shoulder look, glancing at him, his boxers. This was their game. Now he saw her enter the bathroom, Carlo pretending to fiddle with the iron but taking in the sight of her skin and swell of her breasts as she turned and clicked the door shut.

God a'mighty.

God will strike you down. Naw, God didn't give a shit. Carlo's mind spun with everything he had to do today, while he ironed his Hawaiian shirt, getting the sleeve creases tight. He owned about six shirts like this, soft and loose and comfy. Wearing them made him feel chilled out. He wasn't a bad-looking guy if he shaved. So how come he was still single, or no woman was pressing him to ask her that certain question? He didn't know why no woman could ever hold his interest for them to reach that point. He touched up the collar with the tip of the iron, thinking, That's just the way it is, Carlo, you're the fucking Serpent, too cool and slippery to trap.

Hell, he damned well knew why he was single. Unplugging the iron and gazing at Mirta's room door. He stood there a while, holding his warm shirt, feeling adrenaline rising. The house was quiet; her kids were downstairs. He heard her coming out of the bathroom now. He draped his shirt over the ironing board and went to stand beside her half-open door, put his mouth to the space. "Mirta?"

No response.

He pushed the door open wide and said, "Can I ask you something?" walking in before she could answer.

She turned away from the long mirror at the end of the big room, the white blouse spilling down to her hips, the top shirt buttons open. She reached back, fluffed her hair out over the collar, shaking it loose for good measure and because she knew she looked sexy doing it. She said, "What do you want?"

Carlo sat on the bed and cleared his throat. There was a pair of dark jeans laid out. She'd look good in that, with the white blouse, maybe keep a couple buttons open, yeah . . . He said, "You talk to Pedro lately?"

Arms akimbo, she said, "Pedro, our cousin Pedro?"

"Stop saying that."

"What's this with you? Why do you feel you've got to find me somebody?"

He'd fallen into his normal slouch and now he set both hands on his thighs like a little boy, which sometimes around her was what he felt like, he never understood that. He wanted to say, Because if you go off with somebody else maybe then I'll stop thinking you belong to me.

"You have to quit this, Carlo, playing matchmaker," and she paused, looking at him funny, making him realize he was staring at her legs. He'd seen a glimpse of panties under the shirt, moved his eyes away and heard her say, as she was going to the dresser, "What do you want, Carlo?" Carlo watched her select earrings from a vanity tray. Put them on with a toss of the hair and a cant of the head to one side then the other.

Why didn't she put on her jeans, finish getting dressed? Why was she taking her sloooww sweet time now spritzing her neck and the inside of her wrists with perfume? Standing there with her blouse that had ridden up enough to show off her gorgeous ass under the tight panties. Because this was their game. His voice sounded heavy when he said, "Mirta, is it true—" He began another way. "You had C-sections with your boys, so is it true it hurts when you're moving, when it's healing?"

She turned around, put her hands on the dresser and leaned against it, legs out. "Why're you asking?"

"Just asking. Curious."

"Yes. It hurts like hell. Just another thing that women have to go through."

"Is it a big scar?"

She shrugged. "Big enough."

"Can I see?"

She screwed up her face. "No . . ." Then, "Why?"

"I just want to see it."

"Carlo . . ." She gave a little sigh, seemed to think it over, then her hands went to the front of her shirt, she turned her face to the side with a bored expression and lifted the front of the shirt with one hand and turned down the elastic of her panties quickly. Then it snapped back, the shirt spilled down and she said, "Satisfied? It's not pretty."

Carlo said, "I didn't hardly see. You did it too fast."

"Carlo."

"Please, Mirta. I want to see it."

She said, "Jeeesus, Carlo." But she started again then paused, Carlo's eyes all over her, the crease in her panties, her pale thighs. "Close the door," she said.

He got up fast and did it. Sat down again and patted the bed next to him. "Come, I want to see it up close."

She rolled her eyes but she took three big steps, pointing her toes like a ballerina and was there in front of him. "This is as far as I'm coming," she said. "See," and she lifted the shirt, fingers rolling down the panties one fold, to reveal a dark indented line of scar tissue.

It was beautiful. He swallowed, reaching his hand out, looking up at her, their eyes locked.

She said, "Carlo."

He touched the scar with a finger, tentative, tracing it. Back and forth. He was breathing faster. He put his other hand flat against her stomach and she drew in a breath sharply. He pressed his palm against her warm softness, his finger tracing the scar, gentle, then firm. He swallowed, said in a hoarse voice, "It hurts when I do that?"

She shook her head fast and turned her face to the side, Carlo watching her. She leaned into him, her eyes drifting to the walls, face taking on that bored expression, like he wasn't there. His palm roaming upward, to her ribs now, the thumb of the other hand slipping in just under the elastic of her panties. Like he wasn't there, except now *her* breathing had quickened and her eyes were closed.

A door slammed somewhere in the house and that brought her back. Her eyes were open again and she said, "Okay, okay stop," letting the shirt fall and pivoting away before he had a chance to object.

He sat awkwardly, his mind reeling with possibilities. Okay, Mirta, until hopefully another time.

The buzzer outside in the corridor rang, probably Israel from downstairs. Carlo stood up and looked at her sitting on the end of the bed, pulling on her jeans. "That's probably breakfast," he said. She rose, zipping up her jeans, went to the dresser and picked up a brush, flung her hair to one side and began brushing. Carlo jerked a thumb over his shoulder. "I'm gonna go eat breakfast, then." Mirta brushing with smooth down-strokes, not paying him any mind. He said, "Okay, then, I'll see you later, then," and waited for a beat before he left the room, feeling lonely.

The breakfast table was cleared except for Carlo's big mug of coffee and Israel's glass of Metamucil and a plate of sliced avocado. Israel stirred the glass one more time, set his spoon on a napkin and said, "El Padrón wants to move on this deal. He's losing money and patience, and money is time."

"What?"

"You know what I mean. First, let's take care of our problems at home. Riley called this morning and said he has the buckets and is bringing them by, so now as a gesture of goodwill to El Padrón, we do him a favor, okay?"

"How soon, tonight?"

"Of course tonight. In the small hours."

Carlo, hunched over his coffee, said, "You don't want me to hunt for this guy one more day?"

"No, enough of that. We need to move on."

"You want me to do this one myself?"

Israel shrugged, lifted his glass. "If you think you don't need help." He drank half the Metamucil.

Mirta came out with a sponge and started wiping the table, dragging bread crumbs and bits of scrambled egg into a cupped palm. She said, "Excuse me, please," and Carlo had to raise his mug high off the table and sit back. She moved around fast to Israel's side, sponging away, saying, sharply, "The glass," and Israel picked it up and drank off the rest. He looked at her and said, "Please?"

She took the glass without looking at him and put it on the plate between the avocado slices and went back to the kitchen.

Israel said, "What's wrong with *her*?"

"Who the fuck knows? One day she's all syrup, next it's vinegar. Can't figure her out." He sipped his coffee, staring at the table.

"So you'll take care of this thing tomorrow morning?"

"Yeah, if you're really sure."

"The faster we do this, the faster we can make delivery and get paid."

Carlo said, "First thing when that money comes in," and pointed at the ceiling. "Get a fifty-inch flat panel for upstairs, swear to God, get rid of that piece of crap rear-projection junk you can't see shit out of anymore except you sit right in front of the fucking thing."

There was some scuffling from the kitchen, then one of Mirta's boys came running out. He dashed behind Israel's chair when Mirta stormed out with a chunk of avocado stuck on a fork. "Come here, I said come here this instant." The little boy held on tight to Israel's chair, knocking the cane that was hanging off it onto the floor, as Mirta advanced with the fork. "You can't say you don't like it if you don't even try it."

Israel twisted around in his seat and said, "Boy, Stevie— Carlo, I mean, Joey . . ." He turned to Carlo. "Which one this?"

Mirta told the boy, "Don't you move," and he clapped a hand over his mouth.

Israel said, "Listen to your ma. You don't want to grow up big and—"

The boy darted under the table, scurried out on the other side and ran around the corner and back down the corridor. Mirta said, "That little fucker," and stalked after him.

Carlo sipped his coffee and watched her tight jeans disappearing around the corner.

Israel said, "What a circus," and winced, patting his stomach. "You should be happy you don't have kids, let me tell you.
Anyway, I better go and try my luck, that bathroom's got to be
free by now."

Carlo picked up Israel's cane and handed it to him. Israel
clumped away, mumbling, something about his stomach. He
turned at the corridor doorway and said, "You'll take care of
that thing though, right?"

Carlo put down his cup. Took a deep breath. "Yes, Israel."
Jesus Christ.

CHAPTER TWENTY-SEVEN

In the darkness next morning, he said, "I got it under control. I'm here right now and I got things under control. Would you stop stressing and go to bed? I know, I know but you're stressing *me*. . . . Okay . . . okay, Israel . . . I got it . . . okay, bye," and he slapped the cell phone shut and tossed it into the car cup holder. He shook his head and blew hard through his nose.

He punched on the car radio, heard hard rock nonsense, rolled the dial until he came across "Under Pressure," a classic plain and simple if you asked him, and sat back and stared out the open window. It was drizzling, the air cool. The gasoline smell coming from the backseat was bearable as long as the breeze kept moving.

He saw a light flash down the street, and a minute later Barrel came trudging up with his Maglite. He plopped his fat self in the passenger seat, peeling off the sweatshirt hood. "Car still there," breathing heavy. "One verandah light on upstairs, everything copacetic."

Carlo, leaning a shoulder against his car door, said, "Yeah?" nodding and looking sidelong at Barrel. He sniffed and turned his gaze to the windshield. "Sounds like we have time to give it another five minutes, then."

Barrel rubbed his hands together. "Awright, no problem with me."

Like he had a choice. Like Carlo needed him to approve. It was too dark for Carlo to see the bruising around Barrel's temple and left cheekbone that Israel's broken cane had left, but when he saw it earlier it had surprised him; he didn't think he'd belted the man that hard. Thinking about it now, he felt bad, same as when you whip a dog for chewing the bedpost or shitting on the carpet. You didn't want to strike fear so much as instill obedience and loyalty, but what you gonna do? The deed was done and Barrel was here and they had a job to perform. So maybe, if he was going to wait here with the man, it was better to pass the time by being sociable. Show a little humanity. He said, drumming the steering wheel to the beat, "Barrel, Julius told me one time—God rest his soul—he said you had a wide-screen flat panel and home theater system and all this?"

"Yeah, mahn. It sweet, it sweet."

"True high-def and everything?"

"Yeah, 1080p, fifty-inch sharp contrast, all the bells and whistles. My cousin in NYC hooked me up last Christmas."

"Oh, a *gift*. I was gonna say, Barrel's hauling in big cash on the side with something I don't know about, like deal me in." He rattled off a drumbeat on the wheel. "I like this part right here, Bowie, dude knew what he was doing."

"Bowie? No, this that guy, what's the guy's name, Queen?"

"You got shit mixed up. But you know? Every time I hear this beat I can't help but think about that other song. Completely messed it up for me. Fucking Vanilla Ice. Listen to that idiot on VH1 the other day, 'No, I didn't sample. Their groove line goes, Ding-ding-ding-da-dah-ding-ding. My one goes, Ding-ding-ding-*da-duh*-ding-ding.' Asshole, what the fuck is that?"

Barrel chuckled into the side of his fist.

Carlo said, staring at the radio clock. "You know what?"

"Now?"

"Exactly."

Carlo started the car and they drove up a distance until they were directly across the street from the house. Barrel got out, went around and climbed into the backseat. Carlo peered up at the dark house, hearing Barrel say, "Not like I can't afford a flat-panel, you know. I save, every week," Barrel checking out the box on the floor. Carlo pulled out a little baggie of coke from his shirt pocket and helped himself to a pinkie-nail hit. He tipped his head back, sniffing, said, "Ahhh, *shit.*" Cracked his knuckles, smoothed his slicked-back hair with both hands and said, "Let's roll, big Barrel. Yee-haw." He tugged on a black skullcap, feeling nicely nervous.

Barrel was bent over the box, tightening the strings that affixed the tampons to the necks of the bottles. They had soaked the tampons in gasoline and filled each bottle with half gas, half motor oil, the oil being the ingredient that would stick to everything and accelerate this blaze.

They crossed the dirt street carrying two bottles each down by their legs. A moist breeze was blowing off the bay, cooling Carlo's chest, and he thought about pneumonia and night chills and other old wives' tales but he knew this was just nervousness rippling through like a current.

The gate was wide open, the way Barrel had left it earlier. No dogs barking, no sounds except crickets singing in the street-side bush. They came to the Honda in the carport under the house. It was locked, windows up. Carlo said low, "Do this last." He motioned that he was going up, the verandah at the side of the house, Barrel should stay down by that window facing the canal. "Yeah, that one there."

On his way upstairs, Carlo heard a faint meow. He stepped onto the narrow verandah and stood by a metal patio table and chairs to listen, heard nothing now. His nasal passages were clear from the coke and he felt so good in the quiet darkness, like he did just before a good bowel movement. Maybe Israel should try some blow, a tiny bump, couldn't hurt.

He grinned at his reflection in the sliding glass door, checked his distance from it, took two steps back, knocking into the table. Shit. He set the bottles on the ground and moved the table and a chair out of the way to clear a running path. He took a Bic from his pocket, picked up a bottle, and put the flame to the tampon. He faced the glass door again, reared his arm back—brought the bottle down. His scalp prickly, a breeze caressing the back of his neck. He wanted this feeling to last, like long sex.

He said, "Fuck this," and totter-stepped forward and flung the burning bottle, the crashing shower of glass frightening him momentarily, and he pulled back as a ball of flame—*fhoop*—lit up the living room, fire whipping across the carpet, eerie. He remembered, snatched up the other bottle, lit that and dashed it, clumsily because he was already turning sideways, getting ready to run away from the heat.

He raced down the steps, almost tumbling, hollering at Barrel, "Yes yes yes," and saw Barrel send a flaming bottle crashing through the downstairs louvers. Carlo was at the gate saying, "Let's go," when Barrel lit the last bottle and flung it at the car's driver's side window, glass breaking and flames blowing up with a violence.

They drove away from the house, the upstairs windows glowing red and the car engulfed in fire. Carlo was giggling and when he noticed Barrel looking scared he held his belly with one hand and laughed hard. After they turned the corner, Barrel started laughing, too, the relief getting to him just now.

Carlo's hand slipped down and, uh-oh, what's this here? The strongest erection he'd had in months. He adjusted, left his hand there all the drive home, now and again picturing Mirta in her peach bra and panties, her pale soft skin.

CHAPTER TWENTY-EIGHT

After Riley returned the Monsantos' last four buckets, he had a rough week. He was drifty and forgetful, sometimes wandering in and out of rooms; not knowing why he was standing in front of his open fridge; sipping bourbon from his favorite shot glass only to look at it three drinks later and realize it was a small water glass he was holding.

Saturday morning, slightly hungover, he forced himself to rise early, prepare for Turo's trip with the tourists. The only reason he'd remembered was Turo had called him "to discuss the itinerary." Yes, Turo, Altun Ha then Progresso, Orange Walk Town if they want, that's right. Bye, Turo.

He made a pot of coffee and took a mug into the yard. He checked the tire pressure, packed the raincoats in the back, re-stocked the first-aid kit with bandages and a fresh tube of antibiotic ointment. Wiped down the seats with Armor All and swept the floors with a small brush and dustpan. Aware all the while of Candice's bedroom windows looming over him like two huge eyes.

Last night she'd said, "We need to talk, okay?" But when she shifted the conversation by asking him if he'd seen his son lately, saying that she was looking forward to the photo shoot,

Riley realized, with relief, that she didn't want to talk just yet. He said, "I haven't called him," and pointed at his stomach. "Didn't want to scare him." Then Candice pushed him back on the bed, conversation over, and changed his dressing tenderly, whispering as she unrolled the gauze, "Let's see how we're doing here, big man."

Later, at the door, she said, "So are we okay?"

"Yes, Candice. Gimme a week and I'll be a stallion again." Purposely misunderstanding.

"No, I mean we," her hand going back and forth between them, "are *we* okay."

"Yes." He reached for her hand. "Why not?"

Why not indeed. Gazing up at her house he had a sense there was something she wanted to tell him. He'd felt comfortable with her from the start because she didn't talk about herself much and it didn't appear to bother her that he'd followed suit. One major trait of their relationship, living so close together: They respected each other's private selves. He wondered if with marriage up the road, that map would be redrawn.

Back in the house, he found himself wanting a beer or a little taste of bourbon, just to get his mind right. He had a slow shave instead, lathering up thick, using his straight razor—a gift from Candice—to force himself to slow down; pay attention or he'd feel some pain. Not quite halfway through, staring at the mirror, he saw a rifle muzzle flash and Miss Rose falling . . . a dark shape falling . . .

He set the razor down. Sat his ass on the toilet cover and took a minute to compose himself.

More foolish than brave he finished with the straight razor, satisfied that he came away with only two nicks. He rinsed off, heard a banging, thought it was the pipes. But when he turned off the faucet, he realized it wasn't and went to get the door.

Turo rushed in, eyes bulging. "Mistah Riley, I know I'm kinda early, but you didn't hear?" He gestured vaguely outside. "Mistah Harvey's house burned down last night. To the *ground*, total destruction. They're saying no survivors."

Storming into the shop, Riley bumped a woman coming out. She touched her shoulder and said, "*Hey.*"

Riley said " 'Scuse me, 'scuse me," pushing past a man assorting plastic bags of purchase; knocking paperbacks off a wire rack display and not giving a shit; going straight for the back counter where Mirta was tending to a woman, Carlo there chatting with them.

Carlo saw Riley and turned abruptly for the back door. Riley kicked a wheelbarrow out of his way and pointed at him. "No, don't go anywhere."

Carlo racewalked through the back door, slammed it shut behind him. Riley moved around the counter and kept going, hearing Mirta's shrill voice, "Hey what's all this?"

Riley pulled open the door and stepped into the cement backyard. Carlo stood there, maybe ten paces from the door. His hand was a blur and out flicked a knife, down by his side. He said, "Sure you want to proceed?"

Riley pointed, took a step forward. "You said you weren't gonna touch him."

"Come, come," Carlo waving him on, "right where I want you."

"Just dishonorable bitches, what you people are, you and your lying-ass brother."

"We didn't promise you anything, chief, not one thing."

"Firebomb the house, man? That's your method now? Are you people insane?"

"Keep coming, that's right." Carlo in a loose crouch, grinning, the knife going in slow circles. "Yeah, baby, yeah, that's it, step up. You know how long I been wanting to do this?"

Riley stopped, his heart pulsing in his throat, watching Carlo drop one foot back, arching the blade through the air. Riley said, "I want to talk to Israel."

The blade slowed its revolutions, and Carlo's arm drifted down. "We're talking now?"

"We're talking, what else?"

Carlo nodded, relaxing, rising out of his crouch, nodding some more. "Then back the fuck up 'cause I can do 'what else' quick time." He closed the knife against his leg but kept it in his fist, motioning with his chin for Riley to step aside. Carlo walked past, eyeing Riley.

Through the open door, Riley saw him pick up the phone on the pillar in the store. He talked for a bit, came out and said, "Let's go upstairs." He waited for Riley to take the lead and stayed well back going up the stairs.

Israel was on the living room sofa peeling a tangerine, dropping the skin on a saucer in his lap. He seemed amused with Riley. "You pissed?" He slid a plug of tangerine into his mouth.

Riley stood in the center of the room.

Israel chewed, his lips wet with juice, eyes smiling. He raised another plug to his mouth but seemed to pick up on Riley's mood and laid the tangerine down and put the saucer aside. He said, "Sit down, please."

"No, I'm good." Riley's gaze following Carlo as he moved to the other side of the room, leaned in a doorway, arms folded. "Wouldn't want to get too comfortable around you people."

Israel shook his head and said to Carlo, "Hear that now? 'You people.'"

Carlo clucked his tongue. "I believe we've gone and hurt his feelings."

Israel looked at Riley. "Is that right? You're too experienced to think this is anything but a hard business, Riley. Are you slipping? Tell me."

"I had your word," Riley said.

"No no no, you had my word I'd talk to the Mexican, that's it. What's coming home to you today is just how crazy some folks can be."

Carlo said, "No more crazy than your asshole friend. Thinking he could waltz in and out with other people's property."

"Somebody must've put that idea in his head," Israel lifting a finger, leveling it at Riley. "Was it you did that, Riley?"

"You're still on that story?"

Israel wiped his fingers on a paper napkin, one by one. "Let me tell you how it is, Riley. We needed to extend a gesture, a favor for a friend, something on the order of—oh, retribution—call it whatever you want. The way I see it, it was purely a business decision. My Mexican *compadre* didn't take kindly to your supremely fucking foolish amigo stealing from him and then living like it was nothing while," Israel wadded the napkin, pitched it on the coffee table, "his two trusted employees didn't return and are here rotting on foreign soil in unmarked graves, which I have to remind you that it was we who did the digging."

"You mean it was *me* who did the digging," Carlo said.

"I stand corrected."

Riley breathed in deep; there wasn't enough air in the room. He looked at the floor, his hands sort of cupped down in front of him like when he tried in vain to meditate, and at that moment, he knew he could easily hurt somebody again. Starting with one of these Monsantos. "Well hear this, I brought your four missing buckets, so I'm done. You want somebody to make your delivery, look elsewhere."

Israel and Carlo exchanged a glance. Israel said, "I expected you might say something like that."

"I can't trust you. Should I start watching my back now?"

"Settle down, don't get hysterical. You want to listen to me with a clear head, especially since I have a sweet offer to make."

"I'm not doing this run, Israel, I'm not."

"Tuesday morning. Down the New River, you transfer it to their boat, they carry it upriver to wherever, then they filter it across the border by trucks in three or four trips, something like that. We're sorting out the details but I know this much: Nobody's getting the jump on us this time, and I need you to complete this run, you're the man knows all those routes in that river, the twists and turns. We need you, son."

"At what price?"

"There you go. You do this run? The interest on that bar loan? Clear, all clear on my books, you won't owe me a cent more than the principal."

"Maybe," Riley said, "it would be better if it was a cleared debt. For all the hardship this thing has caused, combat pay, you know what I'm saying?"

Carlo let out a whoop. "Ho baby! Listen to this shit."

Riley looked from one to the other, waiting to see how far he could take it.

"You come into *my* house," Israel said, "insult me like this, like it's your due. You have some damn nerve, son."

Riley looked off, nodded, then headed for the door.

"Riley."

"No, let him go."

Riley, a hand on the doorknob, looked at Israel. "This is bullshit, you realize that? All of this."

"Your interest will be clear with me, that's a solid offer."

"But will it bring Harvey back? His wife? He screwed me over, Israel, but he was my friend. My business partner. And I thought I had your word. I need to feel certain you won't go back on your word again. Considering everything? It's better you forget about me."

"Look at me, son, and let's forget the bullshit—since when me and you had problems? All these years, we've been straight with each other, when it comes down to the deals, me, you, and Carlo. Don't let the actions of your rotten, betraying so-called friend cloud your reasoning, Riley. He was the one that started this, not you. He had no place in our affairs, none. He should've known that, so don't feel responsible for him."

Riley exhaled, jammed his hands in his pockets and looked up at the ceiling. He rolled back on his heels. Looked at the floor. "When you say? Hypothetically speaking."

"Tuesday morning. Before daybreak."

"And if I'm dumb enough to do this, who handles the transaction on their side to give me the cash?"

"That's what I'm saying, details to come. As of right now, with all the attention lately, we might need to get creative."

"See now, I don't know what that means."

"I'm saying we might handle the money exchange in another location, but we don't know where yet. Logistics, logistics . . ."

"Communicate with me by radio or something?"

"There you go, that's an idea. Welcome back, Riley."

Riley could not get a full breath. He needed to leave before it started to show. He told them, "You know my number," and didn't have to say any more by way of agreement; they'd known each other so long.

Israel said they'd call him after noon, and Riley opened the door, went out. They might know each other's idiosyncrasies, but what the Monsantos couldn't know was how much his knees were trembling as he walked down the stairs.

CHAPTER TWENTY-NINE

Riley drove all the way down Albert Street and circled left around St. John's Cathedral to head back north on Regent Street. After another circle like this, after he was sure no one was trailing him, he squeezed into a space between two trucks on Regent and got out of the pickup. He walked along Regent in the sticky humidity, hoping he wouldn't meet anyone he knew, anyone who might want to stop and chat. It wasn't until he hooked a right on Prince Street, going toward the sea, that he felt he could relax, breathe deeper.

He turned right on Southern Foreshore and walked along the seawall until he came to Miles's house, a white and green colonial wood-frame, three stories, garage and storeroom downstairs, verandah and living area on the second floor, bedrooms on the top. He opened the front gate, went up the path to the covered stairway, glad for the sea breeze in the shade. He rang the doorbell and said, "It's me, Riley." No one answered; he rang again. "It's Riley."

He heard the door being unbolted. He waited before he opened it and entered.

Across the room, Harvey stood in disheveled T-shirt and shorts. "Riley," he said, raising a cell phone. "My house, I just found out. My neighbor's texting me like crazy. Damn, Riley, these Monsantos don't play."

Riley walked in, hearing sobs coming from upstairs; he took a wild guess that it was Gert. He headed to the kitchen, Harvey slouching in after him, the once cocky Harvey looking beaten down and haggard. He asked Riley if he wanted a cup of coffee, he'd just made Guatemalan Arabica, was all he could find. Riley poured a cup, dumped in cream and sugar, and sat at the rough-hewn table. "Where's Miles?"

Harvey dropped heavily in the chair across from Riley. "Upstairs, fixing a toilet, I think." He planted his elbows on the table, shaking his head. "Lopez, man, he keeps calling and calling."

"You going to answer?"

"I already know what he's gonna say. 'Where are you? Where are the buckets?' It wouldn't be no 'Thank god you're alive,' that's for sure."

"Next time, answer him."

"Yeah?"

"And tell him they took the buckets before they burnt the place, but you managed to put away some of the coke."

"Why would I want to say that?"

" 'Cause some might have accidentally fallen out, like three kilos, into some bags I stashed somewhere. Keep this in mind, Harvey, coke is like money. It got us in trouble, and it might help get us out."

Harvey sat back and stared at Riley. "Don't go getting all crafty, I don't want no part of this."

"Harvey? Let me take this opportunity to inform you that, hello, you're already part of this."

Harvey sagged. Riley tipped his chair back against the wall and studied him. "You said last time you spoke to Lopez, couple days ago, he didn't know that the Monsantos had found you out. Now he does. But tell him I don't believe it, what they're saying about you, and tell him I'm helping you hide out somewhere but you can't say where. Tell him I don't agree with what the Monsantos did to your house and there is confusion in the camp, but I still have to do their bidding and deliver those buckets."

"Confusion in the camp . . . Okay, but look—"

"You know why you're going to tell him you stashed some of the cane away? 'Cause you want him on your side."

Harvey looked like he was in pain.

"You don't want him thinking you turned coat, getting scared and begging me for forgiveness." Riley took a beat for him to get the message. "Especially since, last time you talked to him, things weren't looking too hot for him. Isn't that what he said?"

Harvey shrugged. "He said Minister Burrows wasn't happy. So?"

"The guy needs a friend."

"I don't want to be it."

"Well, guess what, it's either him or the Monsantos, and they don't want you and you can't hide in this house forever."

"What about you, Riley, I'm with you."

"Me? I'm with the Monsantos, buddy."

"Riley, man, this is me," Harvey said, palming his chest. "Me and you, R.J. Why you being like this?"

"Being like what? Like trying to save your life?"

"How is that? You're pushing me away." Harvey's face was getting red.

Riley couldn't deny a part of him was enjoying this. He let the chair down and drank some coffee. "I'd be interested to know, when you talk to Lopez again, what his plans are. The minister giving him a certain access and turning a blind eye, then backing away when it gets too hot? I'd like to know where his mind is. Pick his brain for me, Harvey. Think you could do that?"

Harvey took off his glasses and rubbed his eyes with the heel of his palms. "Hell, man, my life is over."

"Nope, you follow my directions you might get your life back. Open a bar again, start making money again, the honest way. Customers are getting thirsty."

Someone was coming down the stairs and Riley waited. Miles entered the kitchen with a toilet tank ball and flush handle. "Riley." He looked from Riley to Harvey. "I'm interrupting?"

"Nah, we're done."

Miles passed behind him and pitched the parts in the garbage can under the sink. "This house is going to send me to the poor house. Every day it's something else busted. Last week the gutter, now today this. Harvey, listen, you're gonna have to use the downstairs toilet till I get this fixed. Who's Sir Belly?"

"What?" Harvey waking from a trance. "My cat . . . I know, I know, Gertrude . . ."

"She's still crying up there."

In the center of the table Harvey's cell phone started buzzing. He picked it up, checked the screen. "See what I told you, that's him again."

Riley said, "Before you answer, just one more thing." He waited, the phone buzzing. "To make yourself believable, you got to act like you're ready to keep on stabbing me in the back."

Harvey's eye flickered with the hurt, then he rose with the phone and walked out of the room, saying, "Hello? Hey, brother . . . what's that you say?"

Leaning against the sink, arms folded, Miles watched Riley. "You're turning the screws on him, huh?"

Riley raised his cup to his mouth, put it down.

"Making him feel like shit, which is proper, but at least it's better than dead."

Riley drank off the coffee.

"What I can't understand, though, is why you go out of your way to protect a man you don't know you can trust anymore."

Riley turned the cup around and around, staring at the dregs. "Because he's my friend, the oldest friend I have," and he looked up at Miles.

"Okay. Same reason I open my doors to you guys, because you're my friend, and as a friend? I hope we're doing the right thing. I know you, Riley, but Harvey—I'm not too sure about Harvey. I like him, okay, but you know . . ."

"I hear you."

"And as a friend, I know you'll understand why I have my daughter staying at my fiancée's this weekend. This life I'm living with Lani, it's peaceful and predictable and boring, and my house—"

Riley raised a palm. "You don't have to say it." He stretched out his hand and they bumped fists. "If there's even a shadow of trouble at your door we're off like a prom dress."

Miles's eyes crinkled with a smile. "But I've been restless, too, so if you need my help outside these doors . . ."

"I'll holler."

"Cool," Miles said and Riley responded, "Cool."

And that's all they needed to say.

"Lopez is furious," Harvey said, holding the cell phone in his lap with both hands.

He and Riley were sitting in the dark family room filled with old mahogany furniture and dusty photos on the walls of Miles in his boxing days.

"What he say?"

"He wants *get back*. He kept saying he wants to fucking hurt somebody."

"Any plans?"

"One to come, it sounds like. But this is the big news: Minister Burrows cut him off for good. No further assistance. He says they're coming down on her, some kind of internal investigation, he says. Police, people from the DEA involved, all that shit, he doesn't know who else, except the minister's telling him she's out, he's on his own. Until it cools off, but the way he's talking, all defiant and arrogant, he doesn't want to cool off."

"Who's he got with him, did he tell you?"

"Two guys still hanging with him. That's it. One is a cousin of one of those guys that got killed in Caye Caulker the other day, and the other dude is a policeman still wants a big payday. But he's got nobody big behind him. Everybody is scared, he says. His contacts on the BDF won't take his calls. He says the head of the Coast Guard threatened to string him up if he comes by asking for help, and that's why he's pissed, Riley. He says everybody turned their backs on him because of this DEA and police pressure, and he's blaming you and the Monsantos for it."

"So just him and two other guys, no Coast Guard boats, no BDF guns, nothing like that?"

"That's about it. What it sounds like, none of his contacts want nothing to do with him at the moment so he's taking this one up himself."

"How about you, he have any doubts about you?"

Harvey chuffed. "That's the funny thing. He's hardly listening to me. Just keeps giving orders, pontificating. Wants me to keep my eyes open around you."

"Good."

"No no, not good, not good at all. I don't want to be in the middle of this."

"What did I tell you about that?"

Harvey flung himself back against the chair and said, "Shit," shaking his head. "Not good, not good. He's threatening your life, Riley. He sounds crazy. He's talking about taking your *life,* how he knows where you live, what you drive, serious stuff."

"He really said that?"

Harvey nodded, gravely. "He said somebody saw you and two other men the other night at Caye Caulker in that bar." Then, after a moment, "That true, Riley? You did that?"

"Who you gonna believe?"

"I'm just asking."

"What else did he say?"

Harvey exhaled. "He said . . . well, he said something like, 'One gets the sense that Riley James isn't bright enough to see beyond friendship, so let's fuck him.' That's him saying that, not me, okay? Like he wants me to set you up or something. 'One gets the sense that Riley James isn't too smart,' shit like that."

"Juan gets the scents, huh? Who is Juan and what do his scents have to do with me?"

That halted conversation.

Harvey sucked his teeth and waved a dismissive hand, looking away. "You're turning this into a joke? How can you take this for a joke? Man, Turo's rubbing off on you."

But when Riley kept staring at him in mock seriousness, one eyebrow lifted, Harvey couldn't fight it, he chuckled, and for a moment, a brief moment, it was like old times.

"Hey," Harvey said. "We screwed?"

"Not if you don't set me up."

"No, no," Harvey jumping to his feet, "no, that's not . . . Yeah, okay, maybe I deserve that but I can't laugh through this, I'm sorry, it's like, like—I'm dying inside."

"We're going to get through this, man." Riley watching Harvey pace the room. Riley twisted around in his seat, ignoring the

pain in his abdomen, to get Harvey's eyes. "Listen to me," and
Harvey stopped pacing and looked at him. "We're going to get
through this but we need to keep our heads," pressing a fist
against his stomach, "and think from down here. Centered.
You understand? Like a rock. Right down here."

Harvey looked at Riley. "Where did you hear that from?"

Riley shrugged. "Read it in a book one time."

"Really? Like what, some Zen comic book?" Harvey's mouth
threatening to break out into a grin.

"Comic book? No, man, higher learning. A graphic novel."

"A what?"

"Never mind."

CHAPTER THIRTY

The ice rattled when Candice set the glass on the coaster and sat back in the rattan chair. "This is nice."

"The whiskey?"

"Well, that too. I meant out here, this breeze, the view. I don't think I've ever come out here."

Sister Pat followed her gaze out toward the sea and boat lights winking in the distance. They were on the verandah of the Château Caribbean, no one else out there. "How long have you been here, in Belize?"

"A year and a half? Yeah, about that, maybe a few months shy."

"And you like it?"

"Oh, it's wonderful. Now. At first, the poverty, the heat, the dust—it was too much, too much in your face, but now—it's a different story. Just, just look at this. That is a perfectly raw beauty out there. It's been great for photographs. Don't even get me started on the cayes, or the rainforest."

Sister Pat nodded thoughtfully. "Photography, this is the place for some interesting shots, that's for sure. And there's Riley."

Candice reached for her drink, putting on a tight smile. "Who is the reason you're asking me to meet you here, I'm assuming." She sipped the drink, peering at Sister Pat over the rim of her glass. "Mmm, this is so good. I'm not a big fan of single malt but *this* is awesome."

"I can't drink anymore. But I did enjoy it. To a fault." Gazing over the railing, Sister Pat said, "When I first came to Belize, I was about your age. Wow, so long ago. I was stunned when I first came, just stunned. I was a nun, mind you, very sheltered, naïve. Taught school but didn't really understand the culture. Trouble was I was more adventurous, relatively speaking, than the other sisters. I wanted to explore. So I did, whatever chance I got. Went on trips to the Maya Mountains, to the Blue Hole out on the reef, toured all those villages in Punta Gorda, every chance I got."

"That's what I try to do."

"Good. You'll get a good feel for the place. When I couldn't travel, I drank. Maybe to cope with the strangeness, I'm not sure. At parties, school fairs—discreetly of course. I even became an accepted member of the expat community—the Brits, this was before independence, when the British Forces were here and there were so many Americans from the embassy. That's when it really struck me how some of us Americans view the world. I'd do a lot of listening, I'd listen to my acquaintances talk and talk and sometimes I'd see myself reflected in them."

"Okay, I'll take the bait. How do Americans view the world?"

"Like it's our playground. Like it's Epcot. And if it's not what we are accustomed to, well, then something must be wrong with these people. That these aren't real people struggling with real issues just like us, you know? 'How could they not have a mall? Why aren't all these streets paved? My God, their leaders are so corrupt.' We come here and demand that they meet *our* standards. It repels some of us, we won't or can't even imagine what it must be like struggling to make ends meet in a place that's not like Peoria, Illinois."

Looking at Candice as if she might be included in this assessment.

So Candice said, "You think I—being an American—you think I see Belize like that?"

"I sense you have a great affection for this country." Sister Pat holding her eyes. "And one person in particular. But I guess I wonder, I have my doubts, how well you know what you like."

Candice finger-stirred the ice in her drink, deciding simply to listen.

"There's the saying 'Where there's smoke there's a fire.' The locals have one that goes, 'If da no so, da nearly so.' 'If it's not so, it's nearly so.' Let's say you're an expat, you're new to the country and you're driving, like a lot of them, a shiny new Range Rover, something big, you're going to attract attention. Not only are you two shades paler than the average Belizean, but you may very well be living in a pretty nice house, relatively speaking. People notice, they talk. And let's imagine you have a certain kind of job that requires a certain level of secrecy, you're in the DEA, let's say, you must necessarily associate with others like yourself, in government buildings and the U.S. embassy and the like, and people notice that, too. Word travels." Sister Pat's fingers swept up and fluttered. "Like pollen, settles here, settles there. Nothing dramatic, it just happens. Like dust rising when a car rolls by, part of the scenery. People talk, people listen. It's a small country, and soon enough people have heard a little something. No big deal, you might think. But, no, in some situations, it can be a big deal. For me, anyway."

"You're trying to tell me something, Sister Pat, but seems to me you're making a huge assumption."

"I have lived here thirty-five years and I've seen Americans and other expats come and go, nervous white people, quiet and secretive, reserved Brits, I've befriended many of them. Something else—I became their de facto local guide, the—one of them called me this once—the hip sister. True. A tour guide is what I was, I had a universal pass to parties and conversations. I was a dreadful, just a dreadful embarrassment to the convent, but outside—everybody trusts a nun. I was privy to drunken confessions many a night and learned an awful lot about other Americans, just by being the friendly smiling nun at the dinners and cocktail parties and over drinks on those windy sea-view terraces, just like this one."

Candice sipped her drink, no longer tasting it.

Sister Pat said, "There is a young man who works at the embassy, who is a friend of an old friend of mine long gone from here. This friend was once the agent in charge of DEA in Belize. We still keep in touch. And now his young protégé, I believe his name's Henry Malone—he's the person in charge now. Don't ask me how I know, I can't say—just trust me, I know. And Mr. Malone . . . Well, enough of him. Now we come to you."

Candice removed her hands from the table and folded them in her lap. A slow swell of dread rolling over her. "Ask me what you want to ask me." Her tone sharper than she intended.

"Do you love Riley?"

Candice didn't trust her own voice right then so she only nodded.

"What are your intentions? To marry him, or imprison him?"

Candice tamped down the impulse to wisecrack, Aren't they the same thing? Something she didn't believe. Plus, the time for clever retorts was over. "Sister Pat, you've stepped over a line, way the hell over it and I'm beginning to not trust you."

"That's the least of my concerns. I'm here for Riley. You know, Candice, the only kind of delusion is self-delusion. I'm trying to answer this: Who is deluding themselves? You about Riley? Or Riley about you? Whichever way, the consequences, I hope you can foresee this, can be tragic."

Now the wave crashed over her and she reached out and held on to her drink for support. There it was, the wicked truth.

"You're troubled, I can see it."

"Really?" Instantly regretting the weak sarcasm.

"If what I was saying wasn't true, you would've gotten up and left. But you're here, you're sitting there because you want to hear this, and you *need* to hear it."

"Hear what, Patricia?"

"Either you tell him or I tell him."

"And you'll tell him what?"

"Just about every blessed thing I know."

A waiter was standing in the doorway. Candice twirled around and raised her glass. "Another one, please?" After he left, she said, without looking at Patricia, "I never thought I could love somebody like Riley. In fact, I don't want to love him. I wish I could stop." She shut her eyes briefly, then, "This road here," tilting her chin at it. "Sometimes I run this route fast, past here and all the way up Marine Parade and Barrack Road, past Lindy's, up Princess Margaret Drive, all the way home. I play this game with myself, I say, Okay, at the end of these four miles, I'll feel different. I'll get home, hop into the shower and step out washed clean, fresh and rededicated to my career, nothing will derail me. I'll do the job I came here to do with such laser focus, it'll be frightening. Then I can leave Belize, then I can get the hell out and back to my old self."

Candice picked up the coaster and turned it around and around, Sister Pat watching her face intently.

"It never happens of course. When I finish the run, I feel good and clearheaded, like any other hard run, that's it. It's silly when you think about it, it's like expecting to get up in the morning with a new brain."

"You're saying, or maybe it's what I'm hearing, is that you came here as one person but somewhere along the way you fell in love and lost your direction."

"I'd describe it, 'Fell in love and became confused.' I'm still on the same road."

"Then let me help you find your way." Sister Pat with a wry smile.

The waiter came, set the drink down, taking a moment to eye Candice's legs before leaving.

"You speaking to me tonight, coming with this threat, that's supposed to help me clarify things?"

"I love Riley, Candice. I can't condone what he does sometimes, but I don't want to see him go to prison either, so you'd think that the person who professes to love him and promises to be his wife one day would understand that I— knowing what I know—cannot sit by and watch him be betrayed and suffer, watch him be crushed. You've got to be kidding me, my dear, if you don't understand that. So what else is there to talk about tonight? The stars? The barrier reef? Photography? Let's subtract all that unnecessary stuff and examine what's important—in other words, clarify." Patricia pushed back her chair and stood up. "I've said what I've come to say. Now, I'll leave it up to you." She stared at Candice.

Candice wrapped her hands carefully around her glass. "He asked me to go away with him. He's bought two tickets. I don't know what he's thinking, what he has planned. But he has two tickets. Antigua then St. Kitts."

"I see," Patricia said and put a hand on the railing, looking out at the water.

"Maybe this will be all over sooner than you expect."

"By that you mean . . . ?"

"I'll think about what you said." Candice drank a mouthful of whiskey and shut her eyes as she swallowed, stomach burning. "I'll give it lots of thought. If I'm lost, what else do you expect me to say?"

CHAPTER THIRTY-ONE

"I love you, you know I love you," Riley said. "You're my boy and hey, I'll always love you, but you've got to listen to your mother. What? No, she said don't touch it, that's it, that's final, son. . . . Oh, come on, Duncan, don't say that. . . . No, I'm serious, that's not nice. . . ." Riley smiled, holding the phone and listening to his son's delightful Duncanisms. The living room window and the window to the porch behind him were open, the sounds of the street and a breeze flowing in. "Yeah, I *was* worried, your mother didn't tell me Miguel needed eye surgery. So how are you liking it in Mérida? It's big huh?"

"We walked around so much, my head hurts, Dad."

"What? That doesn't make any sense."

Duncan laughed.

"What are you eating? It sounds crunchy."

"Sliced apples. I'd dipping it in peanut butter. The way you eat it. Dad? Remember that place we went fishing that I told you I liked? We went with Mr. Harvey. By the airport?"

"The little clearing by the river? Sure, what about it?"

"When I get back, can we go there again?"

"But of course."

"I want to 'cause the other night? I dreamed I caught a

huuuge bonefish. I think I'm gonna hook one next time I go there."

"You can't catch bonefish in the river, but anyway, you're gonna hook something, I know you will."

Duncan crunched into an apple slice and began a wet spiel with his mouth full.

To sit back and listen again to the timbre of his son's voice delighted Riley. His boy was getting so big. "You took what? . . . Oh, sure, assigned schoolwork . . . so you didn't miss out, I understand. Well, that's smart . . . I know, I know, we'll go to the river when you get back, all right? I love you. Tell your mom I said hi, tell Miguel I said hang in there, okay? I love you, big boy."

He hung up and stayed on the sofa, feeling giddy. The glass of iced Knob Creek in his hand was partly responsible, but considering the events of the last few days, he ought not to quibble with a pleasant mood.

He rose and fixed himself another small one, then went to the bathroom to check his wound, loosen the tape some, while the ice in the bourbon melted just so. He sipped it on the way to the bedroom, feeling the best he had in days, sleep floating up comfortably to embrace him soon. There was a pile of clothes on the bed, shirts folded in plastic bags on the floor, old shoes, a stack of paperback mysteries. He wondered what was keeping Turo, he should've been back about two hours ago. Any of this stuff that Turo didn't want or whatever didn't fit, he could still take and sell, or give to family or friends, Turo's choice. Maybe Riley was impatient because he couldn't wait to see Turo's face when he gave all of this to him. Always a ghost of self-satisfaction hovering behind charity, wasn't there? Riley sipped his bourbon, musing on that.

He had folded a pair of jeans he never used and was sticking

them into a bag when he heard the van pulling up outside
and the gate creaking open. Riley threw on a shirt and went out
to the porch. He watched Turo drive up the tire tracks in the
grass, turning, and the headlights beaming into the carport.

"How'd it go, how'd it go, tour guide extraordinaire?"

Turo stepped out, grinning. "Now *that* was a long day, Mistah James." Immediately he started cleaning up, opening the
back door and tossing out empty plastic bottles.

"So tell me," Riley said.

"Mostly smooth," Turo said and slid open a side door. He
dragged the hand broom and dustpan from under a seat. "I
think maybe it coulda gone smoother, I'd've been back earlier
if they hadn't started touching the beers."

"Don't tell me somebody got sick in there."

"Nothing like that. Just a couple of them turned boisterous
after they got illubricated."

Riley sipped his drink. "Inebriated?"

"Yeah, that too. They couldn't make up their mind which
restaurant they wanted to stop at, one woman wanted Chinese, one man just wanted more beer, kinda nonstop like that
for a spell." Turo ducked into the van and started sweeping.

Riley told him he didn't need to do that, but Turo blew him
off. He told Riley that the tourists had dropped him forty
bucks tip. Riley, on his way in, said well, well, come inside, he
had a little something for him that might top that.

Riley tied up the plastic bags of clothes and brought them to
the living room, hearing Turo whistling outside, doors slamming. He thought about how much he should pay him for the
day. He got his wallet from the dresser drawer and removed
two hundreds, thought it over and fingered out another hundred, ignoring the inner voice whispering the warnings of being too generous.

Turo knocked on the door then entered. "I can please borrow a garbage bag to put all these bottles in?"

Riley told him to get one from under the sink. Turo returned with it and stopped, looking at the bags of clothes on the sofa and by the door. "Going somewhere, Mistah James?"

"I might be. This is for you." Riley handing him the three hundred, folded.

"Man," Turo said, embarrassed, pushing the money in his pocket. " 'Preciate this. This is a lot though."

"Then give me back fifty."

"No, it's cool. Let bygones be bygones." Turo grinning, cruising out the door.

Riley searched his closet for something else to give away. Outside, Turo was singing something so totally off-key it was painful to all life forms. Riley found two pairs of shoes, an old Timberland still in decent shape and a clean Nike. He dusted them off, hearing a motorcycle rumbling close by. He put the shoes in a bag, hearing Turo talking to somebody, a man saying something then another voice shouting, "No, that ain't him," and somebody yelped, then two gunshots split the air.

Riley threw himself on the floor by the bed. Time slowed way, way down, his cheek flat on the musty carpet, fingers gripping the bag, but it couldn't have been more than a few seconds before he heard the motorcycle roaring off and the front door banging open, Turo saying in a choked voice, "Help help, Mistah James? Help me . . ."

Riley jumped up, ran into the living room and collided into Turo. The boy was cradling his left arm, blood soaked through his T-shirt sleeve. Riley said, "Let's go, let's go," and led him into the bathroom, hit the vanity lights and stood him in front of the sink. Turo was saying, "They shot me, they shot me," Riley saying, "It's cool it's cool, you're okay," soaking a washcloth with warm water, wringing it out a tad.

"Let's take off this shirt, Turo," and Riley helped him peel it off. Turo gritting his teeth all the way, chin up.

Blood flowed from a spot on his upper arm, just below the shoulder. Riley wiped the arm down with the washcloth, Turo flinching, a hand raised to stop Riley.

Riley said, "Well, okay."

"Shit shit shit, I don't want to look, man," Turo shaking his head.

"You didn't get shot."

"Huh?"

The phone rang outside.

"You *almost* got shot. See that? Look, look at it, broke the skin but that's all. It's superficial, you're going to live." Riley wiped down the wound again.

"Grazed me? Grazed me, huh?"

Riley exhaled a long breath. He knew. He *knew*. He had questions to ask but he knew, the bullet that nicked this boy was meant for him. The fucking phone kept ringing.

He sat Turo in the living room and served him an ice-cold Guinness Extra Stout in a mug. He peered out the window, Candice's house mostly in darkness—Candice had said she'd be on a photo shoot somewhere—but across the street neighbors stood on their porches pointing this way and that, some milling around outside a fence. The phone started up again, the caller refusing to get the message, so finally Riley grabbed it and said, "What's up, Bill?"

Of course, it was interfering Bill Rivero from across the street, who else?—wanting to know did Riley hear that noise, sounded like gunshots. Was everything all right over there? Riley said yeah, he heard it, too, but didn't know where it came from, and was everything all right over *there*?

Riley helped clean Turo's arm with cotton swabs and alcohol and plastered a big bandage over it. He sat awhile and watched

Turo sip the beer, uneasy. Riley got up, brought back a fresh T-shirt and another Guinness and poured it, Turo holding out the mug, hand steady. Time to have the talk.

After Turo spoke a bit, Riley said, "Two of them?"

"I seen them roll by the first time, so when they roll by again, I'm like, What they want? The guy that bust the shot, from the time I look in his face when he walked into the yard, I could see he was up to something."

"Describe him."

"Beefy, but not like fat, you know? Black dude, short dreads."

"So he comes into the yard and what's he say?"

"Didn't say anything. Like he couldn't see me good 'cause the driver's door was open and I'm behind that wiping the side mirror, so when I step out, I'm like, 'Can I help you?' and he kinda look at me like I'm from Mars and that's when I see the gun."

"Nobody said anything? Nothing like, 'That ain't him'?"

"I don't remember that. All I remember is, man, that's when he bust the shot and I fucking started running, me one way, him the next."

"So he runs, jumps back on the bike and they're gone?"

Turo nodded, idly touching his bandage.

Riley walked to the kitchen to top off his glass of bourbon but once there he lost the feeling and emptied the drink down the drain.

Turo said, "I better go home."

He was scared, Riley could hear it. "I'll drive you home. Take all these bags with you. Most of these shorts will fit you good, some of the pants, those jeans maybe not, but you can alter them. If you want them, that is."

"Definitely." Turo stood up with his empty mug. He looked like he wanted to say something.

So Riley helped him. "What's up, Turo?"

"Mistah James, like now the bar is shut down and things happening here I don't understand . . . Like I'm not going to report this to no police or nothin' but, if I, like, seek another opportunity somewhere else . . . ?"

"No problem. In fact, I'd advise it." Riley reached into his wallet and took out all the cash, two hundred fifty-three, folded the bills and walked up to Turo and pushed them into his shirt pocket. "To help hold you over till you find something else." Partly out of guilt, partly out of a sense of responsibility.

"That other guy," Turo said, "I'm remembering this now."

"What other guy?"

"It's coming to me, his face. I seen him before."

"Who, Turo?"

"The guy that was controlling the bike, he passed under the streetlight, and I *know* I recognized him. I see him round the way sometimes, but in uniform, Mistah James. That dude's a policeman."

CHAPTER THIRTY-TWO

Carlo was hanging out on the sidewalk in front of his store, closed on a Sunday morning, the streets quiet and cool, when Riley pulled up in his truck. He parked as close to the corner as he could so that no other vehicle would obstruct forward movement. He nodded at Carlo, scoping the area as he got out, flipping his shirttail over the .45 stuck in the waistband of his jeans.

Carlo was eating cashews from a fist, shaking them. "What's happening, Riley?"

"I'm late?"

"Naw, Israel's talking to the others in the back. Don't go in yet, we'll talk afterwards. So what's new?" Carlo poured cashews into his mouth and chomped. "You looking jumpy, what's wrong?"

Riley shoved his hands in his jeans, slumped his shoulders, and smiled to act relaxed. "Might be because I have good reason." Looking up and down the street.

Carlo eyed him sideways. "Things cool between me and you, my boy. We ain't go no beef."

Riley said, watching a group of kids in church clothes trailing past, "Somebody took shots at me last night."

Carlo spun to him. "Did what now?"

Riley nodded at a man he knew in an SUV rolling by. "Wouldn't happen to have a clue who could've done it, would you?" and turned his head to Carlo.

Carlo said, "Uh-unh, no, don't even look at me. We got business we need you to handle, how would that make any damn sense?"

"Hey, I'm just paranoid. That's my feeling, maybe I should heed my instinct."

Carlo was staring narrow-eyed at him.

To soften the damage, Riley said, "Could be this guy I eighty-sixed out of the bar last week, full of threats."

"Hey, tell you what though, we wanted to, we would have and could have. Got me?"

Riley couldn't disagree, and left it at that.

The thump of a deadbolt sounded behind them and Riley felt big relief. He was nervous standing out here in the open and overly conscious of the hunk of metal in his jeans.

Three men filed out, Barrel and two others Riley also knew only by their street names, Boat and Jinx. They were wearing jean shorts, flip-flops, sandals, Sunday morning casual, coming up to shake hands with Riley, saying they hadn't seen him 'round a long time, goofing on him that his place was getting too high-class for them. VIP room in the back and all this mess? Look out now, royalty. They lit up cigarettes.

Riley strained a smile or two, not paying much attention, hearing them talk about drinking and some nightclub fight last week. He didn't know much about Boat or Jinx and didn't really care to, except that Boat, the wide-body, was quieter and smarter than Jinx, the handsome one, who considered himself dangerous and liked to say behind his pretty smile, "Jinx is no joke."

After a minute, Carlo said to Riley, "Ready?" and Riley was only too.

They walked through the darkened store and through the back door, crossed the cement yard and entered the storeroom, where Israel sat waiting, legs spread, hands clasped on his cane.

"My boy is here. Grab a seat and let's talk, Riley. Pull that chair closer."

Riley drew a chair next to Israel's and sat down. Carlo told Israel about someone taking a shot at Riley last night.

"Jesus Christ," Israel said. "Who you think did this, Riley?"

For a second, Riley considered telling him. Instead, "There's a guy got kicked out last week at Lindy's. Don't worry, I know where he stays."

"You need some help?"

Riley pretended to think it over. "Let me make contact with him first, see how that goes."

"You need help just say it." Israel belched silently and tapped his chest with the side of a fist. "Damned sour stomach." He said to Carlo, who was just about to take a seat, "Get me a ginger ale from inside the shop, please?"

Carlo shook his head, sleepy-eyed with irritation, but he went to get it, Israel saying if they didn't have that or Sprite then anything with good fizz.

Israel leaned on his cane and regarded Riley. "Come here, Riley, come," beckoned him with a nod. Riley slid to the edge of the chair. Israel said, "How you feeling? How's your belly?"

"Healing. Still tender, but not too bad."

"That's good, that's good. You don't want to be in pain when you work. Such a nuisance when you don't have your health. You don't want to be like me here, hurting all the time and doctors can't figure out what's wrong with my gut. Last night I was in terrible shape, terrible. Nothing worked, antacid, Maalox, nothing. I'm holding a pillow to my belly, like this, see, I'm rocking, moaning, like a fucking baby, and I start worrying,

I'm there groaning and thinking what if this is cancer? Who'll take care of the business? Carlo? *Pffft.* Carlo's not ready. He might think so but"—Israel made a face—"too emotional. Makes him unstable. I'm not lying. You understand what I'm saying, you've seen it. He'd need some help. What I'm asking you is this." He reached out and gripped Riley's wrist. "I have a place for you in my business. You sure, you a hundred percent sure in your heart of hearts that you don't want to stay on with me? Can you look me in the eye and tell me that?"

Riley stared at the floor, then looked up. Israel's grip was steely but his eyes were kind; sometimes the old boy was capable of gentleness.

"I need to know, son. I make a grand offer like this to you, show me the respect of a prompt response, that's all I want. Be honest with yourself, and answer."

Carlo reentered the room. He cracked a can of Sprite and put it on the metal table close to Israel, Riley self-conscious now with Carlo looking on; Israel's fingers bony, his eyes wrinkled and more rheumy than Riley had ever seen. He'd known this man, this rapidly aging hustler, nearly all his life, and Riley had a feeling, looking at him now, that it might be cancer indeed, and felt sorry for him. And yet. "Yes, yes. I'm a hundred percent sure this is my last run."

Israel released Riley's wrist and slowly sat back. He strained to push himself up with his cane and got his Sprite. He took a swig and set it down, looked at Riley. "We know your friend Harvey is alive somewhere, okay. They didn't find a single body in the fire. Aside from the remains of a dog or maybe it was a cat. I hear he might've run up to family in New York, but that's fine, we'll let that slide for now. The important thing, tell him this for me, it'll be good for his health: don't get ambitious again." He'd gone from warm- to cold-hearted in a snap.

Riley said, "The man you want? It's not Harvey. The man

behind all this is a guy called Lopez, drives for Minister Burrows."

Carlo pulled up a chair in front of Riley and sat down. "You want me to tell him, Israel?"

Israel put up a hand and said to Riley, "You don't think we know who planned the setup? But we are not going to touch Victor Lopez. Foolhardy is what that would be if we mess with a man with governmental ties. However, since we had to send a message to people, better it was to people like your friend Mr. Clock."

None of this surprised Riley, and only proved something to him. Let intuition be your boss. He had intuited correctly to keep quiet about Lopez being behind last night's shooting; Lopez was his problem—that's what it amounted to.

Carlo said, "You taking notes?"

Riley's mental notebook said it in bold: The Monsantos wouldn't touch Lopez and Lopez would lay off the Monsantos directly, but everybody could touch Riley. That's how this game worked.

Israel waved a hand. "Enough with all this old business. It's time to discuss current affairs." He hobbled over to the door and turned the lock with a click. "Now then."

Ten minutes later the door opened and Riley departed alone.

And about ten minutes after that he was at Caribbean Hospital, at the bedside of Roger Hunter, who was not doing well.

"How so?"

"Weak," Roger said. "Just a weakness in my arms and my grip." He flexed his fingers a few times. "A general malaise. But I'm glad to see you. Thanks for coming."

Riley dragged his chair closer to the bed. "Listen, Roger. I'm here partly for selfish reasons."

Head propped high on the pillow, Roger stared at him. "You've sparked my curiosity."

"You asked me when I was here if I needed a getaway, a safe place. That was very kind of you. I'm here again because I want to know if you'd be able to assist me with something else."

"You're also flattering me. But I like it. However this dying man can help you, he will. Any friend of Patricia is my friend."

Riley said, in a low voice, "It concerns guns. I was wondering if you knew . . . If you had a source where I might be able to buy a few guns."

Roger sat up on his elbows and motioned for Riley to help him. Riley took him by the hands and pulled him up, helped swing his legs off the bed, so that he was sitting straight, feet on the floor. He pointed a trembly finger at the cup of water on the table, and Riley stood up and brought it to him. He drank and looked at Riley. "Young man, are you humoring me?"

"What? No . . . I'm not."

"Your eyes tell me you're interested, but before I expose myself I need to know you're really interested."

"I am."

Roger twisted around to check behind him, and Riley craned his neck to see the other patient asleep in his bed.

"I won't ask why you need these weapons. I'll assume that they're for your protection?"

"Let's assume that."

Roger nodded, wiped his lips with the back of a hand. "I have reliable information. Information I'm passing on to you without any profit motive, without any stake in whatever may transpire." He leaned his head forward and said quietly, "There's a man who may have several firearms in his possession that he needs—in the parlance—to unload. Is it something like this you're interested in?"

"That's why I'm here."

Hands clasped, Roger leaned back. They looked at each other for several seconds. Roger sniffed and said, "It's a man I've known for some years, a former felon I've counseled, who unfortunately has not turned his life around. Who has an assortment of firearms. This is what he's confessed to me, that he'd like to sell."

"Where did he get them from?"

"From someone's house perhaps."

"Stole them?"

"A safe full of them."

Riley said, "A safe? Do you know how many guns? Or what kind?"

"So you're really serious."

"I told you I am."

Roger said, "The safe has sixteen guns. Thousands of rounds of ammunition, and very importantly, Kevlar vests."

Riley wondered why that sounded familiar. He was about to ask another question when a possibility occurred to him: Brisbane Burns's guns? A safe full of sixteen guns and body armor? Of course they may be Brisbane's. "Sixteen guns. Any assault rifles?"

"So I've been told."

"Handguns? Like any .45s? I'm used to the .45."

"You're in luck."

Then these must be Brisbane's, all right. Riley sat straight and took in the moment.

"I know what you're thinking," Roger said. "*Who is this old guy?*"

"Well . . . yeah."

"Look, I'm a cynical man, Riley. These guns, I understand, were taken from an individual who does not exactly deserve good people's sympathies. Which is why they've probably not been reported stolen. Many of them, I'm sure, are quite illegal to own in this country."

Riley looked at Roger, thinking renegade ex-priest, look at him. Old and seemingly harmless. Riley thought, You are Sister Pat's friend for sure. Maybe that's why Riley felt at ease when he said, "So let's imagine I need these guns tomorrow. This would be between me, you, and who else?"

"A man who knows better than to push his luck."

"That's definitely a requirement."

"A man who keeps quiet when necessary. Who is very careful. In light of how miserable eight years in Hattieville prison was for him."

"And if I say today, yes, let's do this, it's you who will contact him?"

"This very afternoon."

"No names can be exchanged."

Roger gave him a nasty look. "I might be half dead but senility hasn't set in yet."

Riley lifted a palm in apology. "Just making sure." He smiled at Roger, and Roger nodded, and that's how the deal was made.

Sometime later, after small talk, mostly about how vile the hospital breakfast was, Riley helped Roger into his wheelchair and pushed him out into the hall, in front of the screen.

Riley put his hands in his pockets and stood beside him. "Hey, Roger? There's nothing in it for you? As middle man, twenty percent maybe? I could insist."

Roger inhaled the sea air and shut his eyes. "This *is* for me." He looked up at Riley. "I'm doing this for Patricia, too, don't you understand? I know how much you mean to her, and this is for my own sense of justice. Tell me something, Riley, who doesn't hope to God that one day bad men will suffer, suffer and lose it all, even if in real life it's so often the other way around?"

Later, Riley walked into Miles's kitchen. Harvey was clearing breakfast from the table and Gert was at the sink, suds up to her elbows. Riley didn't have to say anything. As soon as he sat, Gert toweled off her arms and huffed out of the room.

Harvey poured two cups of coffee and sat with him. He told Harvey about last night and why'd he just parked the truck in Miles's garage with the intention of keeping it there indefinitely.

"Shit, Riley, if Lopez wants to find you, he'll find you."

"Maybe. I'm hoping to give him reason to not want to look for me anymore."

Harvey sipped his cup, put it down. "How do you mean?"

Riley lifted a slice of bacon off a plate and crunched on it.

"Riley?"

Riley washed down his breakfast with a swallow of burnt-tasting coffee.

"Riley, you got something cooking?"

"You're gonna have to help me."

"You're gonna have to tell me what you're talking about."

"What I'm talking about is the Monsantos are making their run on Tuesday morning. On the New River. It's me transferring the stuff to another boat, and once that's done, I'll radio Carlo and he'll receive payment from the Mexicans, and that's how, Harvey, that's how there'll be an opportunity."

Harvey was shaking his head. "No, no sir, I'm not fooling with that again."

"No, Harvey. Inform Lopez."

Harvey reared back, eyebrows raised. "You lost me." Then, slowly, he smiled. Yeah, I think I see where you're going."

"Tell Lopez he wants a payday? He can have one without the hassle of selling all that cocaine to get his cash. We can give him time, place, all the details he might need but first, first he's got to lay off me. Tell him I can set this up for him but he's got to step far away from me."

"How much—"

"Four point four million cash."

Harvey whistled.

Riley rose from the table and turned on a small radio on the windowsill, a British voice droning about Pakistan sticking to its schedule for parliamentary elections. Riley raised the volume, sat down, leaned across the table and beckoned to Harvey. He put a hand at the back of Harvey's head and pulled him close. "You're in this with me?"

"Yeah, yeah . . ."

"I need to trust you, I need to rely on you."

"Of course, of course."

Their heads almost touching, Riley stared into Harvey's eyes until he started to feel convinced. He sat back in his chair and said, "This is how they're going to do it. Two guys are going with Carlo, two jokers if you ask me, Boat and Jinx. Everybody, and I mean everybody, will be armed. They'll be going to a farm in Orange Walk that's off the Northern and a couple miles down a dirt road, just past an old rum shop. I'll draw a map closer to the time, but anyhow, a house on the farm is the place where money will change hands. One guy will be with Carlo at all times, the other man will be outside as a lookout. The Mexicans usually have a couple guys themselves, maybe one outside, two inside. No reason to think it won't be the same this time. Now, you're saying Lopez has two men still running with him?"

"Yeah, and that's it, far as I know."

"Surprise being the chief factor, nobody ever having done something like this to the Monsantos in all my years with them, they won't be prepared for it."

"I don't know if Lopez's crew will want to do this. Remember before they had BDF and police working with them, but now?"

"Now? Now you tell them they'll get some assault rifles. Pistols if they want that too. And Kevlar."

Harvey dropped his head low and peered into Riley's face. The radio newsman was saying that suicide bombings and other attacks in Baghdad had fallen significantly in the last month. Harvey glanced at the door as though somebody might be there, listening. Amusement creeping over his face, he said, "Riley, what the hell are you cooking up, you crazy fool?"

CHAPTER THIRTY-THREE

Riley and Miles sat in the car across the street from the hospital, Miles at the wheel, Riley dozing. The day was blistering so it was good to be in the shade, catch a wink before events started churning.

Miles said, "How long ago did this guy go in there?"

Riley opened his eyes. "Twenty minutes? About that?" shutting his eyes, dozing off again.

Another minute passed, maybe ten, then Riley yawned and stretched, sat up and looked across the way at the hospital gate. Miles was watching it, too, a hand on the wheel. "He's taking too long," Riley said. "I hate this shit."

"So your contact in the hospital that summoned him has to vouch for you, that's how this goes?"

"Apparently the guy doesn't trust anybody, and I don't think he's got a phone either. People can't reach him unless he wants to be reached."

"Cloak and dagger, huh?"

Riley stole a glance at Miles, assessing how he was handling accompanying him on this deal. He said, "I don't want to beat a dead horse, but I can't thank you enough."

Miles said, "Hey, no problem. Like I told you before, I've

been restless. I don't know what it is, brother." He scratched his head. "Maybe I miss the ring, the training, the whole discipline. But domestic life, that nine-to-five routine day after day—it's wearing me down. Anyway, don't worry, and didn't I promise I'd help you?"

"I know that," Riley nodding, "but it's not like this is something you do every day, like taking out the trash," and his eyes settled on Miles's left hand resting on the wheel. "It's not like you're me. Who's used to the gutter."

Miles shook his head. "Don't start."

"No, it's true. Just funny how we grew up close but life took us down some entirely different roads."

"Boxing, you know? It's because of boxing I struck out on a different path. If it weren't for that, who the hell knows what I'd be today, or where. Jail maybe?"

"I don't believe that for a second." Riley staring at Miles's hand on the wheel, half of his forefinger missing. "The guy that did that," Riley said, "you ever run into him?"

Miles looked at his hand. "I used to see him around. Not anymore though. Might be he's in jail, or somebody finished off that beating I started and killed him. Now, if he'd done this during my career? I really would've killed him."

"But you didn't, that's what I'm saying, we're different." Riley leaned his head back and gazed out the window. "Sometimes I wish I could play it again. Rewind to that day, the moment right before I said yes to running that errand across the bridge for Israel Monsanto. I was sixteen. Damn, I didn't know anything. Don't laugh, but sometimes I wish—I wish I was innocent again."

Miles said, "Why would I laugh?"

"I've hurt people, Miles. I've done some vicious shit."

Miles was silent, giving the words thought.

Riley turned his gaze down the street and saw himself, sixteen and skinny, riding away on a black Rudge bicycle, his pants cuffs clothespinned tight to prevent them catching in the chain; heading over the bridge with a stuffed manila envelope in his backpack.

Riley said, "I've done things that made sense at the time but make me feel like a bully now. That feeling, it sticks to you, you begin to think, That's who I am. All that shit, that must be the real me. You think it defines you, and you wonder if all these things, these things you did, if they were smart moves at the time, why do you get depressed whenever you remember them? And you always think about it, you can't help it."

"If you're referring to something you did in order to stay alive or to help somebody, like save their lives? Don't beat yourself up, man. It might've been necessary. Lots of times when I was boxing, my early days? They put me in the ring with some boy who wasn't in my league, same weight class, maybe similar record but no way, no how shoulda been in there with me. Physically, mentally, skills-wise just wasn't ready. So what do I do? Let him look good? Absolutely not. A couple times, I carried guys for two, three rounds but I still ended up thumping them. Did I feel like a bully? Sometimes, little bit. Listen to me though, Riley, when you're in the game, you've got to be in all the way. Or don't play. Because you can't win half-assing it. That's the mistake people make, they don't *commit*."

"I know you're right but some nights when I can't sleep, I wonder how my life would've been, and sometimes I feel like I'm still waiting for my old man to come home, hang out with my mother and me, and then, I'd let them show me the way."

"The way?"

Riley nodded, looking off. "The way to live a decent life. For once."

With anybody else it would have been awkward. Not with Miles, who had known him since forever.

Miles nudged his leg. "Look, he's here."

A man came out and stood at one of the gateposts smoking a cigarette. He was a cool, skinny black guy somewhere in his fifties in sleeveless T-shirt and dress slacks, red Kangol cap, taking a deep draw on his smoke. He didn't look at them and didn't move from the spot until he'd finished, flicking the butt aside and crossing the street. He traveled with a self-conscious hood bounce, a hitch and a glide, going away.

Miles said, "What, should I follow him?"

"That's what I was told but . . . this guy's still walking."

They watched, the skinny man strolling on.

"I don't believe," Riley said, "this guy's got a car."

"So how . . . ?"

The skinny man kept going.

"Let's follow slow," Riley said.

Miles eased the car out and rolled after him, ten miles an hour. A horn tooted behind them and a car veered around. After another driver overtook them, Miles steered to the far right.

The skinny man turned left onto Daily Street. Miles sped up to the corner, slowed way down into the turn, the skinny man crossing to the right side of Daily Street. He sauntered on, not a worry in his head. Miles hugged the far right, grazing parked cars. Another driver tooted him, zipped around, then another one, a woman shooting him a glare. Miles said, "Okay, this is bullshit."

Crossing Queen Street, the skinny man lit up a cigarette, strolling to where Daily narrowed and became Handyside Street, dirtier and darker, the buildings shabbier, fences leaning. Maybe six houses in, the man stopped, turned casually and nodded, the first sign that he knew they were following him. Then he swung to the right and disappeared down a lane.

Miles parked streetside and he and Riley got out fast, Riley carrying two big duffel bags. They saw the man entering a yard down the lane. By the time they hit the yard, he'd gone around the shambling clapboard house to another one just like it in the back. A dirt yard, a netless basketball hoop on a straight wooden pole. A rusted bicycle, one wheel off under a mango tree, buckets and other trash in the bush behind the corrugated zinc fence.

The man opened a screen door, beckoned them with a nod. "Wipe off your feet."

Miles paused, searching for a mat.

"Just fucking with you," the man giving a half smile.

The room was cramped, dark and dingy, low ceiling. It smelled of sweat and chicken grease and stuff Riley didn't want to imagine. He could make out dishes piled in a washtub in a makeshift kitchen to the right, daylight peeking through a round hole in the wall. They followed the man deeper into the house, where a light was shining. A kerosene lamp on a table. A woman in a headwrap sitting there, half her face in shadow.

Something creaked, and after Riley's eyes adjusted he saw the playpen in a corner, a baby inside tottering around.

"These the fellows?" the woman said.

The man indicated yes with his cigarette.

The woman tipped her head back to appraise Riley and Miles. It was hard to see her eyes in the poor light, but she could've been the skinny man's sister: same sinewy arms, wolfish face. "Mawning," she said with a brief smile, no front teeth. "What's the password?"

Miles threw Riley a look. Riley looked at the man, then the woman.

She flashed her gums. "Joking, mahn, joking."

Same sense of humor, too.

"What you need?"

Riley told her and she nodded at the man. He went into

another room. They could hear heavy stuff being moved around, dragged across the floor. He returned dragging a wooden trunk. Left it by the table and went back to the room, Riley all the while trying to be polite and not look around at the grungy house, the floor filthy, clothes lying about; the woman doing the opposite and being impolite, staring at Riley and Miles, sizing them up.

The man came out dragging a second trunk, a little boy sitting on it. The man shooed him off, the boy skipping over to the woman. She patted him on the back, told him to go play outside little bit till she's done. He left, gaping at Riley and Miles.

The man set the kerosene lamp at the edge of the table and opened the trunks. He threw a length of oilcloth on the table, and one by one he took guns from the trunk and laid them down. Various assault rifles, black carbines, magazines curved and straight, one pump-action shotgun, pistols.

Riley said, "Any more light?"

The man shook his head, moved the lamp to the center of the table and adjusted the flame to better illuminate the hardware. The woman said, "Sorry, sweetie, I have a condition. Too much light's not good for my eyes."

Riley recognized the Garand, the World War II rifle, looking classic and clean. He handled the pistols, checking if the chambers were empty, dropping out the magazines and slapping them back in; locking back the slides, releasing them with a snap; dry firing with muzzles pointed at the floor. He hefted two of the carbines to his shoulder, flipped up the dust cover and checked down the sights. He put them back with a "Hmm," touched an AK-47, nodded.

Half for show. Riley didn't know that much about firearms beyond what Brisbane had taught him. But these, he recognized, were fine, well-maintained pieces. That's because they were Brisbane's.

"My friend said you might need some Kevlar?" The man pulled out the body armor from the other trunk and flopped the vests on the table. Next he set down two boxes of .223 caliber rounds and a military green ammo can.

Riley, faking it, picked up a vest, held it tight to his chest and looked down at it with a frown. "Yeah, yeah . . ." dropped it back on the table. "So how much?"

The woman said, "How much for what?"

"Everything."

"Everything?" glancing at the skinny man then smiling at Riley. "You a serious consumer."

Riley stayed quiet.

"Why don't you name a price?"

Riley waited, before he said, "Five thousand."

The woman produced a soft pack of Newports from her bra and shook out a cigarette. The man took the occasion to fire one up himself. The woman, head tilted back, let out a cloud of smoke. "You gonna have to hit me again, sweetie."

From the playpen the baby whimpered.

Riley gave a deep-thinking performance and said, "Five thousand five. With no ammo."

The woman didn't bother. She twisted around in her chair and reached a finger out to the playpen, the baby grabbing it.

Riley said, "Let me show you something," stooping to unzip one of the duffel bags on the ground. The skinny man quickly shifted his feet, reaching behind his back. Riley said, "Easy, easy, it's not like that." The man lowered his hand, stepping away. Riley brought out a Ziploc filled with cocaine, lifted it high and set it down amid the guns. "Colombia's finest. Two kilos."

The woman turned around and straightened. The skinny man lowered his cigarette. Except for the baby—*ga ga ga*—not a sound in the room.

"Uncut. Weigh it yourself. You got a scale? Over ten thousand dollars right there in that bag."

The man approached it and said, "A little taste?" Riley nodded. The man unsealed the bag, sank a finger in the powder and dabbed his tongue. He looked at the woman, who said, "Lemme see that thing."

While she rubbed some on her gums, Riley said, "That plus a hundred dollars ought to do it."

The woman put the bag in her lap and said, "Wait now," by her tone, sorely disappointed.

"You saying that's not fair?"

And so the real negotiations started. It went back and forth for maybe two minutes, the woman remonstrating, never letting go of the Ziploc, Riley insisting they were taking advantage. "Ain't that right, buddy?" to Miles; Miles, the only words he said the whole time they were in there, "You got *that* right."

In due time a deal was struck, and they came out of the house perspiring. The Ziploc bag and two hundred dollars for everything—guns, ammo, Kevlar. While the man and woman weighed the bag in a back room, Riley and Miles paced the stretch of yard at the side of the house.

Miles palmed his forehead dry and shuddered. "Hoo boy, she got some serious BO. It was like a spirit in there, like a dark presence, sweet Jesus." Walking along the fence, he stopped. "Hey . . ."

The woman, sporting gigantic sunglasses, was standing in an open doorway at the side of the house. She took a long drag on her cigarette, blowing smoke from the side of her mouth. She said, "Price increase. Forty dollars more. Think you could handle that?"

Riley said, "I guess I have to," reaching into his pocket, peeling open his wallet. "Inflation is a bitch."

She snatched the money and said, "Come inside and pack your things," and returned to her cave.

Miles said, "Man, I'm sorry about that."

Riley shrugged. "Hey, the truth hurts."

Minutes later, they crossed Handyside Street to the car, each carrying a heavy duffel bag that occasionally clinked like tools.

That evening at Miles's house, Harvey said, "Lopez just called me. He's in."

Riley lowered the book he was reading. "In all the way? As in tell Riley James he's not a target anymore?"

"That's what he said."

Riley knew that look. "But?"

"Well. Part of it I'm not comfortable with."

"And that is . . . ?"

"He wants me to do the driving."

"To the farm?"

"Yes, but I told him, I let him know, man, I don't want to be involved hands-on like that."

"Harvey? Shut up. Seriously."

Harvey shook his head and released a big breath. "That's what *he* said."

"It's just driving."

Harvey clucked his tongue. "No, it's just me getting pulled along as insurance. Insurance that you, or we, don't fuck him over."

Riley smiled at Harvey. "That's true, no doubt about that. So let's not fuck him over." Getting in a dig, but Harvey was off somewhere in his head. Riley said, "Think about it, then when you have your mind settled, grab two beers from the fridge and meet me upstairs. We'll talk some more and I'll show you the kilo you'll give Lopez as a sign of good faith. Then I'll show you the weapons you'll present to them tomorrow that should put *their* minds to rest."

He lifted his book, his worn copy of the *Tao Te Ching*. Harvey sat like he wanted to say something else, then got up and sloped out of the room.

Riley searched the pages for words that he might find reassuring. It was a habit, but a man had to draw support from where he could find it.

CHAPTER THIRTY-FOUR

Riley drove off the Western Highway and down a rocky dirt road that curved around an overgrown pond and snaked through a row of shade trees and brush in the cool morning light. The truck squeaked and trundled over ruts and splashed through a patch of mud. After a bend in the road, the land cleared, and he heard the gunshots in the distance.

He parked in the field and walked toward the shooting. He came upon a group of young men lounging on camp chairs and perched in the backs of two big-wheel pickup trucks. He traded nods with them as he passed, clean-shaven faces, good-looking guys, some of them he recognized as occasional bar patrons. Brisbane, in boots and shooting jacket, stood poised with a shotgun, facing the skeet field. He lifted the gun to his shoulder, hollered, "Pull!" A clay disc flew out of the high house, Brisbane tracking, tracking, then the gun boomed and the disc exploded in a puff against the cloudless sky. "Pull!" From the low house this time, the disc sailing up to the left, Brisbane tracking, tracking and a boom, the disc shattering into small pieces that sprinkled to the ground.

Brisbane broke open the barrel and moved to the next station, the midpoint of the semicircle. He plucked out the old shells, then fished out two fresh ones from a jacket pocket and fed them to the gun, snapped it closed.

Riley approached and they stood side by side looking out at the field.

Riley said, "I've been thinking how to put this to you. Not like we're strangers and we have to be bashful but why I'm here, it's a business proposition. Concerning your guns."

Brisbane lifted his black straw fedora with a free hand, inclined his head to the left and mopped sweat off on a sleeve. He sat the hat back on neatly and said, "Personally, I prefer direct methods. Talk to me."

"I got reliable information a group of men returning from a robbery early tomorrow morning will have some of your guns."

"Some?"

"Some. But if their morning is a success, they'll have a chunk of cash in the neighborhood of four million."

A smile crept over Brisbane's face. He put his fingers to his lips and whistled toward the high house. A young man scuttled down the ladder and trotted over. He took the shotgun from Brisbane and walked toward the pretty boys by the trucks.

Riley said, "That's Rodrigo? The same Rodrigo used to do your garden?"

"That's him, yes."

"Man, I feel old. Boy's getting tall."

"I adopted him, you know? So what's this proposition?"

Riley said, "I might be able to get all your guns back, if you agree."

"*You* will get my guns from these people."

Riley said, shaking his head, "No, you. You're gonna get them."

Brisbane's brow knotted. He was about to say something, then lifted his chin, eyes narrowing in a smile. "You want me to get that money, don't you." He nodded, grinning now. "Yeah, you're supposing Brisbane wants his weapons bad enough Brisbane will do something reeeeal craaazy."

"I'll give you time and location where this crew will be. You'll get back your weapons—some of them—and get me that cash, of which I'll offer you a fair split."

"Oh?" Brisbane cocked his head. "Me and my boys do all the work and *you* will be the one offering to split with me? I see. For four million? Hell, keep the fucking guns, I'd rather take the money. But let's say I do this, the split will be on my terms."

"Well, like I said. *Some* of your guns. The rest of them, which is most of them, I might be able to locate. If you agree to this today, we split the way I believe to be fair. Or maybe your Garand, your Ed Browns, some of your ARs? You'll probably never touch them again 'cause I happen to know this crew will not have them tomorrow morning."

"So that's what you think you're holding over me?"

"I'm not holding anything over you. I'm making a proposition, Brisbane. Listen to it. I give you all the details, you get your guns and some cash, twenty-five percent of whatever's there. When I have my seventy-five in hand, I'll do everything within my power to bring you the rest of your guns. If I can't, then hear this: I'll pay you for them. Twenty-five thousand on top of that twenty-five percent."

Brisbane looked toward the field and laughed. He put his hands on his hips and squared up to Riley. "I know there's a reason I went and asked you for help, I know it. Something told me, go to Riley, the boy's got an ear to the ground, a hand on the pulse. So look at this now, this sounds very, very nice, but should I be worried that you might be dicking me around, Riley?"

"Think I'd walk in here, middle of your crew, everybody packing but me and do that?"

"I know, I know," Brisbane nodding and looking at the truck, looking away. "When I used to run with the Monsantos, you're maybe the only one I could trust day in, day out."

"Likewise."

"Seeing the feeling is mutual," Brisbane leaning in, "how did you come to find out these people have my guns? Or maybe me and you can talk about where this four mil came from?"

In the long silence, face to face, Brisbane understood an answer was not forthcoming. Eventually, he sniffed, fooling with his hat. He stuck a hand out, Riley took it. Brisbane said, "Let's go somewhere, grab a cold one we can talk further."

At Miles's kitchen table Harvey said, "They took two carbines, six magazines, the shotgun, all the ammo, the flak jackets, and three pistols."

"Kevlar, Harvey, Kevlar."

"Yeah, and, oh, it's three of them, me the wheelman. Lawd have mercy, I can't believe I'm saying that, wheelman. Somebody's van we using, I don't know who. Staging time, one o'clock tomorrow morning."

"It's about to start happening fast. You have everything ready?"

Harvey hunched forward. "Yeah. I guess." Sounding tired.

"Passports, cash? Hotel reservation made?"

"Yes, all that." Same tired note of resignation.

Riley wondered how long this was going to last, Harvey's willful refusal to accept his circumstances. If he couldn't, he stood a solid chance of getting himself hurt. Maybe, more than likely, it was . . .

"Gert giving you grief, Harvey?"

Harvey lifted his glasses, rubbed his eyes. "She doesn't want to go back to Guyana. She doesn't have any family there, not since her sister moved to England and the rest of them passed on."

"She's got *you*. You guys stay here, she might lose you next."

"Yeah . . . no, she understands. We bought the tickets, we're going . . ." He adjusted his glasses, looking at the table somberly. "My whole life is turned around. I never saw this coming."

Riley thought, Then you're blind. He said, "You'll be a richer man."

"Riley? You think this will work? Really?"

"I wouldn't be doing it otherwise."

"Get that money and take off, just like that. Begin a new life you're saying."

Riley nodded. "Yeah."

Harvey reached and snatched Riley's forearm. "R.J., buddy, can you believe we're doing this? Me and you? This, this don't hurt you? The bar, leaving it behind, your home? Your son?"

"Leaving Duncan is the roughest, but what can I do? I've got to have an out, in case it gets too hot for me here. At the moment it's not exactly wintry."

Later on, sitting on his bedroom carpet at home, Riley could still feel Harvey's hand gripping him and it made him feel sorry for his friend. Harvey wasn't made of the hardest stuff, was too fun-loving, too lacking in street meanness for what he'd gotten into. The swell of emotion surprised Riley, had him hoping keenly that he'd come through everything without too much damage to his mind.

He counted out eight thousand twenty in cash, all the U.S. currency he could find in his safe. Arranged two stacks side by side. Picked up the Kimber, checked the magazine, slapped it home, laid the pistol down. Picked up his passport and checked for the second time that day that his visa was current. He sat, encircled by everything, asking himself, hoping to feel it, if there was something missing, something he'd overlooked.

The phone rang and he was tempted to ignore it except he hadn't heard from the girl next door all day.

"Speak to me, baby."

"Riley?"

"Oh, hey . . . Sister Pat."

"Riley, when are you going to get an answering machine? I've been trying all day, you're never home or you don't pick up."

"I've been busy," and he fought a sudden and powerful urge to drop a hint, lay the groundwork for his farewell.

"Are you alone?"

"Yes."

"You have a minute we can talk?"

Riley looked down at the circle of cash, passport, .45, and said, "I was in the middle of something actually . . . but I might have a few minutes."

"Can you come over here tonight?"

"Ahh . . ." He didn't want to show himself on the streets any more than necessary despite Lopez's agreement.

"My friend . . . my dear friend died today," and suddenly Sister Pat was crying. "Roger died today."

Riley couldn't remember if he had ever heard her sound like this. "I'm so sorry. I'm sorry about that, Sister Pat."

"He'd been ill for so long . . . so long, and it's not that I didn't expect this, it's just . . . it's not easy when you lose a good friend."

Riley held the phone tight and listened to her breathy sobbing. He wished he could think of something to say.

"I've lost him, such a good friend, a *great* friend. I've lost him and now I don't want to lose you."

"Sister Pat, you're not going to lose me, what are you talking about?"

"You've been like a son to me, Riley. You've been like my own child, my own boy."

"I know," Riley said, "I know."

"Have I ever judged you? Have I ever let you feel . . . Have I ever let you feel alone or unloved or worthless, or that I didn't value you as a man? Oh, Riley, I . . . because I do love you, I want you to know that."

"No, yes . . . Hey, Sister Pat." Riley wasn't following this tangent.

"I have something to tell you, and I want you to listen to me." Her voice sounded clear, stronger. "You promise you'll listen to every word? To the end?"

"Yes, sure, I will."

"I worry about you. I do, I can't help it. I want you to understand something, okay? I was the one who asked Roger to offer you a place to go, to get away from the trouble you're in. It was me. He said he did, but you refused. Then this afternoon, he said . . . He was lying in bed and was in and out of consciousness, in and out all day. The hospital knew he was dying so they let me stay there, and I was holding his hand, Riley, I was holding his hand and talking to him, and there was a moment when he opened his eyes wide and all the energy he used to have seemed to fill him up again, just for a few moments. He gave me a little smile and . . . and we started chatting. Just chatted away. He was lucid, it was wonderful." Sister Pat's breath caught in her throat, and she sniffled and then was quiet for a second. "He told me what he did. About the guns. He said there were some vests, some bulletproof vests. He shouldn't have done that, I didn't ask him to go that far. He said he did it for your protection. He said you reminded him of himself when he was your age. He also said the deal he arranged went through. Riley, listen to me, please. Would you listen to me?"

Riley closed his eyes. "I'm here, I'm listening."

"I've always told you, Live an interesting life. I haven't agreed with all the decisions you've made, but it was your life and I've always said you're the one who's got to live with the consequences. But now, after today? I can't justify my silence, Riley. I know you have something planned, you're up to something. I know, and I can't keep quiet any longer."

"Sister Pat, you're confusing the hell out of me. What do you want to tell me?"

"Sit down for a second, sit down and hear me out. There's something you need to know. About your fiancée."

Riley felt a jab in his chest. He walked over to the sofa and sat down. "I'm listening," and he thought, Aw, hell, here comes something he knew he'd overlooked.

CHAPTER THIRTY-FIVE

Malone walked through Candice's living room in his bow tie and suit, shiny black shoes, perusing. He roamed the kitchen, touching the stove, peering through the screen door to the back porch, shoes echoing on the tiles.

From the living room, arms folded across her chest, Candice watched him open the cabinet by the fridge, asking, "You wouldn't happen to have any tea, would you?"

She went out to the front porch and looked up and down the street to see where he'd parked. Maybe around the corner? She saw Riley's truck and van parked in his yard, bedroom light on.

She came back inside and said, "You need to be careful. Our friend is awake next door."

Malone lifted the kettle. "You use bottled or straight from the tap?"

"The bottled water's in the fridge. Why're you dressed up like this? And why are you here? I know it's not for biscuits and Darjeeling."

Malone filled the kettle with bottled water, set the kettle on a burner, and turned the stove on.

"How did you get here, Malone? You didn't walk." She rubbed her arms, feeling exposed in her running shorts—when he knocked she'd been lying on the bed reading—and her too-small T-shirt she wore only around the house.

He came from behind the counter into the living room, examining the ceiling, all around, nodding to himself. He hitched up his pants and sat down. "If you had more time, you could've done a lot more for this place, make it seem a little more homey. Kind of bland, isn't it?"

"You didn't come here to insult my décor," she said, "nor drink my tea."

Malone crossed his legs, smiled almost wistfully at her. "I was at a party at the ambassador's house when I received word. So I decided to come and inform you in person."

"Received word about what?"

"You're well aware our work has been hurt by local law enforcement, a certain corrupt bunch anyway. In spite of that, we've gathered sufficient information and we know now that there's something afoot. It'll probably happen—if our contact is accurate—tomorrow morning."

"A shaky *if*," Candice said, sitting down.

"Nonetheless, we must follow through." He scratched his jaw, fixed her with a stare, and it began to make her uncomfortable. "We must follow through and end this operation on a high note since it's coming to a close."

"When? Has it been compromised that much?"

"Candice, listen to me," and he looked away, working through something in his head, then came back to her. "We have reason to believe that your association with"—he tilted his head—"our friend next door is damaging the integrity of the investigation. We'll be shutting down this part of the investigation, the house here, any aspect of it related to your work. By the end of the week, you'll be transferred out of here, first to the Miami office, then after a debriefing you may be assigned to a country of the administration's choosing. If you refuse, you may be asked to reconsider your future with the administration, possibly open yourself to an internal inquiry. It may very well happen, Candice, so this is why I'm here, to tell you personally that what transpires next, we believe tomorrow or the next day, is of the utmost importance to this operation. And to your career."

Candice sat back, arms folded tight across her chest. Her eyes drifted from Malone to the tiles, the brown grout. "What the hell . . . You expect me," she said, "to defend myself against that sorry-ass accusation, you're wrong. I have been here a year, dedicated myself to this operation a full year and now that local police screwed things up, I shouldn't think it's so predictable some of their dirt flies in my direction? Careful how we throw that suspicion around, Malone."

He tapped his feet. "Before you start preaching to me how deeply I've offended your professional sensibility, let me just say—the rumor isn't new. We heard months ago. Certain neighbors told us, during what they may have believed was casual talk, that you and Riley James are an item. You've been seen also in his truck, on more than one occasion, driving through the city, but that's understandable, to a point. Now there's talk of an engagement? I mean, are you insane? Now, wait, hold it, I know the closeness, this undercover friendship is part and parcel of your assignment, but the administration doesn't need to prove the nature of your real feelings in order to make adjustments. It's not about you, it's about results. If enough suspicion is there—and Candice? there is—I believe a change is warranted."

The kettle started a piercing whistle.

Candice stared at Malone for a time, before she said, "How do you take your tea?" getting up to go to the kitchen.

His hand shot out and his palm wrapped around her right thigh, stopping her. He looked at his fingers pressing into the pale skin of her inner thigh.

She said, "What are you doing?" shaking her head fast. "Don't."

He let go, pulled his arm away. His hand settled in his lap.

"What the hell was that?"

He lifted his shoulder and gave a long sigh. "Little bit of cream, one sugar."

She fixed his tea, the spoon clanking against the cup, loudly in the awkward silence.

"A girl, a local girl brought me here," he said, staring at the floor. "She's a secretary at the embassy. A nice young woman." He turned as Candice came with the steaming tea. "I've been lonely," he said. "My wife filed the papers yesterday and all day I've been feeling like shit. It's awful, divorce is plain awful. Do yourself a favor, don't ever get married."

He sipped the tea. She asked if it was fine; he said it was perfect. She arranged herself in the love seat to his left, legs turned away, out of groping distance. "This is kind of an odd way to inform somebody of an assignment change, abrupt to say the least."

He blew on his tea. "This whole operation has been kind of odd." He blew on the tea some more and slurped. He set the cup on the floor and pulled forward. "You'll be getting an official letter . . . I'm thinking, next week?" He wiped the corners of his lips with two fingers and seemed to be waiting for her reaction, then he reached down between his legs for the cup, stopped and looked at her. "Speaking of odd. You haven't asked why you'd be subject to an internal inquiry."

"It's because you think I've been fucking Riley James all this time, isn't it?"

He snorted. "No need to talk like that." He stood up and walked toward her room. "Candice, let me tell you something," paused to examine framed photos on the wall—a pier like a wooden finger in green water at St. George's Caye; a low wide-

angle shot of coconut trees going crazy in a blue-black storm—
and he said, "It's because we believe you're fucking the DEA."

"Didn't you just say no need for that talk."

"It's a different sense of the word, dear."

"Why don't you tell me what I should do, then drink your
tea and leave?"

He clasped his hands behind his back like some general and
strode away, into her room.

She sprang up from the love seat and followed. He was examining the room, studying the photos. He said, passing by the
open bathroom door with a quick peek, "The U.S. government
is paying for all this and I've never taken the time to inspect it.
Where's the other room, over here?" He pasted on a phony
smile, walking by, and instantly she understood why his wife
had divorced him.

In the other room, he put his hands in his pockets and looked
at the photography equipment she'd set up: the white roll of
backdrop paper high on two stands; light stands and umbrella
flashes arranged all around. "How come you've never taken
studio pictures of me?" He turned to her, one eyebrow cocked.
"Always wanted some special pictures done, private session, you
know what I mean? You've never offered, how come?" Leering
at her now, stepping toward her. "You take pictures like that
with the drug runner? Does he pose for you? You pose for him?"

"You need to leave," she said.

He came closer, so close that she had to take a step back.
"Nasty pictures, that's what he likes?"

"Malone . . ."

"Nasty things, you and him? But *hey*," Malone's voice rising, "only for investigative purposes of course." He was almost
touching her, all six feet two, two hundred and odd pounds of
acrophobic, Ivy League, Republican poster boy looming over
her with a glint of mean in his eyes; lips pinched, jaw clenched.

"Stop," she said, a hand up between them; her voice sounded like a young girl's. She *felt* like a young girl, with him bearing down, shuffling closer.

"What? Stop what? Telling you the truth? The hard facts? Like the ones you choose not to tell us whenever we're"—he showed her the gap between his thumb and forefinger—"*this* close? Huh?" He was on top of her now, breath smelling like sushi. "Tell me, what does this man do for you that's got you so completely"—he tapped her on the foreheard—"*screwed* up?"

She recoiled, her left heel touching the wall, and when he bumped her she glanced to the left, reached out and grabbed the heavy zoom lens on the worktable. "You don't get away from me right this second I'm swinging at you so hard you're going to see God."

He cut his eyes at the lens. Stepped back.

"You need to leave now."

He crossed over to the window. He put his hands in his pockets and looked out. After a moment he said, "So this is the view you have. Splendid, you can see his entire house." He craned his neck. "What's that in the backyard . . . a clothesline? A *clothesline*?" He said over his shoulder, "Can't afford a dryer, all the money he makes? Too much tucked away in mutual funds and IRAs, must be. You ever discuss money with him, in the midst of pillow talk?"

"Get out."

Malone did some neck rolls. "Let me tell you something so there are no further misunderstandings, Candice. We will be expecting calls from you this week. One way or the other. This asshole makes any move out that gate, doesn't matter for what—once he's out, you place a call."

"You trust me to do that?"

Malone said, "Now, now," and shook his head. "Don't be so sensitive. I'm ticked off for a reason. You're still a professional.

We need you more than ever to do this. Keep a sharp eye out. He moves, you call, and then report to the office immediately." He turned away from the window. "Any questions?"

"None."

They stared at each other, before Malone exhaled, eyes softening. "Evaluation question. Where do you see yourself five years from now?"

She was still holding the lens and she looked at it, put it on the table. On a beach somewhere, she wanted to say. Snapping photos, in a bikini . . . with a cold bottle of beer waiting in a cooler on a towel, under a huge umbrella.

Malone's lips turned down bitterly. "Me? I want to be doing something else. These people in this piece of shit place don't want to help themselves, then to hell with 'em. But . . . that? That's the future." He checked his watch and walked out of the room. "Yolanda's waiting for me down the street. That's a pretty name, isn't it, Yolanda? She's also sexy. Not as hot as you, I'll admit, but she'll do."

From a distance came the sound of a ringing phone. Malone looked toward the window. "Is that . . . that's his phone you hear so clearly?"

Candice nodded. "When his windows are open."

"Wow," Malone said, with a curious frown like he was puzzling over something, then he dipped his head so that they were eye level. "Make it happen, Candice."

CHAPTER THIRTY-SIX

Harvey said, "Okay then. Sure everything's cool? Okay then, see you later," and he put down the phone. He kept his hand on it a few seconds, thinking, before he stood up.

"What's the matter?" Gert said.

"Shit, I don't know . . . Nothing. Riley just sounds a little strange."

"Nervous, you mean?"

"Like me, you mean?"

Gert took hold of his hand and rubbed it between hers, and massaged his palm, bending and rotating his fingers.

"That feels good."

"Pressure points," she said, thumb-kneading the center of his palm. "Helps you relax. Focus. Don't be nervous."

He closed his eyes and leaned back against the headboard. The window curtains moved in the light breeze. They could hear Miles downstairs locking up the house, TV going off. Miles retiring for the night. Harvey said, "What time is it?"

"Twenty to midnight."

"Time to go." He lowered one foot to the floor and waited for his courage to collect. "Maybe I better have a quick drink."

"No," Gert said, grabbing the other hand and starting on

the palm, rotating the wrist. "Try to feel it, what I'm doing here."

"Just a little toot. Riley left a flask of bourbon in the kitchen."

Gert covered his face with a hand and brushed downward, fingers feathering to his chin and up again. "Breeeeathe . . . breeeeathe . . . Yes, close your eyes . . ."

"I should go, Gert."

"Breeeeathe . . . Oh, Harvey," sounding tearful. "I want this to happen fast and you come back and we go home again, I miss my house, I miss Sir Belly. I just want to go home."

"Hey, Gert, don't do this."

"I'm trying to be strong, baby, I'm *trying* but I miss my home. I don't want to go to Georgetown, I don't know Guyana anymore."

"If I'd've known getting in with Lopez woulda brought all of this I'd never—"

"Shhh," and she clamped her hand over his mouth. "Okay, sorry . . . no regrets. Breeeathe, yeees . . ." Her fingers feathering up and down. "I did everything like you said. I booked the room in that hotel by the airport, I have the bags packed. I'll pray, I'll think positive thoughts."

He smiled at her and let her fuss with his hair, finger-brushing it back, like he was going on a job interview. Finally, he said, "I really got to go now," and swung his other leg off the bed and stood up. "One quick shot of liquid courage and I'm gone."

Leaving the room, he caught sight of himself in the dresser mirror, a shortish man in black shirt, black jeans, a slim and sharp-boned woman following closely with worry on her face. He found the flask in a high kitchen cabinet and had a nip, then two more. Wiped his lips, and retied his boots for no other reason than not to have to look at Gert's forlorn face, which was getting to him, stirring up doubts.

At the bottom of the stairs, just before he opened the door,

Gert told him wait and lifted her gold chain necklace over her head. A crucifix dangled from it. She looped it over his head, having trouble with the fit, working it down and scraping his nose in the process. "There." She flattened the crucifix against his chest. "This'll help."

He looked at her. "Since when you've been so religious?"

"I believe that Jesus Christ our Lord will protect all who humble themselves before him and have faith in his power to protect good people from thieves and fuckers who seek to do us harm. I really do."

Riley lay in bed, arms laced behind his head, staring at the water stains on the ceiling. The map of Italy?

Not really. More like his lack of imagination. How come everybody always described a cloud or maybe a stain like this one as resembling the map of Italy? *See the boot right there!*

For the moment he was happy that his mind was wandering. . . .

He rolled his head to one side. The digital on the nightstand read 12:09. He got out of bed, turned off the lights and stretched out again in the dark, one foot on the floor. He watched the red digits flicker and change. 12:10.

He sat up, looked out his window into the bluish moonlight on the grass and put his head in his hands and said, "I must be stupid." He rose, took a deep breath and stepped over the pistol and cash and passport to go to the bathroom, to concentrate on something, anything else. Like shaving with his straight razor. . . .

No way, he wouldn't dare, not now. He washed his face instead, combed his hair. He picked up his toothbrush and stared at himself in the mirror. "You've been played," he said. "You know that? You have been well played."

He tossed the toothbrush on the counter, marched out and

picked up the pistol off the carpet, jammed it into the waist-band of his shorts. He snagged a semiclean shirt off the bed-post and left the house barefooted, not bothering to button the shirt, the door banging shut behind him.

A light was on in Candice's house, in the spare room. There was nobody on the street, as far as he could see, no neighbors hanging out on their porches or at their front gates or on their steps. Quietly, he opened Candice's gate and left it ajar. He pad-ded up the stairs and onto the porch. The windows were open and he could hear soft jazz lilting through like life was oh so placid, and with the stove hood light on, it was such a mellow little scene. He felt that powerful knot in his throat. He tried the door—unlocked, the knob turning. Careless, Candice, careless.

The door hinges squeaked, and Candice said from the spare room, "Who's that? Who's there?" rushing out to the living room, clutching a camera lens as he stepped into the house and said, "It's me, it's just me."

"Riley," she said, "hey, did I forget to lock the door?"

He closed it and flipped the lock. He stared at her.

"Riley?"

Her voice sounded the same, but he was no longer believing the act.

She said, "What's wrong?"

She frowned, looked at him curiously as he came forward, reached behind. "I'm here to show you what a thug looks like. Want to see a thug?"

He drew his gun and gripped it low. He smacked his bare chest twice when he said, "This is what a thug looks like, special agent. He's here in front of you. See him?" Slapped his chest and grinned, "No, don't be scared, this is what you expected to find all along. What do you think?" He held both arms out at his sides, feet apart. "Go ahead, take a picture, baby. Take your last one of me."

CHAPTER THIRTY-SEVEN

Harvey drove Miles's old Taurus up the Northern Highway to Bella Vista. He turned into the development and hung a series of lefts and rights along cracked and bumpy streets, toward the older houses in the back.

He stopped in front of a split-level with a steep zinc roof and Spanish-style railings. He looked at the radio clock. 12:53. Early. He wanted to wait in the car till 1:00 but he'd seen a figure come to the window and didn't want to seem too eager to please by arriving too soon. Didn't want to get them suspicious either by sitting out here. A man just could not win. He opened the car door and thought, Here goes.

First thing, happened immediately after he stepped inside, wiping his boots and trying to keep his eyes level, definitely not shifty-eyed—they started mocking him, in particular, for the clothes and the crucifix he'd forgotten to tuck inside his shirt.

"The mysterious man in black," Lopez said, slumped in a leather chair under a standing lamp in a corner.

The gaunt-faced man who was closing the door now said, "You a man of the cloth?"

This brought a guffaw from a potbellied younger guy with

short dreads, smoking a blunt by the open sliding door. "Fucking Zorro."

Lopez was working a newspaper crossword puzzle. "Start calling you Father Doolittle."

Thing was, they were all in dark clothes themselves, so now Harvey was annoyed. "It's you told me to dress like this." Directing a hard stare at Lopez.

Lopez gave him a long look and chuckled. "Don't mind us, come and grab a chair."

He introduced the men, Busha the stout one, Tic Tac, the gaunt-face—street names. Harvey said he thought he'd seen Tic Tac before. The man shrugged. "Corporal, in another life,'" he said and grinned, showing crooked bottom teeth.

Busha moved away from the sliding door and offered the blunt. "Hold some, Clock."

Which led Harvey to understand that he was probably going to be the butt of the jokes tonight, the shit-bucket carrier. "Nah, I'm cool," Harvey said, waving it away.

Busha held the thing in front of Harvey's face, smoke curling up. "You sure?"

"Yeah."

"Sure you sure?"

Harvey pulled back from the smoke burning his eyes, Busha smiling down. Harvey said, "Do me a favor, *potner*. Call me by my name. Harvey."

Busha glanced around, grinning, seeing if anybody else heard. Lopez was looking at them, and not smiling.

Busha left Harvey and pulled a chair at the dining room table and sat. Tic Tac picked up a paperback that was lying pages down on the table and sat across from him. Busha smoked; Tic Tac read. Lopez worked his crossword, pencil scratching and erasing. He said, under his breath, "What the hell's Bath separatists?"

What the hell are we waiting on, is what Harvey wanted to know.

Busha lifted himself off the chair and peeked out the window by the front door, returned to his chair.

Tic Tac said, "What this mean—*pantheon*?"

Lopez lowered his pencil and reflected. "That's . . . well . . ."

Busha beat him to it. "I just seen this thing on TV 'bout that. The old place in Rome where the lions used to slaughter the Christians, back in ancient times."

Tic Tac nodded with appreciation.

Lopez turned to Harvey. "You ready?"

Ready? He wished it was over. He said, "Let's do it."

Lopez, who had grown a Clark Gable mustache, seemed obsessed with stroking it, eyes smiling at Harvey. "Then let's do it," and he got up and crossed into the dining room and passed through an arched doorway to the back of the house.

Tic Tac tossed his book aside, stood up and stretched, arms to the ceiling, yawning but stopping abruptly as Lopez came back carrying two assault rifles and a shotgun like firewood. He laid them on the table. Busha stood up, as if out of respect. One more trip to the back of the house and all the equipment lay on the table. The black assault rifles, six full magazines, one pump-action shotgun, three semiautomatic pistols, and the Kevlar vests.

They checked and rechecked the guns noisily while Harvey sat very still and tried not to look nervous.

Tic Tac said, "Don't put that there, Busha, that's where people eat."

Busha moved a pistol off a place mat.

Lopez unfolded a map from his shirt pocket, jerking his chin at Busha. "Enough of that, now."

Busha mumbled something but he stubbed out the blunt in the kitchen sink.

Lopez and Tic Tac consulted the map spread on the table, pointing here and there, Lopez murmuring serious, Tic Tac shaking his head, disagreeing with something. Lopez reiterated, tapping a spot on the map. They hailed Harvey over and showed him the route in Orange Walk they were going to take, the road off the Northern—just a thread on the map—and the road off that, which wasn't on the map, Harvey having to follow Lopez's finger as it slid up to a circle of red ink by the New River.

"That's the property. We went by this morning. One road in, one road out. Three-quarter ways in, this farmer got a house, white maul, thatch roof, pigs in the backyard. I already talked to him, how I'm interested in property in the area, this and that, so that when we show up there again, it's like, Hey, no big deal, they're interested in buying . . . Busha, why you looking out there again? Pay attention."

Busha turned away from the window. "Just . . . you know—"

"See what I told you, that weed gets you all paranoid. Quit smoking that shit."

Harvey reviewed the map, the arrows in red ink that marked the route. They were all looking at him. Lopez stroking his mustache, Tic Tac fondling a carbine. Lopez said, "Problems?"

Harvey shook his head. "Nope."

Lopez sniffed. He tilted his chair back and looked at his watch. "Then we wait." He rubbed his eyes, yawned, and said, "Coffee anyone?"

CHAPTER THIRTY-EIGHT

Broken plates, glasses, and a wire dish rack on the kitchen tiles. A puddle of tea and pieces of a shattered cup that had been arm-swept onto the floor.

Riley held on to the counter with both hands, head bowed. The house was quiet except for the soft unmelodic jazz playing on the stereo, his heavy breathing, and the occasional sniffle from Candice, who was sitting on the sofa behind him. He couldn't stand to look at her, but he couldn't power up his legs to walk out the door either. His mind kept saying, Leave, don't look back.

"Are you finished?"

"Maybe," he said. His .45 lay on the counter. He studied it and had no interest in it. He stuck it back in his waistband anyway.

"Riley, please sit down."

"Hell, no."

"Don't you understand what I'm saying?"

"I could easily kill you, you ever thought about that?"

A long silence from her, and the jazz played on. Then, quietly, "You need to listen. Why do you think you haven't been arrested yet? Why do you think you're still here talking to me?"

"You want me to thank you?"

"You don't believe me."

"Believe you? I don't even *know* you."

He eventually forced his body to move into the kitchen, kicking pieces of a plate out of the way. He pulled a bottle of red wine from the fridge and poured some into a glass. He drank, looking at her wiping her face.

"What a terrible night this has been," she said. Their eyes met. "Riley . . . Riley?"

He shook his head, didn't want to hear this. No time or patience to listen to more bullshit about how she was in love with him and so "racked with confusion" and how she'd been "withholding information from her bosses off and on" throughout the year—no, betrayal was betrayal.

"Last week . . ." She faltered, swallowed hard. "I don't expect you to be anything but skeptical but I need you to listen to me. Look at me."

"I don't really want to. Don't know who the hell I'm seeing."

"Last week? They were on to you."

"*They* were on to me?" He pointed at her. "You mean *you* were on to me. You are *they*, baby."

She closed her eyes momentarily. She said, "Last week you could have been arrested." Enunciating each word. "You made a trip to St. George's Caye and somewhere else—okay, we won't talk about that. What you do not know is, if it weren't for me, you could have been intercepted on your return trip. If I hadn't put in the call late? If I hadn't misled them with photos of the wrong boat at the dock? You and I, we wouldn't be having this conversation."

He threw back the wine. "But see," he said, gesturing with the glass, strolling into the living room, "see, now, if it wasn't for you, I wouldn't be here right now."

"That's what I'm saying."

"No, *here,* in this predicament between me and you."

"You're forgetting the reason I'm here, on this street, is you. And the irony is you're not even the target, it's the Monsantos, their Mexican associates, not you."

"I'm one of their associates. Don't try to tell me you're on my side."

She covered her face with her hands and groaned, then she swept her hair back, opened her eyes wide, seeming to arrive at a decision. She sprang up, came toward him.

He watched her, freckled skin, red hair, those taut legs he was wild about. Now, she was in front of him and took the glass from his hand and let it go, the glass bouncing once off the rug. Now, she was in his chest, searching his face. "You think I'm afraid of you?" She lifted her chin. "Huh? Do you?"

She was beautiful, and he wanted to touch her.

"I'm not afraid of you, Riley."

He stepped back, groin stirring, disappointed in himself because he knew he was still too much in love with this woman. He went to the fridge for more wine. Poured her a glass as well and set it on the counter.

She sipped. "I don't know why you just didn't leave the Monsantos a long time ago. There was no reason for you to stay with them. I know you enough to know it wasn't for the money."

"You don't understand what you're talking about."

"You don't owe them anything."

"Don't owe—" He shook his head and looked away. "Yeah, you don't know what you're talking about. You come here, you think you know these people because of what they do, they're criminals, that's all you see, so you've got them figured out, right? Nah, that's not how it works, though. The thing you don't know is they're the ones, the Monsantos, that fed me many evenings when my mother was so drunk off her ass she could hardly stand up, much less cook a little dinner for her son. Is-rael Monsanto's the one took me in after my old man passed and I had no house to go to, Israel took me in till I saved enough to start renting my own little place, Israel paid my rent some-times when I didn't have the scratch. And now you're saying, after all these years I worked with them, all they did for me in my desperate days, I just drop them and move on, no worries? Sorry, but you're talking like a cop. What they did to help me? Now, that's about respect."

She swirled the wine in the glass, lips pinched. "You have to stop. Whatever else you've got planned with them—you need to stop. Don't do it. Walk away. Please."

"You're telling me something I should know?"

"Listen to me, will you? Just quit. You can choose to quit. You don't have to do this, you're *choosing* this. Me, I'm so far into this I'm a goner. I—"

"You're warning me, Candice. Go on and say it. You're on my side? Just say it."

"They know you're planning another run this week."

"They're right."

"Don't go. Don't do it."

"What're you gonna do? Turn me in? You gonna turn me in, Candice?"

He pulled an airline ticket from his back pocket and slapped it on the counter. A corner of the ticket touched the puddle of tea.

She gave him a pained look. "Do you actually believe we can run off someplace together? Antigua? Do you even know anything about Antigua?"

"Here's what I'm going to do," he said.

"No, no, I can't listen to this, this is a fantasy. We've been living a fantasy."

"I'm telling you reality. I'm telling you what I'm really going to do. Come tomorrow morning, me and the Monsantos will be through. I'm leaving this place, I'll be gone by midday tomorrow. I want you to come with me. And I'm not coming back here." He laid a hand on the ticket. "There it is. It's your move."

He headed for the door, Candice saying wait, don't do this, Riley, think this over. Riley opened the door, where he stopped. He said, "Sister Pat knows me like a mother. But you, more than anybody, maybe 'cause you came along at the right time, you're the only one who knows all of me, the good and the bad."

She refused to look at his face.

He said, "Last week I got dressed up and asked you a big question. But what's clear to me now, you haven't answered it truthfully. You're telling me the last run is my choice. Fair enough. What's your choice? What do you choose?" and he left her considering her glass of wine.

Toads and insects were calling from the high grass. He heard them all through the restless hours lying in his bed. Dull moonlight seeped into the dark room. He rose, found his meditation bench, folded his legs under and sat.

Let the thoughts fall, let the thoughts fall away. . . . He tried to breathe evenly, let his body take over completely. Let the body put the mind at rest.

In his head, he began to compose a letter to his son explaining that he had to leave because of business but he'd be back to see him soon, and one day they'd take a trip to Half Moon Caye, just the two of them sleeping in a tent on the beach, or they could do whatever else . . .

Riley's mind danced on. Soon, he found himself opening the fridge, then drinking a glass of water and staring up at her house through the kitchen window. He had his plane ticket and he was leaving, that's what he knew, so why was he gazing at that house? He thought, Nothing up there for you. Close this window and get some sleep.

She had left her front door unlocked. He walked into her room, and she sat up in bed. Pale in the darkness. They looked at each other. Their breathing filled the dark. She moved to one side of the bed and flipped back the covers. He kicked off his sandals, peeled off his shirt, and got in close to her. Quietly, they fluffed the pillows and adjusted their positions until they were perfectly spooned. His hand wrapped around her waist, chin resting on her bare shoulder. They were comfortable, almost breathing in unison, until after a while, they were asleep.

Some time just before dawn—Candice so used to waking up early for morning runs—she felt his absence and reached behind her. She patted the bed, the sheet just a little cool. She didn't know when he'd left. She stayed still, lying on her side and staring at the nightstand, the lampshade, the photo frames, the telephone.

CHAPTER THIRTY-NINE

The bottle of One Barrel rum they brought for the farmer was overkill. He was already skunk-drunk, deep into a quart of something clear that smelled vaguely industrial whenever he breathed in Harvey's direction.

They were sitting almost knee to knee, the farmer shirtless and short, scars all down his forearms. Machete scars, he said. Lopez and the others stood outside conferring by the river-bank. One of them was smoking a cigarette; Harvey could smell it, and he wished they'd come back inside so the smoke would cover the farmer's breath. Or maybe it was the whole house that reeked, two rooms on either side of this dingy main room, the back door directly opposite the front and opening into—that's it, *that's* the smell, the backyard, a black pig snuffling by the open door now.

They stomped back into the house, Lopez leading the way. He looked with amusement at the farmer, who was rolling a joint with brown paper, dipping a finger into a can of condensed milk and using that for a seal.

Lopez said, "Molina, me and my friends going for a walk. Check out the other side of the property. Entertain my driver here till I get back?"

"But sure." The farmer seemed affronted by the very question. "This man is my guest."

Busha said to Harvey, "Hear that, you the guest of honor."

Lopez turned to Harvey. "What time your watch say?"

"Three forty-two."

"This won't take long. At around three fifty-five, don't matter if you hear us coming or not, you get in the van, wait behind the wheel."

"I got it, I got it."

Busha said, "You *better* get it."

As they walked out, Tic Tac clapped his shoulders. "You doing good, man. Fifteen minutes more and we done with business."

They left, Harvey hearing their boots crunching gravel down the path. He got up and stood in the doorway. He saw them, three dark figures opening the back door of the van parked under some trees. He saw them take out the Kevlar, heard murmuring as they strapped the vests on. Saw them take out the rifles, sling them over shoulders, Lopez carrying the shotgun. They slammed the door shut and went on their way, fading into the darkness.

Harvey turned back to the crazy-ass farmer and sat down. He felt his stomach twist, for the first time that night—he'd been expecting it.

The farmer said, "What can I get for you? You want a drink. Want me to fix you one of these here I'm drinking? Horchata and rum. You know horchata? You make it from rice. Want one of those, splash rum in it? It's good."

Harvey said no thanks.

"Or how about this, coconut water and rum? I put some coconut meat in the glass for you, with some ice . . . I think I might have ice, I don't know, I'll check. But you don't want to drink, look," pushing out a lopsided brown-paper joint, "I'll share this *tubumbu* with you."

"Mr. Molina? I'm not feeling too good at the moment so do me a favor? Don't talk to me about drinks right now?"

"How about some ceviche. Conch ceviche. I could interest you, a bowl of ceviche? I made it fresh myself . . . garlic, limes, onions, fresh conch, peppers, you like peppers? Vinegar—"

"Mr. Molina, food too. Don't talk to me about food."

Molina nodded, blinking slowly. "All right, then." His eyelids drooped, chin going down to his chest. He came out of his microsleep and said, "Music? I can put on some music. Juan Gabriel, *El Unico: Sus Más Grandes Exitos.*"

Harvey said, "Jesus Christ," and wiped cold sweat off his forehead, tensing as his stomach churned.

"You got a headache?"

Harvey shook his head.

"A backache? Oh, is your belly, huh?" Molina snapped his fingers. "I have Alka-Seltzer . . . somewhere." He tried to get up and fell back on the bench, widened his eyes in mock horror. He cackled at his drunkenness.

The pig, round and mud caked, stumbled into the room. It snorted and poked around in the corners, waddled over to a small rusty fridge and nosed it open.

Molina was trying to light his joint, hands trembling. He got it flaming on the fourth match and chortled amid a plume of smoke, pointing at the pig eating something from the fridge. "House trick, see, house trick."

Harvey put his head down, he needed a toilet but he didn't dare venture a request, not wanting to even imagine this man's bathroom.

"Want some rum?"

Harvey just flat-out lost his patience. "Hell, man." Then he saw that Molina, straddling the bench, was addressing the pig.

Harvey leaned his back against the wall, closed his eyes tight.

Yeah, this night was a bad dream, that's what this was. He was definitely dreaming this shit.

Riley stood at the helm of the skiff cruising down the New River. Barrel was perched on the gunwale to the left behind him. The stern sat low in the water from the weight they were carrying: eighteen buckets under a heavy blue tarp.

Hazy moon, a jumble of stars, and the wind shifting to the east and warming already. Dawn was only a couple of hours away; Riley could tell, even if he closed his eyes. He had been out on the river enough to know from the hoots and caws and crackling twigs in the jungly riverbanks, the sounds of animals awaking.

He glanced at Barrel, who wasn't looking too comfortable, only his second or third time accompanying Riley on a trip. He wondered about Barrel; the man hadn't shown much emotion or acted any different since Julius had been killed, and he and Julius were tight, far as Riley knew, but then you can never be too sure about people, especially in this trade. Tight today, enemies tomorrow.

Riley eased back on the throttle for the boat to slide around a slow bend. Up ahead the river was like ink, drifting thickly under the overhang of branches and heavy leaves, plants sticking out of the surface. On a high tree limb, a skinny-legged jabiru, black face and white wings, regally observed them.

The radio on the glove box squawked. Riley, checking out the upcoming bend, turned the volume down.

Carlo's voice said, "Hooligan, come in, Hooligan."

"This is Hooligan, Santa, go ahead."

There was a click click. "How far from the destination, Hooligan? Over."

Riley said, "Ah . . ." A bat fluttered near his face by a wall of trees and he brushed another dark shape away. "Five minutes approximately, over."

Riley continued at the slower speed, ranging the riverbank, ears perked. He had taken off the running lights and didn't expect the other boat to have any either so he needed to be careful. He said, "Hear that?" glancing back at Barrel.

Barrel grunted. "Huh?"

"Listen," and Riley pulled the boat down to idle. They were on an expansive stretch of the river, a wide bend off to the left and you could hear another engine, just beyond the trees.

Barrel joined him at the helm, and they listened.

The boat appeared from around the bend like a shadow, too fast, bow aimed in their direction, a low-riding Panga. Barrel raised a flashlight and blinked it once, then again. The Panga slowed, a light blinked from its bow. It was still about fifty yards off and slowed even more.

Riley steered to the right. Barrel flashed his light; the other boat blinked and steered away.

It could be anybody. Riley reached slowly into the glove box and curled his hand around the .45 lying on its side. Flicked off the safety, turning the wheel farther right with his other hand.

They were coming up alongside the Panga now, engines burbling. *Caw caw caw*—a bird flapped over the river and away. The boats glided past each other, two men in the Panga, faces sliding by. Everyone assessing each other. As the boats drifted apart all heads turned to look back.

Riley bumped the throttle and the skiff picked up speed but he noticed the Panga still drifting, and when he glanced over, Barrel gave him a nod of confidence. He circled back, the other boat rotating to the left, idling.

The exchange was fast, few words beyond "Hey, there," and "*¿Qué pasa?*" No more than five minutes. Riley stood at the wheel with one hand in the glove box on that .45 and watched

Barrel and one of the men lug the buckets into the Panga and arrange them under the tarp, and he watched the driver watching him. He'd never seen these two guys before, young, clean-shaven Mayans who could be farmers or fishermen and perfectly law abiding, which was probably why they'd been chosen. But nobody was harmless, Riley had to remind himself every time out; it's when you got comfortable that you made mistakes, missed a move. . . .

Like this driver fumbling with something on the seat behind him; Riley got ready. Finished, Barrel hopped back in, rocking the boat. Riley said, low, "You're in my way, move out the way," craning his neck, see what the driver was doing, and he'd drawn the .45 halfway out of the glove box before he exhaled with relief.

The man had lifted a radio and was speaking Spanish into it. After some words, he nodded at Riley, and Riley picked up his own radio.

"Come in Santa, come in, this is Hooligan, over."

The boats bumped against each other. "Go ahead, Hooligan."

Riley waved good-bye to the clean-cut gentlemen. They waved back, and their boat roared off, in the other direction, Riley waiting until the noise had faded. Then he clicked in and said, "The fish are biting, Santa, over and out."

CHAPTER FORTY

At 3:55, while the farmer chatted with the pig, blowing weed smoke into its face, Harvey stepped out of the house and breathed in fresh air. He walked directly across to the muddy darkness under the trees and climbed into the van. Key in ignition? Check. Headlights working? Check. He rolled down the window, sat back. Cracked his knuckles. He turned the key, a test if the engine would start; it did. He turned it off, cracked his knuckles.

At 4:00 he figured something must be wrong and got out of the van. He walked down to the riverbank and peered east into the darkness along the line of the river's edge. Way he understood it, the Monsanto place was—that direction? But then maybe—talking to himself, pointing—it could be *this* way. More northeast? Didn't matter, something wasn't right. He said, "This is not cool," and then a burst of gunfire crackled from deep in the trees.

And he ran, didn't know where to go, just ran. He stopped, looked around, sprinted to the van and stumbled inside. Fumbled with the key and heard gunfire again, coming from the east. Far away—far away, Harvey, relax. He let go of the keys and raised his hands high to stop himself from driving off.

Another burst of shots and he saw flashes in the distance. No way. He started the van and rolled out, slow, his stomach churning. He kept going, no headlights, didn't know what he was thinking. He braked and said, "Jesus Christ, man," and thought for sure he was going to lose control of his bowels if they didn't show up soon, and that's when he heard them running up, thank god. When this was over he was gonna chant some Psalms every day, swear to Christ. They were talking excitedly, laughing. He threw the van into park, reached over and opened the passenger door, needlessly because they flung open the back and piled in, rifles clattering, boots thumping the walls.

"Drive, drive!" Lopez said.

Busha hooted and howled.

Harvey stepped on the gas, tires spinning and kicking up gravel before they caught, and off the van flew, bumping and rocking down the farmer's land and onto the dirt road, Harvey smiling widely for some damn reason, maybe feeling their energy.

In the back, Lopez was holding his stomach and rolling around with laughter.

Riley was making good time on the river, enjoying the breeze on his face. He felt wide awake, a sharp thrill.

Barrel was talking a lot, nervous, talking about anything— flat-panel TVs, like which of the smaller ones were better, LCD or plasma? Car stereo hookups, he wasn't sure if he wanted that or maybe he was gonna go satellite, forget all that wiring hassle.

After a mile or so, Riley was no longer listening. Maybe in the past, when he knew he needed to develop rapport with a man he was doing runs with, he might've been polite, but the central focus of his thoughts, as the skiff sliced down that green-black river, tilting as it weaved through the forest, his focus was Candice.

It was her play and he was completely uncertain what she would do. To his core, he feared she would disappoint him.

So when he heard the big engine of another boat coming down the river he wasn't surprised. He jacked the throttle back and aimed the bow at a turnoff. Barrel stood up, hearing it too. His head jerked around, huge eyes asking Riley what was up.

The bow dropped and the engine fell to a rumble, the boat slipping past a stand of trees and into a narrow channel. "No big deal," Riley said, "let's wait this out." Ahead he could see where the channel ended, at a cove in the bank. Trees darkened the passage on both sides and Riley killed the engine and let the boat float on.

Barrel had shoved his hands into the pockets of his jeans shorts, adopting a much cooler pose, looking toward the river and the vessel they couldn't see yet.

It was coming, a heavy engine, a big boat. A big boat on the river this time of morning? Riley moved away from the wheel and stood next to Barrel, both of them watching through a lace of low-lying branches and leaves for the boat to pass.

Barrel said, "Star, we don't have nothing incriminating on board, correct?" He stood tiptoe, scanning. "So we don't need to be doing this, hiding in here, right?"

Riley spat over the side. "I know that. But we don't need to be seen either."

It was coming and Riley held his breath. Tall bow, covered cockpit, streaming by . . . then gone. Riley lifted his eyes, took in the stars. He had been expecting disappointment and now that he'd seen it was an ordinary cargo boat, probably going to some village, what did he feel? To expect disappointment—to expect to have your desires unfulfilled—was a conundrum he'd have to discuss with Sister Pat one day; did it mean he was expecting to fail?

For Candice to fail him?

The skiff bumped into something, and Riley swung away and hopped onto the bow to push it back from branches. He leaned into a thick branch and shoved so that the tree shook and the boat slid back, nearer to the middle of the channel. Bush rustled and something skittered up the soft bank into the undergrowth. The channel narrowing, the other side coming closer. He sat on the bow, legs over the side, to wait for a stout branch to push against.

"Listen, listen," Barrel said. "Hear that?"

Riley stuck his hands out, ready for the tree.

"Sounds like that boat turning around."

Riley glanced back, didn't hear a thing. Barrel was standing at the stern, leaning forward and cupping an ear.

"Think maybe we should wait, hang out here five minutes, star? Be on the safe side?"

Riley said, "No problem," and pushed off on a branch, grunting, but not pushing hard enough. The skiff barely moved, seemed to be dragging on something. Riley said, "Shit," hauling up to his feet and jumping back into the cockpit to get the pole lying on the floor against the wall. He lifted it, maneuvering one end out from under the bow, and going back to the front, he noticed his glove box was still open. His gun was gone.

He looked about on the floor, the seat. The boat jerked and Riley stepped up onto the bow, lugging the pole, saying, "Lift the prop out the water, Barrel, lift it up." He stood at the tip and jammed the pole into the mud bank till it hit something solid, and he pushed, the boat pulling loose from whatever vegetation was trapping it. He stuck the pole into the water, hit bottom, shoved off again, the boat swerving away from the bank and into deeper water. He pulled up the pole and did it again, turning his face to see sidelong into the boat.

Barrel said, "So this is it for you, huh? Last big drop. We'll miss you, you know that?"

Riley said, "Yeah?" sweating lightly, feeling around with the pole, occasionally touching the semisoft bottom.

"That's right." The boat shifted, Barrel moving around. "They say nobody could do it like R.J. It's been an honor, no lie, an honor to do this with you, star. Me and you, we never really got to like hang out or anything but it's been an honor to learn the ropes from you. I'll be the first to admit that."

Barrel's weight shifted the boat again and Riley worked the pole around, swishing water. "You lifted that prop high, right, Barrel?"

A beat, then Barrel said, "Oh . . . yeah . . . yeah, mahn. I follow directions good, star." His breathing sounded heavy, and he was moving around way too much.

Riley said, "Wait, hold still a second," and fast, hand over hand, he lifted out the pole, choked up on it baseball style, pivoted and lashed out, catching Barrel on the side of the head. Barrel staggered to the far side of the cockpit, holding his head, and Riley flew at him. He punched him one-two full in the face, loud smacking noises, and Barrel dropped to one knee and bounced back up and made a big ungainly step to get away before Riley dug a fist into his ribs and jumped on his back, hooking a right arm tight, tight around his neck. Barrel fell forward on his belly, Riley on top, arm locked and squeezing. Barrel's hand shot straight out, slapping the deck, reaching for something. Then Riley saw it, a pistol, and now Barrel had it, dragging it in, and Riley watching it while squeezing, squeezing, Barrel growling and slobbering, raising up on his elbows and knees, scary strong, now curling one arm up over his head and pointing the pistol backward at Riley. Riley edged away from the pistol, the muzzle wavering, Barrel's thick neck clamped in the sweaty crook of his arm. Riley gave it more pressure; if he could pull the man's head off he would. He was straining to no effect, the muzzle flapping, finding him, flapping away. Barrel had lifted himself up. Riley was hooked to his neck like a monkey, couldn't do anything to stop this man. The muzzle was on him again and he let go and slammed his forearm hard in the back of Barrel's neck. Barrel careened forward, Riley's momentum sending him sailing into Barrel, the two of them lurching and hitting the deck. Riley scrambled up, Barrel was still on one knee, swiveled his body around and gave Riley a perplexed look. What are we doing?

Then Riley reared back and kicked him hard in the chin. Barrel wobbled in place and dropped back on his butt heavily. He sat slumped, head lolling. Riley stepped on the gun hand, reached down. Barrel struggled but with no conviction, like he was half asleep, and Riley wrenched it away.

"Don't move," he said, panting. He backed up, winded, pointing the gun. "I said don't *move*." He got behind the wheel and hit the switch to lower the engine. Then he started up, reversed, throttled forward, reversed, forward again, one stiff arm pointing the pistol, the other steering them out of the cove and back into the main flow. Barrel sat dazed.

In the open, Riley juiced it for a short stretch, eased the speed and brought the hull down slowly and dropped into idle. Barrel was stirring, looking at Riley.

"Where's my gun, Barrel?" Riley felt a tug of pain and touched his stomach, reached under his shirt and patted around the bandage. His abdomen was dry but was hurting like a fury.

Barrel mumbled something, gesturing at the river.

Riley said, "You threw it in?"

Barrel coughed, grimacing, put a hand on his throat. "This—this wasn't my idea . . . okay?"

"Then who?"

Barrel, head lowered, was massaging his neck, turning his head side to side. Riley quickly drew the pistol close to his chest—it was a small Glock—pulled back the slide with his left hand, pushed the tip of his shooting finger into the chamber and felt the round there. He said, "Carlo or Israel, which one?"

Barrel kept a hand over his throat and shrugged. "It matter to you? Like two of them, star."

"Why?"

"Aw, man, fuck, this some messed-up shit. I didn't even want to *do* this, man."

"Tell me why, Barrel."

"All I know, they're talking, Carlo the one mostly, that you fucked up things for them with the Mexicans, you and your friend. Now, they got to make things right."

"They already made things right. That's what we just did."

"No, it's you who didn't want to be part of the business. Carlo saying they can't trust you now, the way they see it, they don't feel obliged to shelter you. Look, star, I ain't the one saying this, this is them, they the ones put me up to this."

"Yeah, and you simply had no choice, sure."

"Man, I'm serious, they said I been fucking up so I got to prove my worth, what you want me do, star? Or I get offed, too."

Riley said, "Well, you tried and it didn't work out for you, so guess what's going to happen."

"No, hold up, hold up," Barrel raising a palm. "Slow . . . slow down and listen to me."

"Get up, Barrel."

"What?"

"Stand up."

"Give me time for us to talk this out—"

Riley stepped up and pushed the gun inches from Barrel's nose.

"Whoa shit, awright, awright," Barrel pushing up, slow and timid. He stood up shakily, raised his palms by his chest.

"Go get my .45," Riley said.

"Huh . . . ?"

"Go on and get it."

Barrel shook his head fast. "Yo, look, I can't swim."

Riley motioned with the gun. "You need some motivation? Get in, Barrel."

"Please don't do me like this."

When Riley said nothing, Barrel saw begging would take him nowhere and he sat on the gunwale. After a moment, he threw a leg over. He sat sideways, one foot in the water. He said, shaking his head, "I can't swim, I'm not lying." He leaned over, dipped a hand in. "It's cold." He looked insulted. "It's *cold,* man."

"My heart too. Get in, Barrel."

"I can't swim, I can't swim," and Barrel lifted the other leg up and over and lowered himself in. He splashed around with one hand, the other hand gripping the gunwale. Riley walked up and stepped on his fingers and Barrel let go.

"Help me, it's cold, shit . . . it's cold . . ." Splashing in place, dog-paddling clumsily.

Riley said, "Hear this now, you got about fifty yards to go that way, east. About—hmm, seventy this way. Or, here's an idea, you could go this way, downriver, let the current carry you over there, by that bend? That's only like forty, fifty yards. But you know what, on second thought, scratch that, that's some thick bush in there, real swampy, and you might have to contend with snakes and jaguars and such."

Barrel was dog-paddling, chin dipping in and out.

"But at least you have options," Riley said, and went to the helm.

Barrel stroked awkwardly for the east bank, then went back to dog-paddling.

Riley said, "But look at you, who says you can't swim? I'm impressed."

Barrel spluttered, "Can't swim. Can't swim too good . . . help . . ."

Riley punched the throttle and roared off, looking back once to see Barrel swimming furiously away from the wake, and the waves washed over him, his head disappearing then bobbing up as he stroked erratically, before another wave rolled over.

CHAPTER FORTY-ONE

On the dark highway, hip-hop blaring, the mood in the van was jovial. Lopez was in the front passenger seat and had rolled his window down, smiling into the breeze. In the back, Tic Tac kept asking to take one more sniff of the fresh bread, and Lopez would turn around, grinning, holding open the burlap sack in between the bucket seats so Tic Tac could inhale deep over the U.S. currency stuffed inside. Tic Tac threw his head back and said, "Ahhh," and brayed with laughter.

Lopez folded the sack shut and said, "Enough, enough," doing his best to act professional.

Going through Biscayne Village then Sand Hill, they passed three, maybe four pairs of headlights, that's all, going the other way. Nobody else on the road, they were almost home free. When Busha leaned between the front seats and tried to sniff the money like Tic Tac, Harvey said, firmly, "Do not pull on my seat like that, man, you'll make me lose control," and when Lopez followed immediately with, "Settle down, Busha," Harvey smiled to himself.

Yeah, settle your chubby ass down, Harvey thought, leave me the hell alone, we'll get back in one piece and I'll have some time to think and finish packing my toothbrush and whatnot and meet Gert at that hotel before we catch that flight out. That was the hazy part, though, which had been bugging him: Why did Riley insist that he and Gert check into the hotel? Okay, it was close to the airport—that was the only reason he could surmise. Fact was, he felt comfortable and safe in Miles Young's house. Harvey just wanted things straight and simple so he wouldn't have to worry like this.

"You talk to yourself all the time?"

Harvey said, "What?"

Lopez was staring at him. "Right now. You were talking to yourself, your finger banging the wheel, just did it."

Harvey said, "Nervous habit."

"Nervous? No need to be nervous when the job is done," and he patted the side of the sack. "Tell your friend Riley James he's good in my books. Probably what should happen, tell him, me and him could do business again. Think about it, tell him. Seeing as how his buddy, the Monsanto guy, will be out of commission."

Harvey swallowed. His mouth felt dry. Then he asked the question he'd been scared to ask since they left the farmer's house. "What happened back there?"

Lopez shook his head. "Nothing surprising. That Monsanto guy? The one with the—the shellacked hair—what's his name anyway?"

"That's the one they call the Serpent," Busha said.

"Serpent, huh? Oh-kay. Well," Lopez speaking to Harvey but looking out the window, "the Serpent wanted to strike. Tried to show some defiance—get this—*after* we seized the money. What was he going to do? *Really.*"

"Tic Tac took care of business, though," Busha said.

"That he did."

"Man, I saw his knee go out. Like blood and flesh and pulp just spit out the other side, damn, that was nasty, Tic Tac."

Tic Tac said, "Easier we don't talk about it, then. All I know, you do what you got to do when you're a soldier."

Harvey thought, Listen to these guys.

Lopez said to him, "So after that, we shot up the place, the walls and lights, like that. You know, drive home the point. He was the one seemed to want a show of force, he got it."

Harvey didn't like this talk. He supposed it might be bragging but had the feeling it was mostly fact. They were coming up on a speed bump, a streetlight on the side of the road reflecting off a sign that said Ladyville.

Busha said, "*Daaamn*, what the hell is that smell?" and Lopez joined in with, "Jesus!" fanning the air in front of his face. Tic Tac hollered, "Ho, gimme a window quick," laughing as he leaned in between the bucket seats.

Lopez said to Harvey, "It's you responsible?"

Harvey hesitated. He said, "Sorry, man," and touched his belly. "Stomach's acting up fierce."

Lopez hiked the front of his shirt over his nose. "Another nervous habit?"

Harvey conceded with a shrug. They rolled over the speed bump and after that he lost the exact sequence of events.

Lights flooded the van from up ahead, a monster truck rumbled forward out of nowhere and hemmed the van in to the side of the road, where another truck was positioned. Intense light roared toward them, another big-wheel truck, fog lights, people leaping out from the back onto the road, everything happening at once.

Lopez said, "Back up back up back up—"

The windshield shattered, somebody in the van screamed, and everybody dived for the floor. The van rolled forward and crunched into the truck grille. Van doors flew open on both sides and long guns pointed in followed by faces in bandanas and ball caps, several men. The back doors swung open, two more men standing there with guns.

Harvey saw it clearly, lying with his chin on the rubber mat—dumb-ass Busha creeping toward the shiny Mossberg shotgun behind a seat, and one of the men clubbed him with the butt of a long gun. Busha covered his face, and they clubbed him again.

A voice stabbed the air: "The money, we want the money!"

More men swarmed the van, young slim guys, all wearing bandanas up to their eyes, ball caps or knit caps tugged low.

"Where's the money!"

Nobody answered. Busha moaned, his hand clawed the air. Lopez said, "Take my wallet, take it, that's all the money I got." The voice said, "Screw that," and hands were all over Harvey, patted him down, flipped him onto his back. The voice said, "Close your eyes, don't look at me." Another voice, "Got it!" Then Harvey heard them stomping around inside the van, picking up guns, heard them leaving the van.

Harvey opened his eyes, rolled his head to the side. Headlights were pulling away. The glove box was open, papers were strewn across the floor, dollar bills, a Yankees cap on its side. The trucks rumbled away, but no one on the floor moved. Then everybody started up at once, Lopez cussing and shouting like he'd lost his mind; Tic Tac on hands and knees with a flashlight, snatching up loose dollars, and Busha on his elbows, moaning loudly and palming his nose, blood gushing over his fingers.

CHAPTER FORTY-TWO

Miles unscrewed the cup cover off the thermos and poured the coffee into it. Set it on the dash for Riley and topped off his own aluminum carry cup and stuck it back in the console holder. And they waited.

A pale dawn. Cloudless sky. A hard-packed dirt clearing amid abandoned half-finished houses and mangroves by the bay. Lonesome Point, a place for lovers and secret deals.

The windshield soon fogged up from the coffee on the dash and after a while Riley reached a finger over and drew on the glass. They sipped coffee and watched the smiley face.

When Miles raised his wrist, Riley said, "That's the second time in less than five minutes, you know that?"

"So you're saying you're not worried? They said six o'clock, didn't they say six?"

"They said six, but that could mean sevenish, or whenever they get done."

"And you don't think by now they should've been long done?"

"You've got to trust," Riley said, settling back on the headrest and closing his eyes. He longed for sleep.

Somewhere in his dozing, in a land far, far away, he heard

movement and motors and opened his eyes to see Miles's hand on his shoulder.

"They're here."

Riley rubbed his face, working life back into it. "Didn't I tell you?"

Miles watched in the rearview and turned his head one way then the other as pickups rumbled up on both sides. "I'm not sure if I like this."

"It's all right. I know Brisbane. It's all good."

"Your Mr. Cool act? Starting to annoy me."

Riley grinned.

"Which one is Brisbane?" Miles pointed low, wagging his finger to one side. "Over here?"

"Guy riding shotgun, with the hat."

The engines went quiet. Riley checked left and right. Two pretty boys in one pickup, Brisbane and his adopted son in the other, Rodrigo giving a nod when Riley met his eyes.

"Okay," Riley said, "here's Brisbane now," and watched Brisbane step down out of his truck. "Yeeeah, looks like he got it. Beautiful. Pop the trunk, Miles, let's show this man his guns." Riley opened his door. "And let me go and give him a hug while I'm at it."

Two minutes later, the trucks turned around, Brisbane flashed the peace sign and they roared away, leaving Riley and Miles in the car looking out at the bay.

On the floor at Riley's feet was a burlap sack fat with cash. In one hand was a cup of coffee he was nursing to quiet his mind. Eventually, he scooped up two stacks of cash and tumbled them into his lap and Miles whistled. "Sweet Jesus."

The bills were crisp and fragrant, neat bundles secured with rubber bands. Riley thumbed through a stack, counting, all fifties. When he reached a sufficiently high number, he removed those bills, tucked them into an envelope from his pocket, and handed the envelope to Miles.

"What's this for?" Miles cocking an eyebrow at the weight in his hand.

"For you."

Miles shook his head. "No offense? But you know I can't take this." He moved to give it back, but Riley blocked his hand. Miles shook his head again.

Riley looked away, then came back. "Then do something for me?"

"Anything."

"Deliver that to my ex-wife? Tell her it's for Duncan. Tell her it's child support for the next six months."

"And if she asks where you are?"

"Tell her I'm going to get in touch with them soon."

Miles, nodding, shoved the envelope under his seat. Riley counted some more bills and when he reached a chunk almost as thick as the first, he jammed that in another envelope and handed it to Miles.

"And what's this one for?"

"For a little boy's family. A family that I don't even know if they live at this house anymore," and he gave Miles the address of a house on Manatee Road, an address that was burned in his memory.

Miles frowned and said he didn't understand, so Riley sighed, put his coffee on the dash and told him a story.

It was about how one day, a youth, an ordinary guy with a little street in him, who wanted respect and attention and a measure of thrills and fun like any other guy his age, got himself into a scrape. Well, not a scrape really, more like a mess, something that changed his life, his identity. How he viewed his place in the world. It happened on a dirt road, the Manatee Road—you know it, the one that's still not paved all the way. They cornered him, these two guys, a policeman and a Lebanese, and the youth responded in a fashion that shocked him— the quick violence of it. But truthfully, he shouldn't have been so shocked because all the rough, lonely days of his childhood seemed to have been preparing him for that moment when he took those men's lives.

But the point wasn't the remorse he felt, although that sadness did torment him in later years—his point was what happened immediately after all the blood soaked the road, the moment the youth saw the little boy standing behind a gate of a yard down the way. Standing there sucking a pacifier.

It was the first moment that he recognized, starkly, how much his life was going to change. It wasn't so much that from now on he would see the world differently or that he was beginning to grieve his lost innocence—no, no such philosophical fanciness—this was a down and dirty realization that this little boy had seen him kill two men.

Panic flooded his veins. He and the boy stared at each other across the dirt road in the fading sunlight. His legs carried him over to the gate to look closely at the boy, the curly black hair at the top of his head. Their eyes met and the youth lifted a finger to his lips. He smiled. *Shhhh.*

But because he was so far into self-preservation mode and because he was too frightened to be certain that a finger to the lips would suffice, too young, his hand came up from behind his back with the .45, and after looking down the dirt driveway to see if anyone else was around, he reached over the gate and leveled the gun at the boy's head.

His forearm tightened and sweat burned his eyes. His arm trembled. He whispered to the boy, *Close your eyes, please.*

The boy didn't seem to understand, sucking that pacifier with a blank look on his face. The youth's arm shook until the muzzle came to rest against the little boy's skull.

Miles broke in with, "Let me stop you right there."

Riley waited for him to say something. He shut his eyes. "It's a long time I've wanted to tell somebody this. I need to continue."

"No you don't."

Riley tied off the burlap sack, sat back and looked out the window. He said, "Sorry about all this, Miles. You're a good friend."

Miles nodded. "Don't beat yourself up."

After a moment, Riley said, "I wish I could promise you that."

Miles turned the ignition, started to put the car into drive, then turned to Riley. "For what it's worth, you've said enough." He looked through the windshield, at the clearing and the shoreline and the bay. "It's out there, you got it out of your system, now just let it float away. Let it go, Riley. You're almost free."

On the drive to the airport, Riley lay in the backseat admiring the sky through the rear windshield and talking about the money. Making sure Miles understood the plan they'd discussed last night. It was simple, he said. Two lots by the bay at Lonesome Point, Riley had found out they were for sale. Miles was going to use the money to buy those properties. After Riley got himself situated wherever he was going, he'd set up a legitimate company that exported hardware and home supplies, a company with one customer: Miles. Miles was going to use the money to build houses for Riley on these properties. Miles would import supplies and home furnishings from Riley's company, and Riley would ship them down at vastly inflated costs. Over time, two homes would be built, which would be sold or rented; Riley would get his money, having avoided the banks' red flags; and Miles, if he wished, could keep a few thousand for his troubles.

Again, Miles refused the money. But he understood the plan, and have no fear, he said, he would execute.

The tires hummed. Riley knew the roads so well he guessed by the bumps and turns, the change in the sound of the tires, that they were nearing the airport. He asked Miles what could he see.

The car trundled over the speed hump a few hundred yards from the terminal. Miles said, "Well . . . looks like any ordinary day . . . taxis over there, a couple vans. Okay, parking lot's kinda empty. We're early."

"I know, that's good."

The car slowed, approaching the parking lot on the left. "Travelers unloading . . . workers eating breakfast over there . . . okay, what this? One SUV over here, two dudes . . . they're just sitting there."

The car moved to a crawl.

"What kind of SUV?"

"Looks to me . . . like a . . ." The car turned left into the parking lot. "It's a Honda Pilot. Brown."

"Describe the two dudes?"

"No problem, I'm passing them . . . right . . . now. One really black, like Nubian black, the other one . . . shades on, mixed with Spanish, tight haircut. Think I should circle back, forget parking?"

Riley felt it: They were on to him. It hadn't taken long and it wasn't altogether unexpected. Maybe it was Boat and Jinx.

"Wait," Miles said, "they're backing out. They're leaving. Nah, Riley, these guys are laughing and eating pastries or something, I wouldn't worry about these two."

Miles drove out of the parking lot anyway, heading back on the road to the Northern. When the Pilot sped past him, he told Riley and waited for the word. At a point before the Northern, Riley said, "Okay, do it," and Miles made a sharp U-turn and they drove back to the airport.

It was speedy. Miles parked directly in front of the terminal entrance, opened the door and stood up, a barrier, looking over the top of the car toward the building; Riley scooted out of the opposite rear door onto the sidewalk, wearing his floppy Tilley hat and shades, walking briskly, past porters and taxi drivers into the terminal, a small backpack hanging off a shoulder, $9,990 in two manila envelopes stuffed inside.

"Now act like you own the place and have nothing to hide," Miles had said to him before he left the backseat. The bold move is often the only move if you want to win, Miles said. He learned that in boxing, sometimes in the middle of a fight he was losing. He'd said something else, and it was in Riley's head now as he hustled across the lobby to the American Airlines counter. Miles had said, "That little boy. I guess I ought to know. Did you shoot that little boy?"

CHAPTER FORTY-THREE

The passport and tickets were in his sweaty hand all the way up to the counter. He laid them down, self-consciously. The woman smiled and said chirpily, "Vacation, sir?"

He smiled back. "Some might say so."

Paperwork squared away, he paid his departure tax with some of the Monsantos' money, half expecting the woman to say, Uh-oh, where did you get this from?

He moved with his backpack through the sparse crowd, passport and ticket in his shirt pocket, straight to the security gate for Departures. He changed his mind and turned away. His eyes wandered out to the ticketing lobby, the people sitting in the molded plastic chairs. Riley searched for one face.

Candice, where are you? Are you here?

That was the mystery on Riley's mind as he moved through the lobby—not so much the questions about what path his life would take now, but Candice. Are you with me, Candice?

No woman in the lobby looked like her. People sat stolidly in rows of adjoined chairs. Suntanned Americans in T-shirts and shorts and flip-flops. A group of chattering high school students standing in the ticketing line or sitting on bulky backpacks with North Carolina stickers.

A man in the gift shop was haggling over the price of a box of Cuban Cohibas. Riley browsed a spin rack for a good paperback mystery. He picked one idly, riffled the pages, not reading, feeling lonely.

Was this it? The grand farewell? Was this how he'd leave the Life and his hometown? Nothing to mark the occasion, nobody to bid good-bye to, no tears, no kisses? No nothing?

Maybe it was as it should be for a man who'd shaped a life under the radar. He put the book back. He hitched his backpack higher on his shoulders and walked out of the store, and saw her.

He wanted to cry, but he was grinning too much for that, and then he was over there chuckling with her, the smell of her hair in his nostrils, and hugging her high off the ground.

They sat by themselves in a corner holding hands, their bags on the floor between their feet. He kissed her and said, "I see it but I don't believe it."

She laced her fingers in his and they talked. To other travelers, they could have been summer lovers or newlyweds. Already they were creating new identities, discussing where they might live, what kind of apartment, better yet, a house. Two-bedroom, modest. But where? North Florida maybe? Mostly sunny there, temperate winters.

Miles reached into his backpack and placed a key on her thigh.

"What's that?"

"Miles gave me the key to his house in Miami. He bought it during his boxing days. It's vacant, we can use it for as long we need it, he says. Till we figure out where we're going, get a place of our own."

Candice gave him back the key. "Before we go there? We're going to Antigua, remember? I have a friend of a friend who owns a hotel there. It overlooks a cane field on one side, the sea on the other."

"Okay, okay," he said, nodding and smiling at her. "Whatever you say, boss."

"Then we'll fly to St. John—Gibney Beach or Francis Beach, I loved both of them and there's this house that I rented one time, off Route 20, less than three miles from Gibney."

Riley was content to hold her hand and listen to her talk about places he knew nothing about. The snorkeling—she wanted to tell him about the snorkeling, said there was a fringing reef off the coast of Gibney that was great for snorkeling, floating along. "And maybe a rum drink or two after an exhausting day of lounging?"

And a question popped into his head, which she seemed to sense, turning around and looking at his face, trying to read it. She said, "They *could* come after me, but they won't. You haven't been charged with anything. They don't have enough on you, so why waste their time coming after me?"

He let that sink in. "I was just wondering. When we end up wherever we end up, I was wondering about your reputation, job prospects, things like that."

"I mailed in my letter of resignation this morning. I'm a private citizen, and so are you."

He held her eyes. "On the river this morning, I had a good feeling. It was quiet out there. Did you give them anything, Candice? Mislead them?"

"What do you think?"

He slid into a slouch, nodded, still holding her hand.

"You believe me?"

People streamed by, but he was paying them little attention. He said, "I do, I do. It's just that I didn't figure it would end like this, so matter-of-factly. Candice, can I tell you something? I ever tell you how close I came to destroying myself?"

Quietly, their faces close, he told her the story of the dirt road, the policeman and the Lebanese. Was she shocked? If she was, and if being around him scared her, he'd understand if she said farewell and they went separate ways. Even though he wasn't that kind of young man anymore, he could not hold it against her if she up and left this very minute.

Shocked? Not at all, she said, because she knew that story already. He said he wasn't surprised that she did. Then he told her about the little boy at the gate and putting the gun to the boy's head, and Riley closed his eyes when she squeezed his hand hard. Harder.

In a voice that sounded far away, he told her how his forearm tightened and sweat burned his eyes. How his arm quavered and he whispered to the boy, *Close your eyes, please.* The muzzle came to rest against the little boy's head.

"But you didn't do it," Candice said.

In his mind, Riley saw himself lower the gun and the boy screwing up his face and starting to cry. Riley said that he watched the boy toddle up the driveway and disappear behind the trees, and in his mind now Riley watched the scene fade. . . .

Candice's palm was on his chest. "But you didn't do it. You didn't."

He needed a moment before he could speak again. True, he did not pull the trigger, but sometimes over the years, the thought of how close he had come had tortured him.

She wrapped an arm around his waist. "You've put that all behind you. You'll never go back to those days. You're stuck with me now."

He felt a smile creeping up on him. "A two-bedroom house, huh?"

She caught on. "Can't you see it? In a big yard. It'll have bay windows and a skylight. Maybe a spare room with a cornice roof—that'll be over the garage. And a lanai out back? A vegetable garden? A shed maybe, for tools? A pleasure garden, too."

He wiggled his eyebrows. "I like that. What's in this big front yard?"

She stared off. "I'm seeing like a farm or something. No fences, tall oak trees, and the ground slopes away, tall reedy grass moving in the wind, yeah . . . and there's a quiet road that curves round the yard . . ."

"And there's you, coming back from a morning jog."

"Hey, you see it, too?"

"I hear a dog barking somewhere, coming through the tall grass to greet you. It's running . . . wait, is that . . . Lassie?"

She slapped his arm. "Oh, shut up, you ruined it."

His cell phone chirped and he reached into his pants pocket, checked the screen. Harvey's cell. "Hello? What's that?" He stood up fast. "Really?"

Two teenagers shrieked by, a boy trying to push an ice cube down a girl's back.

Riley stuck a finger in his ear and walked away. "Wait . . . say that again?" He had to go around the group of teenagers and nudge past a man pushing an old woman in a wheelchair to find a quiet spot by the door of a gift shop.

"Go ahead, Harvey."

"I said I don't want to hear you complain I haven't done anything for you. I'm calling about your son. Duncan's waiting to see you. At that place by the river that we went fishing."

Riley tipped his head back and grinned.

When he returned to Candice, he was holding the phone limply and she said, "What's wrong?"

"My son. Duncan's with Harvey. My ex-wife came back from Mérida late last night, called Gert this morning, wanted to know where I was. She told Gert that she woke up this morning and noticed two men watching the house, parked out front, and then they kept passing by. She figured they were looking for me."

"May I ask why they'd be looking for you?"

Riley slipped the cell in his pocket and said, "Okay. There's a little situation."

Candice folded her arms across her chest, cocked her head. "Uh-oh. Do I want to hear this?"

Riley scratched his jaw, looked across the lobby and thought things over. "I've got to see my son. But my ex doesn't want him coming here to see me. She wants me to go there if I want to say good-bye. She's scared."

"And does she have reason to be?"

Riley ignored the question and said, "They're at a quiet spot by the river, near the hotel, she and my son. Harvey'll come in his rental, take me there. Our flight doesn't board for another hour."

Candice's eyes were steely. "Why are these men searching for you?"

Riley made sure he looked at her straight. "They've owed me money for years. They've shortchanged me for years, and I may have helped myself to that money."

"You *may* have?"

"Some of it. Not all. I'll never be able to get back everything I allowed them to take from me."

Candice crossed her legs, one foot bobbing. "Now is when I find out? Any other details you need to share, Riley, any shockers?"

"We'll have all the time for that. I promise . . . I promise I'll tell you everything." He turned around so that he was facing the terminal exit. "But right now, I need to move."

She was looking at the ground, shaking her head. "I am so goddamn stupid. I just don't learn."

Riley said, "Candice . . ." He stepped toward her. He breathed a sigh and looked away. "Candice, there's a whole bunch of stuff I could tell you, but there's only one thing that matters, one thing. I am never, *never*, going back to that life, that business. Two reasons: I'm tired, I'm sick of it. And I have something with you. I've got enough money now to take care of my son for a long while. If I can't be here as a father for him, then he'll be secure in some other way. And you're with me and, now, all I want is to tell my Duncan good-bye, and that's it. You and I'll have all the time to talk, and if you want to leave me then, after you know everything? Well, at least you'll know we gave it a fair shot, and I'll always know that this meant something to me."

She gave him her profile.

He waited, could feel her retreating.

A voice sounded over the PA: "Good morning, ladies and gentlemen. American Airlines would like to welcome you to Flight 3622 to Houston, which will now begin boarding . . ."

Candice stood up in front of him. "So you'd like me to stand outside for you and look out for your friend?"

He smiled. "You're reading my mind. He can park his car and come in to find me, but we'd waste time. I told him to pull up at the curb, as close to the front entrance as he can get."

"What kind of car?"

"A white Honda Accord, he says. Harvey'll pull up, back door opens, I pop out the terminal, slide down in the backseat. I have some recent experience in that area."

She smirked, narrowing her eyes. "I don't know about you, Riley." She looked across the lobby, people passing through the security gate. "I wish this wasn't so risky, but I agree, you should see your son." She bent down, picked up her carry-on bag. "You and I aren't done talking. Not by any stretch."

Riley lifted his backpack off the floor and held it out to her.

"Do me a favor and keep this for a while? It's not that heavy, and I won't be long."

Candice slung the backpack across her shoulder and started walking to the entrance. "We now have fifty-six minutes till boarding. This better be quick, Riley James."

CHAPTER FORTY-FOUR

Riley lay flat on the backseat of the car, smiling at the sky. Wispy clouds, a bright morning. Man, he was feeling good.

"You should be," Harvey said. "If I had children too and at the last minute I get the opportunity to kiss them good-bye? You *should* feel good."

They were speeding down the road. The radio was playing a synthesizer-rich eighties beat that Riley couldn't name but the familiar rhythm, from the days when he and Harvey were coming up, suited the moment like a theme song. It was almost over now and he was thinking all sorts of foolishness, picturing Duncan's smile and picking him up to tickle his ribs and holding that slim body tight. Wondering if Duncan would cry when Daddy told him how long he'd be gone. Riley conjuring an image of a house on a grassy plain that looked like Candice's dream, seeing Duncan in it, in the middle of the field, his black hair ruffling in the wind.

"What's he wearing, Harvey?"

"What?" The car slowed for a curve.

"Duncan—what's he wearing."

"Shorts, plaid shirt with buttons, I think. No, yeah, plaid, khaki shorts. Why?"

"Just wondering." Riley smiling at the sky, seeing Duncan in the field in shorts and a red plaid shirt. *One day, you'll come to visit me.*

That's what he was going to tell him.

You'll visit and we'll take trips, do anything you want.

The car slowed way down and rolled into a right turn and continued along a bumpy road that Riley knew the hotel was on. He could see trees through the windows, the sky sweeping past, as the tires crunched gravel.

"Stay down there a little longer for me, Riley. I don't trust a car that was behind me on the main road."

"A brown SUV?"

"No, looked like a Chrysler."

The car rattled over bumps, and springs creaked. Dust billowed up, momentarily clouding the view of the sky.

Harvey cleared this throat. "You know, I got a bone to pick with you."

"What's that?"

"How come you didn't tell me that guy Brisbane had plans to intercept? Riley, man, that was one rude surprise. I'm still pissed. I almost shat myself."

Riley chuckled. "I apologize, Harvey, but you can understand, I couldn't let you in on that. A trap is a trap only if it's a secret." Riley watched the back of Harvey's head.

Harvey mulled that over and said what Riley was expecting. "So let me understand. In other words, you think I was going to divulge this to somebody?"

"Harvey, let's not talk about this, it's over. Everything went down cool, let's move on."

"It's me talking to you. Me and you, we're supposed to be in this together and you kept me out of the loop."

His anger surprised Riley. If Harvey wouldn't let it go, fine.

Riley would let it go for him. He would not engage him on that subject again.

"You didn't trust me, that's how I see it. You still have your doubts, but that's okay, I see how it is."

Riley kept quiet. The car turned right, onto what felt like a rocky road, narrower, trees closing in, no more lampposts, no more wires.

"They beat up one of Lopez's guys. They didn't mess around, they whacked him with their guns, and don't worry, I know who was behind it as soon as things started jumping off. I said to myself, that fucking Riley, he set us up good."

"What do you want me to say, Harvey?"

"I don't know, man, I don't know, just I never had nobody pull a gun on me like that and I've never seen a man get clubbed in the face like that before. Tell you the truth, I *heard* it more than I saw it, but I'll never forget it."

Riley was tired of listening to this. If it continued, it would spoil his moment with Duncan, so he said, "Do you want an apology?"

Harvey banged the steering wheel. "I want your respect!"

Riley closed his eyes briefly and said, "Okay. I mean this. Harvey, I apologize for not telling you about Brisbane and as a result almost letting you crap your drawers."

The car rolled down a slant and Harvey turned around with a slow grin, the old Harvey again.

They were coming into a clearing. Riley could tell from the sparse number of trees and the sound of the tires. He found himself smiling again, thinking of Duncan. The car rattled over a rough stretch and up a long smoother path. Then it eased to a stop. Harvey cut the engine.

"We're here."

Riley sat up. A clearing of wild grass, a glimpse of the river

down an incline and through the trees. The grass was a beautiful green in the bright light.

The brown SUV came barreling out from behind the trees
and lurched to a sideways stop behind them, blocking their
path to the road. Riley spun back to the front and saw Harvey
pocket the car keys and open the door, and a car and white van
speeding toward them, kicking up dust.

Riley said, "You didn't bring me here to see Duncan, did
you?"

Harvey was halfway out the door and Riley snatched at
him. "Come here, come here you son of a bitch," grabbing a
fistful of shirtsleeve. Harvey twisted away, nearly falling backward.

Thirty yards in front, the car and the van had stopped and
men were getting out.

"Why, Harvey? Tell me why."

Harvey backed away from the open door, fear in his eyes,
his lips trembly. He looked around fast and shrugged at Riley.
"Why do you think? Huh? What the fuck do I know about
Guyana? I told you, man, I told you I never wanted no part of
this operation, I *told* you."

Riley shook his head in disbelief. Up ahead, Lopez stood in
front of the white van, flanked by two men with pistols held low.
Barrel was helping Israel Monsanto out of the car. Barrel, the
man Riley should have killed. He looked over his shoulder and
saw Boat and Jinx standing by the SUV, also with pistols. Then
he looked at Harvey, whom he definitely should have let them
kill, and said, "You were this close. You had money, you could've
created a new life. But instead you made a stupid move."

"New life? Make a clean break, get a fresh start, like toward
better days? Yeah sure, right. I already *have* a life, and this is it
right here, this is my home. I got to do what I got to do to protect

myself if I want to live and prosper here, my country, not no Guyana."

"You think you're so wise but you outsmarted yourself this time, Harvey. This time—"

"I don't want to hear no more, I'm tired of listening to you." He swung away and walked off.

"Hey!" Riley lifted himself off the seat and shouted through the door. "They'll kill you too, don't you know that? When they run out of use for you, you're gone. You can't see that?"

Harvey clapped his hands over his ears like a child and walked on. "I don't want to hear it, shut up shut up, Riley, please." He slouched toward Israel Monsanto, who was leaning on his cane with a wistful smile.

Riley flopped down in his seat and laid his head back. So this was it? He covered his eyes, then he brought his hand down and punched the back of the front seat and kicked a door viciously, and after a moment, he started to regain control. He looked through his window at the slice of river gleaming between the trees, and a sudden calm fell over him.

Candice's field and house took shape in the air and he could picture it right there, right out there by the river. Could see himself lying in the grass by the river, under a tree, staring up at the rustling branches, his head on the tree's buttress. It was a soothing image to hold in the mind. He let it settle into him.

One of the men said something. A door slammed. Riley looked straight ahead and saw Harvey in the backseat of the Monsantos' car. Lopez and Israel, standing a distance apart, were talking, nodding, glancing at Riley. Two foes banding against him. In this equation Riley was the odd number, and maybe had always been.

Harvey was a child, and watching him sitting in the backseat, staring at the floor, Riley gave him four months, maybe five, before one night after locking up the bar, he would put a hand on his car door and hear footsteps behind him a second too late, a second before he felt a gun barrel cold against the back of his neck.

Riley squinted at the glitter of light on the river, seeing himself under that tree on the slope . . . yes . . . A screen door slammed and he turned his head lazily to see Candice on the porch across the field, calling to him. Her voice drifted away in the breeze but he heard faintly, *Time to put the steaks on the grill,* then something else, a question about red wine. . . .

Lopez and his men were advancing. Behind him, a loud *clack.* Boat and Jinx had chambered their rounds and were strolling toward the car.

Riley's body went rigid with anxiety, down to his calves, but his mind was quiet and unafraid. A deep, deep breath and a long exhale and he relaxed.

They surrounded him on four corners, guns held low, fingers on triggers. Lopez turned and spoke to Israel. Israel leaned on his cane with both hands and gazed at Riley across the distance. Then he raised a hand. Good-bye.

Riley nodded.

When Israel's hand fell and he turned away to hobble to his car, Riley realized it wasn't a wave but a signal. One of Lopez's men was stepping forward, big pistol raised.

Riley looked out at himself lying in the grass by the river. Somewhere in that world, perhaps in the field, a dog was barking and he saw his son running through the knee-high grass bringing a frog in cupped hands. If he listened really well, he could hear the river and his heartbeat.

When the fear rose again, he thought of Sister Pat and his bench at home, and he succeeded at the thing he'd been trying to do for the longest time. Breathed evenly, lowered his gaze and let the worries go, let the fear fall. Let it fall, let it fall . . .

All the men raised their weapons and took aim.

Sitting there, picturing himself tranquil in the sunlight on the grass, it was only natural for Riley James to believe that if he had another chance, if he could live his life again, easy happiness would always be with him, even in his dreams.

ACKNOWLEDGMENTS

Special thanks to Kris Dinger and Enrique Noble for patiently sharing their marine knowledge; to Markus Hoffmann, Kelley Ragland, and Christina MacDonald for their editorial assistance; and to my wife, Pamela Vasquez, a dependably candid and astute first reader.